SHADOW OF THE WOLF TREE

A WOODS COP MYSTERY

SHADOW OF THE WOLF TREE

JOSEPH HEYWOOD

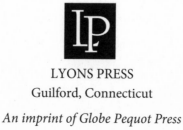

LYONS PRESS
Guilford, Connecticut
An imprint of Globe Pequot Press

Lyons Press is an imprint of Globe Pequot Press

Designed by Sheryl P. Kober

Library of Congress Cataloging-in-Publication Data

Heywood, Joseph.
  Shadow of the wolf tree : a woods cop mystery / Joseph Heywood.
    p. cm.
  ISBN 978-1-59921-900-4
  1. Service, Grady (Fictitious character)—Fiction. 2. Game wardens—Fiction. 3. Upper Peninsula (Mich.)—Fiction. 4. Ecoterrorism—Fiction. 5. Drug traffic—Fiction. 6. Cold cases (Criminal investigation)—Fiction. I. Title.
  PS3558.E92S53 2010
  813'.54—dc22

                                                                    2009043590

Printed in the United States of America   .

10 9 8 7 6 5 4 3 2 1

For Mom: Wilma Catherine (Hegwood) Heywood,
Oct. 31, 1918–May 16, 2008.
Passeth a good woman bravely.

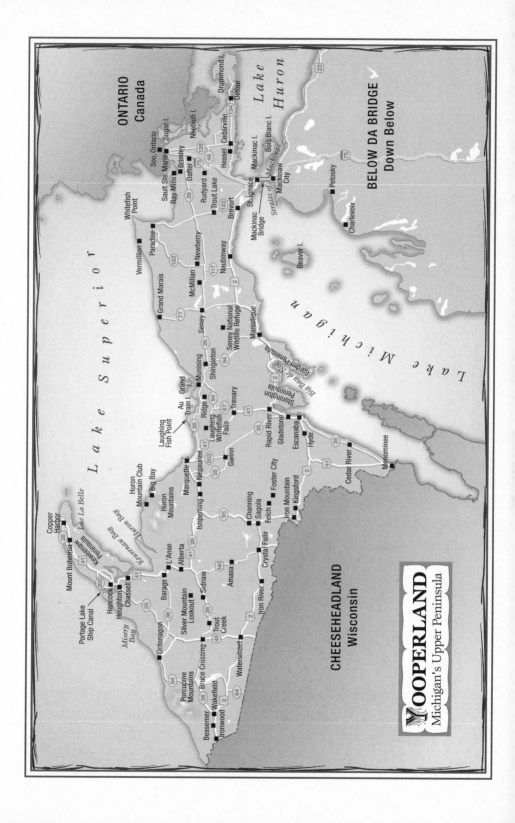

1

South Branch, Paint River, West Iron County

SATURDAY, APRIL 29, 2006

The last Saturday in April was Michigan's traditional trout-opener, and Grady Service began his day mesmerized by the reflection of a battered face, looking down into a mirror of black frogwater. For the first time in a quarter-century he had the time off to actually fish for fish, rather than chase cheating trout fishermen.

What he saw was a man nearing double nickel, loser of the woman he desperately loved and should have married, a widower in concept (albeit, not legally), loser of his only son (by the ex-wife he'd married and shouldn't have), a son he knew only for a short time but loved, an individual with three decades in government service in various branches of law enforcement—including almost twenty-five years as a game warden, a man who had lost count of his broken bones and stitches, had had his face rebuilt, lost all his teeth to trauma on the Garden Peninsula, had been shot and stabbed, had inherited an unconscionable fortune from the woman who had not been his wife. He saw a man who once again lived alone in an unfurnished cabin near the Mosquito Wilderness, slept on thin mattresses placed on army footlockers set end to end, had a giant dog, a foul-tempered cat, and a granddaughter by blood, sixteen months old. In his mind he was a total failure, a sad excuse for a human being. Worse, how could such a fuckup be responsible for enforcing laws that determined right and wrong? *Pathetic,* he thought. *Piece of shit.*

When he thought about it, he had spent his life fighting—as an athlete, as a marine in Vietnam, and as a woods cop—and what had all the strife brought? More violence. He was by some accounts an alpha shit magnet, the sort of rare individual in law enforcement who seemed to naturally attract trouble, and in one way or another always seemed to overcome it. Others in law enforcement called it a gift. He thought of it as a curse.

Best of all, his best friend was with him. Luticious Treebone and Grady Service had finished college the same year, Service at Northern Michigan

University in Marquette and Tree at Wayne State in Detroit. Treebone had played football and baseball in college and graduated cum laude. Service had played college hockey and had been only a fair student. Both had volunteered for the marines, met at Parris Island, and served together in the same unit in Vietnam. They had been through hell and had rarely spoken of the war since. After their discharge from the marines they had joined the Michigan State Police and graduated from the academy with honors. When the opportunity came to transfer to the Department of Natural Resources (DNR) law enforcement division as conservation officers, they had both made the move, but within a year, at the urging of his wife, Kalina, Treebone had left the DNR for the Detroit Metropolitan Police, where last year he had retired as a much-decorated lieutenant in charge of vice. The two men had been best friends since the crucible of boot camp; each considered the other his brother.

The two men lost count of fish caught and released, but each kept four eleven-inch brook trout for dinner, gutting them as soon as they were unhooked and stuffing them into creels lined with damp bank grass, all in all the near-perfect day Grady Service had dreamed of for years. When he began to choke up thinking about what it would be like to have Maridly Nantz and his son with him, he quickly banished the thought and focused on fishing.

They set up a pair of two-man tents on the north bank of the river; made a small fire; pan-fried their trout with brown sugar, shallots, and capers; and sipped Jack Daniel's and Diet Pepsi from tin cups while smoke curled lazily into the sky, blending with their exhalations as the night temperature dropped. Service noticed that the dew was coming early; there could be a hard freeze tonight. The area was without frost only two months a year.

When Newf brought something to the fire, Treebone grimaced and rolled his huge eyes. "That's *nasty,* dog!"

Service stared at the object, a human skull. He rubbed his eyes with the heels of his hands, dropped his cigar into the fire, and tried to will himself to act when all he wanted to do was crawl into his sleeping bag and sleep without dreams.

A second skull fetched by the dog made the two men glance at each other and roll their eyes in unison. "I'm retired," Treebone said. "Not no cop no mo."

"Lucky you," Service said.

"Your mistake," his friend concluded. "You goin' bone-huntin' in the dark, you be on your own," Tree mumbled, picking up one of the skulls. "No skin, no hair, no stink—it's old. This'll wait till morning, Grady."

Service got a flashlight out of his pack and stuck it in his jacket pocket. He didn't really need a light in the darkness, but carried one as a precaution. He patted the drooling dog's head. "Show me, girl."

Treebone grumbled and swore, but followed behind them, muttering.

Newf led them to a low rocky outcrop, two hundred yards north of their camp. There were bones protruding from the rocks, the bones and rocks both white. A few bones lay on the ground. "Cave-in," Treebone announced.

"You retire to a second career as a medical examiner?"

"Handled more stiffs than a lot of them smock-boys. You see the broke finger bones?"

"Yeah."

"I'm thinkin' cave-in—fingers got broke tryin' ta claw their way out. Found a ho one time, Sweet Quim Polinka, she run girls Flint to Toledo, but King Luther Martin, aka Batshit, the downriver pussy boss, he offer to buy her out, set her up in West Palm, retire her with honor, bank account, and pussy intact. She send word, 'Fuck off, nigger!' Batshit, he tell his boys, 'Bury that ho-bitch.' Sweet Quim's hands look just like that when we found her."

"Very instructive," Service said. "Vice handled homicides in Detroit?"

Treebone audibly winced. "Man, don't you know Vice is the *carrier* of homicide. You gonna babysit bones all night?"

"It's a crime scene until forensics determines otherwise."

Treebone grunted, shook his head, and squatted while Service used his cell phone to call conservation officer Simon del Olmo.

"Thought you and Tree were fishing?" the Cuban-born officer asked.

"My dog found two skeletons. You want to call Iron County, get the Troop specialist and deps rolling?"

"Roger that, *jeffe*."

Service gave his colleague GPS coordinates.

"North bank of the South Branch?" del Olmo queried.

"That's affirm, just off the Rec Trail."

"See you there."

"No need for you to come out tonight."

"Elza's on her four-wheeler up that way. Skeletons in the woods? We both gotta see *that*."

Elza Grinda covered west Iron County, del Olmo the east. The two officers lived together in a house near the village of Alpha. The highly competent Grinda was known throughout the DNR as Sheena. She was beautiful, with long, thick hair and intense blue eyes. She had wanted to become a detective and Service had gotten the job she had wanted, which had for a brief time caused hard feelings on her part. Now they were friends.

"We're just at the Rec Trail where it makes a ninety to the east."

"Cool. You got your 800 with you?"

"Affirmative."

"Bump you later," del Olmo said, hanging up.

Treebone looked at Newf. "See what you gone and done?"

A gray wolf howled from a ridge to the north. "One a yo boyfriends?" Tree asked the dog, which ignored him. Last year she had mated with a wolf and produced a dozen pups, all later shipped to a licensed sanctuary in Wisconsin.

Service looked at his friend. *"Sweet Quim Polinka?"* The names of Treebone's criminals and his stories had been a source of amusement for years.

"Swear to Jesus. 'Fore she run her own show as mama-san, johns fly from other continents root-hog that ho, I'm talkin' Saudi princes, Barranquilla blow-kings, Jap business dudes . . . She world-class, had more twisty-ass moves than a dyin' snake, street say. And clean. Busted her once in company of Tripod Kennedy."

Tripod Kennedy had been a longtime, very popular Detroit Pistons bench player in the glory years of Isiah Thomas and Joe Dumars, his nickname reflecting the enormity of a certain appendage.

"Tripod, he made the bail for her. Nice boy, polite, smart, a lawyer in Austin now. I say, 'Tripod, what you thinkin', bailin' that ho?' "

Treebone's stories had long been one of Service's great pleasures, and he let his friend finish with the punch line. With Tree, there was always a punch line.

"He say, 'Real talk—weren't my brain made that decision, say?' "

Service laughed.

Treebone sighed. "This surely will ruin our fishin' tomorrow."

"Not necessarily."

"Bull."

"Like you said, they're just bones, probably old."

"You be the shit magnet of shit magnets," Treebone said. "You and that stinky old dog. You gone sit there in the dark all night or head back to the nice warm campfire?"

"Better hang here. Newf carried away bones. Other critters could do the same."

"Ever the po-fessional," his friend said mockingly as he trundled back toward the river. "Be coffee waitin'."

"Send Grinda and the deps to me when they get here."

"I look like your tour director?"

Grady Service sat beside the bones in the dark, remembering boneyards of the past: a cedar swamp in spring littered with desiccated deer carcasses, and in the crotch of a broken tree, the leg bones of a deer that got stuck as wolves or coyotes stripped its meat, the bones left in place, wedged too tight to be moved, a grisly monument to the sort of violent death that marked life in the wild. Out here Walt Disney was a sick joke.

In Vietnam a Korean unit set up base camp in a Vietnamese graveyard and the monsoon washed out the graves, scattering bones; the Koreans then used the bones to construct their fence perimeter and added fresh heads of enemy soldiers on stakes. Combat shorthand: Stay the fuck away!

The temperature was dropping. Service put on his gloves and slapped his hands together. Why bones here? Lost hunters or fishermen? Not likely. They got reported. Something else then: Trapper, logger, prospector, something old, not new. He reviewed the area map in his mind. They were about two miles east of an old rail junction called Elmwood in West Iron County. The U.P. was filled with names and no histories. Elmwood: a name, a blank, not a town. The bones didn't even have names.

Sheena Grinda came in through the dark, moving quietly, but not quietly enough to elude his hearing. She was a pro, self-contained, thorough, fearless, and showed up with blood caked in her hair and a bloody ear.

"Your four-wheeler buck you?"

"LF Two," she said, rubbing her jaw.

"LF Two?"

"Our Mother Earth offshoot—Let Fish Live Free, technically—but Omears to the core."

Service had heard of Omear—Our Mother Earth—an all-female eco-group labeled eco-terrorists by the FBI. LF Two drew a blank.

"There was information that the greenie weenies were planning something for the second day of trout season, and I got a tip that strangers were seen hanging around a camp near the Tamarack River. So, I went to look. They had battery-powered motion sensors, which I completely missed. I walked into an ambush, a big dry stick, not fresh-cut. The stick broke, they ran, and I started tracking."

"Simon know?"

She shook her head. "He'll just worry."

"He's en route."

"I know. My patrol's done. The trail petered out. Amateurs with sticks, but they know how to hide their tracks and sign."

"How many?"

"Hard to read. I'm thinking four, maybe five."

"Women?"

"Chromosomally," Grinda said. "Little feet."

"I've got ice packs in my fishing pack at the camp," Service told her. "Disposables."

"What have you got here?" she asked.

"Bones." He shone his flashlight against the boulders. "Two skulls at our camp."

She said, "Simon called the county. The deps and a Troop forensics specialist are rolling. He'll lead them down the Rec Trail."

Service nodded.

"The medical examiner in this county doesn't like being called out until the Troop specialist deems it necessary," Grinda added.

"Problem?"

"Tough to get a doctor to take the ME job up here. You'll hear more about it, I'm sure."

The recreational trail was the old Chicago and Northwestern railroad bed, long ago stripped of tracks and ties, and converted to a narrow high-berm roadway for pickups, snowmobiles, and four-wheelers—the so-called Iron County Recreational Trail, or the Rec.

"Make anything out of the bones?" she asked.

"I just find. Others interpret."

"You guys catch any fish today?"

"Until our arms hurt."

"Newf brought the skulls to you?"

He nodded. "The county have any active MISPERS reports?"

"No major open jackets I'm aware of. The usual runaway teens and stray spouses, but no old cases anybody talks about. You know how *that* goes."

He knew. The U.P. had two kinds of history. The first was the public history, that recorded by government records, the media, etc. The second was largely secret, buried in the memories of individuals and families, and rarely talked about outside the circles of the designated tribe—those who also knew. Grady Service was Yooper-born, had lived most of his life in the harsh realities above the Straits of Mackinac. His father had been a CO before him, killed in the line of duty, this the first level of history; the old man died because he was drunk on duty, the second history said—but nobody talked about this history, Service included.

Grinda sat quietly in the night chill. Clouds were scudding overhead, which would help keep any freeze at bay.

"Got a fisher," he said. "Thirty feet, your three o'clock."

"Male or female?" she cracked.

His night vision was legendary, implausible, and medically inexplicable. He had first discovered it one night in Vietnam, along the banks of the Babyshit River, named by grunts for its color and odiferous stench. He, Tree, and a Kit Carson scout had tracked a North Vietnamese agent named Nguyen Tran Nang, who lived as a farmer and fed intelligence to his comrades. They had followed him half of a night and watched him meet a man and a woman. Despite total darkness Service said, "Marlene Bao." The woman was French and Vietnamese, and worked as a translator at the Rat Mountain Helo Base. She was thirty meters away but he clearly saw her face and identified her, and it had been like that at night ever since.

Later Tree asked, "How you see her face in the dark?"

"Dunno. Just happened. You?"

"Nobody see like you at night, man. X-ray vision shit. Gives me the spooky crawlies. You got bat blood, owl?"

Service couldn't explain it.

Ten years into his career, his night-shooting scores had caught the attention of Lansing, which ordered him to an ophthalmologist at the University of Michigan for a battery of tests to determine if his night vision was physiologically that much better than his colleagues, or if he had developed some sort of unconscious techniques that enabled him to see and shoot better in the darkness. They had checked his eyes and made him shoot under laboratory conditions. As long as there was some ambient light he was good, but others were as good or better. But in absolute darkness he shot perfect scores, and the doctors were at a loss to explain it. For most of his career it had been this way, though in recent years it seemed to him his night acuity was not what it once had been. A decade back a tribal warden from the Soo Tribe had named him *Tibik Gississ,* Night Sun, a nickname his DNR colleagues did not know about, and never would—at least not from him.

"Superman," Elza Grinda said, interrupting his thoughts.

"Knock off that shit."

"I'm not talking about your night vision," she said. "Where are you and Tree headed?"

"We planned to yank the yaks at the second Gold Mine Road bridge."

"Good float," she said. "Some real good holes down around the old Uno Dam. It was a nineteenth-century logging structure built to hold logs for branding. Most of it's gone now, but there are some old pilings and ruins in the river," she said, and switched subjects. "You and Candi still scromp-mates?"

"Subject off limits," he said.

"Nothing's off limits among the green and gray. There're no secrets among woods cops. How's your granddaughter?"

"Too young to tell."

"Have we got us the crankies tonight?"

"I don't *get* cranky."

"Right—and your dog doesn't scromp with wolves. What's with the shit rolling around Lansing?"

Under ordinary circumstances this was a rhetorical question, but not nowadays. Leadership in Lansing was in turmoil.

"You going to promote up?" she asked, out of the blue.

"No," he said, quickly and firmly.

"A lot of us would like to see that."

"Am I that big a pain in the ass?"

"I'm serious," she said.

"Me too." He had no desire to talk about his career; in fact, he was rarely comfortable talking about himself. He immediately changed the subject: "Is this state land?"

"Probably. Want me to check? The plat books are in my four-wheeler." Officers rarely worked a single county and carried plat books for their own turf and all surrounding counties—just in case.

Service uprooted a hunk of reindeer moss from the ground, poured water on it, and handed it to her. "Put that on your head."

"Magic poultice?"

"Something like that."

Grinda came back several minutes later with del Olmo in tow and an Iron County plat book in hand. She set the book on the ground and lit it with her flashlight. "Art Lake," she said. "Huh."

"Why the huh?"

"You've heard of Art Lake?"

"Local guy?"

"Not a person. It's a small lake in Baragastan, west of Ned Lake. A foundation owns a couple of sections and has the whole thing fenced shut. No uninviteds get in, and I mean *nobody*."

"Supposed to be some sort of big-shot artist retreat, by invite only," Simon del Olmo interjected. "We've never met anyone from this county, who has been inside. It's close to the headwaters of the Perch River, the epicenter of Baragastan."

Baragastan was what Upper Peninsula COs called the southern reaches of Baraga County, a sparsely populated area that over time had become the site of some nasty confrontations between conservation officers and various violators. "Hazzard hasn't been inside?"

"Never asked Speedboy about it," Grinda said.

Speedboy was CO Nick Hazzard, who had grown up in Bessemer, about ninety miles east of Iron River. He had been an Upper Peninsula sprint champion in high school and was now the CO responsible for Baragastan.

"Speedboy's transferring south," del Olmo said. "Kalamazoo County, I think. Maybe Calhoun. Not sure which. His wife just got a job at a hospital down there."

"Replacement named?"

"Just rumors," del Olmo said as a man approached, his flashlight dancing in the darkness. "We'd better move out of the way."

Each state police post in the state had at least one officer trained as a forensics investigator, and the F-Trooper was often called out before the local ME or the Troop lab team out of Marquette. The Iron County F-Trooper was Cory "No Sweat" Smalt, an almost serene man in his late forties. Smalt arrived with two Iron County deputies who began setting up lights while other deps began cordoning off the site.

Service studied the rock outcrop. If it had been a cave-in, what exactly had caved in, and how? *Not your problem,* he cautioned himself.

Treebone fetched coffee. "We gone fish tomorrow?"

"Don't see why not," Service said.

Two deputies remained at the site during the night, and Treebone kept them supplied with coffee while Grady Service sat by the fire and tried to focus his thoughts. Art Lake? Why the hell had he never heard of it? Eventually F-Trooper Smalt announced that he had summoned lab people from Marquette, and the county ME.

At one point after the Marquette personnel arrived, Service walked up to the site and watched them set up a screen to sift bones from dirt. He'd found the bodies, but dead bodies weren't the DNR's business unless there was a clear and compelling natural resource angle. Tree was probably right; the victims had been caught in a collapse and suffocated. Such things happened, especially in the old days.

When he finally dozed off, his mind was focused on the white bones and the white rocks they protruded from. It seemed to him there was something significant he was missing, but it was not his problem. He tried to turn his mind to something more pleasant, like his granddaughter Maridly. At sixteen months she was already a live wire, and whenever he and Newf showed up, the kid went ballistic with glee. Thinking of his granddaughter made him warm. *Life is good,* he told himself.

2

South Branch, Paint River, West Iron County

SUNDAY, APRIL 30, 2006

Grady Service had gotten less than three hours' sleep, and was glad to be back on the river and thinking about brook trout instead of human bones. Grinda and del Olmo had gone home before first light to catch some sleep before today's patrols. The state forensics team from Marquette had done its work and departed. Trooper Smalt, the forensics specialist from the Iron River post, made a point of telling him the skeletons were old, and therefore came under a different set of regs and procedures for forensics than more recent remains. *Not my problem,* he told himself.

They inhaled instant oatmeal from foil packets, hurriedly had coffee, and pushed their canoes into the river just as the day's first light began to top the eastern trees. It was still dark on the river, the water purple-black. Larger trout would feed until more light began to touch the water, which meant the fishing from now until then could be pretty good.

Always in a hurry, Treebone was floating just ahead of him when Grady Service thought he detected a tiny flash in the middle of the river. It was at eye level and just ahead of his friend. He yelled for Treebone to stop and the big man immediately curled a hard 180 to wait for him.

"S'up?" his friend asked. "You see a fish risin'?"

"Not sure. You see lightning bugs?"

"Man, no fireflies in April. What's your *problem*?"

"I saw a flash downstream."

"Mornin' sun comin' up—there's always flashes."

"This was different," Service said.

Treebone shrugged and shook his head. "You lead. I know how you get when the paranoia starts crawlin' up your butt."

Newf was sitting on a rock at the edge of the river, watching the discussion. "Stay, girl," Service told his dog, and began inching the kayak downstream, his eyes up and locked at head level. When he saw it he first thought it might be the single strand of a river spiderweb, but as he stopped the kayak and gingerly reached up, he felt wire.

"What you got?" Treebone asked from behind him.

"There's a damn wire strung across the river."

Service dug in his pack for his Leatherman tool and cut the wire, which snapped with a twang. Not just any wire, but a twist of razor wire, cured black. Razor wire was designed to be as much of a deterrent as anything else and was made of stainless steel so it would reflect light. But this wire was black and of a design he'd never seen before. He scratched at the metal with his fingernail and some of the black came off. Dyed, he told himself. Black wire wasn't just a deterrent. It was a potential killer, and he knew they were lucky he'd seen it.

Treebone pulled up beside him and wedged his kayak between a couple of small boulders. "Wicked-lookin' shit," Tree said.

"You ever see this type before?" Service asked.

"Sure didn't come off no power line," his friend said, shaking his head.

"Somebody put it here."

"Lop off somebody's head," Treebone said. "Or take out an eye."

"You got any strike indicators?" Service asked. Some fly fishermen used small pieces of yarn to fish nymphs and help them see gentle strikes, which were difficult to feel or see without help. The yarn amounted to a bobber, a term that made purist fly fishermen cringe.

"Somewhere."

Service said, "I'm gonna curl up the wire on shore. Let's mark the spot."

"Drop a marker on your GPS while I get this out of the way."

Treebone handed Service a plastic bag filled with orange yarn indicators, got out his GPS unit, and electronically marked the spot.

"There's a ford just downstream of us," Treebone announced, reading his GPS unit.

Service crossed the river, snipped the other end of the wire, and brought it all to the north shore where he carefully curled it into a coil in the tag alders and tied yarn on the riverside to mark the location. At the time he was thinking that whoever strung the wire had done it with evil intent, and might well have a background as a trapper because the stainless steel was dyed black the way trappers blackened their traps by boiling them in red oak bark or sumac berries. He scraped the wire again with his fingernail.

Definitely and deliberately blackened to make it hard to see, designed to injure, not to warn people away.

"Eyes in the game," Service said tersely. "Let's walk our kayaks downriver."

Treebone grunted, got out, and took hold of the bow handle.

Less than one hundred yards downriver Service saw something else strung over the river, and small wakes in the current below. The thing above had other things dangling from it, and as he reached up to it, he saw that the line across the river was braided fishing line with large black treble hooks suspended a foot apart all the way across the river. A weight had been tied below each hook so that they hung straight down into the water, the weights holding them in position, the hooks set at different heights. Like the wire before, this rig was designed to injure, not to warn.

"What's *with* this shit?" Treebone asked, looking at the treacherous assembly.

Service undid the rig, put it on the bank in tag alders, and marked the spot with orange yarn while Treebone turned on his GPS and marked the location.

There were two more obstacles before they got to the ford—another strand of wire, and another clothesline of hooks. As before, they took down the obstacles, put them on shore, and used the GPS to mark locations.

The knee-deep ford had a four-wheeler trail down to the river on both sides. The two men stood west of the crossing in a rocky riffle, studying the water ahead.

"See anything?" Service asked. The sun was over the trees now and directly in their eyes.

"Can't see shit," Treebone grumbled. "Let's park the yaks on shore, grab a smoke, wait for the sun to get up some."

Service watched as his friend slid over to the north bank, and just as he pulled his kayak toward the opening made by four-wheelers, Treebone yelped a startled "Fuck!" and dropped straight down into the water as a loud thump and blast shredded the tag alders beside him. Service also dropped down into the water, the cold not taking his breath because his adrenaline was pumping.

"You okay?" he yelled at his friend.

"Fuckin' eh!" Tree said. "I felt the trip wire against my shin."

The blast had shredded the tag alders and bank bushes behind his friend.

"Eyes on a swivel," Service said, looking around. *Trip wire? Jesus. What the hell is going on?*

"Damn, this water's freezing," Tree carped.

"Hang tough."

Service had a snub-nosed .38 in his gear, as did all off-duty COs, but he didn't dare reach into the kayak and raise his profile until they could assess the situation.

"Sure it was a trip wire?" he asked his friend.

"I guess we saw enough of them back in the shit."

"The blast came from the south?"

"Yep, from our right."

With the pressure of the river, up with runoff and pressing against his waders, it was a miracle his friend had felt the wire that allowed him to duck the blast. "I'm gonna slide right, see what we've got."

Treebone was in combat mode, suddenly still and quiet.

Service eased over to the south bank and pressed slowly along the tag alders until he saw an opening. Making his way to the bank through the rocks and easing along the damp ground on his belly, he worked his way east toward the four-wheeler trail. The blast had to have come from that general vicinity.

He found the 12-gauge shotgun rigged to a tree with the wire still attached. It was an ancient single-shot, what he and other officers called a spring gun, a weapon that could be tripped by game when poachers were far away.

"Spring gun," he announced as he got to his feet beside the weapon and looked at it. "Single-shot, sawed-off, rigged to a tree." The barrel was about twenty inches long. He looked across the river and saw where an entire swath of trees had been stripped away by the pellets. Tree had been *damn* lucky.

He checked to make sure the weapon was unloaded, left it in place, and waded into the river. Treebone was on his feet and Service saw blood dripping down the top of his friend's fist into the water. "You hit?"

"Maybe barked my knuckles on the rocks."

Service looked at his friend's jacket and saw that it was torn. "You're hit," he said. "Let's get out of the water and take a look."

His friend had been hit twice. "Double-ought buck," Treebone announced without emotion as his friend looked at his beefy arm and blotted the blood with a sterile gauze pad from the first aid supplies in his ruck.

"Need to get you to an emergency room, get the pellets out of there," Service said.

"Told you our fishin' was fucked."

If his friend had not felt the wire he probably would have been done fishing forever. A full load of buckshot at that angle and range would have cut him to ribbons.

Service dug his 800-megahertz radio out of the kayak and called CO Elza Grinda. "Three One Twenty, Twenty Five Fourteen. Where are you?"

"USFS 3470 at the first bridge crossing. Where are you?"

"Section Twenty, T 44 North, R 36 West."

"The ford to the old county quarry," she said. "You guys catching fish?"

"No, we've got a situation here. Can you break loose?" *Professional* radio protocol. *Not a problem—a situation.*

"Negative. I'm waiting for EMS, but Three One Twenty Three is here. He'll be at your location in about twenty minutes. Three One Twenty clear."

Three One Twenty Three was del Olmo, and he arrived in less than twenty minutes. Service and Treebone had by then walked up the four-wheeler trail, over the berm to a two-track that paralleled the river. They could hear del Olmo's truck tires crunching gravel before they saw it fishtail around a bend into sight.

Simon looked at Treebone and narrowed his eyes. "Booby trap?"

"Why'd you say booby trap?" Service shot back. "It was a single-shot, sawed-off, trip-wired," Service added. "How'd you know?"

"Elza's got the same thing downriver. Couple of Chicago guys parked their truck by the bridge. One guy cut east through the woods to get around the rapids. The other guy went in at the bridge to go wade upstream. He went through the shallows, and as he cut around a boulder, boom. Blew out his crotch and belly. His partner heard the shot, came back to see what had happened, found the guy in the water. He'd floated down about thirty feet, jammed into a sweeper on the bank, right above the bridge. Shotgun, sawed-off single-shot, double-ought buck, spring gun. Troops and deps are there with the ME."

"Dead?" Service asked. A spring gun was usually discardable, a lethal favorite of the worst poachers.

"Still alive when his partner found him, bled out by the time Elza got there, and she's feeling bad. I was ten minutes behind her."

"There's more," Service said. "We found razor wire strung across the river upstream in two locations, and then some braided line with suspended treble hooks, also two locations. We took them down and marked the locations with orange yarn. Did Elza or you look upstream or down from where her vic got hit? Tree's got all our lokes on GPS."

"She was too busy squaring away the vick and the shooting site."

"I'm guessing there's more stuff," Service said. "How the hell do we close a river?"

"Gotta check with our sarge." Del Olmo looked at Treebone. "You okay?"

"It don't mean nothin'," the retired Detroit cop said with a wince.

"EMS is at the bridge by now. Let's load your kayaks, get Tree to the EMS people so they can look at his arm."

Service and del Olmo loaded the two kayaks.

Simon del Olmo used his cell phone to call Sergeant Corky Schneider, who had been a CO in Chippewa County before being promoted to the western U.P.

"Sarn't? Simon. You hear about the bridge deal? Good. I've got Grady Service and Treebone with me. Treebone tripped another booby trap upstream. Yeah, same deal. They also found some other booby traps and wires strung across the river. Grady thinks we should close the river. What? Okay. There in fifteen minutes."

"The sergeant says he'll call the Troops, get an announcement on the radio that we are temporarily closing the South Branch to all fishing and watercraft," del Olmo said. "We'll call in officers from other counties, put kayaks in the river, find out what we're dealing with."

"Head west," Service told del Olmo.

"The way out is north and east, then south."

"I told Newf to wait. She'll sit there forever unless we go get her."

With the dog in the truck, they headed for Iron River. By late afternoon, eight conservation officers and six Iron County deputies were on the river. They found various booby traps and wires spread out over almost twenty miles of river, but no more spring guns.

Treebone was at the Iron River Community Hospital, in outpatient surgery, having three pellets removed from his bicep. Service telephoned Treebone's wife, Kalina, who listened quietly and responded with uncharacteristic reserve. "He'll be okay, Kalina," he said, trying to reassure her.

"It's you and that *damn* Upper Peninsula," she said. "You're both magnets for crazy people, Grady Service."

Service cringed, but couldn't disagree.

That night the officers all met at the DNR district office in Crystal Falls. Booby traps were cataloged and placed in the evidence locker.

"Good thing we got us a detective here," Sergeant Schneider announced. "You want everybody to stick around?"

With the Law Enforcement Division's manpower down due to retirements, and no budget for replacements, most sergeants were all too happy to quickly pass complex cases to detectives in the Wildlife Resource Protection Unit. Regular officers were covering a lot more ground than usual, and often without reasonably close backup.

"No need for everyone to stay," Service said, but he motioned for Elza Grinda to stay behind when the rest of the officers departed to head for their homes or to resume patrols.

"The group you tangled with last night," Service began. "You think this is their work?"

"As far as I know, they've never seriously hurt anyone, so if this is theirs, their agenda's drastically changed."

"You want to take me out to where you were last night, walk me through what happened?"

"Sure."

They drove both trucks fifteen miles west to Iron River and stopped at the hospital. Treebone was asleep in post-op; his doctors wanted to keep him overnight to make sure everything was all right.

"Could have been two dead today," Grinda said as they walked toward their trucks with Newf barking anxiously.

"Not your fault the victim died," he said. "A wound like that's a death sentence."

His mind was on the situation. If this was the same group, allegedly nonviolent, and if they had been clever enough to use battery-powered motion sensors last night, why were all the booby traps so crudely rigged, and where did a bunch of nonviolent fish-lovers learn to set spring guns and cure metal with the sort of knowledge only old-timer trappers tended to have? Evidence said this was one thing, but his gut said it was something else, and definitely not a slam-dunk.

3

Tamarack River, West Iron County

MONDAY, MAY 1, 2006

Service followed Grinda into the far west county where she veered off USFS Highway 147 onto the Rec, which stretched all the way from Ironwood to the Wisconsin border, south of Crystal Falls. They made their way a mile or so before coming to a gated crossroad. Grinda parked and came back to Service's truck.

"Camp's to the right."

"This where you had the run-in?"

"No, west of the camp, by the river. I never got this far."

"You saw the motion sensors?"

"No, but what else could it be? Afterwards I was too loopy and pissed to go searching for them."

Service didn't ask her if the gate had been closed last night. Officers had the constitutional right to enter private property if they had probable cause. "What exactly did your informant tell you?"

"She said there were strangers around the camp, and she knows the owners live in Texas and are only up here June through September. They've also got a son from Flushing who comes up only for deer season. She called her son and he said he hadn't given permission to anyone."

"Previous tips from this person?"

"Several. Her son's a longtime Gogebic dep. She lives on Tamarack Lake and walks over here."

Which suggested the complainant herself might have been trespassing, Service noted.

"Let's just walk right in there," he said, "introduce ourselves to anyone we find."

Grinda shrugged, smiled, and rubbed the knot on the side of her head.

They found the camp empty, with no fresh tire marks in the dirt or grass lane that led back through scrub oaks and jack pines. Service looked at the cabin, but it was dark, and without probable cause they couldn't enter; even if they'd had cause he knew he'd ask for a search warrant first—just to be safe and legal. "How close were you to the cabin when you got jumped?"

"I couldn't see the camp, but I think I can find the spot."

"Lead on," he said.

They wended through young tamaracks, and old-growth white pine loggers somehow had missed in the last century. They descended into tag alders and Service could hear moving water. "The Tamarack?"

"Hundred yards," she said. "There's a high bridge on the Rec Trail, and I came across a bend about a hundred yards below the bridge where the river swings west. I was trying to climb up the bank to higher ground when I got jumped."

He didn't ask why she had taken such a circuitous route; good conservation officers rarely went directly to their destinations. When possible, it was better to ease your way into position and get a preview of what you were going to deal with. "Why the hell would they have sensors down in the tags?" he asked.

Grinda shook her head.

"Boots," Service said, his command to Newf to stay by his side and not range ahead.

When Grinda finally located the place, Service found a blurry footprint and the broken aspen stick she'd been struck with. The stick was old, not freshly cut, meaning it probably had been grabbed up in a hurry; the attacker had not been carrying it as a weapon.

He said, "Female?"

Grinda nodded.

"Okay, let's see if we can find any more sign and take it from there. How much of this is private?" he asked.

"Just the forty with the camp. Everything else here is federal."

"Tamarack Lake is southwest," he said. "What's north?"

"Johnson's Lake."

"Anything notable there?"

"Might have some brook trout. There's an outlet feeder down into the Tamarack."

"You ever been back there?"

"Couple times, when I first got up here. It's roughly shaped like a Z. Got a creek running in from the north. Mostly cranberry bogs in the area, but Forest Road 4130 runs in above the creek source, about a third of a mile northeast of the lake. Whole area is a whole lot of nasty walking—sphagnum mats."

Walking on sphagnum was like walking on a trampoline, except that sphagnum sometimes gave way and dropped you into the deep, liquefied, frigid peat Yoopers called loon shit. "You up to this?" he asked her.

"What do you think?"

"Let's get it done." He touched the dog's head and said, "Okay, *find*," and she started ahead of them, her head down, tail sweeping.

It took thirty minutes to find broken tag alders and a rough trail meandering north. At first it looked like a game trail, but Service found another blurred footprint of about the same size as the first one, and they stayed with that, the two of them flanking the trail on either side. Newf sniffed the print and began following.

Two hours later the trail, which skirted the lake briefly before angling due north, led them to the forest service two-track Grinda had talked about earlier. The area was a sprawling black spruce bog with low trees and soft ground. The two of them were tired when they reached the USFS road, and they were running out of daylight. Service said, "We'll come back in our trucks from the east, walk the road in, see what we can find."

He walked around for a few minutes and came back. "Four-wheelers."

"How many?" she asked.

"Two, maybe three."

"First light?" she asked.

He laughed out loud. "We'll be lucky to get back to our trucks by first light, unless you know a shortcut."

"No shortcuts out here," Elza Grinda said.

"A warden's fate," he said, touching Newf's head. "Truck, girl." The dog took off at a trot.

"Does she expect us to keep up with her?" Grinda asked.

"Only if we want to find our way out."

"I thought you had X-ray vision," she said, trotting along near him.

"X-rated, not X-ray," he said. Elza Grinda stopped running and began laughing out loud.

4

Johnson's Lake, West Iron County

TUESDAY, MAY 2, 2006

Grinda had tried to get him to come home and spend the night with del Olmo and her, but Service was distracted, his sixth sense making his soul taut with anticipation that this case was going to fly off in a strange and even more deadly direction.

After convincing Grinda he'd be fine on his own, he and Newf made their way through the maze of Forest Service roads to the one that dead-ended north of Johnson's Lake. He used a small propane stove to heat a can of Dinty Moore stew and fed the dog from a bag of stinky dry food he carried for her. Having eaten, he was restless. There was no point in looking for tracks in the dark because there was a good chance he might spoil them, so he took off on foot, avoiding the two-track, and made his way cross-country, back to the Tamarack River where Grinda had been attacked. Why here? There had to be a reason for the intruders to be here, and the fact that they'd jumped Grinda, and deployed motion sensors—if they had—suggested less-than-righteous reasons.

Even with the night temperature falling, the physical effort of fumbling around in the tag alders was sweaty, unproductive work. Eventually he slid into the river and waded downstream to where the river bent westward. The bottom was greasy loose cobble the locals called snot rocks, and the wading was tricky, but after a while he found a place where something had been crossing from south to north, and on the north bank, a body's length in, he found more: a huge coil of industrial-weight two-inch garden hose. His first thought: dope.

Working uphill from the hose, he made his way north into the cran-berry bogs and waited for first light. Once the sun began to peek over the trees, it didn't take long to find where someone had stashed two dozen large plastic pots. Usually dope growers grew their weed in small forest clearings, but these pots were covered with black canvas, and he guessed they would put them in clusters around groves of black spruce so that spotting them from the air would be difficult. *Dope,* he told himself, almost smiling. *Not a damn thing to do with animal rights. Coincidence.*

He got back to his truck minutes before Grinda and Simon arrived and had just enough time to brew coffee on his portable stove.

"You sleep at all last night?" del Olmo asked.

"More or less," Service said.

"I'll put five on less," his younger colleague said.

"Simon brought a casting kit," Elza Grinda said.

"May not be that complex," Service said. "Easier if we call UPSET and let them take it."

Grinda stared at him. "Drugs?" UPSET was the Upper Peninsula Substance Enforcement Team, which covered most of the western U.P. and comprised personnel from the Troops and county sheriffs' departments.

Service explained. "I found hoses hidden down by the river, and they've got empty pots up in the peat bogs above the lake. Probably just one of multiple sites. Maybe they have the plants growing inside right now, waiting for the last frost to be done. Who knows? The logic of druggies doesn't register with the rest of us. You know anybody on the team?"

"Julie Jenks. She's a dep with the county."

Service could see fire in Grinda's eyes and hear it in her voice, and tried to calm her. "I know they jumped you, but if you give it to UPSET and they make the bust, they can bring the assault into the case."

"She's genetically wired for payback," Simon said, taking a step away from his girlfriend.

Grinda smirked. "It's a woman thing."

Service took them to see the pots and the hose, and by mid-morning they had taken photos and casts of four-wheeler tracks and eased their way out of the area. Was it normal for eco-nuts to be growing dope? He didn't know, but he knew someone who might. Chances were the dope farmers had nothing to do with what had happened on the South Branch, or any eco-groups.

"Why LF Two?" he asked Grinda.

"*FBI Bulletin,*" Grinda said. "You don't read yours?"

"I prefer my fiction to be labeled as such."

"They believe LF Two is up to something this year, specifically day two of the fishing season. They figured there'd be too many of us lurking about on opening day."

"Day two? They must have had something specific," he said. "Did your complainant mention the group by name?"

"No. She just said that there were some skulkers."

"And you added two and two."

"Better to expect four and get nothing than vice versa. Assume the worst, right?"

He couldn't disagree, and they had assaulted her. "Probably just dopers, but there's something I can't dislodge from my thick skull: If this outfit wants to make a dramatic splash and get coverage, why the hell do it up here? They'd get a helluva lot more attention on the Au Sable or one of the famous rivers downstate where there's more activity. If your mission is to sabotage fishing and get attention from the media, why bury yourself in the boondocks?"

Grinda considered the question. "Maybe because there *aren't* many people there, which means body count would be low, but the point still would be made."

He hadn't considered this angle and wasn't sure he bought it, but she had a point, and he acknowledged the possibility with an accepting grunt.

"You going to take the case?" del Olmo asked.

"Have to check with my el-tee," Service said. "But probably it will be mine."

"You seeing much of Captain Grant these days?" Grinda asked.

Now one of only two captains in DNR law enforcement, Grant was on the road almost all the time. "Nope." The captain was in Lansing most days of the week and living in a motel somewhere down there.

"The department's in a state of flux," Grinda said.

"*Bloody* flux," Service answered. DNR law enforcement had not undergone a major reorganization in years, but he suspected the captain would work to change that and try to create a department streamlined to deal with realities on the ground.

"We're bleeding personnel," del Olmo pointed out.

Grinda said, "Maybe they'll try to outsource law enforcement to the private sector."

Service couldn't help laughing. "Good—we'll all quit and create our own organization to bid on the contract. We'll call it Swampwater USA. What private security firm would be so stupid as to want a contract with a sinking ship of state? The feds can print money. Lansing can't. Besides, they'd have to pay us so much more, the state couldn't afford our service."

The conversation and the events of the past two days had left him with a sour stomach. "Catch you later. I'm headed home to get myself organized."

"What about Tree?" del Olmo asked.

"I'll spring him from the hospital on my way back to Slippery Creek. He won't head for home until Kalina raises hell with him. He'll spend the summer at his camp or my place, chasing brook trout. She makes him come home about once a month just to make sure her mojo still has juice."

5

Marquette, Marquette County

THURSDAY, MAY 4, 2006

As soon as Grinda told him about the possibility of involvement by extremist environmental groups, Service's initial thought was of Summer Rose Genova, DVM, herself a bunny-hugging environmental activist and onetime foe, turned prickly friend and ally. He had once interceded on her behalf with the feds, and she remained grateful. Genova ran an animal rehabilitation facility in western Mackinac County, and was highly respected by all the east-end COs she worked with.

"SuRo—Grady," he said when she picked up on the other end of the line.

"They haven't put you out to pasture yet?"

"The end is always just one case away."

Genova laughed sympathetically. "What is it you want?"

"Let Fish Live Free," he said.

The pause on the other end of the line was palpable. "The Twit Sisters," Genova said brusquely.

"You say that like you know them."

"Wun't waste my time on the likes of them. They're cartoons—ignorant, trendily passionate, intellectually lighter than air. They want to live the life of crusader rebels, but all they do is yada yada. I'd guess recovering anorexic, convenience vegan, trust-fund babies—probably left elite schools to find their humanity, and join a way-cool cabal with copious magnum spliffs."

"Not high on your admiration list."

"Too insignificant to make any list other than Twats Turned Twits."

Grady Service stifled a laugh. Intellectually lighter than air? "Don't hold back to spare my sensitivities."

"Rats trying to tear down the establishment maze their kin built, own, and operate. This whole anti-fishing thing is as bogus as Bigfoot. Any fish biologist knows pain comes from certain parts of the cerebral cortex, and sports fans, fish don't *have* those parts, end of science, end of bleeding hearts, full stop. The whole issue is craponey! Some elements of the environmental movement have been hijacked by showbiz, glitz, and fools. Greens once had a modicum of integrity, but this has spun out of control. I mean, PETA is now publishing comic books to show children the cruelty of their evil *fishing fathers?* What in bloody hell are they thinking?"

He had no idea what she was ranting about. "Are you suggesting LF Two is ineffectual?"

"They like to make threats, maybe once in a while throw pebbles to disrupt fishermen near Aspen or Steamboat."

"No violence?"

"Only if you count ruining their manicures." She paused again. "Iron County—one person killed, another wounded on the second day of trout season, case presumably under investigation—is that what this is about?"

"I'm just curious about LF Two." *She doesn't miss much.*

"Bullshit, rockhead! I'll tell you right now, you're going down the wrong damn road."

"Our Mother Earth," he said, trying to redirect her.

"Omears aren't into the anti-fishing sideshow. Small group, single issue—global warming. They stay focused on genuine issues, the shit that really matters."

"LF Two's an offshoot."

"What the hell does offshoot *mean*? None of these outfits are organizations in any traditional or hierarchical sense. They're movements, religions without churches, buildings, bylaws, or appointed clergy. An individual buys into a philosophy and talks a few friends into joining him or her. There's no organization, no home office, no infrastructure, no mission statement, nothing. *Offshoot of Omear?* Jesus, they're more likely the spawn of the Sorority of Needy Doodahs. LF Two doesn't do violence. And they sure as hell don't do anything that isn't tied to a potentially large major media event and audience."

He had instinctively begun thinking down this line at the river. "Nonviolent people can become violent."

"In a shooting war, maybe, but over *fish*? Not so much."

"Unless a group picks up a new member with a different view of the world."

Genova sighed. "I loathe theoretical discussions. You're a detective. Rely on Sherlock Holmes. If it swims like a duck and quacks like a duck."

"That's not Sherlock Holmes."

"This is about Iron County, yes?"

"Yeah."

"Where'd the notion of the LF Two connection come from?" she asked.

"*FBI Bulletin* predicted action on the second day of trout season."

"*FBI Bulletin?* Information from the same folks who failed to show interest in why certain Arab exchange students wanted to learn to take off airplanes but not land them? The same FBI that so recently used you as bait and tried to hang *your* ass out to dry . . . That FBI?"

"I hear you," he said. His own opinion of the FBI was low at best.

"Forget LF Two," SuRo said. "It's got to be some other group and some other issue. Don't believe me, talk to Frodo the Finn, ex–Earth Liberation Front, did seven years in a federal lockup in Wyoming for sabotage."

"Does this Frodo have a human name and address on this planet?"

"Shows how piss-poor your outfit's intelligence is. His name's Sven Lidstrom, and he has an herb farm near Tunis."

"What county?" He pretty well knew the U.P. like most people knew their own backyards, but he couldn't place Tunis.

"Southern Baraga County," she said.

It figured: *Baragastan.*

"You know this Lidstrom?" he asked.

"We're acquainted."

"Think he'd talk to me?"

"He's not a law enforcement fan, but he might if I put in a good word for you and you promise to play nice."

"I'm a professional."

"Attila the Hun used to make the same claim. Seriously, Grady, the man's paid his debt to society. He did the crime and the time, and now he just wants to live his life."

"Don't we all." *Grady?*

"Sugar, not vinegar, *capisce?* I'll call you when I get something set up. He doesn't have a phone."

"Why's he in Tunis?"

"Everybody's gotta be somewhere."

"Does he know anything about LF Two?"

"Ask him," she said, adding, "I'll get back at you."

6

Slippery Creek Camp

THURSDAY, MAY 4, 2006

Neither Cat nor Newf came out to greet them when he and Tree pulled up to the cabin. There was a new white Ford pickup by the house, and as he got out, CO Dani Denninger came onto the porch and grinned. Denninger had been at the Academy with Nantz and had helped him with a couple of cases over the past few years. She was young, attractive, and showed a lot of promise as a game warden. She also sometimes seemed to lack confidence and needed a lot of emotional support. Last he knew, she was working a county below the bridge.

"You lost?" he greeted her.

"Transfer," she said, smiling. "Meet the new Speedboy."

"Baragastan," he said. *Oh boy.*

"Is it that bad?" she asked.

"No, it's a joke—sort of."

"I thought I'd stop by and say hi on my way west. You look good," she added.

Service ignored the compliment. She looked *damn* good, but he wasn't going to go there. "You got a place to stay yet?"

"I'm going to rent Speedboy's place in L'Anse."

"That's good." Finding adequate and affordable housing was often a problem for conservation officers.

"You know Kragie?" she asked.

Junco Kragie was the second officer in Baraga County. Service nodded, saying, "Solid, unflappable." *And cheap.* He kept this to himself.

"Tree told me what happened. You catch the case?"

"Part of it. The state and county want in."

"Is that good?"

"Is how it is. Time will tell. You staying for dinner?"

"If you're asking *and* cooking. I've got wine in the truck."

"You bet," he said, wishing he'd kept his mouth shut. There had been moments when Denninger had come on to him, and he wondered if her transfer had anything to do with him.

"I took the job because this is where I want to be," she said, seemingly reading his mind. "It has nothing to do with us."

"There is no us."

"Did I not just say that?"

Leave it alone, he told himself. "I've got to make dinner."

"Have you seen Zhenya?" she asked, following him inside.

Zhenya Leukonovich was an IRS special agent known in her agency as Super Z, and she'd been a huge help in solving a recent case. She was also one of the strangest women he'd ever met—totally professional, totally unpredictable, probably loony—and had exerted a powerful sexual attraction he had somehow resisted.

"No," he said.

"I thought for sure you two would be an item by now," Denninger said. "She had the hots for you."

"You thought wrong."

"Yo, Zhenya—she's here?" Treebone asked, hobbling in.

"You want dinner or not?" Service snapped.

7

Iron River, Iron County

THURSDAY, MAY 11, 2006

The Iron River State Police post provided a small working room, and the uniquely named Michigan State Police detective Tuesday Friday drove down from Negaunee to join him there. He didn't know Friday, but had heard roundaboutly that she'd been a good road officer, was newly promoted to detective, and just coming off maternity leave. Iron County detective Mike Millitor would join them as soon as he closed a county case he was working.

Detective Tuesday Friday was in her early thirties, small, almost delicate in her movements. She had a pageboy haircut that looked like a bowl of hair, and wore cheaters around her neck on a chain that looked like M&Ms. She wore loose slacks, black flats, and a gold ankle bracelet. Her smile was thin. *More soccer mom than cop,* Service told himself. She plopped a bulging purse on the floor and clawed at her hair before opening the purse, pulling out a notebook, and flipping it open.

"I read Officer Grinda's report," she said. "Who manufactures razor wire? This anti-fishing group, Let Fish Live Free—what do we know about them? Your colleague—where did her tip come from? Where's the evidence, and who's following up on it? The shotguns . . . what make, and were the serial numbers intact, or filed off? What about fingerprints?"

Service held up his hands to stop the onslaught.

"Sorry," she said. "Too much caffeine makes my mouth run. What's it do to you?"

"Gives me the shits."

Her laugh was a dead ringer for the braying of a donkey. When she stopped laughing she sucked in a breath. "I'm sorry. I'd hate to know what you think of me right now."

"Relax. Your questions are all good ones." He saw her exhale. "Maybe delivered a tad fast," he added.

"Can we just start over?"

"How about we wait for Detective Millitor, so we can all start on the same page?"

"Fair enough," she said. "I have to confess that your reputation is as intimidating as all get out."

"My reputation?"

"The professional part. I'm really sorry about your girlfriend and your son. I can't imagine losing a child. God, I *know* I'm making a terrible first impression."

As addled as she seemed to be, his gut told him she was good people, and that he needed to lighten up and ease her into the work.

"Okay," he said. "You're a new detective, yes?"

"This is my first case."

"And you're just off maternity leave. Boy or girl?"

"Firstborn son," she said. "Is there a proverb or something about that?"

"None that I know of. Sit down and relax. There's no need to charge forward yet."

"But someone was killed."

"Our hurrying won't bring him back to life. Does your son have a name?"

"Shigun Wellington Friday," she said. "My ex-husband's aunt married a Nigerian soccer player by that name. The name was his idea, not mine. Go figure."

"Sounds okay to me," he said.

She glared at him. "He'll need a wheelbarrow to carry his name," she said.

It was Grady Service's turn to laugh.

Mike Millitor was Service's age, with a bit of a paunch, white hair, and a neatly trimmed mustache. "Heard good things about you from del Olmo and Grinda," the detective said to Service.

Service introduced the two detectives.

"Who has the lead?" Millitor asked.

"If this is some anti-fishing group," Friday said, "I think that gives the lead to the DNR. I'll take the homicide segment."

Service nodded, and after going through what had happened from his perspective, said, "Tuesday, you want to run your questions by us?"

She went through them one at a time, and when they were done, the work was apportioned. Friday would look at the evidence, including the razor wire and fishing line used in the other booby traps, and try to establish the manufacturers, and, hopefully, the points of purchase—a real long shot. Millitor said he'd follow up on the shotguns.

Service would look into the anti-fishing group. He knew he ought to contact the FBI, but decided to put that off until SuRo Genova got him an audience with Frodo the Finn.

Working the Internet, he found several accounts of Frodo/Lidstrom's crimes and got the name of a Boulder, Colorado, detective who had broken the case. It was clear from the tone of the news articles that the FBI had not been happy to share credit with Detective Sondra Orly. SOP with feds.

A phone call to Boulder revealed that Detective Orly had retired and was now living in Aurora. He had to use his charm to get an address and phone number.

"Orly," she answered the phone.

"Detective Grady Service, Michigan Department of Natural Resources," he began.

"Is Lidstrom in Dutch again?" Her voice was raspy from too many cigarettes.

"Not that I know of. Why would you ask that?"

"Nice guy, but a follower, not a leader. I'm just hoping he can stay clean. I knew he was in Michigan."

"You put him away?"

"He tumbled pretty darn easy. The FBI had all sorts of wacky theories, and when they got one of his prints, they wanted to set up surveillance to see if he would lead them to others, but I went directly to him and he caved right away."

"Did he lawyer up before he confessed?"

"Nope. Waived his rights, the state gave the case to a public defender, and that was that. We tried to make a deal for other names and so forth, but the PD wouldn't let him go that way, so he got a full swing of the sledgehammer of justice."

"You sound disappointed."

"I like Frodo. Nice guy, easily misled. No way he was the ringleader. Is he doing okay?"

"Far as I know. How'd you know he was in Michigan?"

"He sent me a postcard. Some burg called Tunis, right?"

SHADOW OF THE WOLF TREE

"It's hardly a town." He wasn't sure *what* it was.

Orly laughed. "That fits. Frodo's not what you'd call a city guy."

"Are you aware of a group called Let Fish Live Free?"

"Heard of them. Pulled some stunts in some resort communities."

"Violent?"

"Not that I've heard. Not real effective, either. Out here in Colorado we have some flaming environmentalists who know how to play the game and shake up the establishment, and I'm talking seriously hard-green. LF Two isn't one of the ones with real crust. What's going on?"

"I've got someone setting a meeting for me with Lidstrom."

"Why?"

"See if he knows anything about the anti-fishing movement."

"Even if he does, he won't talk. He's sorry for what he did, but he won't rat on anyone. He's a nice guy who has seen the light."

"It's worth a try," he said.

"I wouldn't waste my time," she concluded. "But let me know if I can help in any way."

She sounded like she meant it.

Service drove over to del Olmo's house and threw his bags in the spare bedroom. He'd bunk here until the case was done. Tree would stay at Slippery Creek, where he'd left his vehicle. Eventually his friend would head over to his camp in Chippewa County, or home to Detroit when he felt up to it. Operating from del Olmo's would put him within fifteen miles of the Iron River office and make his life easier and cheaper than staying in a motel.

Elza Grinda was in the kitchen, looking blankly into the refrigerator when he came in. When she turned, he saw that the bruise on her head had changed colors.

She grinned. "I think of it as a beauty mark."

"You talk to your drug team friend—what was her name, Jenks?"

"They have a couple of individuals in mind."

"You working with them?"

"Not directly. They're keeping me in the loop."

"Keep me in it too, okay?"

"Cool. Simon is in a canoe on the Fence River today. He won't be back until late. Just you and me for dinner. We've got our choice between leftovers and leftovers."

"Leftovers are my favorite," he said.

"You meet the other detectives yet?"

"Today."

"Impressions?"

"Could be interesting, "he said. "You ever heard the name Shigun?"

She laughed. "It's unique . . ."

"Apparently not in Nigeria."

"Did Nantz ever tell you that you are an odd man?"

"Regularly. What do you think she meant?"

"Think about it."

8

Tunis, South Baraga County

FRIDAY, MAY 19, 2006

Detective Friday had so far determined that there were eight major razor wire manufacturers in the United States, all of their output contracted to the Defense and Homeland Security departments since January 2004, which suggested the wire had been acquired before then, or stolen since. The state crime lab had analyzed the chemical composition of the blackening agent: red oak bark mixed with carbon. Apparently some unnamed, hush-hush military units used the same process to blacken wire, but end-uses and units were classified. Friday was now talking to manufacturers to determine if there had been thefts since the government contracts took effect. Predictably, none of the manufacturers were in Michigan. The state had once been a world center of major and minor manufacturing, but those times were long past, and unlikely to ever return; and with gas prices rising steadily, the tourism industry was tanking.

Next, Tuesday Friday would go to DOD and DHS, which Service suspected would be an empty exercise on her part. Unless there had been a major theft, small quantities of all kinds of things had a way of walking out the doors of factories and businesses, not to mention government agencies at all levels.

Mike Millitor had traced the shotguns, minus serial numbers (no surprise), to Blunt Dog Arms of New Haven, Connecticut, which produced the model between 1961 and 1980, at which time the company had declared Chapter 11 and disappeared. A blind alley, except that Millitor learned the metal used in the first ten years of the weapon's production was unable to sustain modern shotgun loads, which had to be hand-loaded. Hand loads meant somebody knew about weapons, and the fact that the razor wire had been coated once again suggested the possibility of a trapper's involvement, or someone with trapping knowledge.

It was a slow grind, not atypical of most cases, but a start nevertheless, and Tuesday Friday had calmed down. She was a bulldog, and optimistic, and he liked working with her.

Genova had called two days earlier to report that she had convinced Frodo the Finn to meet with him today at 11 a.m.

He was driving south of Watton on Tunis Road when he heard a call on the 800 megahertz. "Twenty Five Fourteen, Three Two One Niner. Now who's *lost?*"

Denninger! He made a quick decision. "Busy?"

"Not for you."

He pulled over to the side of the road. "I'll wait."

Minutes later she was getting into his truck with him. "What's this about?" she asked.

"Nosiness."

She gave him an innocent look. "I just *happened* to look at my AVL. I'm learning my way around the county."

Might be true, might not, he told himself. *She's a friend. Cut her some slack.* "I've got someone I hope can give us information about LF Two. A friend arranged it. The guy's a felon and former activist, did seven years for blowing up a resort in Colorado."

"Maybe you should go alone," she said.

He appreciated the gesture. "Your observations would be good. Four eyes are better than two."

"I'm in uniform, you're not."

"It's okay," he said, knowing she had a point. Some people tended to get jumpy or uptight around uniforms.

The address was a fire number off Northwest Tunis Road. Exactly where Tunis was, he still had no idea, but guessed it was probably an old railroad stop on the Chicago, Milwaukee, St. Paul and Pacific Line, and his guess proved correct. There was no gate across the entrance—unusual for camps so far out in the bush. Neither were the trees on the property perimeter plastered with no trespassing signs. The two-track had muddy ruts, with a grass hump down the middle. No fresh vehicle tracks showed in the dirt. The road stretched west through a mature aspen grove. The house at the end of the drive was made of ancient black logs, but the roof was green metal, obviously new, and pricey, easily thirty or forty K. No owner's name on the mailbox, no wacky camp name; the place felt sterile. Garden beds flanked the house, the earth in them freshly turned over. Too early to plant. There could be heavy frosts into late June. He had once been caught in a daylong snowstorm in the Mosquito Wilderness Tract on Independence Day.

Grady Service stepped onto the porch and knocked. After a minute or so a voice from the side of the house said, "Is it that time already?" The man was in his mid-forties, thin, wore coveralls and no shirt. His arms were black with dirt to his elbows. His head was shaved clean and he had thick black eyebrows that looked like they had been drawn on with some sort of makeup pencil. He looked freaky. "You Service?" the man asked, still standing at the corner.

"Yessir. Mr. Lidstrom?"

"Who is *that?*" the man demanded, with a glance at Denninger.

"New officer in Baraga County. She's out meeting people."

Denninger walked toward the man and stuck out her hand. "I'm Dani."

The man took a step backwards. "Why can't you cops keep things simple? I explicitly told Dr. Genova I'd talk to one cop, not two."

"I can take the truck and come back," Denninger offered.

The man scowled. "I guess you can stay. Just don't snoop around."

"Not a problem," Denninger said, trying to make eye contact with Service.

"I'm working in my greenhouse," the man said, pivoting and walking toward the back of the house.

The two officers followed. Service saw a small security camera mounted on the eaves of the house roof.

The greenhouse was large, fifteen by forty feet long, bags of peat piled in back, rows of red clay pots on the floor, some of them full. There were clumps of loose peat spilled all over the floor.

"No shoots?" Denninger asked.

"They're under lights in the basement at the house."

"I wish I had a green thumb," she said. "I always wanted to grow plants."

"Learn on your own, the way I had to," Lidstrom said sharply.

"I wasn't suggesting—"

"Sure you were. I know how cops think." The man turned to Service. "Dr. Genova said you're a good man, and fair. You've got some questions?"

"Let Fish Live Free. Heard of it?"

"I still support and follow the environmental movement. I've read about the group."

"What's your view on fishing?"

"I eat fish—does that answer your question? What is it you're after?"

"I'm trying to get a feel for the group."

"Their anti-fishing gig is a sidebar, a nonproductive non sequitur in the movement."

"How's that?"

"Reckless development, sprawl into animal and plant habitat, the rape of natural resources, lethal pollution, global warming: I assume you're familiar with the core issues."

"I am," Service said. "Sadly."

"Someday there'll be condos all over the side of Mount Everest," Lidstrom said, adding, "That's hyperbole, not a prediction."

"You consider bombing a resort hyperbole?"

"That was a statement; nobody got hurt."

"A potentially deadly statement."

"Lots of background noise, clutter, short public attention spans. It costs money to be creative and capture the media's attention."

"I guess you accomplished that. You're lucky no one got hurt."

Lidstrom stared off in the distance. "Wasn't luck. If I'd wanted a body count, there would have been a body count." The man looked at his feet. "It was dumb, but I did it, I admitted it, and I paid for it."

Lidstrom sounded contrite—and something else Service couldn't quite peg. "While others walked."

The man sighed. "Why is it so difficult to think one man lacks competence to do something on his own?"

"Footprints, for one thing."

"Planted by the feds, or someone," Lidstrom said, "to make it look like I had help."

"You don't get the credit if you're one of many," Service said.

"I didn't plan to get caught."

"But you confessed to Detective Orly."

Lidstrom showed real attention for the first time. "How is she?"

"Retired."

"She treated me with respect and dignity. She was the only one."

"She had your fingerprints."

"The FBI had one partial," Lidstrom said. "Off a detonator part. I thought the heat would take care of the evidence."

"It didn't."

"Which is why I confessed. Obviously I'm not cut out to be the lone wolf eco-superhero."

"What got you into the movement?"

"That's a very long story. Maybe I should write my memoirs."

"About seeing the light or being drawn into the darkness?"

Lidstrom smiled. "That's pretty good. Most cops trying to suck up for information avoid making value judgments. Dr. Genova said you were straightforward and blunt. I think the point is my finding the light, don't you?"

"I guess I never thought of right and wrong as a voyage of self-discovery."

"Granted," Lidstrom said.

"Why here . . . in Tunis?"

"I grew up just down the road, in Sidnaw. My old man and his brothers had the family camp here."

"Now it's yours?"

"Not mine. A friend owns it. He lets me stay here."

"Must be a good friend."

"Any more questions? I've got work to do."

"I hoped to get a name, someone who could provide insight into the anti-fishing movement."

"Sorry, I can't help you. That life's behind me. Can I get back to work?"

"What do you grow?" Denninger said, interrupting.

"Basil, Thai peppers, dill weed—mostly herbs."

"You sell them?"

"Some. The rest I give to friends. No dope, if that's what you're driving at."

"You use?" Service asked.

"I have. Now I meditate. It's a lot more effective."

Service stopped as he stepped out of the greenhouse and turned around. "Where'd you learn to handle explosives?"

"Self-taught, like everything else," the man said.

Back in the truck Denninger said, "Nice brows. You catch what he said?"

"Yeah. He acted surprised that we were there, but I got the feeling he'd been waiting and watching. You see the security camera? I think the dirty arms were for effect," said Service.

"What do you make of him? He kept saying he understands how cops think, and from what I saw, he does."

"Don't know yet what to think."

"You want help?" she asked.

"All I can get."

She grinned and said in a low voice, "Good thing I happened to look at the AVL, eh?"

"Do me a favor? Creep his place tonight, see what vehicles he has—you know the drill."

"Yes, boss. This is just like old times. Makes me want to rip off my gear right here, right now."

"Please don't go there, Dani."

"Just teasing," she said unconvincingly.

"Don't. You meet Kragie yet?"

"We talked on the phone."

Service checked his watch. "You want to grab lunch, see if he can join us?"

"Works for me."

He dropped Denninger at her truck and got on the cell phone to Kragie. "Had lunch yet?"

"Not even breakfast."

"Denninger and I are headed toward L'Anse. You want to meet us at the Hilltop?"

"You buying?"

"Sure."

"Be there in thirty minutes."

• • •

Service and Denninger parked their trucks beside the restaurant, which faced US 41, the main route between Marquette and Houghton. The restaurant was famous for one-pound cinnamon rolls, with enough sugar to plug a moose's arteries. The place was homey and well-lit inside.

Kragie came in after they'd ordered coffee and plopped down at the table. He was forty, had fifteen years on the job, and tended to be self-contained, almost a loner. He was also famous for his frugality.

"You two have talked on the phone," Service said.

Kragie nodded at Denninger.

"Shall we order?" Service said.

Denninger got a tuna salad, Kragie two cinnamon rolls. Service ordered coffee and a grilled cheese sandwich on limpa rye, with lots of dill pickle slices on the side.

"You got it, hon," the waitress said, ignoring Junco Kragie.

"The waitress not your fan?" Service asked.

"I probably stroked one of her relatives."

"Or you tip for shit," Service said.

"We don't get tips—why should a waitress?"

Service saw Dani's right eyebrow flutter.

"You know a place called Art Lake?" Service asked.

"Know where it is. Never been inside."

"Some sort of artist colony?" Service asked.

"The locals call it Pussy Pond. It's not on maps and not on our AVL."

"How come?"

"No idea. Ask the USGS, I guess."

"Where is it?"

"Southwest Covington Township. You take Norway Lake Road south, then a two-track off USFS 2460. It's on a dinky feeder creek that dumps into the Perch River. I've flown over it plenty of times, but the owners don't like local law enforcement."

"Pussy Pond?" Denninger said.

"Not my term," Junco Kragie said. "Just telling youse what the locals call it."

"Just women?" she asked.

"Beats hell out of me," Kragie said.

"You ever creep the place?"

"Fenced tight, all kinds of security shit. I've done the perimeter, but you can't see inside. There's two full sections, one helluva lot of land."

"Been like this for a while?" Service asked.

"Since before I got up here."

"You know anyone who's been inside?"

Kragie studied Service. "Guy named Dayton Chodos. Heard him at the bar one night. Said he used to go in there and bang one of the artists, only he got caught, they threw him out, and filed a restraining order."

"Recently?"

"Ten years back. What's your interest?"

"Nothing professional. I heard about the place down in Iron County, thought I'd ask since I had some business up this way."

Kragie was the kind of officer who didn't probe his colleagues for information. Like many COs, he mostly wanted to be left alone to do his job.

Service watched Denninger watch Kragie inhale approximately two pounds of cinnamon rolls, chug his coffee, and get up from the table. "Got fishermen to check out in the west Hurons." He looked down at Denninger. "You want the east county two-track tour?"

"You bet," she said, looking at Service.

"You'll let me know what you find with that other thing," he reminded her.

"Soon as I know."

"You two have fun out there."

"This job ain't about fun," Kragie grumbled.

"You haven't ridden with me yet," Denninger chirped.

Her response caused Kragie to swallow loudly and cough.

Service tried to remain deadpan. Kragie was a humorless tight-ass. Do him good to work with Ms. Free Spirit. And it would do her good to work with him. He was a solid CO.

"Hey Junco, where's this Chodos guy work?"

"Celotex, right here in L'Anse. They make ceiling tiles."

Service watched the two get into separate trucks and pull onto US 41; he ordered another cup of coffee.

Kragie's question was relevant. Why *had* he wanted to know about Art Lake? He had not thought about the skeletons on the South Branch of the Paint River. Why did the folks at Art Lake own property down there? Did they own more in the U.P., elsewhere? He opened his cell phone and punched in Denninger's number. "You catch the conversation about Art Lake?"

"Pussy Pond? Yeah, I heard."

"After you creep Frodo's place, do the same at Art Lake, okay? Just be real careful."

"There a reason for your interest?"

"Just being nosy, I guess."

"I can get on board with *that*. I'll bump you when I can."

"Thanks, Dani."

"Not a problem."

She sounded like his late son and had some of Nantz's characteristics, but only some. The thought made him feel sad, and he called Karylanne Pengelly's number in Houghton. Karylanne had been his son's girlfriend, and the mother of his granddaughter. "Where's the kid?"

"I just put her down for a nap," Pengelly said.

"Her grandfather wants to talk to her."

"She can't talk."

"She can *hear*."

"I'm not waking her, Grady."

"Okay, I'm driving up to Houghton. I'll take my girls to dinner."

"We're cheap dates," Karylanne said.

"The best kind," Service said. "Five work for you two?"

"She doesn't have a say in this. See you at five."

Grady Service cared deeply for the Canadian Karylanne, who was working hard to finish her degree while raising the baby. She had never married his son, but he considered her his daughter-in-law. He had helped by buying her a house, and his friends, CO Gus Turnage, Yalmer "Shark" Wetelainen, and his wife, Limey Pyykkonen, were acting like Dutch uncles and aunt. Given the tragedy of losing Maridly and his son, his granddaughter and Karylanne had come into his life like miracles.

9

Iron River, Iron County

SATURDAY, MAY 20, 2006

Grady Service had enjoyed his night with his girls and felt lighthearted and happy on the drive to the Iron River post. Detective Tuesday Friday was on the phone and waved as he came in, pointing to an urn of coffee. "I'm on hold," she said. "Mike made the coffee and took off to Watersmeet. Callbacks are on your desk."

Service picked up the pink callback slips. His boss, Lieutenant Milo Miars, wanted him to call as soon as possible. There was another slip from someone named Beulah Takala. Miars probably wanted him to file time slips and list current activities from his daily sheets for the weekly Wildlife Resource Protection Unit report. Milo was a good man, but he could wait. He punched in the number for Takala.

He was surprised when it was answered by a woman who said, "Northern Michigan University, Department of Anthropology."

"Beulah Takala?"

"I'll see if the *doctor* is available," the woman said haughtily.

Doctor?

"Thanks for calling back," Takala said as soon as she picked up. "We've not met," she began. "I'm a forensic anthropologist, and I have a contract with the MSP. Whenever they find skeletons in the U.P., they call me. One of my colleagues at MSU in East Lansing handles skeletons below the bridge."

"Is this about the skeletons in Iron County?"

"You betcha. It's taken a while, but the ME and I agree: These were not accidental deaths. He's ruling homicides. One man's spine was severed between the third and fourth atlas with a cutting tool."

"Atlas?"

"Sorry—also called the cervical. We're talking up high, just below the neck. The second vick also had a severed spine, but was literally chopped up. All sorts of cut marks on the ribs and other bones. Both vicks had multiple fractures, but only one victim was chopped. Whoever did that one seems to have had a real woody for vick number two."

Real woody? It sounded like she spent more time with cops than academics. "Homicide makes it a state police case."

"Of course. Most people who find old bones don't think much about them. You were right to treat it as a crime site. You did a great job."

"Standard procedure," he said.

"Trust me," she said. "There are some young Troops up here who don't know standard procedure from Standard Oil."

"Thanks for calling."

"I'm not done," she said sharply. "Vick number one is Native American; vick two is African American. Vick one was roughly forty years old, vick two younger, twenty-five to thirty. We've narrowed time of death down to somewhere between 1925 and 1930."

"I really appreciate the call," he said.

"Will you just *please* let me finish? You're wondering why I'm calling you, right? It's not a courtesy call. The bones of both vicks show evidence of color."

An Indian and a black man. *Of course, they were both men of color.*

"You know about color?" she asked.

"Tell me," he said, not wanting to say something stupid.

"Color means gold, and in this case, it's flour gold—specks to be sure, but gold for certain, mixed in with the bones. There's also magnetite—that's magnetic oxide of iron with some traces of hematite. You understand what this means?"

"I'm about to learn . . ."

She ignored the sarcasm and continued. "Magnetite is an indicator of placer gold. We've had an assay done on the flour gold, and this is *primo* stuff."

"I don't think I'm getting this," he said, having great difficulty putting the woman's information into any sort of useful context.

"The vicks are dripping gold dust, Detective Service. Gold is a natural resource. We can't say that the gold has anything to do with why the two men were murdered, but you can't rule it out. Gold has been the cause of a lot of trouble since the dawn of mankind. The gold angle means that the Troops are probably going to want you to at least assist in their investigation."

Service did some quick arithmetic: 1925 to 1930 was close to eighty years ago. How the hell did you investigate eighty-year-old murders? "I haven't heard anything from the Troops."

"You will," Beulah Takala said. "I just gave them my report yesterday, and sent a copy to your office in Marquette. I learned you're working in Iron County; that's why I called."

"Thanks," he said. "I guess."

She laughed. "I feel your pain."

He found Friday watching him when he closed his cell phone. "Problem?" she asked.

"Not sure," he said. If not a problem, it surely was going to at least be a complication. He didn't buy into the old saw about every problem being an opportunity. A problem was a problem, and not all puzzles got solved.

He got up from his desk and stretched. "What are you working on?"

"The wire companies. I'm not getting anywhere, but one of them out of Cleveland told me he thought there were some smaller companies around, not tied to government contracts. He didn't have their names, but gave me the name of a man at Purdue who might know."

"Purdue?"

"Some sort of metallurgy expert. What are you working on? Get anything from the felon?"

"Not much, but I thought I'd take a ride. Want to take a break?"

"Works for me. Can't lose weight with my butt glued to a chair."

She was wearing low heels today, and a skirt. "You got boots?"

"In my vehicle."

"Grab them and let's burn some state gas."

• • •

Service drove down the Rec Trail from Forest Highway 16 and parked near where he and Tree had camped that night. He'd talked to his friend yesterday, and the big man was still at Slippery Creek, enjoying the fishing out the back door. Friday had kicked off her heels and put on socks and boots while they drove.

He led her to the outcrop where the skeletons had been excavated. If he'd been Sherlock Holmes, he would have had a magnifying glass, but he wasn't Sherlock, and even if he were, he wouldn't know what to look for.

"What's here?"

"It's what used to be here. Two skeletons."

"Yuck."

"My dog found them while I was camped by the river, first night of trout season."

"Bummer," she said.

"It looked like the vicks had been trapped in a cave-in, but that call I got in the office today was from a forensic anthropologist from Northern who works for your outfit. She says she and the ME have ruled both deaths homicides."

She rubbed her nose. "Dr. Beulah Takala—I've met her. How old are the skeletons?"

"Eighty-plus years."

"Geez. How do you investigate homicides that old?"

"Dunno," he said. "I'm a woods cop. Your outfit is going to catch the case."

"It is? Does this have anything to do with what we're doing?"

"What do you think?"

"If it does, I don't see it."

"Me either."

"Why did we drive out here?"

"Sometimes I find it useful to look at a site several times, see if it will talk to me."

"Is the earth talking to you today?"

"Not even whispering . . . but I still want to look around."

"For what?"

"I don't have a clue."

After an hour he still didn't have a clue, and the site remained silent.

He called Denninger on the cell phone. "You got a plat book for your county?" he asked.

"Riding shotgun, right beside me."

"Look at the property where we met Frodo the Finn. Who owns it?"

It took a couple of minutes. "Taide Jarvi," she said.

"That male or female?"

"You guess first," she joked.

"Check around, see what you can find."

"You bet."

10

Redlight Creek, Ontonagon County

SATURDAY, MAY 20, 2006

Detective Mike Millitor called on the cell phone as they were driving south on U.S. Forest Highway 16. "There's an old coot in south Ontonagon County you may want to meet."

"Friday said you had something in Watersmeet."

"Cleaning up an old case. Meet me at the ONF Visitor Center and we'll take one vehicle." The parking lot for the Ottawa National Forest's Visitor Center sat on a hill above US 2 and M-45, and wasn't visible from either highway. Officers often met in the lot, or dumped vehicles there to ride with others.

"Friday's with me."

"Good—she'll find it interesting too. See you at the VC."

Millitor was leaning against the door of his unmarked. He got into the backseat of Service's Tahoe. The Iron County detective put an unlit cigar stump in his mouth and started talking. "M-45 north to Paulding, west on Sleepy Hollow Road, north on Choate Road. Couple miles northwest, Choate cuts a hard ninety west and back to the north. There's a two-track running straight west off this curve. Jump on the two-track, drive down about a mile. There's a driveway running south. That's where we wanna be. Got it?" Millitor asked.

Service nodded, drove out of the visitor center onto M-45, and then drove north through Watersmeet past the Lac Vieux Desert Casino and golf course. Millitor talked while Service drove.

"Twenty years back a guy named Rankin Box was selling conversion kits for AK-47s. He assembled the kits and sold them cheap, strictly word-of-mouth biz through the local scum line and gun show circuit. BATF sent me in undercover. I bought some kits from Box and three semiauto Kalashnikovs from his brother-in-law. Box rolled on the in-law, got fined, and did no time. The B-I-L did three years, until one of his fellow residents cut his throat over a cigarette beef. The B-I-L's death set off a family war. Box sold his place in Marenisco and moved to his hunting camp on Redlight Creek. He's pushing one hundred now, lives on social security, and isn't in the best of health. For some reason the old bird took a liking to me, and we've been chums ever since."

"One of your snitches?" Service said.

"Never cared for that term. He's an eccentric bugger to be sure, but I've never met anyone who knows guns like him. From time to time I drop off venison and groceries for him. Last night his daughter called and said he wants to talk to me about the old days. That's code for he's got information for me," Millitor said.

"His information usually solid?"

"Dead-on so far."

"Our case?"

"I doubt that, but if he's in a talking mood, we can pick his brain. He looks like the walking dead, but his mind is steel-trap."

Service said, "If he's your informant, maybe you should go alone. "Ordinarily I'd agree, but Box likes to be the center of attention. Three of us will inflate his ego more than me alone."

Millitor, Service decided, was an old pro, and typical of a lot of good U.P. cops who could have moved away and had big-time careers, but stayed home for the quality of life.

The camp was at the end of a short two-track driveway through tag alders, the building one story with a steep roof. The undergrowth around the cabin had been cleared. Ricks of cut wood were neatly stacked in rows all around the cabin.

"The windows don't even have cobwebs," Friday observed. "My God, I can't even keep them out of the *inside* of my place."

Millitor said, "He's got his own support system, run by his daughter. They make his wood, clean the place, plow his snow, bring him groceries and prescriptions. Usually he cooks for himself, but that's about it," Millitor said.

The detective walked into the cabin without knocking. "Mr. Box?"

Service looked around. Rifles were mounted on the wall, intricate, ornate wood carvings all over the place, the furniture circa 1970s, and a big-screen TV. Red-and-black-check woolen hunting coats were draped on wooden pegs on one of the walls.

The old man was sitting in a rocking chair, looking out the back window, where there was a salt block and a dozen deer milling around, still in their gray winter coats.

The salt block was supposed to be broken up and spread around to reduce disease transmission through nose-to-nose contact, but Service kept quiet. No matter what the regs called for, it was the rare Yooper who ever broke up a salt block.

Millitor grabbed a chair and placed it in front of the old man, whose head bobbed. "Youse finally come, eh?" Box said.

"Keeping busy?"

Box pawed at his head with a finger deformed by arthritis. "Up dere."

"Your daughter called me last night."

"What can I do for youse?"

"You wanted to see me."

"I did?"

"You had your daughter call me."

"Oh, dat's right."

"So?"

"Who's dose pipples youse got wit' youse?"

Millitor introduced Service and Friday. Box stared at the DNR officer. "Game warden, eh? You got a problem wit' salt block out back?"

"I'd be a lot happier if it was broken up."

The man smiled. "Youse mebbe had kin was game warden?"

"My father."

"T'ought so. Beat bejezus out of me over Gwinn one time. Shot me a red. Musta had a tip, 'cause dat bugger was right dere waitin', an' when I went ta gut 'er, he went ta town on me. Busted hell outta my noggin. Din't write no ticket. Said ta me, 'You need dat deer?' I did. He told me, 'Den take it. Don't never come back Gwinn.' Never did. Game wardens dose days din't give no breaks. Youse're like your daddy, eh?"

"I think we can skip the beating," Service said. The old man guffawed with such energy that he began to drool. The last thing Service wanted was to be like his father.

Box wiped spittle off his chin and looked up at Millitor. "Heard dere's a young buck over Kenton got fifty cal, been shootin' up woods some. Word out, piece's for sale. Full auto, not no one-shot sniper rig."

"The young buck have a name?"

"Christian Stempi, bout t'irty, hothead, lives out Peterson Road on da Jumbo."

Jumbo was the diminutive Jumbo River, barely a river in size.

Millitor said, "There were Stempis who ran a chop shop south of Trout Creek. This kid one of those Stempis?"

"Chop shop, dat's his ole man's, but da hull family's allas up ta shenanigans."

"Other weapons?"

"Wun't s'prise me none, eh."

"I'll talk to the ATF," Millitor said. Then, "Back in your day, you make any spring or dump guns?"

"No need. Use lighter load in cartridge, get less noise, no need for t'rowaway gun, eh? An' dose bloody spring guns too dangerous. Mighta could wing da old lady or somepin."

"Anybody making a business out of spring guns nowadays?"

The old man shrugged. "Reckon pipples up here can make dere own easy enough."

Detective Friday interrupted. "Mr. Box, you've got some beautiful wood carvings here. Who's the artist?"

The man held up his crooked hands. "Was me before dese tings become claws. Go barn out back. Chuck-full of 'em."

"I'm not an expert," Friday said, "but I think these could be worth something if you wanted to sell them."

Box fixed his eyes on her. "How much, you tink?"

Friday pointed to a porcupine clinging to a ceiling beam. "Several hundred for that, I would think. Maybe more."

Box's eyes became slits. "Dat so . . . ?"

"I've got a girlfriend who owns a wildlife art gallery in Marquette. I could ask her to drive over and do an appraisal, give you a better estimate of their value. If she likes them, and you want to, she might sell them for you."

"She buy for cash and resell with markup?"

An unexpectedly precise and focused question for Box to ask, Service thought.

Friday said, "Consignment, I'd think, but I really don't know the details."

"Umm," Box said. "Youse bring 'er, give 'er da look."

"You're okay with that?"

"Youse want, go out back, look in da barn."

The detective excused herself, leaving the men to themselves.

"Dat girlie done just spit out a kid," Box said.

How had he seen that? Service wondered.

Box looked at Millitor. "Was Paulding girlie come here once, want me teach her make spring guns."

"You help her?"

"Too old, da hands no good. I sent her to old chum."

"The chum have a name?"

"Allerdyce."

Service lurched at the name. "*Limpy* Allerdyce?"

"Dat's him."

"When was this?"

" 'Ninety-seven, '98, mebbe 'round dat time."

"Allerdyce was in prison then."

"Din't say he wasn't. Sent 'er Allerdyce's way. His crew kep' workin' while old man was inside, eh?"

"Did the woman meet with them?"

"Never heard. Somebody tell me later she join up."

"Join up?"

"Army," Box said. "I know somepin' else."

"What's that?"

"Dat Vernors soda pop dey make down Detroit is made from nigger piss," the centenarian said.

Millitor made a puffing sound and looked at Service. "What was the woman's name?" he asked the old man.

"Lemme tink . . . ," Box said. And after a moment, "Penny . . . Penny Provo."

"From Paulding?"

"Furt'er nort'. Youse know Pecker Lake?"

"No."

"Humanka Hill. Youse go down bottom, take two-track sout'. Few miles down dat way."

"You just met Provo that once?"

"Come, make wood, ast me 'boot guns, gone."

• • •

Back in the Tahoe, Tuesday Friday said, "You can't believe what's in that barn. There's a full-size bear carved out of bird's-eye maple. Must be two hundred carvings. The workmanship is astounding, the best I've ever seen. My friend is going to flip out."

"Valuable?"

"Like I told him, I'm not an expert, but I think they're worth a lot in the right hands. If he's just living on social security, those days could be over."

"You know Pecker Lake?" Millitor asked Service.

"Nope, but we'll find out." He used his cell phone to call Lars Hjalmquist, retired Gogebic County CO. "Lars, Grady. You know Pecker Lake?"

Hjalmquist chuckled. "Formally it's Pickle Pond."

Yoopers were forever attaching their own names to places and things. "Off Humanka Hill Road?"

"South of there, I'd think."

"Does the name Penny Provo ring a bell?"

"Vaguely. I can check my patrol diaries—if I can find the bloody things."

Most COs kept daily diaries, often with the intent of writing a book when they retired. The writing rarely happened, but the diaries were rich troves of memories and information, most of it never shared with anyone.

"Appreciate it, Lars. Call me if you find something. How's Joanie?"

"Givin' me her evil eye. Wants shop grocks."

"Sorry to interrupt."

Service told his colleagues, "Friend of mine, retired CO, lives in Ironwood. Says the name Provo is vaguely familiar. He'll check some records, get back to me."

Millitor said, "Let's call the Ontonagon County sheriff. He's an old chum."

Millitor made the call and Service listened.

"Yeah, Danny, it's Mike. You guys have any dealings with a Penny Provo, lives in the Paulding area? Yeah, okay. When was that? She still in?"

Millitor snapped his phone shut. "She was a schoolteacher, Trout Crick, some kinda stink, quit her job, joined the army. In Iraq now, he thinks."

"You want to go find Pickle Pond?" Service asked.

"Dere a reason?"

"I guess not if she's in Iraq."

"On that note, let's call it a day," Service said. "Where are you staying?" Service asked Friday.

"AmericInn. I miss my kid, but I'm actually getting uninterrupted sleep."

On the way back to Iron River, Friday's cell phone rang. "Friday," she answered. Then, "Yessir. Tomorrow at nine. Right, I'll take care of it," she said, and hung up.

"That was my el-tee. Those eighty-year-old skeletons—guess who catches the case?" she said to Service.

"You?"

"Us," she said. "You found the damn things, and we're already on this case."

"Da bones got found over Elmwood?" Millitor asked.

"He and his friend found them," Friday said with a nod toward Service.

"Technically it was my dog."

Millitor said, "Was me, I'd sit down with Theokkilur Petersson. Theo was our sheriff forty years, and he knows more Iron County history den anybody I know."

Last thing I need is a wild goose chase, Service told himself. The bones had been there a long time. The Indiana fisherman was newly dead and had priority.

11

Iron River, Iron County

SUNDAY, MAY 21, 2006

Service and Friday drove to the Knotty Pine Café in Gaastra, an old mining town six miles from Iron River. They took a table by the wall. The counter seats were filled with elderly gents in plaid shirts, suspenders, scuffed boots, and faded baseball caps, all of them smoking hand-rolled cigarettes and yakking in light-speed Yooperese.

"I called the retired sheriff last night," Friday said. "He can see us this morning after mass, tennish."

"You tell him what it's about?"

"Broad strokes only. He said perhaps we can help each other."

"Meaning?"

She shook her head, shrugged, turned her attention to the menu.

"No reason for you to be here weekends," Service said. "It's not like either case has critical mass."

She stared at him. "You ever hear of postpartum blues?"

"I've heard."

"I'm the poster girl. Right now, I need sleep, time to get my head straight."

"Just trying to help."

"Which I appreciate," she said, "but I'm good to go. My sister's taking care of the baby. "

His cell phone started to sing just as breakfast came. It was Denninger.

"Your boy Frodo keeps a four-wheeler back in the woods. There's a four-wheeler track that crosses a creek and comes out on Tunis Road, about a half-mile south of his driveway. Looks like it gets used a lot."

"You follow it?"

"Not yet. I'm at the four-wheeler right now, maybe two hundred yards behind the camp. No surveillance out here. I got the VIN number off the ATV. It's registered, and I checked the records. It belongs to Lidstrom."

"Cast the tires?"

"Didn't know you wanted that."

"Me either, but I do. Anything else?"

"There's a load of big-ass old clay pots under tarps down near the creek, beyond the parking spot. They look new."

"Get photos, and, if you can, the manufacturers' names, lot numbers, whatever you can find."

"Okay, boss."

"Send the digitals by e-mail to Grinda and hold onto the plaster casts."

"You bet, boss."

"I'm not your boss."

"If you were, I'd have to do *anything* you ordered me to do . . ."

"Stop!" he said wearily.

"Joke," Denninger said.

Service hung up. "Women," he said.

"Present company included?" Friday asked.

"Sorry, not you."

"Day-to-day life can be hard," she said. "The job's a lot easier to cope with."

"That *was* work-related. I don't need a pep talk."

"Just trying to help," she said.

They both laughed. She fumbled with her pants and undid the top button. "Just eight more pounds to lose," she said, "all loose skin."

"It doesn't show," he said.

"With clothes on."

He changed the subject. "You talk to your girlfriend in Marquette?"

"Last night. When I described the bear and porcupine, she wigged out. She said bird's-eye wood alone is worth thousands. There are dozens of bird's-eye carvings in that barn. Box is lucky some lowlife hasn't hauled them away. He may have a small fortune there."

"Never know when the sun will shine," he said, thinking about the unexpected fortune Nantz had left him. It had been worth $80 million more than a year ago, and with the stock market going the way it was, no telling the value now. He rarely thought about it. Money had never held much meaning for him.

Service thought about Box sending Penny Provo to Limpy Allerdyce. He'd have to make a point to visit Limpy, a distinctly unpleasant thought.

• • •

Retired Iron County sheriff Theokkilur Petersson lived in a well-kept brick house a block from the Iron River City Hall. There were ramps up to the porch, and Petersson came to the door in a motorized wheelchair. He let them inside and led them back to his office, the paneled walls covered with certificates and photographs of a considerably younger Petersson in Marine Corps dress blues. A tray with a coffeepot was sitting on a low table. "Help yourselves," the retired sheriff said.

"Been to mass?" Friday asked.

Petersson pointed at a TV set. "Mass for shut-ins. If the homily gets boring I just hit the mute button."

Service poured coffee for Friday.

Petersson said, "Them skeletons out in Elmwood really grabbed my attention. My great-grandfather and namesake disappeared out that way in 1927 and was never found."

"The skeletons were those of a black man and a Native American," Friday said.

The retired sheriff didn't look surprised.

"Let me tell you a story. Just before Christmas, 1927, my great-grandfather and a priest took a train to Elmwood to check on some black families who had come up the year before to work potato fields planted in logging cutovers in exchange for their own land. The folks were in real bad shape. One child had already died from malnutrition and exposure. Great Granddad saw this and arranged to get them out of there and back to Chicago where they'd come from. A half-breed named Roland Denu owned the land," Petersson said, taking a deep breath.

"After the survivors were on the way to Chicago, Granddad went back to Elmwood to look for stragglers or more bodies, but he disappeared. The postmaster at Elmwood wired the authorities here, but there was a helluva blizzard going on, and then a real heavy winter settled in and no search was made until spring. The searchers found nothing."

"Any ideas about what happened to him?" Service asked.

"The usual theories: He got hurt, snow came, he froze, end of story. Or he got lost, snow came, same result. The fact is, winter kills people up here. Killed a lot more back then than now."

"What do you think happened?" Service asked.

"I don't know. Family history says he was a careful man, and a good man in the bush—with an internal compass second to none. He'd been a longtime timber cruiser before he became sheriff. I'm named for him," Petersson said, moving his wheelchair to an open rolltop desk and fetching a large envelope. "Granddad was ahead of his time and kept a journal of daily law enforcement activities." Petersson took an old black journal out of the envelope and handed it to Friday, who took it to a table where she and Service could look at it together.

There was a page marked. Friday opened it and read the text out loud: "December 28, 1927. The Negro families are on their way back to Chicago. Some are pretty sick, but they should all make it. We sent the body of the deceased child with them. The train's taking me to Elmwood tomorrow to look for stragglers and other survivors, which are unlikely, but I still have to go. Of the original group only the man called Lincoln is unaccounted for. Father John O'Neil escorted the families south and will return next week. Going out to Elmwood will give me a chance to talk to G. Bernalli. The day we found the families, Bernalli indicated he knew the priest, and the tone of voice he used makes me curious. Probably nothing, but people here don't just spit out things without reason. The hard part is getting them to open up, and you need to be patient if you want to collect useful information. Timber cruising made me a very patient man," she concluded.

"G. Bernalli?" Service asked.

"Giuseppe Bernalli, Elmwood's postmaster back then."

"Who's the priest your great-granddad refers to?"

"That's one of those sixty-four-thousand-dollar questions. In previous entries, Granddad wrote about a priest named O'Neil who turned up in May of 1927 to take over the St. Agnes Catholic Church. My great-grandfather had a lot of respect for O'Neil. The county commissioner for the poor died that summer, and the priest volunteered to take on the job without pay. Church records burned up in 1928. When I got interested I made inquiries to the dioceses in Chicago, Green Bay, and Marquette, but none has a record of any priest being sent to Iron River in 1927."

"A priest named O'Neil?"

"*Any* priest," Petersson said. "Bloody odd, eh?"

"Does your great-grandfather's journal have any more information on the priest—where he came from, his age, where he went to seminary, anything?" Service asked.

"No, and neither do the old newspapers. And since my great grandfather has also passed away, we don't know if the man he thought was a priest ever came back from Chicago, eh. The Crystal Falls *Diamond Drill* was published throughout the period until 1996. Crystal Falls is the county seat now. But Iron River was the seat then, and had spotty news coverage back in the 1920s. Publications would fold and disappear, or merge. The merged Iron River *Reporter* and Stambaugh-Caspian *Reporter* operated from 1927 until 1968. There was a period in 1927 when the papers came out intermittently, or were short of news. Both the papers in Crystal and here reported the priest's arrival, but gave no biographical information.

"What I do know from the papers is that St. Agnes was a much-troubled parish. In 1910 the Poles left the church to form their own congregation. Three years later, parishioners from Gaastra and Caspian formed their own churches. What remained of St. Agnes was in pretty rough shape for the next thirty years, and pastors pretty much came and went through a revolving door. In the early 1930s things hit bottom when a priest named Lenhart was murdered on the church grounds."

"What happened to the man who owned the property where the Chicago people settled?" Friday asked.

"Roland Denu disappeared about the same time as my great-grandfather. I've been through all the old papers, but there's nothing about him."

"Did he actually own the property?"

"Land records from early in the century got lost during the Second World War. My great-grandmother told my mother that Denu was a troublemaker. People called him Snake. As a kid he used to bite the heads off live reptiles."

"Did the local papers write stories when the black settlers arrived?" Service asked.

"None that I could find. Lots of people were passing through in those days, individuals and groups, and Elmwood isn't close to town. The postmaster was the Elmwood correspondent for both papers, but all his stories covered only the news about the Italian families out that way. Back then immigrants and ethnics didn't mix with each other socially, unless you count scraps."

"What happened to the postmaster?" Service asked.

"He died in a fire in his store in 1940. He had four sons. Two died in logging accidents in their twenties, and pneumonia got the oldest. The youngest son, Vito, served as a ball turret gunner in a B-17 in Europe, was shot down, and spent almost three years as a POW in Germany. After the war he came home to Iron River and married an Italian gal whose family had immigrated from the old country just before Pearl Harbor. Vito and his bride moved to Iron Mountain where he opened a grocery store and ran it until he died five years ago. No kids, but his widow lives in a nursing home in Crystal Falls."

"You ever talk to her?"

"Tried, but she wasn't around in 1927. She was polite but tight-lipped about her husband's family. I have to confess, I'm disappointed one of those skeletons isn't a white man. When a family member disappears it leaves a hole, even if the events were eight decades ago. So what is it you two want to talk about?"

"The ME has ruled homicide for the remains," Friday said.

"You don't say!"

Before Friday could answer, Service said, "Was there much gold mining around here?"

Petersson raised an eyebrow and smirked. "More of that to the north where the big copper mines were—Marquette, Keweenaw, up that way. Gold and silver show up in trace amounts with copper as I understand it. Why?"

"Sorry," Service apologized. "My mind's not focused right now. I just wondered."

"You know, now that I think about it, there was one gold mine around here, but we never took it seriously," Petersson said after pausing to collect his thoughts. "It was called Peter Paul's, out on the South Branch of the Paint River. Gold Mine Road is named for it. Old Peter Paul found color, and claimed he struck a rich, pure vein, but he didn't have cash or capital to develop it, and didn't want to share with partners. He tried to raise some money by selling blueberries to locals, but that was like trying to sell ice to Eskimos. Blueberries grow wild all over the bloody county. The old guy was never taken seriously, and died intestate as one of the town's eccentrics."

Service thanked the retired lawman for his help and led Friday out to his Tahoe.

On their way to the Iron River post, Friday said, "Your question about gold mines came out of the blue."

"I didn't want to tell the sheriff, but the forensic anthropologist who called me said there was gold dust all over both skeletons."

She looked confused. "I haven't gotten the case file yet. You think gold's involved in this?"

"Doesn't seem likely, but who the hell knows?"

"Both cases are complex," she said.

"Let's not get deflected from the first one," he said.

"That means back to the phone for me," Friday said. "What about you?"

"Not sure yet. I'll call Mike and we'll huddle tomorrow."

• • •

Grinda and del Olmo were home when he got there. "Did you get photos from Denninger?" Service asked Elza.

"Better. I met her up in the north county, and she gave me her memory stick, the tire casts, and some product information off the clay pots. I'm passing it all to the Drug team."

Service felt uneasy, decided it might be a good idea to pop in unannounced on Frodo the Finn and see what he had to say for himself. Summer Rose Genova had more or less endorsed the man, and he trusted SuRo's opinions. But she had also once been involved with some real wackos, which showed she wasn't perfect.

12

Tunis, South Baraga County

SUNDAY, MAY 21, 2006

Days were stretching out. In a month it would be light until 11 p.m., the nights short and star-spackled. Grady Service pulled down the driveway to Lidstrom's camp with his headlights on, and parked. His dash clock said 10 p.m.

A porch light came on, and Lidstrom came to the door and stared out. "Detective?"

"We need to talk."

"I told you I don't know any of the idiots in the anti-fishing movement."

"A friend lets you stay here?"

"I also said that."

"Taide Jarvi?"

Lidstrom nodded.

"Do you own a vehicle?"

"Neither car nor truck. Carbon emissions are suffocating the planet. I keep a four-wheeler out back. It's a compromise. Most of the time I ride my bicycle."

"There are no tracks in your driveway."

"I use a four-wheeler track out back, not on the driveway and roads."

"To go where?"

"I don't like your tone of voice."

"Just answer the question," Service said. "To go where?"

"Wherever I need to go." One of the man's painted eyebrows raised. "Are you snooping?"

"Are you afraid of what I'll find?"

"Of course not."

"I'm trying to figure you out. SuRo vouches for you, but I keep getting funny vibrations."

"Our feelings are our own," Lidstrom said.

"You've got clay pots hidden out back."

"Stored, not hidden."

"You sure you're not growing something other than garden herbs?"

The man looked irritated. "Nothing illegal."

"This place has all the smells of something way off the garden path."

Lidstrom's shoulders slumped. "Come inside, please. I have no coffee to offer, but I've got sassafras root tea."

"No thanks."

"It cleanses the body."

"So does Ex-Lax. I'll take water."

Lidstrom gave him water in a mason jar. "I try to minimize the use of plastics," he said. "The water is from an artesian well near the Perch River. That's what I haul in my four-wheeler."

"I asked what you're growing."

"*Hierochloe odorata,* Latin for sweetgrass."

"The stuff Ojibwas call 'the grass that never dies?' "

"The Ojibwas and many other tribes use it for medicinal purposes, to purify themselves and the air, drive away evil spirits."

"People with cancer also smoke dope."

"You're fixated, Detective."

"Goes with my job."

"I guess it does. No offense taken. The shoots are in my cellar under black light, if you'd care to look."

"I'm not questioning your integrity, but I'd better look."

"Understood."

Service stood in the underground room and stared at the rows of pots and lights. "Why sweetgrass? It grows wild."

"Indeed, but always mixed with other plants, and the local Ojibwas don't like sharing sweetgrass plots even when they're on public land."

"You can call the law if there's a problem."

"I don't narc."

"You just did by telling me about the problem. And the fact that you say you don't narc suggests there were others involved in Colorado."

"I gave you generalities, not specifics."

The man didn't address Colorado. "Why grow sweetgrass?"

"Finndian herbs. I had time to do a lot of reading and research in prison.

I found there's a real market for sweetgrass—New Agers, old hippies, lots of niches. If I try to harvest on public land, I'll be in conflict with the tribes. Worse, you have to look all over to find it, and that takes time. I figured if I grew my own, it would be to my advantage. Finndian herbs will be marketed on the Internet. I lost everything I had when I went to prison. This is a way to get well, and it's legal."

"Finndian?" This was a legendary blend of Native American and Finnish blood.

"My heritage on my mother's side."

"You're tribal?"

"No, my blood's too diluted for the local rolls."

"Ergo, no annual check from casino operations."

"How it is," Lidstrom said.

"You could get a lawyer."

"I'm done with lawyers. I've even done all the legal work for Finndian by myself."

Service mulled over the situation, what he'd heard, what he'd seen, and what his gut said, which was that he probably was hearing truth.

Upstairs Lidstrom took a braid of sweetgrass out of a paper bag, lit the tip, blew it out, and waved it around, making the smoke curl in the air.

"Smells vaguely like vanilla," Service said. It would be interesting to see if the evidence Denninger had gathered matched anything from the Tamarack River. Either Lidstrom was the best liar he'd ever met, or he was what he claimed to be.

"Sorry to have bothered you."

Lidstrom handed him a bag of sweetgrass braids. "Our secret until my little company is launched, right?"

Service held up the bag. "Is this a bribe?"

"A gift isn't a bribe."

On the way north to Watton he called information in L'Anse with his cell phone and got an address for Dayton Chodos, the man who claimed to have been inside the Art Lake commune, or whatever it was. L'Anse was close. Service figured he might as well drop in on the guy, see what he had to say.

A minute later his cell phone warbled. A thin, wavering voice on the other end said, "Grady."

It was Denninger. "You watching your AVL again?"

"*I need . . . help!*" she said, her voice feeble. "On foot, away from vehicle . . . just hit . . . *panic button!*"

Service looked at his computer screen, saw the glyph for her vehicle flashing the silent electronic alarm. "What's wrong, Dani?"

No answer. The panic button was a feature built into the AVL system. An officer in trouble and on foot, away from the vehicle, could push the button and the computer system would alert the entire state, with the AVL providing the vehicle position courtesy of GPS satellites. What the fuck was going on? He'd never actually seen a panic button go live before.

He got on his 800. "Three Two One Niner, Twenty Five Fourteen is rolling. If you are near your truck, toggle your 800. One click if close, two if not."

"Twenty Five Fourteen, Three Two Twenty, I'm also rolling. It looks like that place we talked about earlier." Kragie had seen the signal too. The place was near Art Lake.

Grady Service floored the accelerator and turned on his blue lights.

"Twenty Five Fourteen, Three One Oh Three is passing Kenton, on M-28 coming your way." This was Sergeant Willie Celt out of Houghton on the 800, which made three COs en route. As he flew along he heard del Olmo and Grinda also check in, and two Troops. A panic button, the system's designers had assured the state, would bring officers swarming toward the problem. They hadn't lied.

He was first to get to Denninger's truck, which was nosed into some white pines. The hood was cold. Kragie joined him three minutes later, Celt a minute after that. Service continued trying to raise Denninger on his 800, but she wasn't answering. He flashed his SureFire into the cab of her truck. No handheld 800. Had to be on her belt. "She called me on her cell," Service told the other officers, "but I lost her. Let's find her track."

Celt got a rifle out of his truck. Kragie brought his shotgun. Service found a boot print, and told the others, "I've got her."

They moved south at a fast, steady pace known as the recon shuffle. Service stopped briefly every few minutes and used his green light to make sure he was still on her trail, his X-ray night vision working better for living things than for tracks. Kragie flanked left, Celt right.

"Fence," Kragie reported over the 800. "To my left, eighty yards, maybe."

Service kept moving south, saw that the distance between prints was getting smaller. She had started out walking fast, but had slowed. Why? "On me," he said into the 800. The others joined him. Service shone his light on the ground. "She got cautious here. Let's snail-walk from here."

Grady Service's night vision had clicked in. He stayed just left of Denninger's tracks, was able to move his head to keep branches from slapping his skin. Time slowed. He felt keyed, but calm. Heavy vines and low trees with spikey, sharp, three-inch thorns. He keyed his radio. "Thick wall of hawthorns dead ahead. Use gloves if you have them."

Service moved slowly through the dense foliage, moving branches where he could, ducking and sliding sideways when he couldn't. When he broke through to an opening, he stopped. He could faintly hear Celt struggling through the heavy cover off to his right.

"Jesus—fuck!" Kragie yelped from the left.

"Stay *back*," a faint voice said from ahead. He poked his head out of the thicket, looked, saw a silhouette. "Dani?"

"Use light. Dropped mine."

Service turned on his SureFire, pointed it at her. She was on the ground, on her side, up on an elbow.

"Stay where you are," Denninger said. "Trap's got my leg. Really . . . *hurts*."

Trap? He studied the ground between them. It looked clear, and he started to ease ahead slowly.

From his left, Kragie said, "There's a goddamn trap over here! I triggered it with a stick."

"Got one by me too," Celt said from the right. "Damn-near invisible."

"Great," Denninger moaned. "Am I the *only* one who can't see the fucking *things*? I think they're in a circle. Look at the big tree behind me."

Service redirected his light. There was a deer draped around the base of the tree. His light caught the reflection of a cable, and his heart nearly stopped. He'd heard of such things but had never seen one. "Everybody freeze and watch my light," he said. "We've got a wolf tree."

Two firsts in the same night—a panic button and a wolf tree. There were no odds on either, much less both. He moved to Denninger, got down on one knee, used his green light. What the hell kind of a trap was it? Not one he'd seen before. It had her above the ankle. Blood everywhere. Cloth tourniquet around her thigh, a pencil twisted in it for leverage. She'd been thinking, he thought, but its being there also put the foot in jeopardy.

"You been loosening it?"

"Uh-huh," she mumbled. "I think . . ."

"How long?"

She shook her head, showed him her watch. "No idea. You like my lipstick shade?"

"Shut up, Dani." She was shocky, her skin clammy. *Not good at all.*

"Willie. Can you see your trap?" Celt had trapped since he was a boy and was one of the department's most knowledgeable in that area.

"Holy smokes! It's a modified Conibear 330, a big fucker. It's a kill trap."

"It's got Dani's ankle. How do I open the damn thing?"

"You have to turn up the end of the trap."

"Dani, this is going to hurt—a lot. You've got to shift over to your other side to help me."

"My God!" she yelped, trying to roll. He helped her with his hand.

"Got it," Service said into his radio.

"Put your boot on the lower frame, reach down, and pull up hard on the upper spring. This trap maintains pressure until it's reset. You'll have to wrench it off."

Grady Service sucked in a deep breath, put his foot on the trap, took hold of the spring, and pulled.

Denninger screamed and thrashed momentarily.

The 800 crackled. Service hit the volume so he could hear. "Grady, Simon. I'm at Dani's truck. Where are you guys?"

Service radioed, "Call EMS. Look for our trails behind her truck. We're south. Come the way we came in your vehicle. Turn on all your lights and stay on your radio. I'll flash my light in the treetops. Let me know when you see it."

Service bounced his light beam off the trees just east of their position.

"Got it," del Olmo reported.

"We're ten yards in front of the lit tree. I'll leave my light on it until you get here. You're going to have to bash your way through some hawthorns. Take it slowly."

Service checked the tourniquet, decided to let EMS loosen it. He got behind Denninger, rested her head on his leg, rubbed her forehead.

"Can you believe I stepped on that stupid thing?" she asked.

"Be quiet."

"And I just ordered fuck-me heels from Victoria's Secret," she said. "Just for you."

"Stop it."

"Am I going to lose my foot?"

"No, just your nail polish."

"Oh good. Two feet, two shoes, no spare. It *really* hurts, Grady."

She was loopy and shocky. He looked up, saw patrol truck lights. "I know. Hang tough. Simon's almost there." He said into his 800, "Keep coming." To Dani: "We're gonna get you out of here. Everything's gonna be fine."

"That poor deer," Denninger muttered. "Why would somebody chain a dead deer to a tree?"

"Relax, Dani. Stop talking."

"Easy for you big macho types to say. Try being a girl."

The steel deer guard of del Olmo's truck nosed through the hawthorns. "Stop *there*!" Service radioed.

"Am I bleeding out?" Denninger asked.

"No, you're okay. Hang in there."

"I see her," del Olmo said, getting out of his truck.

"Don't move," Service said. "Wolf tree."

Service heard del Olmo moving equipment from his backseat to the front.

"Junco, Willie, we need to clear a path to her."

The two men came over, started forward.

Service took off his coat. Del Olmo came forward with two aspen poles he always carried in the bed of his truck. They put the poles through the arms of the coat and zipped it up to form the bed of a stretcher.

The four men carefully lifted Denninger onto the makeshift litter and carried her to the truck, easing her into the backseat, back-first. Kragie got in from the other side, got her by the shoulders, and eased her across. Denninger winced, but didn't cry out. Tears streamed from her eyes. "I dropped my flashlight. All my stuff's back there."

"Don't worry," Service said, rubbing her neck. "We've got you covered."

"Take it slow," he told del Olmo as he slid behind the wheel.

The three officers walked beside the truck in case it got stuck.

Grinda reported in on the radio. "Covington EMS is two minutes out."

The EMS personnel worked quickly, loosened the tourniquet, got

Denninger onto a gurney and into their ambulance, and started an IV drip.

One of the techs leaned close to Service's ear. "Compound fracture."

Service patted the man's arm to let him know he'd heard. He'd seen the protruding bone when he'd found her, had said nothing about it.

"We'll bring a bottle of wine to the hospital," Service said as they began to close the ambulance doors.

"White," Denninger said. "Seen enough red for tonight. I just bought fuck-me heels," he heard her tell one of the techs, who said, "Way cool."

Two Troops came bouncing up the road in their patrol units. The five conservation officers and two state policemen took del Olmo's truck back to the site and the COs began disarming the seven traps that hadn't been tripped.

"This is some deeply disturbed shit," a young Troop said as he watched the conservation officers work.

They took photographs of each trap and its location, and when the traps were cleared, got photos of the deer cabled to the tree. Kragie brought up his handheld GPS and dropped markers.

"Where's the Art Lake fence?" Service asked the Baraga County officer.

"Over that way. Close."

The two men stood by the fence, which was less than a hundred yards from the wolf tree site.

Celt joined them. "Junco and I will hang here tonight, look this place over closely in the morning. Any idea what this is about?"

My fault. I sent her here. Service shook his head ruefully, and checked his watch. It was just after 4 A.M.

Service, del Olmo, and Grinda drove to Baraga County Memorial Hospital in L'Anse. Some years back Service had spent some time in their emergency room after a nasty fight with a mentally unbalanced man north of Baraga.

Captain Ware Grant called on the cell phone while they waited outside Emergency.

"You find her?"

"She's in with the docs right now. It was a wolf tree, Cap'n. She stepped on a wolf trap."

"Leg?"

"Compound fracture, right at the ankle. Don't know the extent or what else yet."

Silence from the captain. Then, "The people who did this, Detective?"

"Sir?"

"No quarter."

Three hours later she was in Recovery. She would keep the foot and have full use if rehab went right. Service told the doctor no sedatives until they could talk to her.

"Make it quick," the doctor said. He had blood on his smock. "The tourniquet saved the foot."

"I'll tell her."

"Drink?" Denninger said, when he stepped in with her.

Service tipped a cup of water with a flexible straw to her lips, adjusting the straw for her. "Just a sip. You did good out there."

"No, I didn't. I really fucked the pooch."

"Just bad luck. We've all had it."

"Not me. I'm naturally lucky."

"What happened?"

"You told me to snoop the place. That's what I was doing."

Service felt sick to his stomach.

Denninger grabbed his sleeve. "I swear I never saw it."

Service looked at the nurse and nodded. She added something to Denninger's IV. "We'll talk again when you wake up," he said.

"I'm totally *serious* about those shoes," she whispered.

"C'mon," Service said to the other officers.

The captain says no quarter. So it shall be.

13

Iron River, Iron County

MONDAY, MAY 22, 2006

The drive from Baraga seemed to drag as Service made a mental list of follow-up tasks, trying to make separate lists for each of the three incidents. It didn't matter how or if the wolf tree was related to the other cases; Denninger had been hurt, and he wasn't going to let go of that until someone was held accountable. Eventually the details got too confused to keep organized in his head. He pulled off the road in northern Iron County and typed a preliminary list into his computer:

Paint River homicide: wire source, spring guns, woman who went to Box for help and was sent on to Allerdyce; Hjalmquist's records?

Skull case: Bernalli's widow. Black immigrants. Who were they, what did family lore tell (if anything) about their aborted adventure in the U.P.? Can descendants be found? How? Not in papers at the time, or just not found? Records somewhere? Catholic priest O'Neil—real or fake, and does it matter? Flour gold in remains? Germane?

Denninger and the wolf tree case: Who set the traps, and why there? Were there others? What about Art Lake, what's the deal there? Who pays their taxes? He underlined taxes several times.

Kragie and Sergeant Celt were still out at the Art Lake property.

He called Kragie's cell phone. "Service. Anything?"

"Found a couple more sites where there might have been wolf trees, chain marks on bark, that sort of thing; nothing definite, but possible," Kragie said. "There's no crossing we can find through the fence to Art Lake, and no beaten-down trails, but not that far from Denninger's spot, there's a path cut along the fence and another coming from the north. Looks like both get traveled a lot. We can see a couple of surveillance cameras in trees inside the fence. Pretty well hidden, no doubt professionally installed.

"One path may be for internal perimeter security," Kragie continued. "No footprints outside other than Denninger's and ours, but we pretty well trampled the ground getting her out, and if there were prints, they're history. On the other hand, good trappers don't leave tracks or scents, and it seems to me that only an experienced trapper could put down a wolf tree. The Troops took the traps to dust for fingerprints. We should be clear of here noonish."

"Anyone from Art Lake come down to see what all the lights and ruckus were about?"

"Didn't see anyone, but that doesn't mean they weren't watching."

Service updated the wolf tree case list: *Private security at Art Lake? Bodies—primarily passive technology, or a mix? If bodies, who and how many?*

Passing a large facility on the left on US 2, a mile west of the DNR district office in Crystal Falls, Service saw a sign that said Victorian Heights. He swung the Tahoe into the parking lot and called Friday. "Petersson said the Bernalli woman is in a nursing home in Crystal Falls. Call him and get the name of the place and let me know, okay? I'll wait."

Half a cigarette later, she called him back. "Said he misspoke. The woman is in assisted living, not a nursing home. The place is called Victorian Heights."

Assisted living, nursing home. What the hell is the distinction? "I'm there now. I'll pop in and try to see her."

"Push back our meeting again?"

"Nope, we should be okay."

"You going to have time for lunch?"

"Not sure."

"Mike and I are picking up some stuff from Angelli's deli. We'll have something for you. Any preferences?"

"Calories."

Friday sighed. "Me too."

Friday and Millitor were easy to work with.

Service walked into the lobby and showed his badge at Reception. "I need to talk to Mrs. Bernalli."

"Let me call her."

A minute later the receptionist pointed down a hall. "Room 140, on the right."

The woman said "Come in" when he knocked, but didn't get up to greet him.

He found her in a small apartment decorated with fabric flowers, with a stove, fridge, and microwave, and no dust anywhere. She was seated on a small love seat with a red-white-and-blue-plaid afghan draped over her legs. He sat in the only other chair, maple wood, a frilly cushion with Italian flags needlepointed into the fabric.

"I'm Detective Service with the DNR," he introduced himself. He took out a business card and held it out, but when she ignored it, he put it on a small table by the love seat. Maybe she was arthritic. "I'm sorry about your husband," he began.

"It's been five years," she countered.

High titers of prickly, and absolutely no trace of an accent. "I believe Theo Petersson talked to you about your late husband's father."

"He talked," she said through tight lips.

Why the attitude? "We've got a difficult case," he said.

"The skulls near Elmwood, or the man shot the second day of trout season?"

"Elmwood," he said. The woman might be elderly, but she was mentally sharp and obviously keeping track of area goings-on.

"Can't help you," she said. "My family brought me to America in 1941. I never lived in Elmwood. Mr. Bernalli and I lived only in Iron Mountain."

"I thought you might have heard some things about black families who lived in Elmwood in the 1920s."

"Ancient history," the woman said. "You move to a new place and you either adapt or perish. It's the same everywhere."

"Which means you did hear things."

She glowered. "I didn't say that."

"But you knew they had moved here, and that wasn't in the papers."

The woman glared at him, the corners of her mouth drooping, and he knew the interview had ended. Like Petersson, he had gotten nothing.

He touched the business card on the table, nodded, thanked her for her time, and stepped into the hall. A bent woman with hair like coarse blue straw was standing in a walker outside the room. "Real social, ain't she?" the woman said. "I'm Helmi Koski. Heard youse're DNR."

He hadn't been in the building ten minutes; word here traveled more quickly than on the normal Yooper word-of-mouth grapevine, which rivaled fiber-optic cables in speed. "Nice to meet you," he said.

"Nobody talks to the old biddy. Thinks she's better'n everybody. To live here people gotta cooperate and help each other. That one. . . ." She shook her head and didn't finish. "Something I can do to help youse? I'm the nose-tube crew's social director." She put two fingers to her nostrils and made heavy breathing sounds.

Nose-tube crew? He had to swallow a laugh. "I doubt it. How long have you lived in the county?"

"Born right here Crystal Falls, 1917. I'm eighty-nine years young next month!"

"So you would have been ten in 1927?"

The woman laughed. "That some sort of arithmetic question for senior citizens?"

"No, ma'am. Just wondering."

"Ten in 1927, that's right."

"Do you recall hearing about a group of black families who moved to Elmwood in the west county in 1926, to grow potatoes?"

The woman scratched her chin and rolled her head. "We never heard they was there. But we heard there was some trouble, and that the sheriff went and brung them to town. I went down to the station when the sheriff brought them in. He took them up to the poor farm for medical care and food. Believe it or not, the poor farm was right here where this building is now. They looked terrible, poor things. I run home and got some of our old coats and boots and took them to the poor farm for a couple of girls our age.

"Thing I remember is that bad as things were for those folks, they looked proud, looked you right in the eye. They stayed three days. I got to know a girl named Rillamae Garden. Same age as me, almost to the day. We got to be good friends, Rillamae and me. We both cried when she had to leave. We promised to write each other every day for the rest of our lives."

"Did you?"

She puffed up her chest. "Helmi Koski don't make promises she don't keep. We still exchange Christmas cards. Both got bad backs and eyes now, but we *always* get out our cards. We both lived hard lives."

"She's alive?"

"Still kicking last Christmas."

"Do you have an address or a phone number for her?"

"Follow me," the woman said. She started off down the hall in her walker at a pace slower than a snail's. Fifteen minutes later Grady Service had an envelope in his hand, the address on an AARP sticker. A shakily written phone number was scribbled diagonally on the face of the envelope, the writing so erratic he could hardly read it.

As he started through the lobby, he spied Mrs. Bernalli, who frowned and made an obscene gesture with bunched fingers. *Okay, then. No arthritis in that hand.*

• • •

Back at the office, he dropped the envelope on the table in front of Friday and said, "Some days it pays to be nice to old ladies."

"Bernalli's widow?"

"With her attitude she could have been Mussolini's mistress."

Millitor picked up the envelope. "Mrs. Rillamae Thigpen?"

"Married name. She was Rillamae Garden when she was in Elmwood. She was still alive last Christmas. There's a woman in the assisted living home named Helmi Koski. She met Rillamae Garden when they were both ten. They've been writing to each other ever since."

Millitor began to smile. "Holy cow. Only in the Yoop, eh?"

Tuesday Friday pushed a bowl of cottage cheese toward him. "I guess the legend's got substance," she said.

"Elmwood?"

"No, *you.*" Friday then announced that she had gotten the name of a small wire manufacturer in Eagle River, Wisconsin. Service took a spoonful of cottage cheese. "Maybe there's more than one legend in this room."

"I just want to get the scum who did this," Friday said.

"That's exactly what fuels legends," Service said.

Mike Millitor took out a cigar stump, stuck it in the corner of his mouth, and grinned. "Haven't had this much fun in years, and I ain't done doodly-duck yet."

"Lunch first, then let's make us a list of things we have to get done, and start really pounding this case," Service said.

Allerdyce Compound, Southwest Marquette County

TUESDAY, MAY 23, 2006

Friday was en route to Eagle River, Wisconsin, for an early morning meeting with the senior sales VP for Eagle Specialty Steel and Wire Fabrications. Millitor had driven down to Iron Mountain for the annual Retired Upper Peninsula Law Enforcement Officers Association spring benefit golf scramble, whatever the hell that was. Grinda was working a designated trout lake in northwest Iron County, and Simon del Olmo had been dispatched to the south county to investigate a wolf depredation allegation.

Grady Service sat on the porch smoking a cigarette when Lars Hjalmquist called. "I found my daybook. Penny Provo taught elementary school in Trout Creek. She had two DUIs and was invited to resign. She was also in the 1776th Military Police Company out of Kingsford. When the blowup came in Trout Creek in '02, she was on some sort of deployment in Colorado, went over the fence, and hasn't been seen since—except for an unsubstantiated report from somewhere in the Colorado area two years ago."

"You had all that written in your book?"

"No, I had my own stuff, but after that, I pulled a clipping from the Ironwood *Daily Globe* about her resignation from Trout Creek. I remembered the name, stuck it in my book, just in case."

"She was an MP?"

"Yeah, a sister cop," said Hjalmquist.

"You said, 'Just in case.' "

"I had contact with her for alleged hunter harassment south of Bessemer in November '98. It was alleged that she threatened two hunters with a shotgun. When I found her, she denied it, and when I interviewed the hunters they were both blotto, and didn't want it getting out that a woman had scared them out of their hunting blinds."

"You remember the contact?" Service asked.

"Especially after I read my notes. She was pretty, petite, and polite, look-you-straight-in-the-eye, nossir, yessir, very formal, very correct, the whole drill. She denied the allegations, said the men had been drinking and the whole thing was a mistake, that she didn't own any personal firearms, and didn't hunt. I checked the Retail Sales System and found she'd never bought a license. She insisted she was walking where she always walked, and that the two men got abusive when she showed up. Since the men didn't want to press charges, I gave all of them a warning and cut them all loose."

There was something in the old game warden's voice, a hitch maybe. "But?"

"Couldn't peg it. She looked good superficially, but there was something off about her. My last note was, 'Full deck?' "

"Huh," Service said. "You and Joanie finish your shopping?"

Joan was his wife and constant companion. Hjalmquist grunted and said, "Shopping is never *done,* pal. It's only suspended for lack of cash or tapped-out credit cards."

"You warned Provo in '98 in Bessemer. Was she living over there then?"

"Nope. She said she'd only been in state four months, was living down in Kingsford, and looking for a teaching job. She had a valid Colorado driver's license, no wants or warrants. She was clean as a whistle."

"In '98? How long did she teach in Trout Creek?"

"Don't know for sure, man. Until '01, I guess. Wish I could have been more help, buddy."

"You ever encounter a wolf tree, Lars?"

"Never even heard of one until after I retired."

How did she end up in the Michigan National Guard only four months in state? Had she transferred? "Did you see her military ID?" Service asked.

"Didn't need it. Her license was okay."

"How'd you know her outfit number?"

"It was in the newspaper article about her resigning to 'pursue other career opportunities.' "

"Did the article talk about her desertion?"

"No, that musta happened after the Trout Creek deal."

"Thanks, Lars."

"Anytime, pal."

Service lit another cigarette. If the woman was living in Kingsford in

1998, why had she said she walked regularly near Bessemer, which was 150 miles west of where she lived—in deer season? He thought he understood what had happened. The woman denied the charges, the men didn't want to prosecute, and Lars was ass-deep in deer season with too many other pressing things to do. Deer season was the craziest time of the year for almost all officers, and his friend had not listened carefully enough to what the woman was telling him and maybe he had missed something. It would have helped if he'd asked for her military ID. His gut said the hunters were telling the truth.

A lot of things didn't add up. Box claimed Provo came to him in 1997 to "learn guns," and that he'd heard later she had "joined up." Yet, according to Lars, she'd been living in Michigan for only four months in the fall of 1998. Millitor said Box had always been credible as an informant. When had she joined the National Guard? Something tells me Penny Provo's what other cops call a "person of interest."

The mere idea of talking to Limpy Allerdyce made his stomach roll. Allerdyce, the allegedly reformed poacher, had played a key role in helping conclude a lethal case two summers ago. Allerdyce, his extended family, and their hangers-on lived in a compound in the distant reaches of southwest Marquette County, a place you had to know about in order to find it.

He'd already made one questionable phone call today, and so far no callback on that one. This would be his second of the day, and after dialing it and letting it ring and ring, he hung up. No surprise: Allerdyce and his low-life crew moved around the U.P. like fog. Here and gone, invisible blood trails in their wakes.

Willie Celt called from L'Anse. "Thought you'd want to know they're moving Denninger to Marquette tonight."

"Something wrong?"

"The reality of modern health care: They need her bed. But the doctor here also thinks it would be a good idea for specialists in Marquette to check her leg. He says the bones should heal fine, but he's a little worried about permanent nerve damage."

"Moving her tonight?"

"Yeah."

"I'll stop and see her tomorrow morning."

"Long drive for you."

"I've got business in southwest Marquette County tonight, and I need to check on my animals and stop at my office."

"Southwest Marquette County . . . Allerdyce?"

"Bingo." COs tended to know who all the worst poachers in the U.P. were, and Allerdyce was the worst, his crew oozing all over the peninsula.

"You want Kragie and me to visit Art Lake, knock on the gate, say we're just out meeting folks?"

"No, leave them be for now. We've got some things working to figure out a more direct way in."

"Okay. Later."

Why a wolf tree, and why that particular spot?

• • •

Service pulled into the parking area a half-mile from Allerdyce's camp just after dark, locked his truck, and made his way through the dense mature basswood, hemlock, and white cedar forest to the compound. There was no marked trail, and you had to know the way, otherwise you'd find yourself lost in some of the nastiest, wildest swamp in the central Upper Peninsula.

Service knew he was being watched as he walked into the dark camp and went directly to Limpy's cabin. All the buildings in the compound had burned three years ago, but they had since been rebuilt. He knocked on the door and Allerdyce himself answered.

"Youse run outta gas and lose your state get-gas-free card or somepin', sonny?" the old poacher asked with the grating cackle that invariably made hair stand up on Service's arms.

"Penny Provo," Service said.

Allerdyce stared at him. "What about 'er? You gettin' some of dat, too?"

Allerdyce claimed to have had sex with just about every female he'd ever met, true or not. Ironically, a lot more of his claims were true than most people understood. "We need to talk."

Allerdyce held open the door and let Service step inside. Two years ago the old man was keeping company with an author-professor from Northern Michigan University. "Where's your *soul mate*?"

"Gone back North Cargoliner. Up here for da year semenatical, write da book."

The old man's twisted syntax, offbeat vocabulary, and frequent mala-props made him seem a fool, but conservation officers knew him to be smart, his behavior no more than an act honed as sharp as a flensing knife.

"Cuppa mud?"

"If some's made."

"Always got mud," Allerdyce said, taking a pot and pouring two cups. "Been a while since I seen youse, sonny."

Some years back he'd caught Allerdyce, gotten into a scuffle, and acci-dentally been shot in the leg by the old man, who spent seven years in prison before being paroled. Since then Allerdyce had tried to be his snitch, with mixed results.

"Provo back U.P.?" Allerdyce asked.

"Did I say she'd left?" Service countered. Any conversation with Allerdyce was a joust, each probing the other for weakness and information.

"Was Natural Guard, Kingsford. Was off ta some trainin' ting when she got canned Trout Creek. Heard she trew away uniform, bugged out. Wim-mens," the old man added, as if gender explained everything.

"Rankin Box," Service said.

Allerdyce lit up. "Howse dat ole coot doin'?"

"You know him?"

"Go back long time."

"Colleagues?"

Allerdyce chuckled. "Just chums. Box is gun guy, not no real cedar swamp savage like youse or me."

"He claims he referred Provo to *you* to learn guns."

"She in the army; why she need me learn her guns?"

Indeed, Service thought. "Don't bullshit me. I'm not in the mood for your asshole games."

Allerdyce held out his hands. "Trut', sonny. When was it she was 'posed ta come over dis way?"

"Late nineties."

Limpy shook his head. "Yeah, sure, I got pass from warden down Jack-town, droved up here jes to meet wit' 'er."

"She was directed to your camp. I thought maybe she dealt with one of your people."

"Only one it woulda been back den was Jerry."

The son, Jerry Allerdyce, a career criminal and philanderer, had been murdered in 2001 by perpetrators of a diamond mining scam.

"Was Jerry, won't never know, him bein' up heaven, or some such," Limpy said. "You got case in fire?"

"I don't need your help, old man." *Jerry Allerdyce in heaven*?

Allerdyce had his teeth out and rolled his jaws for a minute. "Lemme guess. Dis about dose booby traps down Sout' Branch Paint, hey."

"What booby traps?"

"Wasn't in paper, but word gets 'round, eh? Ain't no secrets You-Pee. Spring guns, I heard. Also some cables strunged crosset river."

As it always was, the accuracy of the old poacher's intelligence network was both astounding and depressing.

"Say dis, sonny: Only shit-balls use spring gun."

Service was fairly certain that the booby trap information had been effectively buried. He also knew he'd probably heard all he was going to hear from Limpy without applying some real pressure. "Thanks for the help," he said sarcastically. When he stood up, he added, "So when was it you and Provo mixed bodily fluids?"

"Gen'leman don' 'posed ta say."

"You're not a gentleman."

"Could be she heard how good Limpy is."

Service poked his finger at the poacher. "The question is, *when*?"

"Sonny-boy pissed?"

"See, I'm thinking you saw her *after* she left the army, and I'm just guessing here—that Army CID will want to talk to you."

"I'm pubic-minted citizen," Allerdyce said. "But army got no say my life."

Service looked over at the old man. "What do you know about wolf trees?"

This seemed to catch Allerdyce by surprise. "Know what dey are, 'course."

"But you've never set one?"

"I *like* wolfies," Limpy said. "Dey make it easy find deer. Why I catch poor tings in traps?"

Service believed him about the wolves. "If you hear anything about a wolf tree, give me a call."

Allerdyce broke into a huge grin. "Holy wah—youse're askin' Limpy's help?"

Service hung his head. "Don't gloat."

"Bin waitin' long time dis day, youse betcha!"Allerdyce said, slapping his hands together. "Youse finally 'cep Limpy changed."

"Not for a Mackinac minute," Service said, getting up. Allerdyce would never change. He couldn't. "When your memory improves on Provo, give me a call; otherwise, I'm passing the information on to CID, and you're on your own with the feds after that. Call by five today, or adios, motherfucker."

Limpy's mouth hung open.

Service drove from Limpy's camp to Slippery Creek, got mauled by his dog and cat, and slept uneasily on the footlockers that served as his bed.

15

Three Lakes, Baraga County

WEDNESDAY, MAY 24, 2006

First thing in the morning Service stopped early at the hospital in Marquette. Denninger was in a semiprivate room.

"You doing your physical therapy?" he asked.

"It hasn't started yet," she said.

"Make sure you do it."

She rolled her eyes. "That's what I've been telling you," she said, laughing. Then, in a serious tone, "The doctors are telling me I could be out of action for six months. Will I get laid off if I'm out that long?"

"It doesn't work that way. They'll stick you in an office with a phone, and give you light duty until you're ready to go back to a regular schedule."

"Thank God," she said. "I *love* this job, and the other night I didn't mean to make this sound like your fault. I chose when to check out that place, and I stepped on the stupid trap. My fault alone."

"All jobs are *about* mistakes, especially our jobs," he said. "The trick is to not make the same ones, and learn from those you do make."

"Have you learned from yours?"

"Tried to. That's the best any of us can do."

"How's Little Mar?"

"My granddaughter's fine."

"She reading yet?"

Service smiled. "Only at sixth-grade level, but she'll get better."

Denninger waggled a finger at him and reached up with her arms. "C'mere, *you*."

He went over to her, bent down, and reciprocated with a long hug. She whispered, "I know I can be a bit of a pain in the ass."

"A bit?"

"You haven't even been to bed with me yet," she said with a wink.

"If you need anything, call Fern LeBlanc at the regional office, or Candi McCants."

"Your thing with McCants—it's really not a thing?"

"No."

"And you're still friends?"

• • •

Baraga County sheriff Bruce "Pinky" Barbeaux had been elected in a landslide after retiring from a distinguished twenty-five-year career as a conservation officer, having finished as the lieutenant for a district in northeast Michigan before moving back to his hometown of Herman, one of the snowiest, coldest places in the U.P.

After visiting Denninger, Service dropped Cat and Newf at Kira Lehto's vet clinic and headed west for a talk with Barbeaux. They rendezvoused at the Moseying Moose in Three Lakes, just a few miles into Baraga County.

Barbeaux's county SUV was already parked and the sheriff inside, holding court with the local morning coffee klatch, regaling them with stories of the exploits of his "boys." Barbeaux was a gregarious, natural leader the DNR had sent to a prestigious FBI school for non-federal law enforcement officers. Service had always thought that Barbeaux would become the DNR's chief when Lorne O'Driscoll retired, so the fact that Lorne was still on the job and Barbeaux had retired five years ago—and had subsequently been elected to sheriff the year after that—had come as surprises.

"Folks," Barbeaux bellowed when Service walked in, "meet Grady Service. You don't ever want this big bugger on your trail."

The people stared at him as Pinky pumped his hand. "Sorry for your loss," Barbeaux whispered as they sat down. "What brings you over this way?"

"I think you know."

"Yeah, I heard. A wolf tree, for chrissakes. How's your officer?"

"Her name's Denninger, and they moved her to Marquette last night. She should be okay."

"I'm thinkin' the boys and girls in green and gray are gonna hammer a giant-size pole up someone's keester."

"It would help to have a suspect."

Barbeaux nodded. "I feel your pain."

"Art Lake," Service said. "What do you know about the place? Seems to me the sheriff of the county would have more insight than anyone."

"Seems that way to me, too, but we'd both be wrong. Got no clue what goes on over there."

"You ever been inside?"

"Once, right after I got elected, I got a letter inviting me on a certain date. I drove over and a Chicago lawyer named Evers Gorsline met me, took me through the gate to a giganto lodge, and a spread of chow that a sumo with a tapeworm couldn't get down. Middle of the bloody day. Gorsline's in his sixties, fit, tall, smooth, makes small talk, the man-for-any-situation type. When we're having coffee and brandy and cigars after the meal, he says, 'We of Art Lake relish our privacy. In the unlikely event your department gets a call for assistance, you will check with me first. I am available by telephone twenty-four/seven.' "

"You agreed?"

"He handed me a check that paid for three new cruisers for my road patrols. I told him I'd keep his request in mind. If there'd been a call I wouldn't have called him, but there's been nothing. So I never had to make that particular decision. The place is quiet."

"They have a gate with security?"

"Electronic. Di'n't see any people. Honking big fence all around the place. My people tell me they've seen surveillance cameras on some of the stanchions. What's your interest?"

"The proximity of the wolf tree, my gut, curiosity—not sure. You still got Gorsline's phone number?"

"The Van Dalen Foundation has bought us new patrol vehicles every year I've been in office, and all sorts of commo and equipment upgrades. Without their generosity, my department would be hurting worse than it is."

"Officer down, Pinky."

Barbeaux gnawed his bottom lip, took a deep breath, grabbed a napkin, and wrote a number with a Chicago area code.

"You ever see him again?"

"Just the one time."

"Anybody else there with the two of you?"

"Just us, but I saw three vehicles."

Service raised an eyebrow. "And you didn't jot down their plate numbers?"

Barbeaux grinned. "I think I got 'em in a file somewhere. I'll call you with them—fair enough?"

"Thanks, Pinky."

"Don't be shittin' in my honey hole, Grady. I know you and your people got a job to do, but try diplomacy. It actually works."

Me and my people? He retired as one of us. "What was your impression of Gorsline?"

The sheriff bobbed his head. "Limpy Allerdyce in a three-piece suit. If he could scare you off with just a cap gun, he'd use napalm."

Service said, "Diplomacy."

"Good lad. Keep me tuned in, eh?"

Interesting, Service thought. *Pinky met the man only once, but doesn't have to look up his phone number?*

16

Redlight Creek, Ontonagon County

All sorts of things seemed to be dancing just out of view in Grady Service's brain, and having gotten a name from Pinky Barbeaux, he knew the only way ahead was to follow every lead, talk to every person with even the thinnest theoretical relevance. One thing a cop learned was that the old thing about six degrees of separation between all people was more true than not. If you kept poking, it was amazing the connections you could find. What he needed was to find a flash of red under the ice, but he doubted it would happen this time.

There were two kinds of history in the U.P., and this was of the second type, by far the most difficult to bring to light. Someone had nearly killed Tree, and had killed another man. Tree was recovering and had moved over to his camp in the eastern U.P. Two skulls had been found by Newf, the skeletons sprinkled with gold dust. And Denninger had been attacked. His gut whispered: *Linkage!* The evidence, however, remained mute.

Detectives Millitor and Friday were good partners, but he was pretty sure that somehow the outcome of all this rode squarely on his shoulders.

All of this played through his mind during the one-hour drive from Three Lakes to Rankin Box's camp on Redlight Creek.

It was just after five when he got there, and as soon as he pulled down the drive and parked he sensed that something was seriously wrong. The cabin's front door was open, and two coyotes were sniffing around the opening.

"Beat it!" he shouted, and started forward. He smelled death and heard flies inside before he got to the door. He took a deep breath to calm himself and moved inside. He found Box still in his chair, slumped forward in a dramatic final bow. Flies were swarming all over the house. *Don't touch anything,* he told himself, backed out, and got on the radio to Ontonagon County to report the body.

A female Troop named Stone was first to arrive, soon followed by two Ontonagon County deps. Service held up his badge, took a hit on his cigarette, and pointed. "By the back window," was all he said.

"You touch anything?" Trooper Stone asked.

He shook his head.

Stone came back out quickly, looking a little green. "I'm calling our forensics tech. The deps are calling the ME. It will take everyone a while to get here. You were smart to not touch anything."

She's what, twenty-something, green behind the ears? Then, chiding himself, thought, You were a rookie too. Back off.

When Trooper Stone stepped over to her cruiser to vomit he didn't look at her, and when she had composed herself, he offered her a cigarette and she took it. "First murder?"

"How do you know it's a murder?"

"You'd have to be double-jointed to commit suicide with a shot directly in the back of the head. Rankin Box could hardly move, and couldn't hold anything." Service curled his hands into claws and held them up. "Arthritis."

"Box—that's his name? You knew him?"

"Met him once."

"Cyndi," she said, holding out her hand.

"Grady," he said, accepting it.

"You're DNR?"

He nodded. "Detective, Wildlife Resource Protection."

"What are you doing here?"

"Save the questions until we find out who catches the case. I don't like repeating myself."

By eight o'clock the camp yard was littered with vehicles. Tuesday Friday stopped on her way back from her Wisconsin meeting and looked concerned. "You all right?"

"Better than old man Box. He took one round to the back of the hat," he said. "Looks small-caliber. The ME's just about done."

She asked, "What brought you back here?"

"Hjalmquist called and told me about a contact he had with Penny Provo. Due to circumstances, I don't think he saw the holes in her story, but I did, and some of the dates Box gave us didn't seem quite right. I also talked to Allerdyce. He was in prison, and the most likely person Provo would have dealt with was his son, Jerry, now permanently dead. But I think Allerdyce has met her since then. When is still at issue."

"Were you going to press Box?"

"Not press. I just wanted to clarify some things, see if I could jog his memory to glean more details."

Friday went away and came back after a few minutes. "Odd. The barn is open and it looks like some of the carvings are gone, but not the bear, and that's the most valuable thing in there."

"Too heavy to lug, maybe. Or maybe it wasn't a real robbery," he said.

She stared at him. "Does this have something to do with us?"

He shrugged. "I don't know yet."

A minivan came rushing down the driveway. A woman in her forties jumped out and came running forward, screaming, "Dad, Dad—oh my God!"

A deputy blocked the way. Friday stepped toward the woman. Service said, "Not our case, Tuesday."

She ignored him, and huddled with the woman, who shuddered and cried silently.

Friday called over a deputy. "Get somebody to drive her home?"

"Not a problem," the deputy said.

"His daughter," Friday said. "Works at the casino. Hadn't talked to her dad since she called Mike for him."

"How was Eagle River?"

"Productive," she said wearily. "The company uses jobbers, thirty of them all over northern Wisconsin and the U.P. Two other companies sell wire up here. That's the bad news. The good news is that only one company makes the model wire you found on the river. It's made by Peachtree Enterprises out of Milwaukee, and is used almost exclusively by corrections departments for max-security facilities."

"That's *great* news."

"Only nine prisons in the U.P., and only Alger and Baraga are maxies. Do cases ever stop feeling like they're all uphill?"

"Only when you feel like you've stepped off a cliff. When that happens, you can't wait to hit the ground, chute or not."

"Well, it's something, right?"

"Something," he said, not wanting to discourage her. He filled her in on all he had learned about Penny Provo.

When he had finished, she said, "I see why you wanted to talk to Box."

"Your friend with the art gallery. You'd better cancel her visit."

"She was here yesterday afternoon," Friday said. "She called me afterwards on her cell phone, said there was too much value to calculate without spending more time. She took photos of everything to use for the appraisals."

"What time did you talk to her?"

"Six-ish."

"Obviously Box was still alive then."

"Makes you wonder what's going on," she said wistfully.

"It always feels like this," he said, lighting another cigarette, "especially when you get blind alley after blind alley after roadblock. We can try to talk to the army about Provo, but she's a deserter, or at least AWOL, and they don't like to talk about such glitches when national recruiting is under such pressure."

"Do we have *anything* positive?"

"Your kid still loves you," he said.

"Only because I feed him."

"Same for my dog."

She smiled. "What do you do when *you* hit the wall?"

"Get blind drunk," he said. "It makes me think I can break through."

"And that works?"

"Nope, but there's always hope."

"I guess hope's better than nothing. Drinks are on me tonight. No work talk."

Allerdyce called ten minutes before the deadline. Service walked up the road to talk privately to the old violator. "Was last year, I seen dat Provo piece one night," the poacher said.

"Where?"

"Motel over Gwinn."

"Name?"

"Starry Inn."

Service knew it. A real hole in the wall, a sometime hangout for Sawyer and Modeltowner crank freaks. "Who paid?"

"Her."

"How?"

"Cash."

"She tell you about her situation?"

"Din't meet ta chew fat, eh."

"If you didn't know her, why'd she call you?"

"Din't call. Sent message."

"Why?"

"Heard I was good at tings."

Service growled. "I'm not buying your shit tonight, Limpy. Truth, or I drop a dime."

"Wanted ta talk traps."

Service felt his heart race. "What kind of traps?"

"Big traps."

"Why you?"

"Coulda been mebbe I come into some 'boot den."

"*Legal* traps?"

"When I had 'em."

"Your ass is in deep trouble."

"I give you address, change tings?"

"Depends on the address and what we find."

"Mead Road, Iron County fire number 9122."

"You've been there?"

"Little bird said."

"Her place?"

"Belong friend, I tink."

Service hung up and played with his AVL until he found the Mead Road in northeast Iron County. No idea where the fire number was located, and no way to tell from the rolling map. He glanced at Friday as he started the engine and pulled around to leave the camp. "Have to take a rain check on drinks. We've got a lead on Provo."

"Solid?"

"We'll see."

Friday said, "You want company?"

"Yah, we'll pick up your wheels later. Get in."

He had heard what seemed like genuine conviction in Limpy's voice. This was as solid as it got.

He knew several state COs who had served or were on active duty with the National Guard, but didn't know who was where at the moment. A lot of COs were military vets, but rarely had official police business with the military, and he was at a loss for a name.

He finally decided to call Lieutenant Lisette McKower, his former sergeant, one-time lover, and old friend. She answered, "Lieutenant McKower, District Four."

"It's Grady."

"How's that granddaughter?"

"No time to make social, Lis. I'm brain-farting. Who do we have in the Army Guard?"

"Jimmy Cleary, District Ten, Monroe County. He's just back from Iraq, returns to duty June first."

Cleary had been a CO for a decade, made sergeant a couple of years back. "Got his home phone number?"

He could hear her fingers clicking keys on the computer. She came back, read the number to him, and said, "I'll put it in an e-mail too."

"Much grass," he said.

"Nice talking to you too," she said with a chuckle, and hung up.

Service stopped the truck and dialed Cleary's number.

"Sarn't Cleary, Grady Service."

"How goes the battle above the bridge?"

"Hooah! I've got a tip on an Army Guard deserter. I think it's solid, and she may be part of a case I'm working. If I pinch her, how do I play it?"

"She do a runner from a military prison?"

"From her unit."

"Not a deserter then. You have to be convicted to be a deserter. Army regs require the individual to be listed as AWOL for thirty-one days, then reclassified as DFR, Dropped from Rolls."

Cleary had always been a deliberate, by-the-regs officer, and would be no less as a sergeant. *Patience,* he told himself. "Who do I call if I grab her?"

"What unit is she with?"

"MP company out of Kingsford, I forget the unit designation."

"When did she go missing?"

"Summer '02, I think."

"Okay, give me a few minutes. The way the process works is that USA-DIP feeds accumulated DFR data to the NCIC Wanted File."

"USADIP?

"United States Army Deserter Information Point—single source for all related data. NCIC—"

Service cut him off. "I know. The FBI's National Crime Information Center." Two years ago he'd been in a case involving the FBI and found that some federal databases had some critical and mostly unpublicized flaws.

"Right," Cleary said, unfazed. "What's the soldier's name?"

"Penny Provo."

"Rank."

"No idea."

"Let me query USADIP and give you a call back."

Service gave the sergeant his cell number and e-mail address, and lit a cigarette.

Cleary called back fifteen minutes later. "Okay, she's in USADIP and NCIC, warrant outstanding, all civilian law enforcement agencies requested to apprehend and hold until custody can be transferred. Specialist Penance Provo, age thirty, has been gone since July 2002. The person you should call is Major Joseph Sutschek, CID out of Lansing. I gave him a heads-up and your number. He wants to talk to you."

"Can I get her photo?"

"Sutschek is sending it."

"Thanks. How was it over there?"

"You were in Vietnam?"

"Right."

"Then you know. Hooah!"

Friday looked at him. "Do you always operate at this pace?"

"We're just warming up," he said and mashed the accelerator. It was nearly midnight and they had a long drive to get where they needed to be, and there were no shortcuts.

17

Near Hermit Lake, Northeast Iron County

THURSDAY, MAY 25, 2006

Mead Road was a misnomer, more a minefield of loose, sharp rocks than a seriously graded route. The army man called on the cell phone just as Service and Friday turned southeast on the road.

"Major Sutschek, CID."

"Grady Service."

"A photo is in your e-mail; also a copy of the warrant, though our people will bring real paper after you apprehend."

"You wanted to talk to me? We're in the area now, close to where she's alleged to be."

"Specialist Provo has been on the run almost four years, Detective. She doesn't use cell phones, the Internet, or credit cards. She knows how to stay under the radar. Most of our runners are caught, or turn themselves in within a year."

"Why'd she run?"

"We don't know. She was a good soldier, excellent skills, bit of a loner. Her comrades called her Nympha."

"What's that mean—she sex-crazy or something?"

"No, it's just what they called her."

"Spell it."

"Roger—nora-young-mary-paul-henry-adam."

Service wrote the word in his notebook. "Did she do Iraq?"

"No, her unit's just in the pipeline now, in California."

"Did she join up in Kingsford?"

"No, she was a transfer from a Colorado unit."

"MP out there?"

"Yessir, since 1987."

"Is it hard to get transfers these days? In my day it wasn't easy."

"Manpower's down in a lot of units. Recruiters are struggling to reach goals, and standards are quietly being lowered, which means soldiers can move around a lot easier than in a normal peacetime," said Sutschek.

"Why'd she move?"

"Finished her degree at Adams State College, in Alamosa, Colorado, got a job in Michigan."

"She has a college degree and the rank of specialist?" *Not to mention a decade and a half of service. Odd shit, all this. When Lars dealt with her, she didn't yet have a job, or was it a place to live? Getting old,* he told himself.

"Not uncommon in the all-voluntary military."

"What's her degree?"

"Secondary education major with minors in history and environmental science. She told her commanding officer she came here because she wanted to teach in Michigan."

"Colorado girl originally?" asked Service.

"Nossir. Army brat, born in Germany and moved around. Her old man was Special Forces in Kuwait and Iraq during Desert Storm. He retired as a senior master sergeant in 1995 with twenty-eight years of distinguished service. Took sick after he retired, and was part of a large class-action Gulf War Syndrome lawsuit. He died of cancer, January '02."

"His health—or his death—have anything to do with her behavior?"

"We don't really analyze such things, Detective. Just like civilian law enforcement, we just get the warrants and go get 'em. The Judge Advocate takes care of it after that."

"Why Michigan?" Service asked, thinking out loud. "The economy's in the crapper here."

"You should ask her if you find her. We've been close to her a couple of times, but she's got almost a sixth sense about incoming heat. The last sighting was in Colorado. If you grab her, we'll come get her. Thanks for checking with us."

"Sighted where in Colorado?"

"Let me check my file . . . okay, town called Penrose," said Sutschek. "That's south-central. She was training there when she bugged out."

"What sort of training?"

"Survival, Evasion, Resistance and Escape, SERE Course D-2G-0014, part one. Not Special Ops SERE, but tough in its own right: Five days of classroom and field training in physically hostile terrain, especially mountains and desert. Her company commander sent her, planned to use her to augment training for the rest of his people. Part two was to be winter survival, six months later."

"Where was the training?"

"A closed section of Great Sand Dunes National Park, north of Alamosa."

"So the Michigan Guard sent her back to Colorado to train, near where she went to college, and she bugged out?" SERE had been called Escape and Evasion in Service's day. *E & E—Jesus!*

"Pretty much," Sutschek said.

"I'll get back to you, Major."

"Good hunting, son."

Service shut the phone. *Son?* He guessed he was older than the CID man.

"Do we have a plan?" Friday asked.

"You stay with the truck while I creep the place."

She said, gesturing left, "Fire number 9122."

He kept driving southeast, found a place to pull off the road, made sure he had his spare keys in his coat, and got out.

"Two is better than one," Friday said.

"You ever work the woods at night?"

"I can learn."

"I'm sure you can, but not tonight. I need you here in case she comes out in a vehicle. I'm going to call for backup."

He gave her a quick overview of his AVL, which was slightly different than that used by the state police. He saw that Kragie was about ten miles north of their position just into Baraga County and called him on the 800.

"Three Two Twenty, Twenty Five Fourteen. Your AVL up?"

"That's affirmative."

"Think you could start moving in my direction? I'll be on foot. Check in with my partner when you get here. Twenty Five Fourteen clear."

"Moving your way. Thirty Two Twenty clear," Kragie replied.

"A CO named Kragie is coming," Service told Friday. He grabbed a bottle of water, stuffed it in his pack, and headed cross-country toward the camp road that he'd seen running north from the red fire number.

Light was fading slowly, creating smudges of shadow he used to cover his movement. Day birds were silent and night birds seemed not to have found their voices in the cumbrous air.

The modest cabin looked relatively new, one story, a screened porch on three sides, huge windows. There was a lone outbuilding near the woods. He moved to the smaller building and saw that it was nearly all windows, roof to floor, with a steep, peaked roof. He looked inside, saw a large object . . . the silhouette of a tepee in the center of the open room. *No, not a tepee. Easel, like artists use,* he corrected himself.

He had an overpowering urge for a cigarette but fought it off. He stood near the tree line to observe, let it get darker, and began to feel a nip in the air. *High forties tonight, but damp and dewy already. No light in the cabin, no music, no sign of life. Easy does it,* he reminded himself.

He had installed his ear mike as he'd made his way from the truck. The transmitter was beneath his coat. He tapped it, whispered, "Dark, no movement inside. Click once if you copy."

He heard one click. *Attagirl.* Friday was on the ball.

He saw three doors into the cabin, all of them up on the veranda. From his vantage near the woods he could see two of the three. He waited until the dark was nearly complete and started slowly across the grass toward the cabin. Three sets of steps led up to the porch. He went to a set of stairs, got on his knees, and looked for motion detectors, any kind of sensors. *Stairs clear. No cameras on the roof corners. Maybe out in the trees? Damn things were ubiquitous nowadays. Too late and too dark to check for them.*

He crossed the porch slowly, looking around, until he was next to a storm door, the outer glass etched opaque by wind and weather. *Difficult to see inside. No flashlight,* he reminded himself. He stared through the storm door, saw that the inner door was open about a foot. *Somebody in a hurry getting out, or someone losing their short-term memory? That last one describes you, pal.*

He moved on, checked all three doors, found the same thing at each of them. Don't believe in coincidence. *Neither someone in a hurry, nor with a forgetful mind. All three doors left open suggests purpose, intent, a plan. Why? Bad vibrations.*

Back at the wood line he took a position so he could see two of the three doors, and weighed his options: *Obviously nobody here.* He had a grab-and-hold warrant for Provo, but not a search warrant for the camp. That had to be issued locally. *Can't go in without supporting paper.*

He hit the transmit button. "Three Two Twenty, you close?"

Click.

"I want you to run the entry road dark. When you break into the open yard, hit your blue lights and music. My partner will follow you in, pull to your right. Copy?"

"Copy. When?"

"Now works for me."

He could hear the tires whoosh on the grass before he could see the trucks. When the lights came on, the camp area was flooded with steady and rotating blue and white lights. No one tried to bolt or skulk from the cabin. *Fuck. So much for Plan B.*

He walked over to Kragie's truck. "I had a report of a military deserter here."

"It's always something," Kragie said. "Figured you were trying to flush someone."

"Nobody home."

"What now?"

"Pull your truck forward toward the south door and put a spot on it."

Kragie did as instructed. Service went onto the porch, backlit by the spot, turned on his own SureFire, and looked at the open door inside. The wire was dark but visible.

He went back to Kragie and lit a cigarette. Kragie held out a thermos of coffee.

Friday joined them. "We've got a trip wire inside the door and I'm thinking there could be wires on all three. We need a search warrant and we need to get inside. You know this place?"

"Think so. Let me check my plat book. I don't get down this far too often. It's Simon's turf, but sometimes we work it together."

Service poured a cup of coffee for Friday, took a sip, handed it to her.

Kragie said, "L. Charfoosh—comes up for deer season, lets people use it at other times. Good man, no problems, retired military. Army colonel, I think. Simon and I have had coffee with him."

"Can you call him, ask permission?"

"Can try. You want to get a warrant?"

"Yep, even if the owner says okay." With a reliable snitch you might chance an entry. But Allerdyce was in the category of totally unknown as far as informants were concerned. "You got the magistrate's name in Crystal Falls?"

"Somewhere in my truck."

"Call him, tell him we need a search warrant, and go pick it up. Friday and I will hold down the fort." *Everything by the book,* he told himself. Not a posture he liked.

"Going to take some time. Did the information come from a good informant?"

"Impossible to answer." Surely Allerdyce was the most knowledgeable poacher in the U.P., but was he reliable as a snitch? That was far from certain. "We've got all night," Service said.

"All night, and no beer," Friday said, passing the cup to him. "You want me to call the bomb squad?"

"Yeah," Service said. The state police had the only bomb squad in the state, with technicians dispersed to various posts.

"The BSRV is in Marquette. This will take a while." The Bomb Squad Response Vehicle; COs called it the B4: The Big Blue Boom Box, or sometimes the Shrapnelmobile.

"They can use their AVL to find us, but give them the address too."

"On it," she said, trotting toward his truck.

• • •

At 4 a.m. someone from the bomb squad went through a window and found the trip wires connected to igniters attached to bundles of cheap and harmless sparklers. The lead bomb disposal technician from the Marquette regional forensics laboratory came out in his blastproof suit and held them up. "We're all set for the Fourth of July picnic," he said drily. "Shit," Service said. *Mind-fuck time. Someone playing with us—Limpy, maybe?*

"You talk to that retired colonel?" he asked Kragie.

"He was glad I called, and said it was okay to go in."

"Can you get him on the line for me?"

Kragie popped the numbers into the cell phone and handed it to Service. The man sounded wide awake. "Charfoosh."

"Colonel, Detective Grady Service, DNR. I'm with Officer Kragie at your camp in Iron County. Do you loan out your cabin?"

"From time to time, but only to people I know."

"Recently?"

"No; last person up there was me during deer season. Why?"

More than six months ago. "Somebody's been inside, Colonel. Doesn't look like there's any damage, but you'll want to do an inventory. The county will keep the case open until you can verify nothing's been stolen."

"I appreciate it, Detective."

"Retired Army?"

"Yessir. Special Operations."

Service rubbed his eyes, disbelieving. Outfits like Army Special Ops and Navy SEALS were small, discrete worlds. *Go ahead, he urged himself.* Ask. "Ever hear of an NCO named Provo?"

"Sure have! Helluva good man to take your six in a fight. Really sorry when he died. He used to take his family up to the cabin for vacations. Why?"

"Are you an artist, Colonel?"

"That was my late wife. She passed two years ago. She loved it up there, and I can't bring myself to clean out her studio."

Service choked up at the mention of the dead wife and terminated the call without another word and looked at Friday. "We need a drink."

"I think we missed last call by several hours."

A county deputy came out of the cabin and said, "No prints inside—*nada.* This place is cleaner than the pope's privy."

Service rolled his eyes and shook his head.

"Do you think Provo's living rough?" Friday asked. "Off the land, breaking into cabins? Got a bunch of safe houses?"

He hadn't thought about this. "No, she knew about this place. She didn't have to break in. If we ask the owner, I'm sure he'll tell us where he hides the key. I think someone's aiding and abetting here, maybe wittingly, probably not. She almost has to have help." *Escape and evasion—E & E—with minimal assistance.*

"Safe houses?"

"Doubtful, but I guess it's possible."

Friday was looking at a note Service had made during one of his phone calls. "Nympha?" she asked.

"That's what the soldiers in Provo's unit called her."

"She must be funny-looking."

Service turned to look at her.

"Nympha," she said with a grin. "You know, cattails—the weeds you see growing along roadsides in swamps?"

A light came on in his head. Grady Service wanted to kiss her. *Nympha's a weed!*

Later he saw her yawn. "What about the old woman in Chicago?" she asked.

"Lower priority than this."

"She's not getting any younger."

"You want to take it?"

"Not alone," she said. "I don't care for big cities."

"Ditto."

"We can parse the angst," she said.

18

Silver Lake, Dickinson County

THURSDAY, MAY 25, 2006

Service took M-95 south, with the intention of going east to Crystal Falls from Sagola. Five miles north of Silver Lake in Dickinson County, Tuesday Friday growled, "Food, dammit! I *need* food."

"You'll never lose those eight pounds."

"You have a *problem* with food?"

"I like food—I just hate to waste time eating it."

"Abnormal," she carped. "Did you check your messages?"

He looked over at her.

"Two came in while we were waiting. I kicked both of them over to your voice mail."

He pulled over, checked his voice mail. Milo Miars again, and Zhenya Leukonovich. He called Miars instead of listening to his boss's message. "Grady here, el-tee. I'll have that report to you this afternoon."

Miars sighed. "You make supervision a sentence, Detective Shit Magnet."

"Look at the bright side: It's not for life."

"I heard about Treebone. LeBlanc told me you're working out of Iron River, but the post dispatcher told me you're never there."

"Can't detect with my butt in a chair."

Another sigh. "Report, end of day—yes?"

"Absolutely, yessir, Lieutenant Miars."

"You make rank sound perverse."

"Meanings are in people, not in words."

"End of the day," Miars repeated, trying to sound menacing but failing, and hung up.

Her machine answered: "Zhenya is battling the forces of darkness. She also is greatly interested in hearing what Detective Service may have to say. He may call Zhenya at the following number at his convenience."

Service wrote down the number. Her voice did something to him, something inexplicable. Leukonovich was a very strange woman, intelligent, professionally intense. There had been sexual chemistry, real and powerful. That they both had resisted it when they had worked together did not make the attraction less potent.

Service and Friday went into a little restaurant overlooking the black-water lake. The sign outside the place said only FOOD. A middle-aged man with a gut and splotchy white beard brought them menus and glowered.

"Let me guess," Service said. "You don't like wolves."

"You got it, fish cop."

Hating and second-guessing the DNR was the unofficial state sport, especially in the North Country. Service ignored the man, ordered two eggs, over easy, American fries, and unbuttered rye toast. Friday ordered the same, plus a full stack of pancakes.

"Damn DNR," the man grumbled when he took the order, not bothering to hide his disgust.

Service got up, followed him back to the kitchen, and looked around. "The health inspector been around here recently?"

The man handed the order slips to a woman with a red gingham apron and stepped outside.

"Don't see trout on the menu," Service said to her.

She didn't look back. "Ain't nobody wants trout for breakfast but old-timers, and they all come in early, eh. Ask tonight."

The man was outside, sitting on a stump and smoking a cigarette. Service stepped outside with him. The red pickup was parked nearby. Service felt the hood, which was still warm."

"I got a license and registration for it. You gonna rag on *me* now?"

"Your cook says you've got trout on the evening menu. I hope you have a bill of sale for it."

"I don't know nothing about no fish, and dere ain't no evidence says different."

"This time," Service said. "Make sure we get those breakfasts—without spit seasoning."

He rejoined Friday. "Is it always like this for COs?" she asked.

"Pretty much," he said.

"And I thought Troops had it tough."

"They do," Service said. "Same menu, different entrees."

"Something you ought to know," she said. "My sister's taking care of the kid—that's why I'm not going home weekends. There's a father who used to be a husband, but he's not in the picture anymore. When he found out I was pregnant, he beat hell out of me, so I filed charges and sued for divorce. My sis loves the kid."

Service said. "You seem to be maintaining."

"Appearances can be deceiving."

"You want, I can probably get you some help for the kid, or get your sis some help. Or you can spend weekends with them."

"Not your problem," she said. "But thanks."

19

Norway, Dickinson County

FRIDAY, MAY 26, 2006

They had worked the phones all yesterday afternoon. A call to Major Sutschek of CID got Service the name and phone numbers of two Guard soldiers not being deployed to Iraq—one because she was pregnant, the other because he had a slot in Officer Candidate School in July. He called both soldiers, and they'd agreed to meet for breakfast that morning at Nardine's Mining House Restaurant in Norway.

Friday called Rillamae Thigpen in Chicago and learned that she lived in Hyde Park, in an upscale neighborhood that included most of the University of Chicago campus. Friday said the woman talked slowly and seemed to take some time to process information; speed aside, she seemed competent—even anxious—to talk about Elmwood.

Their plan was to interview the two soldiers in Norway and afterwards, drive to Chicago, 320 miles south. In any other location, flying would be faster and probably less expensive, but flights from the Upper Peninsula's few commercial airports to major hubs were priced beyond belief, and by the time plane changes were made, if everything ran on time, which it rarely did, it would be faster and cheaper to make the five- to six-hour drive. Friday made arrangements for them to stay with a friend of hers in Lincoln Park.

"The zoo," he said. "Marlin Perkins, his sidekick Jim; see, I did have a childhood!"

She rolled her eyes.

The restaurant in Norway was in an old mining company row house, the interior filled with iron-mining memorabilia.

The soldiers were in civvies, seated and waiting. Both stood when the police officers entered. Specialist Aimee Balto-Shillito, Service knew, was a month short of her due date, but looked two months beyond it. Sergeant Harris Griz was tall and straight-backed, with a lantern jaw—a billboard soldier. Both soldiers made direct eye contact.

The soldiers and Service ordered light breakfasts. Friday ordered more than the other three combined. Service thought, *She learns fast.* Once he got working, it irritated him to stop. She was adapting.

"This is about Specialist Provo?" Sergeant Griz began.

"You both served with her?" Service asked.

"Yessir," they said in unison.

"Soldiers in the company called her Nympha?"

"Sir, the name was her idea, sir," Balto-Shillito said. "Sir, she acted like it was a private joke, sir."

"What's it supposed to mean?"

Both soldiers shook their heads.

"What kind of soldier was she?"

"Sir, she was pretty good at doing things, but not cooperative," the specialist said. "Took care of her job, but not real interested in the team, sir."

"Okay," Service said, "I was a marine a long time ago, and an NCO, not an officer, so let's shit-can the sirs and all that formal crap. I'm Grady, she's Tuesday."

"Yessir . . . ma'am," Griz said.

"So, Provo wasn't a slacker?"

"Not exactly," Balto-Shillito said with a glance at Griz. "It was like she could do everything faster than most of us, and with minimal effort. Some of us felt she could have been the best soldier in the company, but being best didn't seem to motivate her. It was like we all had eight gears and she had ten or more, but always operated at six or seven. You agree, Sarn't?"

The sergeant was slow to answer. "Sure, pretty much."

"Was she close to anyone? Who did she pal around with?"

"Stuck to herself," Griz said. "The company's pretty tight, but she never partied with us."

"Was that a point of contention in the group?"

"No, but it would've been if she were still here. Now that the company's deploying to Iraq, nobody wants to wade into the shit with someone they haven't seen all sides of."

Service understood this, but thought the sergeant a little melodramatic. "She had a couple of OUILs, which cost her a teaching job."

"Not from drinking with us," Griz said.

"I don't drink," Balto-Shillito said. "Does that make me suspect, Sergeant Griz?" The sergeant blushed.

"Did she ever talk to anyone about her teaching?" Service asked.

"I couldn't see her as a teacher," Balto-Shillito said. "She never shared, didn't seem interested in others. She wasn't what I'd call a helpful person."

"Any hot buttons?" Service asked.

"Just one," Griz said. "DUs."

DU meant depleted uranium, the basis of a number of modern military munitions. "Arty and Air Force," Service said. "MPs don't handle DUs."

"Correct, sir," Griz said.

Balto-Shillito intervened. "But sometimes we're around that stuff. We were at Camp Grayling for summer training and were assigned security on the armor range. M1E1s were firing DUs, and when Specialist Provo heard this, she started asking lots of questions, and no matter what answers she got, she posed more."

The M1E1 was the Abrams tank. "What kind of questions?"

"About downwind radioactive dust potential."

"*Is* that a problem?"

"Nossir," Sergeant Griz said.

"What Sergeant Griz says is *probably* true," Balto-Shillito said, "but there have been a lot of scientific reports, and results vary from no effect to severe effect, depending on proximity, time, and dose of exposure. For us, probably nothing, but no one knows for sure. It's a source of concern for a lot of soldiers."

"She afraid?"

"More like she was pissed," Griz said. "We were still in formation, and she went off on the platoon sergeant. He ended up taking her off the duty roster for the day."

"Was there disciplinary action from the blowup?" Service asked.

Balto-Shillito said, "Nossir. She apologized later, said it had been a bad day, and we moved on."

"That's all—nothing else?"

"Practical jokes," Griz said. "Stupid, high school stuff. One day she filled the company coffeepot with carrot juice. She thought it was funny. The rest of us didn't get it."

"There was the range thing," Balto-Shillito said to her colleague.

"Right, also at Camp Grayling,"Griz said. "We were like scheduled for the range with M16s. The night before, our sergeant brings out the ammo can and gives us ten-round stripper mags and tells us to load them, which we did. Next morning we get on the line and not one round will fire. The range sergeant took one of the unfired rounds and pried it apart: The gunpowder had been replaced with sand. The weight of the rounds felt normal, but they were duds. Someone had taken all 840 rounds out of the can and done a switcheroo. It was like totally strange."

"Repercussions?" Service asked.

"They couldn't pin it on anyone. Grayling's security people couldn't even figure out how the hell someone breached their secure area to do it. No prints, no nothing. It was slick. We were all pretty sure it was Provo, but we were all questioned and nobody reprimanded."

"The ammo was in a secure area?"

"When we go to Grayling they control and manage all ammo. Ours is secure back in our armory here."

Service looked at Friday to see if she wanted to ask something, but she was chewing bacon and only smiled.

"Were either of you surprised when she was DFR?"

"Nossir." Two voices as one again.

"You thought she was what—unreliable, unstable?"

"Just Nympha," Specialist Balto-Schillito said.

Griz nodded agreement. "Nympha, out there . . . like, way out there."

"Was she afraid of Iraq?" Service asked.

"Sir, Iraq was not on our deployment horizon when she was in the unit, but Provo was not a coward," the specialist said.

"Mountain," Griz said. The specialist nodded, and Griz continued. "We had this soldier named Hartz, a humongous, very tough dude. We called him Mountain . . . you know, Hartz Mountain? One day at drill he started running off his mouth about being unbeatable in a baton fight, and he challenged us to prove him wrong. Nympha called him out."

Balto-Shillito said, "Mountain didn't get in a single lick. Within ten seconds it looked like she was going to kill him, and we had to pull her away."

"Hurt bad?"

"Bloody and sore, but nothing crippling or anything like that," Balto-Shillito said. "But when Hartz's stint was done, he didn't re-up. I think she broke him. She was quick," the specialist added, "but the difference in the fight was her emotional control. I'm talking stone-cold. I guess that's the only time we saw her tenth gear," she concluded.

"She lived in Kingsford?"

"She had a duplex here for drill weekends, but I think she actually lived in Trout Creek, or the Ewen area," Balto-Shillito said.

"Maintaining two places seems extravagant on a teacher's salary."

"Winter," Griz said. "Several soldiers keep rooms here, either apartments or cheap motels, several to a room, to keep costs down."

"Did she share?"

"Never," Griz said.

"Either of you ever wonder how a soldier with fifteen years' service was still at specialist grade?"

Neither soldier reacted.

• • •

As they drove south, Service said, "You were quiet."

"I was listening."

"And packing away the chow."

"That too," she said with a grin.

"Observations?"

"First of all, 840 rounds with their powder switched to sand: That takes know-how, planning, patience, nerve. Why does a person like that need Box or Limpy to teach them about guns? Second, if the room here was only for drills, where did she actually live? Third, the concerns about depleted uranium seem a little out there . . . and my first thought was that's the sort of thing an environmentalist would go ballistic over. Fourth, and finally, I think they're sending the wrong soldier to OCS."

Her last observation made him laugh out loud, but what was hanging in his mind was what the soldiers had said about Provo having ten gears. The CID major had said Provo seemed to have a sixth sense. *Six senses, ten gears, E & E training. Not a great combo for law enforcement,* he told himself.

20

Kenwood Avenue, Hyde Park, Chicago

SATURDAY, MAY 27, 2006

They had spent the night with Friday's girlfriend, Tara, in an apartment (the size of a box on the back of a move-it-yourself moving van) on the seventh floor of a building in Lincoln Park.

The friend had a thirty-pound dog the color of a caramel with sinister pale blue eyes and floppy pointed ears, a cross between a Jack Russell and an extraterrestrial. Head on the thing looked like something out of a *Star Wars* bar scene. It was named "Cooper." *Like some third-grade nerd-in-training whose uptight helicopter mommy carries his viola to school for him every day.*

Friday slept on a couch, Service on the floor with the dog sitting by his head, staring at him all night long, snarling whenever he tried to roll over.

The newspapers this morning were full of anguish and anger over the Cubs losing the previous afternoon to the Braves.

"Mistakes," he told Friday as they had sour coffee and sweet rolls at Starbucks on North Sheridan. "You make too many errors, you lose. No mistakes, maybe you win or maybe you lose, but too many errors and you lose, end of discussion."

"Are we talking baseball or something else?" she asked.

"Life," he said. Why hadn't he married Maridly Nantz? This failure was the major regret in his life.

Their appointment with Rillamae Thigpen was set for 10 a.m. They were on Kenwood Avenue a half-hour early and found on-street parking a half-block from the address, a four-story gray-stone building, whose architecture reminded Service of the homes of mine owners in Calumet a century ago. The Kenwood Avenue houses reeked of money.

"This what you expected?" he asked Friday.

"No way," she said. He wasn't sure what he'd expected.

They went up a steep set of stone steps to the main door of a four-story town house and knocked on a door that wouldn't have been out of place in Buckingham Palace.

A small woman came to the door. She was barely five feet tall and bent over by scoliosis. She wore a black tracksuit and gold workout shoes, had short white hair, manicured fingernails with red polish, dangling gold earrings, and sparkle-arkle rings on several fingers. "Mrs. Thigpen?"

"I've spent my life in a classroom and thus value punctuality," she said in a soft, sure voice. "Welcome to my home. Please come in."

She pointed them to a room with twelve-foot ceilings and lined with bookshelves, all full. The ceiling was done in ornate plasterwork outlined in what appeared to be gold leaf. Friday rolled her eyes.

The woman pushed a tea cart into the room and set it between her wing-back leather chair and her guests. "I'm sorry, but it's decaf," she apologized. "You know how doctors are. Shall we begin by reviewing your credentials so I can ascertain your authenticity?"

The two officers took out their badges and identity cards and passed them to her. She studied each set and passed them back with a thank-you. She then poured tea for her guests and herself, took a sip, set it on a saucer, and sat back. "I believe you're interested in Elmwood."

"We got your name from Helmi Koski."

"How is she?" the old woman asked with shining eyes.

"Buzzing around the nursing home," Service said. "In charge."

Thigpen's eyes flashed pleasure. "That's my Helmi."

Silence, more than a minute of it. Neither Service nor Friday spoke.

"We met Christmas Eve, 1927," Thigpen began. "The sheriff commandeered a train to take us to Crystal Falls, and from there by wagons up to the poor farm, where they fed us and gave us clothes. Helmi and her sister, bless their hearts, came up the hill from town through all that snow to bring us coats and winter boots."

More silence.

"She had never seen a black person and wanted to touch my skin to determine if it was different," Thigpen said without rancor. "It wasn't an insult; it was the purest curiosity from a young girl in a small town. Helmi is very candid, entirely honest, a woman of absolute integrity. Two minutes after we met, we both felt we would be friends for life."

Another interval of silence, and Thigpen said, finally, "And it's true: We have been friends for life. Who would think a little white girl from the Upper Peninsula and a little black girl would be friends all these many decades?"

The lugubrious pace was driving Service crazy, but he took his lead from Friday, who seemed in no hurry to push the woman along and get to their questions.

"You left Crystal Falls and returned to Chicago," Friday said during one of the intervals.

"Yes, but not back to where we'd lived before. You must understand—my father was a proud man. We left Chicago to follow his dream, and having failed, we repaired with tails between our legs to an even more humble venue."

Repaired? Service thought. *Humble? Who the hell is this woman*?

"Can you tell us what you mean about following his dream?" Friday asked.

"He was from Arkansas, a country boy. He worked as many as three jobs at a time to support us, but always with the idea that he would one day buy land in the country."

"His dream was land?"

Long pause before a response. "Isn't that true for anyone who's never owned it?"

"He *bought* land in Iron County," Friday said.

"It was to be legally ours *if* we worked it and successfully harvested potatoes for five years."

"That didn't work out," Friday said, prompting the woman gently.

"One winter was all we could manage. The land was poor, the weather extreme, life difficult, and the culture foreign. All of us were hardened by life, no matter our ages, but those winters. . . ." Her voice trailed off.

"You didn't qualify for the land," Friday said.

"Of course not, dear. There's no doubt in my mind we all would have succumbed had we stayed any longer."

"How do you feel about what happened? It must have been terrible."

The woman looked at Friday and smiled. "I know this must sound foolish, but it was, nonetheless, the *most wonderful year* of my childhood. We were in those big woods. We picked berries in summer, had fresh fish, deer meat—wonderful. In spring and early summer, the fields were filled with a plethora of wildflowers."

"What about potatoes?"

"They grew. They were about all that *could* grow in that rocky soil," she added with an ironic chuckle. "The problem wasn't the crop; it was the short growing season, and the other farmers. We lacked the emotional tools or the technical expertise to do what we went there to do."

Service sensed there was a lot more story buried in the woman, and that it wasn't going to come out easily. He poured a decaf tea and wished he could smoke.

"I think my father realized very quickly that we were doomed, but he tried to endure, and he tried to keep up my mother's spirits. My sisters and I were happy enough, but my mother was decidedly not. We once had a mother bear and her two cubs by our cabin, and Mama locked herself inside and wouldn't come out for a week. From then on, she walked around with a firearm, even when nature compelled her to use the privy."

"Did you live east of Elmwood, or north?" Grady Service asked.

The woman tilted her head and looked at him. "North, with the Reverend Browning's group."

"There were groups?" Friday asked.

"Not officially, but the land was distributed in two general areas, you see, part of it east of Elmwood and part of it to the north. My father thought the land to the north would be better than that to the east, and he was prescient. The eastern section was lower, darker, less productive."

"Reverend Browning?" Friday asked.

"A godly man," Thigpen said. "He was our pastor in Chicago and my father convinced him to be part of the undertaking. We promised to build him a church when we got stabilized, which never happened."

"Browning was the leader, or was it your father?"

"Neither. The leader was Mr. Washington Lincoln, a golden-tongued scoundrel."

Another agonizing silence passed before she picked up the story.

"He came to our neighborhood in 1924 and told everyone he had served with Pershing in the Great War and been decorated for valor. He even had three medals and a handsome doughboy uniform to prove it. It was Mr. Lincoln who brought Roland Denu to Reverend Browning's church to tell us about the land in Iron County." The old woman sighed and closed her eyes. "We didn't even know Michigan had two parts! Can you imagine our geographic naivete?"

"Scoundrel?" Friday asked.

Geographic naivete? Service thought.

"Mr. Lincoln never served with General Pershing in France. Did you know that his nickname Black Jack came about because the general had commanded black soldiers in the Southwest when he was a young officer?"

Service didn't know, and didn't see how it related.

"Mr. Lincoln did serve with the general in 1916. He was in the Twenty-fourth Cavalry, the Buffalo Soldiers. They pursued Pancho Villa into Mexico, but Mr. Lincoln deserted during the expedition, and years later appeared in Chicago, claiming he had served in France. I can't imagine why, other than to arouse sympathy."

The woman took another sip of tea. "My father was initially skeptical of Mr. Lincoln, but he was so fixated on having land that he convinced himself the adventure would be to our family's benefit. He worked tirelessly to convince others to join us. We left Chicago in the late spring of 1926 with eight families—about fifty people, if I remember correctly. Each family was promised two hundred acres of land, a mule, and a modest monthly supply of staples—flour, sugar, molasses, that sort of thing. If we worked the land for five years, the title was to be ours, free and clear."

Service couldn't stand it anymore. "Who actually owned the land—Denu?"

Rillamae Thigpen exhaled deeply. "That was certainly a commonly held belief, but patently untrue. My father learned that Denu was only a figurehead. The land was actually owned by a Chicago man named Van Dalen, a lawyer and land speculator—what today we'd call a developer."

"Why keep ownership secret?" Detective Friday asked .

"Who knows the heart of another?" Thigpen replied. "Or the heart of a white businessman, to be more to the point . . . no offense intended."

"Did any of your group ever meet Van Dalen?"

"Yes, of course. He came around regularly, but was using a different name, passing himself off as a Roman priest, Father O'Neil."

Service and Friday exchanged looks.

"My father knew right away that Father O'Neil wasn't a real priest. My father was Roman and we had been raised in the church. After our return to Chicago, we became Methodists."

"I don't understand," Service said.

"Of course not, Detective. This was more than eighty years ago and I believe that I am the last survivor. Mr. Lincoln, of course, did not engineer the expedition to raise potatoes."

The officers waited for further explanation, but none was forthcoming.

"If not potatoes, what?" Service asked.

"Will you excuse me for a moment?" Rillamae Thigpen said. "The Lord has blessed me with the mobility to answer nature's calls, but not a bladder to allow me to sit too long between those calls."

Friday got up and wandered around, looking at bookcases, and at one point said, "Holy cow!" with no explanation.

When Thigpen returned, she sat down in her chair, this time perched on the front edge.

"You have a lovely home," Friday told the old woman.

"Thank you. My husband Charles and I acquired it 1970. By then I was a full professor at the University of Chicago and he had built a successful practice as a thoracic surgeon, working out of Northwestern University Hospital."

"What did you teach?" Friday asked.

"Mainly contemporary African American literature. I earned my bachelor's from the university in 1941, my master's in 1944, and my doctorate in 1950. Early on I was fortunate to realize that teaching was my calling, and that Chicago was where I was meant to be. I retired in 1982, but until two years ago still conducted lectures emeritus to graduate students. It's too much of an effort to get out of the house now. I wouldn't trade my life for any other. Charles's family also was in Iron County, you see. We met there when we were children. When we returned, our families went their separate ways. I didn't meet Charles again until many years later when he was trying to get into medical school. We were not childhood sweethearts, but when we fell in love as adults, it took, and lasted until he passed on in 1988."

"Do you know that happened to Washington Lincoln?" Service asked.

"No. You see, he did not return with the rest of us."

"No?"

"He was never interested in farming. He was always gone into the deep woods."

"Hunting and fishing?"

"Yes, to sustain himself, but that wasn't his passion either." She held out a fist and opened it to reveal a small white rock.

Friday accepted the rock, looked at it, and passed it to Service.

"It's quartz, with a paper-thin seam of gold," Professor Thigpen said.

"Are you telling us that Lincoln discovered gold?" Service asked.

"Indeed I am. My father followed him once and brought back several small rocks and nuggets. Naturally, my mother wanted to know where he'd gotten them, but he refused to say. He insisted gold was the source of all evil, and that the true value of land was in the life it nurtured," she said wistfully. "My father was unschooled, but a true romantic."

"Can we borrow this?" Service asked, the stone in his hand.

"If you wish."

"We'll bring it back. Why did Lincoln need others to come north with him if gold was what he sought?" Friday asked.

"I can only speculate. After we returned, my father refused to talk about it, but I believe that Lincoln and Denu were convinced that by having a group of black families among all those white folk, mostly foreigners, we would be left alone, which would enable Lincoln to have the privacy to do what he went there to do. One black man would stand out, but not a group."

"You said earlier that Van Dalen—Father O'Neil—came north to keep an eye on things. Was he aware of the gold?"

"I don't know the answer to that, but I don't think so. It was Denu and Lincoln. I believe Van Dalen was looking to us to farm the land, fulfill our contracts, and settle in permanently. If this happened he would promote other places. America's cities were filled with the uprooted and immigrants in those days. But our experiment failed, the stock market crashed, the Great Depression set in, and I suppose Van Dalen lost his passion for such plans."

Tuesday Friday smiled, leaned across and patted the old woman's hand. "You're the author," Friday said.

Thigpen smiled shyly. "An author—one point in my life—but it was long ago."

"*The Two of Us Are One*," Friday said. "The story of the friendship of a white girl and a black girl in Minnesota during the Great Depression, written by R. G. Thigpen."

"In those days the publishing community was not keen on female novelists; thus the initials."

"Rillamae Garden Thigpen," Friday said. "Garden was your maiden name."

"Yes."

"You wrote three books about the same characters. Helmi Koski is the model for the white girl."

Thigpen's eyes showed her pleasure at being recognized as an author. "I couldn't write about Iron County, but it was the basis of the books, and certainly they were based on Helmi and me. Of course, we knew each other not quite three days, but became friends for life, and it was wonderful to use my imagination to write what the friendship might have been like had we lived in and grown up together in the same town."

"Father O'Neil disappeared after he accompanied your group to Chicago," Service said. "So, too, did Sheriff Petersson."

Thigpen looked concerned. "I don't remember the priest being with us on the train," she said.

"What about Lincoln and the man, Denu?" Service asked.

"We never saw either of them after the sheriff rescued us from Elmwood."

"There's no record of what happened to them," Friday said.

"Not with us, but I know for certain that Van Dalen eventually came back to Chicago," Thigpen said. "He became a successful and prominent businessman in Chicago, and amassed a fortune in real estate. I used to read articles about him in the *Tribune,* and when he died, there was a long obituary with a photograph of him as a young man."

"Did you happen to keep a copy?"

"As a matter of fact, I did. My packrat ways used to make Charles *crazy!*"

She excused herself again, returning twenty minutes later with a yellowed clipping in a nine-by-eleven envelope. Service pulled out the clip and looked at the photo.

"This is Father O'Neil?"

"Yes. Charles agreed that this was him. I wish I knew the fate of Lincoln and Denu."

"Photos?"

"We were too poor for photographs in those days, but Lincoln had only one arm." She made a line just below her left elbow. "Gone from there, supposedly from the war in France—which, as I said earlier, was patently untrue. And Denu, he was impossible to mistake for anyone else."

"How was that?"

"He was a giant, nearly seven feet tall, and to us children he looked even taller."

Thigpen and Friday chatted on about writing and books, and Service tuned them out. He had sat long enough. On their way to the truck he said, "Do we have the autopsy reports from the two skeletons?"

"Back in the office."

"Did they mention a missing arm, or a giant?"

"I don't remember. Are you thinking . . . ?"

"I'm not sure what's rolling around in there, but we're in Chicago, maybe we should look into Van Dalen. The obituary called him a philanthropist of the first order, whatever that means. Most fortunes get fortified by lawyers so that they continue to flourish long after their makers are gone."

"Works for me, as long as I get lunch and maybe a little undivided attention."

"Up north I know some good eating places. Down here in the cement woods, I'm clueless." Undivided attention?

"I'm sure we'll manage," she said.

What kind of cretin had Friday married? he wondered. The sparks she emitted made him sweat. No, he told himself. *Absolutely not!*

Friday insisted on plump Chicago hot dogs from a street vendor. They took them to a park that overlooked Lake Michigan and sat on a stone bench as people roller-skated and jogged past them.

"How old do you think I am?" Friday asked.

"A wise man knows what questions to never answer."

She laughed. "I've been a Troop eleven years—one at the Academy, three in Paw Paw, three in Jackson, three in Wayland, and the last one up here. My marriage lasted all of fourteen months; that is, until he discovered I was with child. Below the bridge there's lots of action for Troops. Road patrol in the U.P. is boring. Down below you're too tired and busy for bullshit. In the U.P., Troops feed on rumors and backbiting. I heard all sorts of horror stories about you," Friday said. "Great cop, loose cannon, unh-unh king, glory seeker, loner, yada yada, all bull," she said. "You're a terrific partner, Grady."

"We aren't partners," he countered. "We're a temporary woods cop, Yoop-Troop mixed marriage."

"I've had partners, in marriage and at work," she said. "And I know the real thing. You work well with women and men. I just thought you ought to know that."

Where was this going? "I've only been a detective for a little more than three years, and I haven't had all that many cases," he told her.

"I didn't say you're a great detective," she said, "just a good partner."

He caught her laughing and laughed with her. "Seriously," she said, "you seem born to it. Me, not so much."

"No one's born to this, and a lot of my cases seem to end up in never-never land," he said.

"But there's the rush of gratification in closing a case," she said.

"I wish. Maybe one case in three gets tied up. The rest seem to leave wads of loose ends and doubt."

"How do you deal with those?"

"I move on to the next case and try not to look backwards."

"So you run away from any feelings that put you outside your comfort zone?"

"Pretty much," he admitted.

"In my opinion, you don't really care what others think of you."

"I can't control what others think, or feel."

"You let me take the lead with the professor. Why?"

"Did I?"

"You didn't jump in and you didn't push her, or me. You let me deal with the timing and pressure. She was so slow I wanted to scream, but you sat back and let it happen naturally."

"The point of an interview is to get information. You were good with her."

"You really think so?"

What's going on here? he asked himself. "Yeah, really," he said.

"Are we spending the night in Chicago?" she asked.

That had been the plan, until he began to get vibrations that made him uncomfortable. "No offense, but not in your friend's apartment."

"Wasn't very comfortable, was it?"

"Not with demon dog in my face all night. It's Saturday. We can probably get into the library and get a computer at one of the cop shops, but tomorrow's Sunday, and everything will be shut down. Better we head home and work the phones from there, get Mike involved. We can come back to Chicago if we need to."

"Picnic sky," she said, looking up.

He held up the hot dog. "This *is* our picnic."

"Why did I *know* you'd say that?"

"Thigpen wrote books?"

"Very popular ones, for young adults. I read them when I was a kid—even collected them."

"I'm wondering how she knew about Lincoln's military history, and why?"

Friday shrugged.

"She said she couldn't write about Iron County. How come?"

"Do you absorb everything you hear?" she asked.

"I'm sure I miss a lot more than I capture."

Friday finished the last of her hot dog and wiped her lips with a paper napkin. "You're thinking I should reread her books, look for parallels?"

"Yes. You know where your copies are?"

"In a box. There's still a lot to be unpacked at my place."

"A good reason for you to go home tomorrow," he said. "Unpack and see your kid while you're at it."

"And you?"

"I'll start looking at Van Dalen."

"Another night here wouldn't hurt," she said, avoiding eye contact.

"I'm good to go," he said. "You're fed, the truck's gassed, and it's not *that* long of a drive. There's no good reason to waste state money here."

"Maybe you don't listen as well as I thought," she said.

"Postpartum blues, swimming in the jetsam and flotsam of divorce," he said. "Back in my playing days, my hockey coaches told us to always settle a bouncing puck before trying to do something creative with it."

"*Bouncing puck*?" she said, her eyes flaring.

"Monday's Memorial Day. Stay home, enjoy your kid."

She refused to look at him.

21

Iron River, Iron County

SUNDAY, MAY 28, 2006

His idea of hell: All day in a cramped office, staring at a computer screen, sorting through arcane bureaucratic bullshit and self-serving trash, and talking on the damn telephone to clueless people. Sometimes the Internet had its uses, but this didn't seem to be one of them. Unless you had passwords to pay-for-use databases, the bulk of what was available for so-called serious research was crap.

He reread Van Dalen's obituary several times. There was no mention of the Iron County venture, if indeed it was his. On that point: No evidence either way. One woman's word—maybe good, maybe bad. If it had been his show, why wouldn't there be a mention? Van Dalen was about success, not failure, big into charities, a "philanthropist of the highest order." Jesus. Lots of labels, but no clue when or why the man's generosity began. Obituaries never told the real story of the deceased, only those parts someone wanted remembered. The Van Dalen Foundation was one of the five largest in the country, and the obituary writer noted that Van Dalen had "pioneered the use of trusts for social issues." *Whatever that means.* He scribbled notes in his notebook.

Mike Millitor came in. "Saw the Tahoe. How'd it go in Chicago?"

"Thigpen's alive and claims she was here, backing up what Helmi Koski told us. You think Sheriff Petersson would see us again?"

Millitor checked his watch. "Mass for shut-ins is done. I'll give him a call."

"Friday said the autopsy reports are here somewhere."

"I'll get them," the Iron County detective said. "Where's our third musketeer?"

"Went home to see her kid."

"You hear about her divorce?"

"No details."

"Her ex got her and two other women pregnant at the same time. He beat hell out of all of them. Friday could defend herself, the others couldn't. One of them died. The ex pleaded to manslaughter and is inside now."

She'd given no indication of any of this. "Who's the ex?"

"Defense lawyer in Grand Rapids, big shot in the Republican party, lots of dough." Millitor handed him the file with the ME's preliminary reports.

"You read them?" Service asked.

"Bones, not much meat."

"Anything about the height of the vicks?"

Millitor shook his head. "I recall that the skeletons are sixty and eighty percent complete. How many bones *in* a human body?"

Service thought for a moment. "A lot?" Then corrected himself. "Two hundred or so, something like that, which means more than a hundred and forty missing in vick one and more than one-sixty in vick two."

"You game wardens need all the bones to get a story from an animal's bones?"

"Not all . . . just the right ones."

"Do we have a problem?"

"Maybe. Let's go talk to Petersson."

During the drive Millitor said, "Keep an eye on Friday. A sergeant stopped to see her during her maternity leave. She claimed he hit on her and she went ballistic, called the cops: alleged rape, sexual harassment, the whole deal."

"You saw a police report to this effect?" *Not the Friday I know, he thought. Correction: Think I know.*

"No," Millitor said.

"That sound like our musketeer?"

"Just saying what I heard."

Service had learned in recent years that female law officers were often the subject of vicious gossip. He didn't understand why. Female COs had it especially rough. "Let me guess: You heard it from a Troop not at her post."

"Yeah."

"Find a police report, and then we'll believe it." What the hell was wrong with Millitor? He was too seasoned to listen to such crap.

Petersson seemed glad to see them, took them into his den/trophy room, and listened raptly as Service recounted the interview with Thigpen in Chicago. "You ever run across anything about Denu's height in your research?" he asked the retired sheriff.

"No, but tall fellas weren't uncommon among the Ojibs in the old days; lots of chiefs six-six and taller. The autopsies say something?"

"No. The bones aren't all there."

"You going to talk to our ME?"

"Thought Mike and I would drive out to the site first, see what we can see. Last time I was out there I wasn't all that focused."

"We?" Millitor said.

"You got something better to do?"

The Iron County detective grinned. "Heck no. The old lady wants me to fuss with the yard. That's too much like real work."

"Good. We'll need a shovel, a sledge, and a pick."

"Maybe that yard work doesn't sound so bad . . ." Millitor whined.

22

South Branch, Paint River, Iron County

SUNDAY, MAY 28, 2006

Service sat in the Tahoe for a long time, studying the topographical features depicted in the onboard computer. Millitor stood outside, launching blue smoke rings with his cigar.

They hiked to the rock formation where Newf had found the skulls and looked around. "Dig here?" Millitor asked.

"Nah, let's climb."

"I don't do heights."

"Gradual slope, not to worry." Some scree with woody debris, a log here and there. The computer topo showed an elevated knob above the site, which they eventually reached. Millitor sat down and rubbed sweat off his forehead. Service took in the scene. *Fifty yards, here down to there. Would've been snow and ice in December. Visualize,* he told himself, looking around. *Kill up here; why not leave the bodies right here? Less chance of discovery. In a hurry, maybe? Or jacked up on the cocktail of fear and adrenaline? Not used to such work . . . panic? All possible; no way to know. Multiple fractures in both sets of remains, but only vick number two, the Native American, had been hacked all to hell.*

"You thinking or what?" Millitor asked.

"You in a hurry to dig?"

"Just asking."

There was a log fifteen feet from the edge, at an angle, there a long time, moss-covered, rotting. He tried to move it, but no luck. It was wedged in dirt and leafy decay, as good as cement. He took the pick, drove it hard into the weakest-looking place, and broke through. *Hollow*! He dropped the pick, picked up the sledge, and smashed his way through the rest of it, the log disintegrating into soft, brownish-orange shards of wood, redolent of decay. There was a natural scallop in the rock face behind the log. His flashlight beam lit more white rock in the darkness. "Quartz?" he asked his partner.

"The stone? Yeah. Not a lot, but there's some here and there in this part of the county."

Service got on his knees with the shovel, scraped at the earth where it had accumulated under and behind the log. He got a chip of something right away and picked it up. Bone. Then a larger piece. *Evidence bags,* he reminded himself, but he kept scraping and sifting with his fingers. Eventually, a long, heavy bone. Gnawed by porkies at some point, but mostly intact, a porous, yellow-gray knob on one end. *Part of a socket or a joint?* He peeked out. "Mike, go back to the truck, call Trooper Smalt, and tell him we need forensics again. Wait until he gets here and show him up."

"You mean I'll hafta climb all the way back up this bloody hill?"

"He won't get here right away. You'll have time to rest."

"You?"

"Gonna take a little walk."

When Millitor was gone he used the sledge to chip off some pieces of quartz, which he put in an evidence bag labeled with a permanent marker and tied to his belt. The topos said the low ridge ran mostly east-northeast. He followed it nearly a mile, breaking off specimens to add to his collection wherever he could find outcroppings.

Before going back to the truck he took samples from where Newf had started the whole thing.

He found Millitor in the truck, napping. "You get hold of Smalt?"

"He ain't in town, and holy smokes, I called the ME and he wigged out. He was out to George Young smacking one of them little balls around. Said to call him when Smalt gets here, only I can't, 'cause Smalt ain't around, so I called the Iron Mountain post and they're sendin Micro Sjovall to cover for Smalt, and now Micro's pissed off too."

"Is forensic support always like this around here?"

"Every doctor in the county is empowered to be a deputy ME, but he's the only one who's taken it seriously, so I guess we shouldn't complain."

"How long until the Iron Mountain Troop shows?"

"One hour at the outside, but I went ahead and called Marquette, and they're sendin' a team too."

When the Marquette forensics people finally arrived, Service gave them the bag of quartz samples. "Assays."

"We looking for anything in particular?"

"Kryptonite, whatever."

The ME showed up and puffed up the hill behind Service, not hiding his dissatisfaction. "*Now* what? I was playing the best golf of my life."

"We think we've got the rest of the bones."

"Why'd you look way up here?"

Why hadn't the others looked up here? "You said multiple fractures in both skeletons, only one hacked up. Falls equal fractures."

"Maybe I should resign, save the county's money, let you game wardens do my job."

"Whatever floats your boat, doc."

Service got an evidence bag from Sjovall, who had arrived minutes before the Marquette contingent. It contained the long bone Service had found earlier.

"Leg? How the hell did Sjovall get the evidence? It should have been locked up at the Iron River Post. You sign for this?" the ME asked the Troop.

"Yeah. Custody trail's pristine."

Service felt a little better. The doctor held out the bag. "Tibia," he said, "hip to knee."

Grady Service told the ME, "Your report didn't indicate any heights."

"Needed this and/or a femur. Artists can estimate height, but I am compelled by science in my work."

The doctor's a blowhard. "Artists?"

"They measure the length of the head. The average body is thought to be eight heads long, four heads from hip, measured laterally at the navel, down to the ankle. Ergo, head times eight gives you a ballpark, which is entirely unscientific and not in the least precise."

Service listened to the man, who was obviously enthralled by the sound of his own voice, lecturing the untutored. "Currently the consensus is eight, perhaps because humans are growing taller."

"Eight, huh, not seven?" Service asked, deadpan.

The ME glared at him. "In the Renaissance it was seven."

"Bit of a diff between seven and eight," Service said.

"Exactly my point. An artist seeks only *relative* proportions, not scientific verisimilitude."

"What was his name, Michelangelo? He seemed to get things pretty close. Listen, Doc, just between us, what's your best guess on vick two's height?"

"Six and a half feet on the eight-head model, but this is, as you put it, a guess, not a measurement. I will call you when I can be more precise."

"When will that be?"

"Good science takes time."

Not good vibes here. "When?" Service pressed.

"When I have something, Detective," the man said, standing his ground. "Tomorrow's Memorial Day."

"You know why God invented golf?" Service asked the ME, who shrugged. "To keep assholes off trout streams," Service said, heading downhill with Millitor chuckling and wheezing behind him.

"Don't mind the doc," Millitor said in the Tahoe. "He's an equal opportunity asshole."

"I couldn't care less about his religion," Service said. "All that matters is how good he is . . . and how fast."

"He was good enough to have been the ME in St. Joe County a few years back. He moved up here to hunt, fish, and play golf. He took the ME's job as a favor to the county commissioners. Nobody else wanted to do it."

"You think the county could get people to volunteer for our jobs as a favor?"

Millitor stared straight ahead. "Nobody's that crazy."

23

Crystal Falls, Iron County

MEMORIAL DAY, MONDAY, MAY 29, 2006

Simon and Elza were on patrol. With unseasonably mild weather, CO short-ages, and the three-day Memorial Day weekend, they would be knee-deep in fools and idiots. Service got up early, ran, came back, showered, and sat down in front of his friends' computer to surf the Internet with no expecta-tion of results. The question of skeleton height was bothering him. He didn't like the arrogant ME, and didn't trust him to do what was needed. He spent two hours poking around in a site called "Osteoarchaeology," jotting down notes as he went. Mostly it made no sense.

When his eyes got tired he sat on the porch and called Karylanne to talk to his granddaughter, who slobbered a wet "Bam-pee?"into the phone.

"Goddammit, Karylanne," he yelped. "We *talked* about this! She can call me anything but *that!*"

"Yes, *we* talked about it, Grady, but now that your granddaughter is learning to talk, I'm out of the equation, and you'll have to negotiate directly with her. Aren't you proud? Her first word is about *you,* not *Mum.* I'm the one who should be bent out of shape."

"But *Bampy*?" he whined. "Besides, I'm pretty sure she's got a couple of words, and at least one of them is mum."

"A woman of any age is quite capable of making her own decisions about terms of endearment."

"She's sixteen months old, not a woman."

"How little you know . . . Bampy."

He heard Karylanne laughing as she hung up, and found himself grin-ning. Karylanne wanted games? Fine; he'd teach Maridly a few words of *his* choosing. *See how Mum likes that!*

He finally summoned the courage to call Leukonovich around noon and listened patiently to a series of clicks and fiber-optic burps as the call pinballed its way to wherever the Poland-born IRS special agent was working. Leukonovich practiced yoga nude, and rarely spoke in anything but the third person.

"Zhenya finds herself vexed and groping for verbiage to adequately express her emotional exhilaration," she greeted him. "How goes the detective's battle against the forces of darkness in the taiga?"

"You sound wired," Service said. There was no denying his attraction to the strange woman's blend of raw and refined emotions and mannerisms.

"Does the detective sense my joy in hearing his voice?"

"It would be easier to sense in first person."

"Nonsense," she said with a dismissive laugh. "Joy is an emotional force—a state of being, albeit temporary—not a construct of language."

He felt sweaty. How could a woman who was far from beautiful have such an effect on him? *Keep to business,* he told himself. "I need help."

"Zhenya would know if such help would be of a professional or personal nature?"

"Professional."

"Zhenya is listening with a heavy heart."

He talked her through all the cases and events, starting with Newf finding the skulls, the interview with the professor in Chicago, what she had to say about Van Dalen, his death and obituary, and the prominence of the Van Dalen Foundation.

Leukonovich possessed the closest thing to a photographic memory he had ever encountered, and, as expected, asked him to repeat nothing. "Zhenya is quite aware of this organization and its oleaginous namesake, an early giant in the Windy City oligarchy."

Oleaginous? He wrote down the word to look up later. "Is the special agent suggesting there's IRS interest in the foundation?"

Zhenya said, "The accumulation of assets in any form is always of interest to the federal government, especially when said accumulation is alleged to have an undeclared political focus."

"Does that describe Van Dalen's foundation?"

"Zhenya chooses her words most carefully—except during copulation. She understands what is expected, and will, of course, be in communication with the detective, for whom she maintains an interest outside the bounds of the professional. Zhenya also observes that the detective's financial condition continues to improve, and she salutes the astute management of his personal assets and investments."

When they had worked together, the IRS agent had taken the questionable initiative of auditing his personal financial situation, something that had irritated him at the time. That she continued to monitor his finances no longer concerned him.

"Zhenya has past satisfactory collaborations with one Captain Isaac Funke, and will confer with the captain regarding the detective's interrogatories. The captain will undoubtedly be in direct communication with the detective."

"Will you?" he asked.

"Alas, Zhenya is neither seer nor oracle, and cannot predict the future, but all things are theoretically possible, and, given this reality, she would no doubt otherwise welcome telefornication, but pleasure has no priority this day."

The call was terminated on her end and left him laughing out loud. *Telefornication?*

Someone named Funke would be in touch. Leukonovich was aware of the Van Dalen Foundation, and, despite her convoluted syntax, he sensed her excitement. Of all the personnel from the many federal agencies he had worked with during his long career, Leukonovich of the IRS was far above all the rest in professional competence, connections, sense of mission, and trustworthiness as a collaborator. Zhenya was not about heaping credit on her own star—only on getting the job done. Credit was irrelevant, which in his experience made her a truly unique federal creature.

Elza Grinda arrived home after dark, showered, and changed clothes while Service was putting the finishing touches on a dinner of Aztec potato salad, Thai corn fritters, and jumbo prawns marinated in extra-hot dried shrimp Thai chile sauce and grilled over charcoal. Simon del Olmo dragged in fifteen minutes after Grinda, with Tuesday Friday in tow.

Friday looked him in the eye and said, "I need a drink—something strong, straight up, undiluted, and *now!*"

Service pulled a bottle of Absolut Peppar out of the freezer, poured several fingers into a small glass, handed it to her, and watched her drain it, making a sour face.

"She schmucked three deer on M-95," del Olmo said. "I was two minutes behind her. Man, she blew them up! Her veek's being towed to Iron Moun-tain. Not totaled, but major damage, man."

"*Trois un coup,*" Friday said, holding out her glass for another hit, her eyes welling with tears. "A mama and her babies, two itty-bitty fawns. I feel like a mass murderer." She shook her glass for a refill.

"Let the first one settle," Service said. "Dinner's on, Simon—five min-utes, tops."

"Into my phone booth now," del Olmo said.

Friday wiped her eyes with the back of her hand and looked around the kitchen, sniffing. "You are *cooking,* you who never *eats*?"

"It's my day off," he said.

Friday picked up the vodka bottle, poured herself another drink, and sat morosely while he plated the shrimp, fritters, and potato salad. He brought the plates inside and drizzled sweet pepper sauce around the rims. Elza opened a bottle of Coppola Rosso and poured while he put the plates on the table.

Simon tasted the shrimp, closed his eyes, and said, "When you retire, will you become our personal chef?"

"You don't like *my* cooking?" Grinda challenged.

"You don't like mine," he countered.

"Everyone knows you're a terrible cook."

"I have saving graces," he said.

She rolled her eyes. "That's what you keep telling me."

Tuesday Friday ate so slowly that Service found it almost painful to watch. "If you live up here," he said, "there's two classes of people—those who have hit deer, and those who will. If you work as a CO, you *will* hit a lot of deer. You've never hit one on road patrol in your blue goose?"

"Never; I'm a careful driver," she said. "And realities aside, I still think it's sad."

"A dead human is sad," del Olmo said. "A dead deer is just roadside protein for other critters."

"You people are so insensitive," Friday said.

They didn't deny it.

"You're supposed to be home," Service said.

"Tomorrow is a work day and it's a two-hour drive. Better tonight than early morning."

"How's Shigun?"

She took a drink of wine. "Cuddly, thank you."

Service rinsed the dishes after dinner and loaded the dishwasher. Friday tried to help but he shooed her away. Simon and Elza sat in the living room, talked a little about their day, and fell asleep next to each other on the couch.

"I'll take you to the AmericInn," Service told Friday as he started the dishwasher, but when he looked up he saw that she was asleep in the easy chair.

He clapped his hands together. "Okay, kids, everybody go night-night."

Simon nuzzled Grinda's neck as they shuffled toward their bedroom, looked back, said, "Bags in truck," and disappeared. Service guided Friday into the room he'd been using, and turned back the covers. "Drank too much," she said. "Bet you never do that."

"You'd lose that bet."

"I did good," she mumbled, looking around. "This isn't AmericInn."

"I'm sure you did," he said, to appease her. "No, it's not."

"Poor, poor baby deer. Bad mommy."

"Yes," he said. "Poor baby deer," and closed the bedroom door.

He fetched Friday's bags, smoked a cigarette, curled up on the couch, and awoke to find a ghost hovering near him—Friday with a sheet draped around her like a toga, her hair askew. She reached for his hand, said nothing, led him into the bedroom, patted the bed, fluffed pillows on both sides, and got in. "Just cuddle," she rasped in the dark. "Newbie sex and drink not good."

He lay down beside her and listened as her breathing changed to a sound not unlike a mourning dove.

When he awoke early he found Friday on her side, propped up on her elbow, her head on her hand. "I have a *really* low tolerance for alcohol," she whispered. "But never a hangover." She leaned close to his ear, her voice barely audible. "Grady, there's something I'd like very, very much to do with you, but it's been a long time for me, and if we're to do this thing, I would be consigned to Jell-O mode, and that would be a terrible thing on a work day." She added, "Correction: Not terrible; more like disastrous."

Jell-O mode? He had no idea what she was talking about.

"Three deer," she said.

"Elza's count was at fourteen last I heard. You're just getting started."

"*Fourteen?*"

"She's very hard on vehicles."

"And deer," Friday said.

"And deer," he agreed.

"I need caffeine," she said.

"Coming right up."

Grinda and del Olmo were in their stirruped uniform pants and bullet-proof vests, still in their stocking feet, and said nothing when he joined them in the kitchen, though Grinda gave him a playful hip-bump as he poured coffee into a cup and took it back to the bedroom.

Friday was on her side, sheets at her knees. Her left shoulder had a softball-size patch of pink scar tissue, as did her left hip. Her work clothes hid a lot more than the scars, and he tried not to look. "Shower's in there," he said, pointing at a door. "Full breakfast or a quickie?"

He immediately regretted his words.

"Is both an option?"

"What about that Jell-O mode thing?"

"Might be worth it," she said, winking.

He tossed a towel at her. "I'll get things started."

"I think I already did that," she said as he closed the bedroom door.

24

Iron River, Iron County

TUESDAY, MAY 30, 2006

Millitor was already in their cubbyhole at the MSP post, feet propped up, unlit cigar clenched in his teeth, coffeepot full. Service poured a cup. Friday sat down, looking smug, and Service wondered if the look related to last night.

Nothing happened, he told himself. *Really.*

"I was busy over the weekend," she said, opening her briefcase and hauling out a sheaf of papers. "There's this man I sort of know? He grew up in Negaunee, went to U of M, Stanford, and retired as vice chairman of Northern California Equities. He moved home for his so-called golden years. He's only fifty-five, but came home with a whole lot more than he left with. I asked him if he's aware of the Van Dalen Foundation. He is, and he told me it's the most complex organization in the country—that California Equities had done an in-depth study of it, and he can get us a copy of the Van Dalen Foundation's organizational charts, including contact names and numbers, current as of three years ago. It will take him a week or so. He's got to go to San Francisco next week for a board meeting and will bring the information back with him."

"Did he offer an opinion of Van Dalen?"

"Too long in big business politics, too diplomatic, but he's eager to help, and maybe that says something?"

A week's not bad, Service told himself.

"That's my *first* item," Friday said. She gave each of the men some papers stapled together. "Here's the second: Provo's transcript from Adams State College. I used a highlighter to mark some of the more-interesting courses she took."

Service read through the transcripts, trying to categorize. Under history: Twentieth-Century Revolutionary Movements; The Lessons of Sun Tzu: Direct Action and the Global Environmental Movement; Roots and Antecedents of the French Revolution; Guerrillas, Resistance & Public

Opinion in Open and Closed States; Trends in Counterrevolution; and the History of Colorado Copper Mining.

Under anthropology: Native American Culture and Aboriginal Healing Practices.

Under geography: Advanced Map Reading for Outdoor Professionals.

Science: The Ecology of *Salmo Trutta*, and Botany of Midwestern Lacustrine Ecosystems.

General studies: Community Action Workshop.

From physical education: Orienteering in Extreme Environments and Climates.

The rest of the classes looked like basic college requirements that all students had to complete, and a heap of ambiguous, stupid-sounding education courses for her major.

Provo's final GPA had been 3.87. *Not an average student.*

"The curricula have changed since my day," Service said.

Millitor quipped, "Curricula—is that a Cuban dance, or what?"

Service found Friday watching him. He said, "Sort of reads like a blueprint for activism, eh?"

"Ya think?"

Pleased with herself.

"How'd you get this?" he asked.

"I called the college last week and made nice with Shirley in Records. We're pals now; you know, sisters in an increasingly oppressive male world," she said, looking directly at him with a conspiratorial grin.

"The last item isn't written down," she said. "The only Army Guard Military Police Unit in Colorado is the 220th MP Company out of the Denver-Globeville Armory, unit strength two hundred souls. Denver's less than two hundred miles from Alamosa, easily doable for weekend Guard drills."

"Call them and see if they'll confirm the dates she served. If not, we'll talk to Sutschek in CID and get him to run interference for us."

"Heckuva job, kiddo," Millitor said.

"Thanks, Mike."

Service nodded, saw her grinning at him.

After the meeting he took Friday with him to the Iron River Community Hospital to find the ME. "Who's your corporate snitch?" he asked as he negotiated the streets.

"Jinger Flamms—and I wouldn't call him a snitch. Right after I moved to the U.P., his wife and eighteen-year-old son were in a rollover south of Marquette. I was first on the scene, smelled gas, and pulled them out. It never really ignited, but the husband thinks I'm a hero."

"I saw scars on your hip and arm," he said.

She blushed. "I show you everything under the big top, and all you look at are the *sideshows*?"

"Tuesday," he said. "Focus."

"Okay, maybe it went off a little, but it wasn't like a conflagration or any-thing. Ever since then he's been trying to reward me—a week in Cabo San Lucas, an invite to join the governor for the Mackinac Bridge Walk, weird stuff. He's constantly telling me he wants to help me. What is it with men—they find a woman who does the same things men do, and it turns them on?"

She's ducking. Obviously she had acted heroically and gotten burned in the process.

"The wifey's a dingey-thingey, cling-on type," she continued. "I think Mr. Flamms wants to get in my little cop pants, but I called him when I got back Friday and told him he could help me by getting me the Van Dalen Foundation information."

"I bet that went over big."

"Men and hope," she said. "Go figure. Said he'd take care of it, and that's what matters, right? Aren't you happy with all this?"

"Absolutely, but I'm also wondering why a reportedly bright, obviously gifted student and future activist creates a course trail that screams, 'Here I am, look at me!' "

She tilted her head. "Maybe there was a magic transformational moment, but I hear what you're saying."

They found the ME in his office, drinking chai. Service said, "Are we keeping you from your work?" The doctor did not offer to share.

"Lab time is minimal," the ME said. "The important work is intellectual."

Yogi Berra, he thought. *Baseball's 90 percent mental and the other half is physical.* The ME was a pretentious asshole, and Service thought about shooting the Yogi quote at him, but decided to behave. *After I jab his ass.* "Intellectual, as in guessing TSH?" he asked.

The ME looked irritated, but Service pressed on. "That's Total Skeleton Height, right, Doc? You're right about needing long bones, but using which estimation method—Bach-Breitinger or Trotter-Gleser? Am I reading this crap wrong, or are these more or less algorithms for educated guesses? Am I off base here?"

"It's extremely complex," the ME said defiantly.

"Including the fudge factors used to account for bone density loss? Doc, we're not trying to yank your chain, and we respect what you do, but please don't be blowing smoke up our asses. We get enough of that every day from the bad guys. We're supposed to be on the same side. We stopped by to see if you might have a ballpark . . . measurement."

"Six-seven, at least," the ME said, his face flushing to the color of a ripe plum.

"Great—thanks. Listen, did you happen to look at vick one to see if he's one-armed?" he asked, adding a slashing motion for emphasis.

The doctor opened a folder, browsed, looked up, and said, "No bones from the arm or hand."

Service said, "You might want to look at the left elbow socket or whatever you call it and see if there was an amputation."

The ME began looking through the folder and didn't look up. "I'll call you," he said. He closed and picked up the folder, gathered his lab coat like a skirt, and disappeared down the hall.

"Adroit," Friday said.

"Is that like using a jackhammer to drive a carpet tack?"

"Pretty much," she said.

Millitor looked perturbed when they got back to their office. "I talked to the MP commander out in Denver and he kicked me upstairs. He says the Army JAG is concerned about privacy matters."

"Provo's RFD," Service said.

"Don't matter. She ain't separated from the service, which means she retains a right to privacy," Millitor said.

"Did the CO give you any sense that there might have been problems with Provo when she was in the 220th?"

"That was before his time. He just took over. Seems more a policy deal than anything personal."

New-guy-in-charge syndrome. Service gave the detective Major Sutschek's telephone number. "Tell him we need his help." Then, as an afterthought, "Fax Provo's transcript and ask him what he sees."

Millitor headed for a fax.

"Why the transcript?" Friday asked.

"If you were doing a background on Provo for Troop School, wouldn't you have some questions about her motivations and intentions?"

"Point taken."

"In my experience, investigators need to look at every angle, not just those that support what we think."

"Even if it destroys our hypothesis?"

"Especially then. Better to know we're wrong now than way down the road."

"Pearls of wisdom?'

"More like grains of sand that need to irritate a clam's guts to become pearls."

"Are you thinking we're off course?"

Not thinking. But possible. "This is about doing all the work."

The ME called later. "Definitely an amputation on vick one. I should have seen it, but didn't. Glad you said something. I'll have TSH on vick two tomorrow morning."

Attitude transplant? "Thanks, Doc."

He looked over at Friday after turning off his cell phone. "Amputation on vick one."

"Washington Lincoln?" she said.

"Two skeletons: a one-armed African American, and a very tall Native American, alleged partners in life, found together in death. What're the chances it's *not* them?"

"Do we publicly release tentative IDs on the two vicks?"

Good question. "Let's leave it as is for now, and wait for the TSH from the ME. Meanwhile, what can we do to get a background on the two men? Place and date of birth, police records, whatever. I know it was eighty years ago, but there had to have been some records kept, somewhere, sometime." *I hope.*

"There's not much of a physical component to detective work, is there?" she said.

"In the old days it was fallen arches and worn-out shoes," Millitor said. "Now it's carpal tunnel, hemorrhoids, and calluses on your fingertips."

"Is there an upside?" Service asked.

"We burn less taxpayer gas?" Millitor said.

• • •

Elza Grinda came by the office late in the afternoon, poured a cup of coffee for herself, and sprawled in a chair. "Any progress on the Paint River vick?"

"Zero," Millitor told her. "Wrong place, right time, or vice versa. Ficklefinger-of-fate shit."

"Shame," she said. "Fate works for me. His fishing partner seemed like an okay guy. He calls me every day asking about progress. He's really broken up by this, told me they'd never even heard of the South Branch of the Paint until they got a flyer in the mail about how it's one of the best early-season trout streams in the Midwest."

"Flyer?" Service said.

Grinda went out to her truck and dropped a folded leaflet on the desk. Service read through it quickly. Sent out by a man named V. Korov, owner of the Mad Russian's Guide & Outfitting Service. Address in Amasa, fifteen miles north of Crystal. Service read out loud, "Guided fishing trips, either float or walk-in, $400 a day, results guaranteed." He looked up at his colleagues. "Trout fishing guide?" Service said. *"Here?"*

"It's a big deal below the bridge," Grinda said.

"We're not below the bridge. We're up *here.* Did the dead guy and his pal talk to this guide?"

"Nope. They got the flyer and came up on their own."

"Have you talked to this Korov?"

"Thought about it," she said, "but you know how it goes. If it's not on the front burner, it doesn't get done."

He knew exactly what she meant and held up the folder. "Can I keep this a while?"

"All yours," Grinda said.

Service looked at Friday. "Take a ride?"

"Lunch along the way?"

"Deal."

He started to pull into McDonald's but she said, "No way, buster. Pull into Angelli's and I'll run into the deli. You won't even have to get out of the truck."

"I hate waiting," he said.

"Be good practice for you then," she said as he pulled into the grocery store's huge lot and watched her hurry through the revolving door.

25

Amasa, Iron County

TUESDAY, MAY 30, 2006

They took three trucks, Service's, del Olmo's, and Grinda's. The address from the mailer was a fire number on Basillio Road, a little more than four miles north of Amasa, a former logging town that in its day had been one of the rowdiest, most lawless places in the western U.P. Basillio Road had been bypassed by US 141, was no longer in use and showed it, the old macadam bed peeling likes scabs under the assault of seven-month-long winters.

It was almost noon. The cabin had not seen paint in a long time, but the roof looked new, as did several windows. A slender, low-slung wooden boat of at least twenty feet in length was on an as-long trailer in the side yard, both of the trailer's tires flat, and a gaping wound in the side of the boat. The boat's state registration sticker was good until next year.

"You know this camp?" Service asked Simon.

"Been by it once in a while, but I've never seen anyone here."

The front door was boarded up, and before they got to the back door a muscular man in jeans, boots, and weathered brown Carhartt overalls stepped outside and glared at them. He had long matted blond hair and a full beard that shone reddish in the daylight. "I am here, by God!" the man shouted. He wore a large handgun in a holster on his right hip.

Service held up the brochure. "We're looking for V. Korov."

"Korov stands before you and God almighty!"

"Korov . . . the fishing guide."

"You think Venyamin Korov writes lies?"

The man's voice was deep and loud, his neck veins taut. Service held out his hands in a gesture meant to placate. "We're just interested in talking about your business."

"Business! You see boat, trailer! What business is it you wish to discuss?"

"You hit a rock or something?"

"I am making wood at Fence. I come home, you see what I find!"

"Somebody did this while the boat was here?"

"Yes, of course!"

"When did this happen?"

"Why do you wish to know this? I called no police. Let me see badge!"

"Boy, this is fun," Friday whispered behind Service as he took out his wallet and showed the man his shield.

"Umm," was the man's sole response. Then, "The others with you! You are responsible for them?"

"We're together . . . partners," Service said.

"I think I am reading state of Michigan is low on fish militia. Yet you are here—I count one, two, three—what is the significance of so many assets together? Answer me this, please."

"We saw your brochure, wanted to talk to you."

"You want to hire guide?"

"No, we are seeking information."

"I have no time for just talk!"

"Did you report the vandalism?" del Olmo asked.

The man tapped his chest and glared. "Venyamin will take care of this matter."

"That's not a good idea," Service said.

"They-et boat is costing me ay-et thousand, U.S. dollar—Grayling, Michigan, special-built."

"It's a nice boat," Service said, "but about the vandalism . . . ?"

"They-et boat is shit now, puts me out of business! People with money are lazy, do not want to walk in and wade, just to float—like fucking czars!"

Service guessed the man's age at around thirty. Despite the gruff exterior and excitable manner, he sensed the man was honest. A bit aggressive, perhaps, but honest. He'd met such types many times before. The U.P. was a magnet for eccentrics. "When were you vandalized?"

"Night before opening day of trout is to begin."

Service had studied some Russian in college and retained a smidgen. Last year a Ukrainian-born snitch had helped him break a major case that led him all the way to New York City, where the Ukrainian mafia was dealing in illegal and contaminated salmon eggs.

"Is your weapon licensed?" Service asked in Russian, hoping it was adequate.

"No CCW," the man said in English. "I wear in plain sight. I think this is legal to wear in this way, yes? Venyamin does not break laws!"

"It's good," Service said in English. "Your boat is registered, and of course you've got permits to harvest firewood."

"Yes, of course. I drive Crystal Falls to DNR. They give permit. Nice geerl at desk."

"Would you rather speak Russian?" Service asked.

The man laughed. "Your Russian is for shit! Is my English not so good to understand?"

"Your English is fine." *My Russian's shit? Rusty maybe, but not shit.*

"Good, English. I come to America to be American, speak American, think American, smell American, everything American. I study engineer-ing, Michigan Tech-no-log-i-cal U-ni-ver-si-ty. I have degree—you want to see?"

"I don't think that's necessary."

"Why not look?" Friday whispered, goading him.

"I am study hard at university. I study hard and fish brook trout. This is disease, I think."

Service found himself smiling. "I'm a victim too. Your brochure seems to focus almost entirely on the South Branch of the Paint."

"Venyamin *loves* this Paint River. I feesh Ontonagon, Brule, Iron, Fence, both Sturgeons, both Blacks, all Foxes, Yellow Dog, Slate, Silver, Otter, Salmon Trout—all of them. South Branch Paint is best. If I were rich man I would buy all the land for myself."

"You're not rich?"

The Russian smiled, sweeping his giant hand across the area. "Look around, see for yourself the kingdom of Korov."

"Did you have clients opening day?"

"I have no clients any day. I make brochure with computer, buy com-puter mail lists, send thousands of copies. Even at kopeks, it costs fortune to be entrepreneur in America."

"Did you fish the opener?"

"Yes, main Paint, Blockhouse Creek—you know this place? Is very good early season. When water warms, trout go away. Venyamin fishes alone."

Service could sympathize. "Why not the South Branch?"

"Opening day, I think perhaps too many people."

"What if you had had customers?"

"No problem. I would take boat, go past people, find good places without company, but boat is kaput. I do not fish South Branch often. River is like woman: Use too much and you wear her out."

Friday whispered to Service. "*Some* women; *not* all women."

"Did you hear about trouble on the South Branch?"

"Yes, on second day this is on radio. Police say no fishing there. Man is keeled, I think."

"Have you ever been harassed on the South Branch?"

"No, never," the man said touching his holster.

"Why a guide service *here*?"

"There are no competitors. Is virgin market."

"There're no clients here."

"Yes, I am learning this. When I am in engineering, I think only of brook trout. When I am with brook trout, I do not think of engineering— you understand?"

"I think I do. Did you come to the U.S. as a student?" Service asked.

"Yes, after my father was here as diplomat of sorts."

"And you came to Iron County specifically to open your guide business?"

"No, I move here to live, to trap fur, to fish brook trout, collect mushrooms and berries, hunt deer and birds, and bear. Guide is way to make money to pay for such palatial estate."

The man was wry, even funny. Service hoped the others were picking up on it. Korov's blustery manner decried a more whimsical soul.

"Would you like to give us details of the vandalism? You can file a formal report," del Olmo said.

"Why not!" the man said enthusiastically. "No offense, but militia in Russia are pigs and pricks, all with hands out. You seem like nice guys."

"Too long alone in the woods," Friday whispered. "Do I *look* like a guy?"

"Do you have insurance?" Service asked.

"No, I do Russian way, I fix myself."

"Simon's pretty handy with wood," Service offered.

"So am I," Friday whispered, her voice trailing off.

"You have eaten, my new friends?"

"We just stopped to introduce ourselves, we've already eaten," Service explained.

"Bullshit! Is Russian custom, guests will take food or is insult." He poked Service forcefully. "Maybe Russian food will improve your Russian language."

A bit later, the Russian served beavertail stew. "Is aphrodisiac in the Motherland," he said.

"Oh goodie," Friday whispered. "Like I *need* a booster."

The man still wore his handgun. "What make?" Service asked.

"*Pistolet Makarova*. Russian Makarov is cannon for the hand. You are *Makarovniki*?"

"Geez," Friday said with a whimper. "Make him stop! I can't take any more of this."

"No," Service said. "First Russian pistol I've ever seen."

• • •

After lunch the three officers met Grinda just outside Crystal Falls, pulled up a two-track, and stood by Service's truck. "Was that guy for real?" Friday asked.

"The U.P. tends to attract eccentrics and individualists," del Olmo said. "Always has, always will—as long as there's wild land and the possibility of privacy."

Service's mind was swimming in other directions. "How many people did you check on the South Branch opening day?" he asked Grinda.

"I saw eight or nine, maybe ten. But I only actually checked three, no violations. Fly fishermen," she said. "Boy Scouts. Most of them release what they catch."

"Different this year than last?"

"Good weather this time. Last year's opener sucked. There's never much traffic on the South Branch. Come late June you can have it all to yourself."

"Did you map the location of the crap we picked up on the second day?"

"Sure, dropped markers on my AVL. Want to see?"

He leaned in the truck and looked over her shoulder as she brought up the map. She had marked each danger with a red X. Service studied what he saw. "The fishing below where the man was killed—that's good water, right?"

"It can be *great* this time of year. Deep holes, lots of cover, better than upstream, unless you go *way* upstream."

"Only two Xs below the bridge."

"Right, the concentration was higher."

"But the better fishing is *below.*"

"This time of year."

"It *is* this time of year," he said.

"Maybe somebody thinks the upper section is his personal water."

"I thought this was about anti-fishing," Service reminded them all. "How many camps up there?"

Grinda and del Olmo glanced at each other. She said, "Forty, fifty—I never really counted. They're mostly seasonal camps with only a handful of year-rounders, and most of them are strung out along Basswood Road."

"Maybe we should knock on some doors, see if anyone saw anything in the days before the shooting."

"Probably not that many people around."

"Some of the people over there must be trout fishermen."

"I suppose."

He could see Grinda trying to figure out how she could knock on doors and do all the other things she had to do.

"Friday and I will get Mike and we'll take care of it. You want to loan me your plat book?"

Her relief was visible as she fished the book from the backseat and handed it to him.

• • •

"So," Friday said, when they were alone in his truck, "I suppose we'll start knocking on doors today?"

"Tomorrow," he said.

"Thank God."

"I thought we'd take a little hike tonight. You like campfires?"

"In a *fireplace,* with a bottle of champagne nearby."

"Think campfire outdoors."

"I don't think so," she said, lowering her eyes.

"We'll be spending the night."

"Are you expecting me to stand up and shout hallelujah?"

"Why would you do that?"

"Exactly," she said.

"Not a real long hike. Ten miles; double that with the return."

"You want to hike ten miles into the bush and ten miles back—at night."

"It's only 4 o'clock. We've got a lot of daylight left. If you hadn't killed those poor deer, we'd have a second vehicle to spot and walk to." He saw her trying to catch a breath. "Don't worry, the woods are my home."

"My boots are in that car we don't have," she reminded him.

"You and Grinda are about the same size," he said. "She'll borrow you some stuff," he said, borrowing a Yooper expression.

26

South Branch, Paint River, Iron County

TUESDAY, MAY 30, 2006

After a fast stop at Grinda's, Service drove to the west county, pulled off the road a half-mile north of Elmwood, where Forest Highway 16 sliced through a low ridge, got out, fixed sleeping bags to two packs, and tossed long johns, wool socks, and a wool chook to Friday. He studied the topography on the AVL while she sat in back, changing clothes, complaining. "It's *after* Memorial Day," she said, holding up the wool items.

"Trust me, it's not summer yet."

"I thought we were going to the river."

"Is that a lyric in a hymn?"

"Seriously."

"What if this *isn't* about fish?" he said, looking back and catching her trying to spear one pant leg of the long johns.

She stopped struggling and looked at him. "Want to tell me what this *is* about?

"We'll know when we find it," he said, and got out of the truck.

He hoped. He didn't have a clear hypothesis; more a notion, an irritating kernel of something, alternate thinking, back-dooring the problem. Booby traps kept some people away, but attracted others. The DNR had closed the river after the killing to keep people away and to prevent further injuries. Did closing the river both prevent something and enable another—the law of unintended consequences? The property where Newf had found the skulls belonged to Art Lake. Art Lake / wolf tree / booby traps—a sequence becoming a mantra. Linkages, or your own imaginings? They seem to be connected. Seem. Not sure.

They hiked through the hardwoods, working their way through tangles of blowdowns and new and decaying slash, leafy compost, like walking on sponge in some places—sponge that hid rocks and made the footing dicey, hard slogging. "Slow down," Friday muttered sharply from behind him. "What's the point of searching at night? We can't see shit."

"Other stuff is more obvious at night," he told her, and began moving again. "Besides, it's not even close to night yet. We still have plenty of light." It was only 9:30 p.m.

"You call it light," she grumped. "I call it twilight."

Service saw the porcupine scuttle in front of him, heading for a tree, thought, *Big porky, big liver.* He got to the animal just as it headed up the trunk, took out his .40 caliber SIG Sauer, and killed it with a single round, pulling his leg back as it dropped heavily back to the ground.

"It's okay," he called to Friday.

She came forward with her own weapon at the ready in the two-handed position. "Put it away," he said.

She looked at the animal on the ground. "You shot a *porcupine*?"

"Dinner," he said.

She said, "I'd rather eat dirt."

He ignored her. Porky meat could be good if it was properly marinated for long enough, but he had neither the time nor the materials. The fast food from a porky was the liver. The animal was not an overly active creature, which produced a relatively large liver. He put his boot on the animal and rolled it onto its back. He slid off his pack, got out a plastic evidence bag and a bottle of water. He knelt beside the creature, delicately slit the belly, just breaking through the skin with his folding knife, reached into the cavity, and delicately felt around until he found the liver. He pulled it through the opening to be sure he had the right thing, and when he was certain, used the knife to sever it from the connecting tissue, and held it up for Friday to see. It was the size of a swollen baseball, perfect for what he had in mind.

Friday sat on a log watching him. "You're gonna get quilled," she said.

He chuckled. "The quills that come loose are mostly in the tail," he told her as he emptied the bottle of water into the plastic bag, sprinkled three salt packets into the water, put the liver into the water and shook the bag, turning the water a color between pink and brown. He put the empty bottle and the bag back into his pack, wiped his hands in the dirt, put his pack back on, and looked at her. "This is great. It can soak while we hike."

"Yeah, that's important," she said.

Thirty minutes later he had dead-reckoned his way back to the knob above where Newf had found the skulls. "Picnic?" he said, setting his pack down.

"Picnics are done in daylight, not in the dark."

"Don't knock it until you try it," he said.

"That's what my ex used to say about anal sex. We haven't hiked anything like ten miles," she pointed out.

"You want to make a fire?"

"More appropriately, you should ask do I know how to make a fire, to which the answer would be, uh, *nooo*. And this is *your* house, right? You come to mine, I'll turn on the stove. That's a promise."

He assembled a small ring of stones, gathered a pile of sticks the diameter of pool cues, and tore some birch bark from a rotting tree. He opened his pack, took out a quart-size pan, and emptied two bottles of water into it. The liver bag sat beside the pan. He made the fire by putting twigs and tinder on birch bark and igniting the bark with his lighter. Birch burned like a candle, and would ignite when wet. In winter he often carried a bag of birch and tinder in his pack.

"Tuesday, when the water boils, put the liver in and let it boil about two minutes."

"I'm not *touching* that thing," she said.

"C'mon, be a sport."

"Yeah, my ex used to say *that*, too."

He took his pack to a boulder with a slight depression about eight inches across and pulled a sheet of paper towel from his pack, along with a plastic cylinder. He used his folding knife to cut some green sticks, a quarter- to a half-inch in diameter, and set them by his pack.

"It's starting to boil," Friday said. "What's in the plastic gizmo?"

"Spices."

"You're joking. Who're you supposed to be, Julia Child?"

"Try Euell Gibbons," he said, but she was a bit too young to remember. "I keep this in my pack. He tapped dried thyme and basil onto the paper towel, and most of the small container of ancho chili powder, and looked over at the pot. "Put it in," he said.

"Isn't that my line?"

She didn't make a face, and clearly did not like handling the liver, but did as he asked and put it in the pot.

"Two minutes," she said.

He handed her one of the green sticks. "Spear it."

She sighed, held the handle of the pan, gingerly stuck the stick into the organ, and held it out to him.

He set the liver on the boulder beside the spices and lit a cigarette. "It needs to cool," he said, adding, "Stoke the fire."

"Yours or mine?" she said.

He shook his head and trimmed yellow membrane and gristle off the cooled liver, cutting it into quarter-inch slices. He tossed green sticks to Friday and began rolling slices in the spices. When each was done he passed it to her. "Thread it like shish kebab."

"Shish kebab has real meat, veggies, fruit. This isn't shish kebab."

"*Tuesday.*"

"Yeah, yeah, don't use that tone of voice with me. We haven't even slept together."

"What was last night?"

"Don't go semantic on me . . . you know what I mean," she said, threading the liver slices.

All the meat on skewers, he took them from her and lay them across the fire rocks.

"This is dinner—all of it?"

"You won't be disappointed," he said. "It beats venison liver."

"Now *that's* a ringing culinary endorsement to get my taste buds quivering."

"Why so uptight out here? You were a regular comedian at the Mad Russian's."

"I saw humor there, none here."

"There's a reason for us to be here," he told her. "Put aside everything we think we know. Think outside of the box."

"This whole experience is way outside my box," she said.

"I know, but try to bear with me. Someone sets booby traps, not on the entire very fishable stretch, but only above the bridge where the man died. My friend and I hit the first razor wire just below here, but this is great water, so why put the wire and booby traps where they did?"

"They're anti-fishing nuts. They want people to leave the fish alone."

"Why?"

"I have absolutely *no* idea."

Take another angle. "Okay, pretend you're a kid playing hide-and-seek. The searchers are moving in, and you have to *do* something."

"I'd surrender. It's a lame game, Mom's calling me in for dinner—and it's goulash."

"Okay, you're a cop in the middle of bad guys; if you come up shooting, you're dead. What do you do? If you hunker, you're done."

"Diversion," she said.

"How's the meat doing?" he asked, poking at a slice with his finger and leaning down to look.

"How would I know?" she said. "Liver's not meat, anyway—it's guts . . . or something."

"What kind of diversion?"

"Throw a rock?"

"That would work. What happens when you throw it?"

"They turn toward the sound."

"Exactly—which buys you time and space, and then you can do whatever you need to do," he said, checking the meat again.

"If not an anti-fishing group, what?" she asked.

"We're not ruling them out. We're just trying to look at the picture differently. If this was a diversion, what happened, and why?"

"Having the DNR on the river and keeping fishermen away saved others from getting hurt, or worse."

"Right, our people were mobilized, and showed up in force—but *only* where the danger was found. The skulls were found directly below us, and if I wanted to be in this area with minimal chance of interference, having a bunch of woods cops just downstream would provide the ideal shield. *Jesus,*" he said, and grabbed the cell phone out of his pack.

He hit the speed dial for Grinda. "Hey, it's Grady. Any word from UPSET?"

"I'd forgotten about all that with everything else that's been going on."

"Can you call your friend, find out what they have?"

"What was that about?" Friday asked after he'd finished the call. "UPSET is about dope, right?"

"The night we found the remains, Grinda had a bit of a scrap with unknown perps less than seven miles west of here. We found tracks of four-wheelers, which means they could easily have been anywhere in this area and seen something."

"All this could be about *dope*?"

"Twins: Dope and violence."

"Sad but true," she said.

"Which makes it worth looking around this area, right?"

"Wouldn't daylight make more sense?"

"Not for what I'm thinking."

He handed her a skewer. "*Bon appetit.*"

When she balked, he picked up another skewer and bit into the liver.

She still balked. He picked up a handful of dirt and held it out to her. "Your alternative entree, I believe?"

Friday finally tasted the liver and said, "Okay, I'm woman enough to admit I'm half wrong."

"Half?"

"It's delicious, but there's not nearly enough."

Fire extinguished and tamped, packs on backs, he said, "Let's boogie."

"Are we carrying sleeping bags for a reason?"

"The night's just beginning."

"I'm usually naked and in bed when I like to hear those words."

"You'll love walking at night."

"If I don't lose an eye."

"Put on your safety glasses and move steadily."

Four hours later they were midway down a low ridge and he began kicking sticks off the pine duff to clear a space. Area cleared, he dropped his pack, undid his sleeping bag, and rolled it out.

"This is it?" she asked.

"Listening post," he said. "Maybe I'm wrong and wasting our time. I'm not seeing anything. Which makes it time to sit and listen. Sometimes ears are a lot better than eyes in the woods."

"I'm too tired to think or listen," she said, "but sometimes the obvious is obvious for a reason," she said, spreading out her own sleeping bag. "Do these bags zip together?" she asked.

He knew she was right about the obvious, but this didn't seem to fit. "Separate sleeping accommodations."

"Naturally," she grumped. "The bones you found," she said, "they're separate from the killing, and the other stuff?"

"So many dots and no pencil to connect them," he said, and heard Tuesday Friday in her cooing mode. "You're supposed to take off your clothes before you get in your bag," he said, but she was beyond hearing.

27

South Branch, Paint River, Iron County

WEDNESDAY, MAY 31, 2006

Vibrations somewhere, genesis of sound, movement, something—muted and mechanical, not that close, but out there for sure. Grady Service awoke and opened his eyes. First light, heavier dew than he had expected, sleeping bag damp. He touched Friday's shoulder gently, saw her eyes open, trying to shed sleep, whispered close to her ear, "Something east-northeast of us . . . can't judge distance."

She fluttered her eyes, nodded.

"Slide out of your bag," he whispered. "It's wet."

He handed her a bottle of water, watched her pour some in her hand, splash her face, take a sip. She held it out for him, but he shook his head. "Leave everything," he said quietly, touching forked fingers to his eyes, raising his eyebrows to see if she was taking on board what he was saying. He got a nod, saw her breathing evenly, not jacked. *Good.*

They rose as one, left the flat place under the trees, and moved slightly downslope. The flag of a large deer waggled ahead of them, 180 pounds of animal moving without sound. Service's eyes took in everything: To the left a swale, last year's deer grass, some spruce and small white pines, skinny cedars. Bedding area, game trails in the high brown grass flattened and radiating outward like tentacles.

Nearing the next crest, lower than where they had spent the night, he heard sound. Not just heard it, but felt it, something moving slowly right to left. Below them, a motor gunned, twice, and again. *Four-wheeler: Fuel-line problem?* Fighting the urge to charge on an intercept angle. *Cool it.* Nodded Friday to the left of him, watched her, watched the ground, tried to track the motor sound but it was gone. *Gone.* He pointed down, north, touched his eyes, saw her nodding, touching her ear. *She had heard it too.* They stepped in unison, watching everything for anything. Saw Friday halt, look down, scrinch her face, give him a questioning look.

He made his way over to her, picking his way.

"There," she whispered, pointing. *Something green, small, size of a biscuit, dull green, but with a sheen. Plastic?* He got down on his knees, looked at it. *Definitely plastic.* He looked left and right, saw more, scattered irregularly in a ragged line, perhaps three feet deep, both left and right of them. Six feet downhill he could see nothing. Barrier, he told himself. *Blocking the route up or blocking the way down? Moot for the moment.* The Ojibwas and Menominees in the U.P. used to build miles-long fences of stumps and debris to funnel animals, position their best hunters at the openings, and pick them off as they came through. *Were they being funneled? If so, by whom? And why?*

"What?" Friday asked in a barely audible voice.

"Can't tell. Something man-made. Good eyes. They're left and right and below, clear behind, if we didn't inadvertently already step past some."

He moved left, maybe twenty yards, could still see green lumps below him. Paralleled the line, was startled when a deer bounded up from its bed and raced downhill in a panic, followed immediately by a wake of pops and flashes. He instinctively lifted his arm to shield his eyes, saw the deer, running through a small opening, fire coming off its back hooves, like afterburners.

He made his way back to Friday.

"Did you *see* that?" she asked with disbelief.

He used his knife to trim off a green stick four feet long, a half-inch in diameter, sharpened one end, touched the point to the nearest package, added pressure, saw the point break through. Nothing. Let out his breath, rubbed his eyes. Heard sounds to the right. Pops and flashes and pops, like a light wave mixed with sound, and a familiar smell—garlic. *Vietnam. Willie Pete! Fuck!*

"Run!" he hissed, grabbing Friday and pushing her up the hill. "*Move, move, move!*"

He careered against a log, rolled over it onto the crest, dropped to his knees, and pushed her forward. Looking back, he saw a carpet of billowing white smoke and sparks that had moved right to left. *Same track the sound had followed,* his mind noted. Flames were licking some of the undergrowth. He unholstered his radio, called the Iron County dispatcher, reported the fire, asked for DNR fire suppression, gave directions. *No way county equipment can get back here,* he told himself.

They stayed on fire watch until help arrived, a DNR man in a yellow Nomex shirt, first on the scene, his face all business. "Rocco Solenetti," the man said. "You the one called it in?"

"Grady Service, yeah. Willie Pete."

Solenetti looked skeptical. "You *sure*?"

"Guessing, but I've seen it before. Bad on the skin."

"Got that right. Later," Solenetti said, moving to join the others grinding relentlessly through the woods in a gigantic red tanker truck.

He sat on a log with Friday, not speaking.

"I like morning fireworks," she said. "But not like this."

Grinda came through the woods and joined them. "What set it off?"

"A deer."

"Only in the U.P.," she said.

None of this is about fish, Service thought. "We're dealing with someone who knows how cops think, how we run toward trouble, only this time we didn't take the bait. They gunned an engine, like a bugle calling hounds to a bear."

"Willie Pete?" Grinda asked.

"Need techs to tell us for sure." He knew white phosphorus burned upon contact with air, but not water. On skin it often kept burning until it went all the way through, or until the moisture in blood dampened it. He didn't like to think about the damage it left, if you lived through it. *How did you pack Willie Pete in a vacuum in plastic? Not from a damn Internet formula, that's for sure. And why?*

28

South Branch, Paint River, Iron County

THURSDAY, JUNE 1, 2006

Tuesday Friday looked exhausted as they got to his truck and stashed their gear in back. Service used the cell phone to call Millitor. "We're gonna start canvassing camps along the river. We'll start at F.S. 3270 and work downstream. You want to start downstream at the 3470 bridge and move up? We'll meet somewhere in the middle."

"Rolling your way," Millitor said. "Heard you had some trouble out there this morning."

"Minor fireworks," Service said. When he looked over at Friday, she was asleep. He looked at his AVL and a plat book and mapped out a rough route in his mind.

Nobody home at the first camp they went to, and no sign anyone had been there in months.

Friday blinked as he got back in the truck. "Where are we?"

"Checking camps."

She rubbed her eyes. "Okay, I'm back. You can count on me."

The fourth camp they went to was not far from the ford where he and Treebone had encountered the booby trap. A sign out front said *nordkalotten*.

"Any idea what that means?" he asked Friday.

"You're the native," she said, shaking her head.

The cabin was bit larger than normal, 1,500 square feet, he guessed. Well maintained, the wooden walkway freshly swept, windows sparkling and clean.

They went to the door and knocked. A woman eventually answered. She wore a bright blue tunic, had white hair pulled back and braided. Her skin was a strange hue of pink, almost orange, and her eyes were blue and alert. The rest of her looked ancient.

"Yes?" she greeted them, a thin smile on her face, her hands behind her.

Service held out his badge. "I'm Detective Service."

The woman squinted, said nothing.

"We're asking people on the river if they saw anything unusual around here in the days before or leading up to April 29, the trout-opener."

The woman smiled and nodded. "In the old days they burned the women."

Service glanced at Friday. "Beg your pardon, ma'am."

"You know—men always kill what they don't understand."

"Ma'am, do you live here alone?"

"I have *this*," the woman said, and suddenly Service found himself looking down the gaping barrel of a large-bore revolver.

"Ma'am, is that weapon loaded?"

"Would be no point to having it for protection if it weren't," she said.

"I'm Tuesday," Detective Friday said to the woman.

Service knew she was trying to distract the old woman, but the gun remained pointed at him, and both of the woman's hands were shaking.

"My son said to shoot first. Will it make as much noise as last time?" the woman asked Friday.

Last time? Service thought.

Tuesday said, "It will be pretty loud, but we're both wearing armored vests that will stop the bullets, so there's no point pulling the trigger."

The woman looked sadly at Friday and Service gently wrested the revolver from her. It was indeed loaded.

"Ma'am, who *are* you?" Friday asked.

"You don't understand. I saw *Stoorjunkare*," the woman said. "All in black, but I wasn't afraid. When it saw my gun, it ran away."

"Ma'am, can we come in?" Friday asked.

"I have no fear of death," the woman said. "If I let you in, can I have my gun back?"

"Is it your weapon?"

"My son's."

"Where is your son?"

"Where he always is—whoring around town."

Service's cell phone buzzed in his pocket and he stepped away from the women to answer it.

"This is Mike," Detective Millitor said. "I shoulda told youse before. As you work your way downriver, youse're gonna get to a camp with a sign that says *Nordkalotten.*"

"We're there now."

"Geez, oh boy. It means 'northern skullcap,' the way we'd say "up north," only it refers to the northern reaches of Norway, Sweden, Finland, and Russia's Kola Peninsula—which all comprise Lapland, home of the Sami people. The old woman's name is Jusakka Noli. Her name means 'goddess,' as she will no doubt let you know. She believes that her late husband rescued her from evil spirits and brought her to the U.P., but the spirits have been able to read her brain waves and track her. She thinks there are miniature 'locators' in snowflakes, which she calls white bees. She greet you at the door with a hog leg?"

"She did. Sounds like you've had a lot of contact with her."

"Not me—our deps, and it runs in streaks. If she takes her meds she seems to do okay, but she doesn't always do what the doctor wants. She looks harmless, but be damn careful. She's shot at people before, at least two. She should be in a facility, but her son can't control her. She not only carries that pistol, but she's usually got two or three knives stashed on her. Few years back she winged a trout fisherman in the leg, claimed he was a demon. She got off scot-free on that one. Sorry I didn't tell you about this before you got out there. There's a standing officer safety caution on her."

"It's okay. Is her son in Iron River?"

"He owns Sam's Organic Nursery."

"Let him know we're here and want him to speak to his mother. We need help."

"Will do. Good luck."

Service shut off the phone and turned back to the women. "Mrs. Noli," he said, and the old woman took a step backward.

"We haven't been introduced. Who told you my name?"

"It's on your camp sign."

The woman looked confused. "It is?"

"Yes," Service lied.

"I don't remember that."

"I called your son. He's on his way out here now."

"I don't want *that one's* help," she said. "My gun's enough. Can I have it back now?"

She walked over to a small table in her kitchen area, sat down in a white wooden chair, began slapping the tabletop with her hand and making a sound somewhere between a chant and yodel, mostly comprised of single syllables that sounded to Service like gibberish. "*Na-we-na-we-en-le-na-WE-na-we-EN-le-na . . .*"

Service looked over at his partner, who raised an eyebrow.

"Mrs. Noli?" he said.

The woman continued making her bizarre sound, and suddenly she seemed to levitate from the chair. Service saw a flash and instinctively threw up his arm to block, and as the woman came forward, he stopped her arm, gripped, twisted firmly against her wrist, and eased her to the floor as the big knife went skittering across the tiles.

"Jesus," Friday said.

"You need to frisk her," Service said. "That was Mike on the phone trying to warn us. He said she may carry as many as three blades in addition to the pistol."

Friday cuffed the woman and carefully frisked her, the search producing two more knives and an autoloader for the revolver.

They took the old woman into a small living room and helped her onto a chair.

"No one believes me about the *Stoorjunkare*," the old woman keened.

"Tell us," Friday said encouragingly.

"*Stoorjunkare* hide things from women," the old lady said.

"Such as?" Friday asked.

"They think I don't know, but I do. I've always known. I've watched them up there with their false idols, out there in sin, the hull buncha them."

She's totally bat-shit, Service thought. Tuesday was patient and encouraging.

"You've seen them?"

"My son is one of them."

"And you saw one today."

"By the river." The woman pointed toward the front of the camp.

Friday made eye contact with Service, who went outside and walked toward the river, looking around. Close to the water's edge he spied fresh bear tracks in some soft earth. It had taken down a bird feeder, and scattered seeds across the yard. Not unusual for hungry bears this time of year. *Most likely a young male.*

He went back inside. "Bear tracks," he said. "A bear hit your birdseed."

"Not a bear," the woman said. "*Stoorjunkare.* All animals derive from them, and they can come in any form."

"This was a bear," Service said. "Not a large one."

The woman let out a hiss and turned her head away.

Her son, Tikka Noli, arrived twenty minutes later, white as a sheet.

Service and Friday introduced themselves and explained why they had dropped by and what had happened. Noli was immediately apologetic. "She can't help herself," he said.

The man's mother stared at him, made a face, and waggled a finger. "I told them about what you and them other sinners do."

Noli said, "She's talking about the Audubon Society. There's an eagle's nest up on the hill, and we have a great observation place on my property. People come out here to take photographs and observe the nest."

"Jarvi, the sinner," the old woman said, her voice high and nearing a shriek.

"She's not rational," the son said.

Service recognized the last name and had a first name to go with it: "*Taide* Jarvi?"

The intensity of the old woman's shriek was such that even Service took a step back.

"Don't listen to her," Noli said. "She's not well."

"Then *you* explain: What about Taide Jarvi, eh?"

"What about it."

"*It?*"

"Taide Jarvi is Finnish. It means Art Lake."

"The artist colony?"

"Taide Jarvi is the name of their real estate operation. They want to purchase property down this way."

"Where the eagles live!" the old woman said with a laugh. "Where the eagles live!"

Service exchanged glances with Friday.

"Mr. Noli, I think we need to step outside and talk."

"I haven't done nothing wrong," he said.

"I haven't accused you of anything." Service pointed at the door.

"What is all this nonsense?" Service asked when they were outside.

"She doesn't want me to sell the land. She wants me to give it in her name to the Iron County Wildlands Conservancy, but it's my land too, and I've got a right to make a profit from it."

Service knew immediately that the business between the old woman and the son was off his playing field. "Tell me about Taide Jarvi."

"It's a nonprofit company. All of its land becomes part of Art Lake, which means no future development. It's the same thing my mother wants, only they'll pay us."

"Have you sold the land to them?" Service asked.

"We're still negotiating, and I don't think they're too happy."

"Who exactly are you in negotiations with?"

"A woman named Chelios."

"Out of Chicago?"

"Milwaukee."

Back inside, they found Tuesday Friday and the woman talking calmly and sharing bread and jelly. "Wild U.P. cranberry," Friday said, her mouth full. "Puts the jellies up herself. Her name, Jusakka, means goddess-warrior. Isn't that interesting, Grady?"

The old woman suddenly scrambled to the sink, tore open the cabinet beneath, turned abruptly, and slid a green object across the floor like a curling stone toward her son. The object skidded to a stop and Service looked at it. "That yours, Mr. Noli?"

"I got no idea what you're talking about," the man said, barely squeezing out the words.

Grady Service went to a closet, found a wire clothes hanger, and began to straighten it. When he had a long wire he held the tip close to the green package.

Noli sighed. "Don't break it!"

"Read him his rights," Service said to Friday.

He had no idea how any of this connected, but sensed strongly that it did—somehow. *Frodo the Finn claims he had no contact with Art Lake, but gets his house courtesy of Taide Jarvi. Frodo has some explaining to do.*

"Why the pyrotechnics?" Service asked Noli as they walked him out to the truck in cuffs.

"I want my lawyer."

"I hope he's a good one."

"The best there is," Noli said.

"Let me guess: Sandy Tavolacci?"

"You know Sandy?"

Tavolacci had built a practice defending the biggest scumbags in the U.P. Service intertwined his fingers. "We're like *that*, Sandy and me."

29

South Branch, Paint River, Iron County

THURSDAY, JUNE 1, 2006

Service and Friday lodged Tikka Noli at the Iron County Jail in Crystal Falls, but Noli refused to answer questions until his lawyer joined him. After lodging the prisoner, Service dropped Friday at her motel to get a bath and sleep and headed back to the woods above the Noli camp. *Taide Jarvi is Art Lake, which allegedly is trying to buy Noli's property—for Audubon access to an eagle's nest? I don't think so!* He laughed out loud.

It was dark when he moved onto the sloping hill where he and Friday had encountered the Willie Pete devices and the deer with burning hooves. The state police bomb squad and DNR Fire Response Team had cleared the area. There was no doubt in his mind that the incendiary devices had been a kind of barrier, but the purpose was impossible to determine without further investigation.

He reached the point where they had fled, hunkered down, and lit a cigarette. He could smell the remains of the small fire in the woods. He cupped his cigarette in his hand.

Service walked slowly southward, along the gently sloping ridge to where it intersected a higher ridge, and as he began to climb higher he heard an eagle's shrill shriek to his east, the animal obviously not appreciating his presence. All raptors tended to make a fuss when people got too close to their nests, or they just flapped away to wait until the coast was clear again.

The four-wheeler he'd heard had come from the southeast, though he saw no discernible trail in the darkness. That was the thing with ATVs and snowmobiles and dirt bikes: They were easy to follow—if you could catch their track. *Tomorrow morning,* he told himself. *First light.* He paused at the edge of a drop-off. His night vision might be superior to others, but it seemed more attuned to living things than inanimate objects. He cleared a space next to a downed tree, took off his pack, and sat down to wait for morning. He surrendered his senses to his ears, but there was nothing human out there.

Nighthawks made their burring sounds, diving for mosquito meals over the river south of him. Coyotes picked up his scent downwind and let loose a cacophony that ended as abruptly as it began. At the end of the log a raccoon appeared, stood on its hind legs, and sniffed at him with consternation.

Eventually he shut out the night and slipped under a veneer of sleep, a thin layer that he could will away instantly. He momentarily thought about his granddaughter but pushed the thought away. Philosophical dreaming had no role on the job or in the woods.

Art Lake, Chicago, National Guard, spring guns, Elmwood, Taide Jarvi, Tikka Noli, Frodo the Finn, gold dust, a wolf tree—so fucking many details and events and factoids, he could hardly maintain a meaningful or complete list, much less organize the whole damn thing so that he could sort it out. He had dealt with eco-terrorists before, and understood that unrestrained ideals could lead to bad decisions. But his intuition told him violence was for only the most extreme activists—the fringe. And at the same time he knew from experience that old-fashioned, unchecked greed drove most of the natural resource crimes he dealt with. Was all of this a matter of ideals gone amok, or was it simple greed? Or was "all this" many things being wrongly lumped together because of serendipitous timing?

A cardinal's song jarred him at first light and he rubbed his eyes, lit a cigarette, and wished he had coffee.

With morning light spreading steadily across the landscape, he found the four-wheeler track, which he followed to a ledge. Judging by the beaten-down grass, he guessed this had been a parking spot. It took several minutes to see that four feet below the rim there was dark dust all over some white rocks.

Easing his way down to the quartz outcrop, he knelt beside it. The white stone ledge was nearly six feet long, close to three feet high, and extended slightly from the hill like a platform. Lots of dirt spackling the crystals. *Don't just look,* he commanded himself. *See.*

Two cigarettes later he knew he needn't bother pinpointing the location of Tikka Noli's eagle's nest. This had nothing to do with birds.

30

Fence River Road, Iron County

FRIDAY, JUNE 2, 2006

He considered a nap, shower, and fresh clothes, but nixed it all; his mind roiled with too many questions. He called Simon and asked him to meet him on the Fence River Road northeast of Crystal Falls.

They pulled their trucks up, one facing north, the other facing south, and put down their electric windows. "You hear?" he asked del Olmo.

"I talked to Elza. *Willie-fucking-Pete?*" He shook his head in disbelief.

"I can't figure out if it was aimed at us or we just stumbled into it."

"Professional situational awareness," del Olmo said.

"You guys use Willie Pete in the Gulf War?" Service asked. Del Olmo had served with the marines in Desert Storm, during the reign of George the First.

"All the time. I *hate* that shit."

"It was ubiquitous in Vietnam, in mortar shells, arty, grenades, rockets, everywhere. What form did you guys use?"

"Infantry, man—M15 grenades, now obsolete," said del Olmo. "Eggshell-thin and serrated so they'd come apart, spread the shit. Cup and a half of pure white phosphorus, twenty-meter kill zone, with some fragments reaching beyond."

"Any way to extract the phosphorus?"

"Why?"

"I'm thinking out loud here. Manufacturers load grenades. What goes in must come out."

"Manufacturers, sure, but grunts? I don't *think* so. Only a psycho would screw with that stuff," said del Olmo.

"Point conceded . . . but what would it take?"

"In addition to severe psychosis and a lot of know-how? Nerves of steel, steady hands, some specialized equipment, chemical knowledge, a room with no air—hell, I *don't know.*"

"How about M16 rounds? If you wanted to play a joke, how difficult would it be to switch the gunpowder for sugar, or some other substance?" asked Service.

"Possible and not really dangerous, but what would be the point? The whole idea of a joke is max effect for minimal effort, right?"

"How about a whole case of ammo?"

Simon del Olmo laughed out loud. "Are you shitting me? Eight hundred and forty rounds? How the hell would you get ahold of that much, even in a free-fire zone?"

"For argument's sake, this is just a theoretical."

"Could be done, but real labor-intensive, and what do you do with all the powder after you make the switch?"

"Average marine could do it?"

"Semper fi—the average marine is better than the top army pud. Does all of this have a point?"

"Maybe. If you and I had a grenade, could we do it?"

"Not me, no way. Like I said, you need to keep air off it."

"But manufacturers do it."

"They get paid, have tools, equipment, special buildings, all that good stuff. I had a gunny tell me once about World War Two. The Krauts had arty shells with Willie Pete. Air bursts. This white snow would start falling and the grunts would start running like hell to get out from under the shit."

Service said, "The stuff we hit was in soft plastic, about the size of biscuits. Punch a hole, air gets in, it ignites. They were sealed to keep air out."

"Good thing for the sealer. Maybe they were made underwater, but then I don't know how you get the water out without leaving some air. All this is over my head technically. Just be glad you guys didn't step on one," said del Olmo.

"We found only one intact. I sent a Troop to the lab in Marquette with it." Service then related the story of the deer with flaming feet.

"Elza told me. That was some weird shit. Somebody is out there with a major fucking personal malfunction. I wish I could be more help."

"I'm thinking all this stuff is like fishing. Right bait, right time, right presentation, right place. You just gotta keep casting, one throw at a time, until we hook up. And I think we got lucky earlier today."

"Lucky how?" del Olmo asked. "Is that like a metaphor or an analogy?"

"Ask Elza—she's smarter than both of us."

Del Olmo laughed. "Got that right. Semper fi, *jeffe*."

"You ever encounter a guy named Tikka Noli?"

"My God, did you run into his whack-job mother?"

"Gun and all. We found what looks to be Willie Pete packages at their place on the river."

"No shit," del Olmo said.

"Noli or his mother active in environmental groups?"

Simon del Olmo laughed. "This is Iron County, not Marquette or Houghton.

Dots-dots-dots, caught in his mind like a tightly closed loop, *moving like atoms. I can see the orbits, but not the particles, and absolutely not how they are connected, if at all. Keep casting,* Service told himself.

He found Friday in the office, her eyes sunken with a vacant stare. "Mike gave me a lift," she said.

"You need sleep."

"I need a lot of things. You don't?"

"Less than most."

"Discouraging words on several levels."

Tired but still playful. He liked that. "That steel wire company you talked to?"

"Peachtree Enterprises, out of Milwaukee; they make that special model. I've also got a call in to Department of Corrections Purchasing in Lansing to get their take on the vendor. Meanwhile, I'm talking back and forth with a Milwaukee cop, who let me know that Peachtree has reported thefts. He's sending me the written complaints and police reports. Soon as I get the paperwork I'll call Peachtree, tell them I know about their problem and I'm working a capital case; if they don't want to cough up customer lists, we'll bring a warrant."

He had no idea she'd thought it through so well. *She thinks in logical plans, not tasks, Service thought. She has the natural instincts, and she's going to be a helluva detective. Can't say the same about myself. Pay attention, ya mutt. You can learn from her.*

She added. "That's the plan—if I don't get hauled out for overnight campouts or keep reducing the deer population. My vehicle won't be done until next week." She added, "We're making progress."

"That's what the Russians told their doggie astronauts."

"Seriously, there's progress."

"Such as?"

"I don't have a lot of specifics, but my intuition's strong. That package in Noli's kitchen is the same thing we ran into in the woods," she said. "I know it."

"We don't know that until forensics tells us so. It's hard to write intuition into a report." But he was glad they were on the same beam.

"For the record, that porcupine liver was actually tasty."

"With more time, the woods would give us a seven-course-meal."

"I'll dream of that day," she said, turning back to her computer.

He turned to his, but couldn't deal with it. He picked up his cell phone, walked out to the parking lot, and watched the traffic going up the hill on US 2 out of town, right by a fieldstone Seventh-day Adventist church facing a McDonald's—an odd, yet somehow normal Yooper cultural juxtaposition. It made him laugh as he lit a cigarette and called the Michigan State Police forensics lab in Marquette and asked for the lead bomb squad technician, a man named Pirdue.

"You again," the man greeted him. "We've got bomb squad guys who don't see in five years the shit you've seen in a month."

"Wire and fishing hooks aren't bombs."

"Iceberg, Goldberg," the man said. "You hear the latest rumor?"

"I doubt I've heard the old ones."

"If the governor can't bring in the state budget, we may get shut down."

"Not for long," Service said. "We've been through this before. The state announces layoffs and shutdowns, the people get pissed, the legislature finds Jesus, and life goes on."

"I mean they may shut down the Marquette lab. If so, that will mean no forensics support for *any* law enforcement agency in the U.P. The closest lab will be in Grayling."

He had *not* heard this, and it sounded ludicrous enough to be true.

"Lori's got a real mess to deal with," Pirdue said. "All agencies are gonna get hit hard even if the budget comes through."

Governor Lorelei Timms had morphed into Lori for a large number of Michiganders, who liked and respected her, and sympathized with the fiscal crisis she had inherited with little role in its making. Timms, through some odd circumstances, had been close to Nantz, and was also his friend. He rarely called her.

"If we shut down and the systems we support get adjusted to it, we may never see light again," Pirdue said.

The man had a point. "It's only summer," Service said. "She's got until October."

"For this year, but I'm hearing the real budget nut-cutter is coming in '07."

He needed to get the man on track. "You get the sample I sent over?"

Pirdue laughed. "The Troop who brought it looked like he was ready to piss his pants."

"I saw that stuff ignite," Service said. "Don't blame your guy."

"Someone said something about a deer with fire shooting out its ass."

"Hooves," Service said. "I saw that too."

"Okay, this is a prelim, but whoever designed this device is damn clever. I'm thinking the perp built them in water and found a way to remove the air to leave dry crystals inside."

"Hard to do this?"

"Damn hard, unless you've got big balls, chemical training, and some high-tech support."

"If I wanted to get my hands on white phosphorus, could I do it?"

"Hell, with enough cash, you can buy a fresh kidney on the black market."

"Seriously."

"White phosphorus isn't a natural substance. It's made from apatite, a form of phosphate rock. China and Russia mine the shit out of phosphates."

"Mined here?"

"Michigan? No way. The geology's all wrong. Florida, Texas, Tennessee, Idaho, Montana—those are our big producers."

Idaho and Montana. Proximity to Colorado. He made a mental note. "Mined for what?"

"You name it: rat poison, munitions, fireworks, toothpaste, fertilizer, food additives, pharmaceuticals—it's used in all sorts of stuff. Even coating for steel wire, and I think the steel industry also uses it as a deoxidizing agent."

Toothpaste? He was glad he had false choppers. *Coating steel wire? Another hit—another dot?* "The mines extract the phosphate rock and sell it to chemical manufacturers, who then make white phosphorus that they sell to companies who use it to make different products."

"You listen pretty good, Detective. I wish other clients did."

"Is the stuff hard to steal?"

"Like I said, kidneys, but you don't have to steal it, see. If you know what you're doing, you can make it yourself."

"How?"

"You take red phosphorus—which is more stable, easier to get, and less volatile—and you use heat to turn it into the white stuff. Red's a little safer, but the gases from it will take you into DNM."

DNM—Dirt Nap Mode, techies' idea of cool talk. "Conversion's easy?"

"Meth cooks do it sometimes. They call the red stuff Red P. I'm not talking about your run-of-the-mill scuzzbagger, using the Nazi recipe, but the talented ones—who could probably make a decent living in the legit chemical industry if only their heads weren't all fucked up and stuck up their butts."

"Meth labs?"

"I expect you've seen a few of those?"

He had, and they scared hell out of him. "Thanks."

"I'll have more on device design early next week. Do me a favor: You see another deer with its ass on fire, take a photograph, or better yet, a video, and we'll both get rich."

"Hooves," Service said.

"Whatever. But fire shooting out its ass would be worth more."

"I'll keep that in mind."

He went back inside and waited until Friday got off her phone. "Can you call that wire outfit in Wisconsin and ask them if they use white phosphorus to coat their wires, or if they know any company that does?"

"Are you serious?"

"I just talked to the bomb squad in Marquette."

"I'll get right on it," she said. "A lot of the cop shops I'm talking to want written requests for police reports, and they charge a fee."

"Cheesehead frugality," he said.

She lowered her eyes. "Really?"

He went outside and found Millitor. "You get a lot of meth in this county?"

"More over in Dickinson."

"Know any cooks?"

The Iron County detective pointed at McDonald's and chuckled. "They do."

"Meth."

"Yeah, there's a pretty good one in the county lockup in Crystal right now, waiting for a transport downstate."

"Your bust?"

"No. He rolled on his distributors for a reduction in time."

"Still talkative?"

"Depends if there's a deal involved, and if his attorney approves."

"Let me guess: Sandy Tavolacci."

"Yep—the Mouthpiece for Morons."

Service had dealt with Tavolacci before. Meth dealers, Tikka Noli; Sandy's record was at least consistent. "Pro bono, I bet."

"Sandy?" Millitor laughed so hard he went into a coughing spasm.

"Tell Friday I'll call her later."

"You heading to Crystal?"

"This cook have a name?"

Millitor said deadpan, "Kareem Abdul-Jabbar."

"Black?"

"Blond hair, blue eyes. Was in school up to the community college in Ironwood and cooking meth for ski money and pussy. His old man's a big shot at Toyota in Detroit. The first time I interviewed the kid, I said, 'Good morning, Mr. Lew Alcindor,' and the kid stared at me and said, 'Who that, motherfucker?' "

Millitor laughed at his own story, adding, "Make sure you call Sandy, or that little shit will go ballistic and complain to every judge and magistrate in the county."

31

Crystal Falls, Iron County

FRIDAY, JUNE 2, 2006

"Tavolacci Law Offices," the lawyer said, answering his own telephone. Sandy Tavolacci had for years been the defense attorney of choice for the U.P.'s most notorious criminals. He was a small man by all measures except ambition, and told people he answered his own phone as a symbol of frugality; the truth was, nobody could work for him for more than a week.

"Sandy, Grady Service."

"Long time, no see. Heard you been hanging around town."

"From Tikka Noli."

"Be unethical to reveal my sources," Tavolacci said.

Service stifled a derisive laugh. "You've got two clients—Kareem Abdul-Jabbar and Noli."

"What about them?"

"We'll get to Noli in good time, but I want to have a little chitchat with Abdul-Jabbar."

"Aboot what?"

"Nothing personal. I've got another case and I'm interested in talking about meth cooking—the process, not his personal transgressions."

"*Alleged* transgressions. What's in this for my guy?"

"He's been found guilty, and there's nothing unless he's also poached a deer."

"Not sayin' he did, not sayin he didn't," Tavolacci said. "I'd have to confer with my client."

What a pompous idiot! Service couldn't help laughing this time. "No deal, Sandy. I just want to talk to the kid. You want to be there, fine by me."

Silence. "When?"

"Tomorrow morning."

Another silence. "What the hey, I'm tapped out on billables with the kid's old man and the guy's like a total prick. You want to talk to his asshole kid, no sweat off my balls, but I want some respect when we get to Tikka Noli."

"Thanks counselor." Sandy's young client had morphed almost instantaneously into "the asshole kid." For Tavolacci, billable hours trumped all.

Service was sitting in the parking lot of the Crystal Falls County Courthouse and jail when he made the call. Tavolacci would stew on the meeting all day and probably show up tomorrow looking for an angle to help his client, which he could then sell to the kid's father in order to bill more hours. He'd be out of luck.

Service picked up a folder with information on the kid, including a photo, and went to an interview room to wait. Yellow walls, freshly painted, no marks, no chips. The landmark courthouse had been beautifully refurbished.

A uniformed jailer brought the prisoner in an orange jumpsuit and flip-flops. The kid had gotten a haircut since his booking photo had been taken. He was tall, the haircut conservative, the effect that of a nerdy-looking kid. "Kareem?" he greeted the prisoner.

The boy poured himself into a chair. "Man, my name is Alan Hudson."

"That's not the name in your jacket," Service said, tapping the folder. "Kareem Abdul-Jabbar."

"Like, my lawyer is working to change it back, sir."

"I'm Detective Service, DNR. Tavolacci told me your old man has cut off his hours." *Unethical to tell him this? Who gives a shit.*

The boy suddenly shifted from lethargic to agitated, holding one hand flat and chopping at it with the other, like a hatchet splitting his words for dramatic effect. "I *need that name changed, man*!"

"Why's it so important to you?"

"I keep hearing how white guys with black names get turned into gray-bar bitches."

The convicts in each prison had their own cultures, and there was a lot of rumor and misinformation about inmates and how they lived. "I can understand your concern," Service said. "I asked your lawyer about your DNR violations."

The kid's head bobbed. "*What* DNR violations?"

"Tavolacci wouldn't confirm anything you did, or didn't do."

"This is, like, *totally* bogus, dude! Ax that motherfucker lawyer."

"You can talk to me."

"Man, I ain't done nuffin' wrong. I don't fish, I don't hunt, I don't even look at the fuckin' birds in my neighbor's feeder."

"I thought maybe you went Crankenstein out in the woods, got out your rifle, tweaked, and shot something."

"Man, I just cook shit. I don't use."

"That's hard to believe."

"You can't ride the white pony and make it too. The shit is, like, totally moody."

"I'll take your word for it. Where are they sending you?"

"Ain't it in the jacket? Bellamy Creek, Ionia County."

"Could be worse," Service said

"Niggers all over the system," the prisoner lamented.

"I were you, I'd worry about your white brothers looking for payback on a cook who dimed his customers."

"I didn't dime nobody, *man.* Cops come through my door like God-fucking-zilla."

"How many dealers you trade?"

"I don't remember."

"Ten, I heard. That's a heap of pissed-off, Kareem."

"I told you, my name is Alan Hudson."

"Sorry, Al."

"*Al-an, not Al,*" the prisoner said.

"You really didn't use?"

"Man, I'm not stupid. That stuff makes spaghetti in your head. I just make the shit, ya know?"

"Word is that you're not just a cook, you're a veritable chef who makes primo shit."

Ego fed, Hudson-Jabbar bobbed his head. "How it is, dude."

"Nazi?"

"Man, I ain't white trash. Nazi's for amateurs. I run strictly Red P."

"Really?"

The kid nodded. "Real talk."

"You ever cook red down to white?"

"Dude, white shit is, like, totally crunk."

"You know anybody who does this?"

"Cooks ain't got like a crank union, man. There ain't no annual conventions."

"What about Detroit?"

"What about it? Nobody wants to make red to white, man. Even splibs too smart for that."

"You did all your cooking in Iron County?"

"Yeah—more space, fewer people."

"Home base or a rolling lab?"

"Neither, man."

"Got to be one or the other."

"See, you people don't think creative. I do sequential fixed base. I just moved from one cabin to the next."

"Friends' places?"

"Cook can't have friends, dude; gotta do this thang alone. Why I'm talking to you—what you gonna do for me with Bellamy, sayin'?"

"If not your friends' cabins, you were using cabins that didn't belong to you?"

"Talk to my lawyer, man. What about B.C.?"

"You're on your own there, Kareem."

"Man, you, like, *promised* to help me."

"I lied. Bitch to Tavolacci."

"My old man won't pay."

"You've got a problem, chief."

"You *played* me, man."

"Yeah, I did. You didn't give me shit. Here's some advice: Don't do drugs, Kareem. Good luck inside."

Service stepped to the door and made a dramatic turn. "Nobody ever came to you to buy white?"

The kid made an X with his arms. "Cross my heart, dude."

"If I step out the door, I'm done with this. You're certain?"

"Wait, man . . . I knew this toolbox down Fuck Creek tole me one time she knew a guy made white from red and liked to blow shit up."

Familiar words. Like many young people, this one used a vocabulary that eluded Service. "Toolbox at Fuck Creek?"

"Watersmeet, Duck Creek Bar. Wins-day night, it be like all-wall-pussy-night—toolbox time, ya know?"

"A meat factory."

"What I just said, dude."

"This particular toolbox have a name?"

"Annie Bonner . . . Anyboner—ev'body *know* Anyboner. Now what you do for me about B.C.?"

"Nothing."

"You lied to me *again,* man?"

"Which, oddly enough, isn't against the law. But selling drugs *is,* asshole. And by the way, don't let people box you in, or you'll get the Four Corners."

"Say what, dude?"

"A black dick in each hand, one up your ass, and one in your mouth. Have a nice life, *dude.*"

• • •

Service called Millitor from the parking lot behind the jail. "Mike, are you familiar with a joint near Watersmeet called Duck Creek Bar?"

Millitor laughed. "Wednesday night is ladies' night, and they call it Fuck Creek with the Gogebic County trifecta: sex, drugs, and rock and roll. The Go-Deps are *always* there. You talk to Kareem?"

Go-Deps—Gogebic County deputy sheriffs. "It's Alan Hudson now."

"I bet," Millitor said with a laugh. "The jailers have been feeding him a rash of shit about what black guys do to white guys using black names."

"He told me about a woman called Annie Bonner, aka Anyboner. I'd like to talk to her."

"I'll call up there, see if we can get an ID on her. I'll be back at you."

"Thanks, Mike. Friday call it a day?"

"Nope. She's still there, working the phones and computer. Said she'll walk to the motel when she's done. She's a workhorse, that one."

He called Tuesday Friday but got her voice mail, and left a message. "It's Grady; I'm knocking off. You should too."

32

Kenton, Houghton County

FRIDAY, JUNE 2, 2006

The plan for the night was simple: talk to Karylanne and the baby, call Kira Lehto and check on his animals, sleep. Grinda and del Olmo were still on duty in the woods, and he was trying to decide on food when his cell phone sang to him.

"Grady Service, Hike Funke."

"Hike?"

"I played some head-buttin' ball at the Point, center. Leukonovich said she talked to you. You hit the mess hall yet?"

"Just starting to think about it."

"I'm headed to Kenton, Hoppy's Bar—you know it?"

"No."

"Can't miss it, right on M-28. You're about an hour away. Meet me and we'll let our beloved Uncle Sam pick up the tab."

They arranged to meet in an hour or so, give or take. Service took a quick shower, changed clothes, and headed west. Halfway to Iron River he called Friday's cell phone.

"*What?*" she answered.

"You had dinner yet?"

"Your call got me out of the shower!"

"Get dressed, there in fifteen minutes. We'll get food."

"More of Mother Nature's natural fare?"

"Bar food."

"Works for me. Is this place dressy?"

"Is *anywhere* up here?" *Did she think this was a date?*

She was in the lobby when he pulled up. Shorts and sandals, a tank top, and a sweater wrapped around her waist. Fragrant perfume and soap fumes filled the truck as she pulled down the sun visor and began fiddling with her makeup.

Hoppy's Bar didn't look like much from the outside, and there were only a few cars around the building, but it was still early, and most fishermen would be on the streams until dark or later. Every Yooper bar had some sort of angle: This one's was a ceiling plastered with old hunting camp signs. Two old-timers were at the bar right inside the door drinking draft beer, and there was one man at a table to the left. He was built like a fireplug and reading something. Even from across the room Service could see the man's face was disfigured and covered with waves of shiny scar tissue.

"Hike Funke?" Service asked.

The man snapped his book shut and looked up. His hard brown eyes were nearly closed by massive scars.

"This is my partner, Detective Friday; I'm Service."

No hand offered. "Park your butts," the man said. "I ordered jalapeno poppers. You want booze, feel free. I never acquired the taste. Wouldn't want to ruin my perfect complexion."

Comedian, Service thought.

They sat down, ordered Old Milwaukees and burgers when the waitperson (it said so on her nametag) brought the poppers. Funke slathered hot sauce on one and shoved it all in his mouth. "Z says you're the real deal, and if she says it, I buy it."

"You work with her?"

"Collaborate; we trade back and forth. She tells me you're interested in the Van Dalen Foundation."

"You're not IRS?" Service asked.

"Nope. What about you and Van Dalen?"

"It's a long story."

"One of my strong points is listening to long stories. Wind 'er up and let 'er roll."

Service talked the man through everything: the skulls, booby traps, Peachtree Enterprises, the dead man, Box, Provo, Elmwood in the twenties, Helmi Koski and Rillamae Thigpen, the Willie Pete, Art Lake, Denninger and the wolf tree. *Slight eye flutter, only at the mention of Art Lake. Otherwise, passive—career flatliner.* When he saw the reaction to Art Lake he withheld information about Tikka Noli, the suspected device in his camp, and his connection to Taide Jarvi. Even though Zhenya had sent this guy, something about him didn't smell quite right.

Funke said, "Okay, my turn. Parts of the Van Dalen Foundation do a lot of very good stuff: education, health care, all positive, all socially important. Because of their size, they wield a shitload of clout. They're also the most complex outfit the IRS has ever looked at. They've got more not-for-profit offshoots than Carter's got little pills—I mean, out the wazoo—most of them legit with alleged well-intentioned social purposes."

"Most?"

"You ever see a scan of a human brain after strokes?"

"No."

"Little black spots all over the place. Docs aren't sure what causes them. Ostensibly, the black spots are dead tissue, but in some instances, with certain treatments, and sometimes spontaneously, they regenerate. Van Dalen Foundation is like that brain: The little black spots are various boxes on a big ole org chart, and like that brain, some are defunct and no longer working, but others go dormant and later quietly reconstitute, all done legally, all done too fast for the government to keep up with the big picture in any real-time way. Warrants would help us open up their guts, but the IRS can't make a good-enough case to create the magnitude we'd need to get Justice off the starting line. Van Dalen pioneered the use of social-issue political action committees, and their people are the best around at picking winners. There's nothing illegal in this."

"You're Justice?"

"No."

"What's your interest?"

"Some aspects of their environmental dealings and interests."

"You're EPA?"

"No. You said you read Van Dalen's obituary."

"We both did," Service said.

Funke said, "Made his dough in real estate, but where his first big nut came from is unknown. You can't make a fortune without some sort of a financial nut to launch your ass."

"Were you aware of his deal in Iron County?"

"Broad strokes only. You've added some new details. Iron County wasn't his only ride down that road. Montana, Idaho—he tried a lot of wacky schemes that never panned out before he settled down to build his wad in Chicago."

"Did he masquerade as a priest elsewhere?"

"Not that I know of, but Van Dalen was the original micromanager, a hands-on guy with every project he ever got into. That Willie Pete deal you had, I can identify with that shit. Desert Storm, Medina Ridge—we had the Republican Guard hauling ass for the safety of Saddam's skirt. Second Brigade, First A.D. We found the rags with their tanks dug in. We stuck our noses into them and started whacking them at close range. A round hit my tank in the ass, lit us up inside, killed my driver, and made me the marshmallow man. Mind you, not the enemy—it was friendly fire! Medics hauled my ass out, and I ordered my boys to keep rolling and killing. A year later I'm at Walter Reed for more surgery and one of my tank commanders stops to see me to apologize. He's the one who lit me up. I told him he was a total fuckup, that I trained all my boys to kill what they shoot at, and there I was in Crispy Critter Land, still alive!" Funke said, laughing. "Poor bastard. You don't really understand Willie Pete until you've got it melting off your nuts in the desert."

"So, you're . . . *military*?"

"Retired early on a medical. Nobody wants to ride in a tank with a freak."

Who is this weirdo? Service wondered as the waitress brought the burgers.

"You ever heard the term 'hard green'?" Funke asked.

Service shook his head. "Money?"

"Maybe in Fairyland long ago; now it refers to environmental activists who aren't interested in fucking around with publicity and winning public sympathy. The motto of my outfit was 'Strike hard,' and that's also what these assholes believe. They don't believe in change from within. They want to blow the whole system to fucking kingdom come and invent and run the new kingdom themselves."

"You know who these people are?"

"Some of them. Very few. What Leukonovich is looking for is their funding sources so we can choke the cocksuckers."

He's some flavor of national security, but which agency? ATF, Homeland Security, FBI, NSA? The federal government's security system rivals the organization Funke attributes to Van Dalen Foundation.

"You think we're dealing with some kind of hard green outfit here?"

"Not an outfit. Think al-Qaeda and the Animal Liberation Front. No dues, no oaths, no secret handshakes. You just go out and stir the shit, help foster chaos with body count, and you're a member. Nobody gives you orders or directions. We call this style of organization 'terrentrepreneurial.' "

"Chaos?"

"The perfect habitat for terrorists."

Something he's not telling us, Service thought. *Maybe a lot he's not telling.*

Funke said with a growl, "Don't bother wasting your time trying to figure out what outfit I'm with. You've never heard of it and you never will, unless we fuck up, and we don't plan on that happening."

"Art Lake?"

"Tonight's the first I've heard that term."

"Part of Van Dalen?

"Leukonovich has a scent. When she gets a good trail, I expect she'll be in touch."

Funke ignored my first question. "The name Gorsline ring a bell?" Service asked.

"Ring one for you?"

"I think I understand what Zhenya is doing. What about you?"

"I never know what Z is up to, and I'm just passing through. I wanted to meet the man Z talks so much about. She says you're like an alpha wolf tracking his last meal."

"I'm not sure that's a compliment."

"Fuck compliments—it says what it says. That's enough for our kind!"

Our kind? Service wasn't sure he liked the term or its vague emphasis.

• • •

Friday was quiet in the truck afterwards. Twenty miles south she said, "Leukonovich?"

"An IRS agent I once worked with."

"According to Funke, whom I would note is one particularly creepy individual, it sounds like Leukonovich has a pretty keen interest in you—for someone she just worked with *once.*"

"She's different," he said.

"As in good different, or not-so-good different?"

He looked over at her. "Interesting different, scary different."

"Did you sleep with her?" She held up her hands, "Sorry, sorry, that's none of my business."

Five miles later she looked at him. "Have you heard the rumors about me?"

"There are always rumors and gossip about female officers newly transferred or promoted."

"Knowing that doesn't make it less unsettling. The word on you is that you're a player and a shit-disturber, but what I see is a man who works well with women and treats them as equals. It's not always that way in the Troops."

"There aren't that many COs, and we all do the same job and share the same risks. The challenges on the Indiana or Ohio border are qualitatively the same as they are here. We judge by performance first, personality and cooperation second. Plumbing isn't relevant."

"Now Funke," she said in an abrupt change of subject and direction. "He really gives me the willies."

"Leukonovich vouches for him, and no, I haven't slept with her."

"I said it was none of my business."

"But you still wanted to know. Now you do."

"Now I do, but my uneasiness about Funke persists."

Unknown branch of government, overly breezy style, a sense he knows more than he cares to share, asked no penetrating questions, no follow-up on anything he'd been told. "I have reservations, too," he admitted.

33

Ironwood, Gogebic County

SATURDAY, JUNE 3, 2006

Friday called Service on his cell phone as he drove west from Crystal Falls. "Peachtree Enterprises has filed theft complaints on two occasions," she said. "Several hundred pounds of wire were stolen from their plant in the first instance, and just under a ton from a delivery truck a year ago March. That truck came to the Baraga Maxie Unit. The Wisconsin State Patrol handled both investigations. The first one they got an employee for. The second remains unsolved; the driver of the truck was a long-term employee of a contract transportation company Peachtree had used for years."

She added, "The driver made a delivery to a max-control facility in Wabash, Indiana, crossed the Mackinac Bridge, overnighted in Manistique, and got to the prison the next morning. The goods were gone when he got there."

"Sleeper truck?"

"Motel. Everything checked out, and the Manistique city cops and Troops there helped the Wispies by canvassing the area. Nobody saw anything."

Wispies—Wisconsin State Patrol members. "How bulky is a ton of wire?"

"Requires a fifteen-foot bed or box. I checked the databases and called Negaunee on the off chance they had a report of a stolen or abandoned truck that would fill the bill. No hits yet."

Service thought for a minute. "Probably happened in Indiana, not Manistique."

"Really?"

"Goods were unloaded in Indiana. The truck was open and vulnerable there."

"Theoretically it could be either," she said.

"Yeah, but the thing about stolen goods is that the further you move them, the greater your exposure. It's also possible this hasn't got a damn thing to do with our case."

"I had the lab send a wire sample to Peachtree to verify the lot. We'll find out if there's a match."

"Have you talked to the manufacturer yet?"

"As soon as we're done. I'll let them know to expect the sample and ask them about white phosphorus."

She didn't forget. I did. "Mike there yet?"

"Should be by the time you get here. Sorry about last night. Your personal life is none of my business. I still don't like Funke."

"There in ten," he said, terminating the call.

• • •

Millitor looked exhausted. He drank an entire cup of coffee in one pull and immediately refilled the cup. "I spent last night at the Duck Creek Bar. Annie Bonner was a no-show, but the Go-Deps all seem to know her. She's nineteen and already has a pretty nasty-looking sheet: possession of dope, misdemeanor larceny by conversion, two Minor In Posessions, and a DWI. The court suspended her license and sentenced her to traffic school and five days' public service. The Go-Deps think she hooks part-time, which they think is ironic because she's pretty much available free of charge most of the time."

"She complete traffic school?"

"Scheduled for today and tomorrow in Ironwood, eight to five. She has to get her license back before she can do her public service component. The county won't pay for her gas."

"Want to take a run up that way, see if we can catch her at lunch?"

Friday said, "I'll be talking to Peachtree and D.O.C. Purchasing. I still want to know if Alger or Baraga has had any wire pilferage."

Another angle that had slipped his mind.

"We'll be back this afternoon," he told her. Ironwood was about ninety miles west of Iron River, pretty much a straight shot on a good two-lane highway with wide shoulders, which helped you see deer, bear, moose, wolves, and other sundry critters crossing at night.

Service checked his AVL to see if Three One Eighteen was active, but his marker didn't show. He called him on the cell. Three One Eighteen was Loren Barr, two years out of the Academy; he'd been a Chippewa County road dep before catching on with the DNR.

"Loren, Grady Service. You in service yet?"

"Yeah."

You know Annie Bonner?"

"You mean Anyboner? Every cop over here knows her—no doubt some of them biblically."

"Out of control?"

"Trending."

"You ever bust her?"

"Not yet."

"Where's traffic school over there?"

"Gogebic Community College. They've even got a driving course in Parking Lot D, and a classroom in the Lindquist Center. You need backup?"

"No thanks."

"You haven't met Anyboner yet."

"Thanks for telling me."

"Not a problem."

Sandy Tavolacci called while they were en route to Ironwood and was not a happy man. "Where the hell do you get off harassing my client?" the lawyer demanded.

"Which one?" Service answered. "The paying one or the nonpaying one?"

"You think this is a joke?"

"What the hell do you want, Sandy? I'm busy."

"I want to meet with you about Tikka Noli."

"When I'm ready."

"We're ready now."

"That's what Custer said, and look how wrong he was."

Tavolacci hung up.

There were nine students in Parking Lot D, either young or elderly, the two ages when driving skills seemed to cause the most problems. Service spotted an attractive young woman in Lycra shorts, more body doodads and things stuck in her face than he could count, and a long-sleeved sweatshirt, stenciled in red with an arrow pointing down: meet my samson. She leaned against a light pole while the instructor negotiated the course with an elderly student who took out every orange pylon she was supposed to avoid.

The young woman paid no attention as Service and Millitor approached her, but said, "S'up, fuzzy-wuzzies? I'm here eating my shit. You see that old bitch? She drives like a total fucking glooey, man."

"Annie Bonner?" Service said.

"You don't know, you're the only swinging dick in the county," she said with a gutteral growl.

Service showed his shield, but she barely looked. "Cracker Jacks or the Dollar Store?"

"Pretty hot out here for long sleeves," Millitor said.

"Gotta breeze comin' off Lake Superior," the girl said.

Millitor held up a finger. "Musta hit a calm."

"Happens, dude."

"I'm thinkin' you ought to shed that shirt, enjoy the sun," Millitor said. "You look pale."

"I've got, like, seriously sensitive skin. It stays on," the girl said. "Free country."

"For some people, the trick's to stay free," Millitor said.

"What the *fuck* do you want, dudes? I'm trying to concentrate here."

"That's the sound bite of the day," Millitor said with a grin.

She turned and faced Service. Eyes sunken, folds of skin from too-rapid weight loss. "I'll talk to youse," she said, "not Old Dirty Harry."

"I think Clint's got the bigger gun," Millitor said, obviously enjoying himself.

"There's a news flash," she said, holding her forefinger and thumb about an inch apart.

"Kareem Abdul-Jabbar," Service said.

"Am I supposed to know her?"

"*He* knows you."

"Don't 'zackly put the dude in exclusive company," she said.

"You're on the nod, girlie," Millitor said.

Her nostrils flared, but no explosion came. "*Man.*"

"Just a few questions," Service said.

"Kareem Abdul-Jabbar," Service repeated. "If we have to haul you over to the cop shop, your class will be done, and you'll have to do it all over again. You want *that*?"

She sighed. "Okay," she said with a glare. "So I, like, know the dude—what's the big deal?"

"He's headed south to the graybar hotel," Millitor said.

"Shit happens, man."

Service said, "He told me you told him about someone you know who cooks meth, Red P, maybe likes to cook red to white."

"Mostly I'm, like, totally color-blind, man," she said. Then, "I talk, what do I get?"

"We'll let you finish your class and your sentence, and get out of your way."

"You got a fag?" she asked.

Service held out his pack and lit one for her. She inhaled deeply and exhaled explosively.

"Big dude, hung like the Hulk, southern guy. Likes to blow shit up."

"Got a name?"

She pursed her lips. "Brett Fav-ree," she said.

"It's Favre," Millitor said, "Packer quarterback, and that tip ain't gonna fly."

"I'm not talking to him," she said to Service, and stomped her foot in frustration.

"One more chance," Service said, "or you're out of here."

"Just know his first name, man. Jericho. I made that boy tumble down good," she said with a leer.

"Local?"

"Marquette, dude. Said he teaches chemistry or ebonics or some-such shitology up at the college, but you know men, *man.* They lie about the number of dicks they got to get some, ya know?"

"Address?"

She shrugged. "Did him at the Fuck Creek Bar," she said. "Can I get back to my class?"

"He a regular down there?"

"What's regular?" she countered.

"You're there a lot."

"I seen 'im now and then."

"Recently?"

"Couple of weeks back, maybe."

"Taller than me?" Service asked.

"Wasn't that kinda big I'm talking about. Hang it out and get it up, and I'll tell youse."

"Cook or candyman?" Millitor said, reaching for her sleeve.

She yanked her arm away and nearly fell. Service caught her and put her back on her feet. *Eighty pounds max,* he thought. "Maybe he multitasks," she said.

"Maybe?"

She twitched a shoulder.

"I'll take that as a yes," Service said.

• • •

The two drove to the Gogebic County sheriff's office in Bessemer. A prisoner in a jumpsuit was washing a patrol car. The shift sergeant was inside talking to another resident.

Service introduced himself and gave enough information to encourage cooperation. "You guys ever deal with a crank cook called Jericho? Could be an aka."

"Talk to Casey, he's our UPSET guy—knows all the scumbags."

"But you've never heard the name?"

"UPSET plays things tight. Casey's in back right now. You can catch him if you hurry."

Casey was Levi Casey, complete with facial hair, months since his last haircut and fingers stained yellow by nicotine. "The sergeant sent us," Service said, and went through his story again.

Like a lot of narcoppers, Casey was laid-back, used to wading in ambiguity. "You talked to Anyboner? Real sweetheart, ain't she?"

"Jericho," Service said.

"Guess I heard that name, the dude with the alleged legendary long schlong. We looked for him for a while, but he never showed."

"Marquette-based?"

"Could be from anywhere, or he could be total bullshit. Druggies make up all sorts of names and throw them around to get us off their scents. Tell so many lies they can't remember what's what even when they try."

"You check with Marquette?"

"Don't have the time or budget for that kind of follow-up. We put it in an e-mail and sent it over. If they can make something, good for them."

"You ever hear he likes to blow up things?"

Casey grinned. "He's a cook, and the odds are he'll get his wish sooner or later."

Millitor said, "Bonner's wearing long sleeves in the sun today."

Casey pursed his lips. "I don't think she's a spiker unless she started this weekend. But I'll stop over and check her out."

"Tell her if this Jericho thing turns out to be bullshit, we'll be back," Millitor said.

"Anyboner don't scare," Casey said.

• • •

On the way west, Millitor lit a cigar. "I got offered the UPSET lead in Iron and passed on it. Sometimes the gut is right," he said smugly.

"The girl looks bad," Service said.

"Classic clinical signs. Won't be long till she gets way out there and can't get back. Brain's already toasted. *Addicts*," Millitor said with a tone more sympathetic than accusatory.

Service held up his cigarette. "You'd think we could emphathize."

"You'd think," Millitor said.

34

Crystal Falls, Iron County

SUNDAY, JUNE 4, 2006

"How many times I gotta say it?" Tikka Noli whined.

They were in an interrogation room in the Iron County Jail. Service's lab contacts in Marquette had called as he headed for Crystal Falls to let him know the package from Noli's place was made from the same plastic that they got from the woods, and that the contents were also white phosphorus, though the tests had not yet been done to reveal if they were chemically identical and from the same batch of chemicals. Service wasn't sure how they would go about doing such tests, but it sounded dangerous.

"Had a white phosphorus fire in the woods not that far from your place, Tikka. Plastic from your package is the same as those in the woods. What else can I conclude?"

"Man, you have got to believe me," Noli said. "That shit is my old lady's. She's crazy as a shithouse rat."

Service glanced at Tavolacci, who was looking nervous, probably needing to puff one of his stinky little cigars. "Is 'shithouse rat' an official mental health classification?"

"Seriously," Noli said. "If I could I'd put her in a nice facility where they can give her her meds and watch after her, but my old man's will sets it up so that if she's incapacitated, a lawyer becomes her executor *and* controls the power of attorney, and she inherits *everything*."

"So she stays out in the free world, even if she's sick," Service said.

"My old man died and I've been taking care of her ever since. She's fucking insane—and mean. Yeah, she's out, I sell the property, then we put her inside and everybody's happy."

"Even her?"

"Nutcases are incapable of happiness."

Grady Service's mother had died in childbirth. He wondered if he'd be thinking of her the same way if she had lived. "Still not buying, Tikka."

"I hate to do this, but that shit belongs to my mother. I was just leaving the place one day when two broads showed up to deliver it."

"Two women?"

"Yeah, spikey-dykey types."

"I don't think I know that term. Do these women have names?"

Noli rolled his eyes. "Thelma and Louise. How the *fuck* am I supposed to know? My old lady didn't formally introduce us; I saw the packages in the back of their truck."

"Right, someone's carrying exposed white phosphorus in a truck bed. That's certainly believeable."

"No man, not naked in the bed. There was a metal box in back, stenciled with 'Danger: Explosives!' in red paint. You know, the kind of box you usta see around the old mines."

Service didn't know.

"You get a mine name?"

"No."

"Thelma and Louise?"

Noli shrugged. "You'll have to ask my old lady for their names."

"Write down a license plate?"

"I'm not crazy. One of the bitches looked like the kind who'd cut my throat, she caught me doing something like that."

"Okay, let's assume this is the truth, and these women brought these packages. How many did you see?"

"Just the one, sitting on top the box."

"So it *was* exposed, not inside the box?"

"*Dude.*"

"None in the house afterwards?"

"No. I don't like snooping, the old lady packing and all."

"So why would she want explosives?"

"To fuck up my plans, of course. She runs with a bunch of nutcases, old women who think they're environmental activists because they want all the world's cats and dogs spayed."

"How could she fuck up your plans?"

"Hey, the Taide Jarvi people are hinky about attention. The old lady starts a fire, Taide Jarvi will back off."

"Have they?"

"Not yet, because I called them up soon as I heard about that shit and told them I'd take their offer."

"Which was?"

"Half-million for twenty acres."

"At the river?"

"No, up the hill."

"The hill with the eagle's nest?"

"No, further east—the one with the quartz outcrops."

Service stepped out to the desk and got a plat book, brought it back inside. "Show me what we're talking about, Tikka," Service said.

The man used a pencil to draw in the property line and put an X on the outcrop. It was the ridge with the outcrop he'd found.

"You own a four-wheeler, Mr. Noli?"

"Don't everyone?"

"Do you keep it at your mother's place?"

"It's at my place in Gaastra."

"I'm going to want to get some tire casts."

Noli shrugged.

Tavolacci suddenly looked interested. "Are we . . . like, getting somewhere here?"

"Maybe, Sandy."

"You gonna charge my client?"

"Still waiting for forensics," Service said.

"Can he go tonight? You already held him as long as you can without charges."

"Sure, he can go."

Meeting done, Grady Service drove to the South Branch of the Paint and made his way up into Noli's property, where he used a hammer to knock off some samples. He put them in an evidence bag, marked them, and headed back to the office to fetch Friday, whose vehicle was still in the shop. He'd told her he'd take her to Marquette for the weekend but the weekend had evaporated because of work. He intended to now drop her off on the way to his place.

35

Big Bay, Marquette County

MONDAY, JUNE 5, 2006

Friday's vehicle would not be ready until June 9. Before leaving Iron River, Grady Service called Marquette County Sheriff Department Sergeant Weasel Linsenman. The two had known each other for years, and Service had dragged him into some unsavory situations, which had left the deputy more than a little leery of him. Then, a year ago, Linsenman had saved his life after he'd been attacked by a tweaking crank addict in Gwinn.

Service had stopped at the house in a snowstorm to do what seemed a routine favor for Simon del Olmo and he'd been ambushed. He would have died had Linsenman not happened along, seen his predicament, and intervened decisively and quickly. The deputy had been promoted to sergeant a month ago. It had taken years to learn that the new sergeant's mother had inexplicably named him Weasel, and, because of this, virtually everyone who knew him referred to him in first and third person by his family name.

"Linsenman," the man answered his phone.

"Not sergeant, just Linsenman?"

"I was sitting here thinking about a cloudless warm day, flying silk kites, nubile young women cavorting buck naked on the beach, letting my mutts run, chase Frisbees—you know, paradise kind of shit—and then I hear your voice and my blood turns cold, and all I can smell is trouble."

"That hurts my feelings."

"One cannot injure what one does not possess," Linsenman said.

"I need help."

"That's been obvious to most of us for many years."

"I'm looking for a meth dealer-cook who goes by the name of Jericho, which may not be his name at all."

"Last time you had contact with a cranker he just about took off your head with a baseball bat. I never heard of a Jericho, and I *hate* dealing with the druggies. Even our UPSET people give me hives."

"Word is he might be on Northern's faculty."

"I doubt that, but I know the campus chief. Let me give him a bump and see what I can find out. I think campus cops spend more time with druggies than deps. I'll get back at you."

• • •

Friday lived in a small ranch house in Harvey, on Cherry Creek Road, southeast of Marquette. Service took her bags in, met her sister Angie Lee, and found himself holding a baby.

"Meet Shigun," Friday said.

The bobble-headed infant looked like his head would come off, and Service supported him with his arm and hand to keep the head from moving, the way Karylanne had taught him to handle his granddaughter. He liked how babies smelled—when their diapers were clean. Shigun Wellington Friday had alert, serious eyes. "Eyes of a cop," he said.

"*Don't even*," Friday said, taking her son back.

• • •

Friday delivered, Service next stopped at the Roof, which is what DNR employees called the regional office just outside Marquette. and found Captain Ware Grant in his office."Two pigeons back to the roost," he told the captain, who turned and smiled.

"Have a seat and bring me up to speed on your case." The captain reached into his desk drawer and brought out a bottle of Coleraine's single malt Irish whiskey, filled two jiggers, and set one in front of his detective.

They picked up their glasses and Service said, "May a virulent plague rot the testicles of all violets." This was Grady Service's personal word for violators.

"I visited Officer Denninger today," Grant said.

"She's worried about being laid off."

"I tried to allay her fears, but we each have our own demons."

What the hell does that mean? "How's her ankle?"

"Pins in it, but she's young and she'll heal."

Unspoken message: You and I are not young, and this is a business for youth, not men our age.

The captain said, "McCants interviewed for a sergeant's position in Clinton County."

"She'd abandon the Mosquito?" It had been his old territory, before McCants, and his father's before him.

"Promotion, not abandonment. We'll make sure a good person gets it," Captain Grant said.

Jesus, she's going to be promoted! My fault she's leaving? Not going to think about it. Too much going on to juggle emotions now. "You here for a while, Cap'n?"

"Heading back to Lansing today."

"Things going all right down there?"

"Ample challenges," the captain said, leaving it at that. "I saw the governor last week, and she asked after you."

Jesus, Service thought.

"She's a fine lady," Grant said. "You should give her a call."

"I'm not comfortable with that, Cap'n. Politics isn't my suit."

"She's your *friend,* Detective."

Change the subject. "Great whiskey."

Service left the Roof to go to the hospital near Northern's campus.

All things considered, Denninger looked pretty good, and had the sparkle back in her eyes.

"You been ignoring me?" she greeted him.

"You're a little tough to ignore."

"You damn betcha. What's happening in the case?"

"None of your business. Your job is to heal, not worry."

"You make it sound so easy."

"Nothing's easy," he said, rubbing her shoulder.

• • •

He fetched Newf and Cat without having to talk to his one-time girl-friend, Kira Lehto, and took them to Slippery Creek.

• • •

Linsenman called late Monday night. "There's no Jericho on Northern's faculty, but there's a student with that handle. The campus cops have had some contact with him. Actual name is Necho Wagenschultz."

"Chemistry student?"

"Career-student type. Been around campus seven or eight years. In school for a semester, out for a year, like that."

"How do the cops know him?"

"Student activist, very outspoken on the Kennecott boondoggle, shows up at public meetings, makes a lot of noise, veiled threats against the company and such, and disappears. Campus snitches claim he's not an actual member of any campus or off-campus group."

"Got an address?"

"Big Bay right on the county road, heading into town. He tends bar weeknights at the TBI." Linsenman gave him the man's address.

TBI—Thunder Bay Inn. "Thanks, Stripes."

"Funny. You're next."

Service laughed and hung up. *Me a sergeant? No way—but if McCants is transferring south, that means the Mosquito will be open again. Something to seriously think about. The old turf. My old turf.*

• • •

He did not sleep well, and got up early Tuesday morning and stared at his free weights. *That's not going to happen.* But he did get in a halfhearted five-mile run, and in the afternoon went down to the creek and caught a sixteen-inch brown with a muddler fly. *When this case is over, it's back to pushing iron and a regular running schedule,* he admonished himself.

He called Friday after his run. "I've got to make a run up to Big Bay tonight."

"Good. Pick me up and we'll head to IR from there."

Something in her voice. Smug? Something. "Five?"

"Works for me."

"What about Shigun?"

"Angie Lee has my six."

• • •

He called Friday on the cell phone as he drove north, explaining what had happened in Ironwood, and with Noli, and how he and Millitor had gotten Jericho's name from Anyboner, and how Linsenman's contacts had converted Jericho to one Necho Wagenschultz. He had no idea what to expect from Wagenschultz, but based on what Linsenman had said, he was the sort to shake the trees and split. Confronted by the law, he might do the same.

Big Bay was one of those places that irritated him. It had been made famous by Judge John Voelker's best-selling novel, *Anatomy of a Murder*, and the movie made from the book in 1959, the story a fictional account of an actual murder in Big Bay. Old-timer locals still rambled on about the days when the Hollywood crew and actors had come to town. Since then the village had been steadily yuppifying, locals being bought out by younger people with trust funds, mountain bikes, kayaks, cross-country skis, driving Japanese hatchbacks and fuel-efficient miniature SUVs. Even the business names creeped him out: Ski-Touring Wilderness Outfitters; Green Guides Lake Superior Kayak Tours; the Eternal Organic Emporium. *Hippy-dippy hell made in the faux-earth style of Yippy-Yuppie-Yumyum.* He hated the feel and look of the whole place.

The latest uproar and cause célèbre was Kennecott Mining's application to the state to blast a tunnel beneath Eagle Rock on the Salmon Trout River, and for over a decade after that, to extract copper and nickel from sulfide rock. Opponents feared the mine would create sulfuric acid and heavy metals, which would leech into groundwater and streams. The Salmon Trout itself was home to the only known spawning population of coaster brook trout on the shore of Southern Lake Superior; sulfide contamination would end that. Opponents of the mine had brought together a wide range of allies: Native Americans who insisted Eagle Rock was a sacred site, Audubon, the Sierra Club, Trout Unlimited, and several land conservancies.

Governor Timms was a member of the exclusive Huron Mountain Club, which owned a major portion of land north of Big Bay and was opposed to the mine, but so far she had not publicly expressed personal concerns or objections.

When he pulled up to Friday's in Harvey, she was waiting with her bags, which she threw in back, slid in, and fastened her seatbelt.

• • •

The Thunder Bay Inn sat in the village center. He'd never stayed in the B&B, but had heard it was nice—with prices to match. The TBI had a dining room that had been built to accommodate the filming of *Anatomy of a Murder*; Henry Ford had once owned the place and had maintained a personal suite that overlooked the company's long-gone sawmill across the road.

He parked in a lot behind the dining room, took out his false teeth, and dropped them in a plastic bag in the truck's console. Friday's mouth hung open. He said, "What—you're hearing dueling banjos?"

They got out of the Tahoe and went inside. Low ceiling, low lights, the usual clutter of beer company memorabilia, dartboards, pool table, large-screen TVs, all on, nobody looking at them. A banner across one wall read SAY NAH TO DA SULFIDE MINING, EH?

The place was fairly busy for a week night. They took a seat at the bar and a waitperson (HI, MY NAME IS ROSE) gave them a menu entitled, "Anatomy of Our Sandwiches." It featured the Lee Remick (charbroiled chicken breast), the Jimmy Stewart (shaved sirloin), and the John Voelker (breaded cod filet). He grimaced when he read the Voelker entry. The former Michigan Supreme Court judge-turned-author exclusively ate brook trout. *Breaded cod? Jesus H.!*

They sat at the bar and ordered beer. Only one bartender: male, six-two, ax-handle shoulders, bulging biceps under a T-shirt emblazoned with SUL-FIDINIACS NOT SERVED HERE. Weight-pusher. Gold wire-rimmed glasses, longish hair, an earring, small hands for his bulk.

The bartender smiled at them, but kept his eyes moving, scanning the room. Service watched the man shift his feet constantly, either nervous leg or prone to running.

"Showtime," he whispered to Friday, who nodded. He hoped she'd get into the moment. There were times when he'd wished the Academy had included some acting classes.

"That's so much liberal bullshit!" he said forcefully, and loud enough to be heard by people sitting at all the tables. He slapped the bar for emphasis. "The damn state's dying! You want *that*?"

"Less than half the jobs are for locals," Friday countered. "What about the coasters and the rivers and the acid? If we lose a river, we can't get it back. I refuse to sell the U.P. one place at a time for a few bucks. We don't need this, and we will not accept it!"

Her staged instantaneous ferocity and passion were impressive.

"We're talking about a mining company. With *real* engineers, not a bunch of limp-dick motherfuckers trying to exhume the sixties and all that shit!"

"You're wrong!"

Service raised his fist and the bartender stepped toward them, his chest puffed out, neck red. "Maybe you should, like, listen to the lady, and maybe you should, like, also lower your hand, dude. Like *now*?"

Service made eye contact. "Maybe you should, like, fuck off and, like, go wash a glass or something? Like, who the fuck asked for your input!"

Wagenschultz said, "You ever hear of aging with grace, old man? You need to chill, sayin'?"

Service leaned across the bar and stabbed at the man with his finger, careful to not touch him. "You ever hear of standing back, collecting your minimum wage, and keeping your mouth shut, *pretty boy!*"

The last words did it. *Weighing his options.* "Get a haircut, you pussy," Service added.

Wagenschultz exhaled loudly and stiffened. "Sir, you are cut off and you are leaving the premises. *Now!*"

Service drained his beer. "Says who, *girly-boy*?"

Wagenschultz came around the end of the bar and pointed. "That way, sir."

Service grinned and presented his fist and the bartender grabbed it and started pulling him toward the exit. "Sorry, lady," he said over his shoulder. Going through the door, Service bent his knees, grabbed the bartender's hand with both of his, bent over, and pulled the man over his back, flipping him down the handicapped-access ramp. Friday was immediately on Wagenschultz, twisting an arm behind his back and snapping cuffs in place.

Service jerked the man to his feet and showed him his badge. "Let's, like, take a walk, Jericho."

"My name's Necho."

"Whatever," Friday said.

"Man, you wanted to talk, all you had to do was say so. What the fuck's up with the Batman SWAT shit?"

The man didn't resist, but kept talking. "I was just doing my job; your profanity was disturbing other customers."

Service jerked the man to a halt. "This is not about your bartending job, asswipe. A little bird told us you like to cook."

"I don't know what you're talking about."

"A witness says different."

"You . . . ," Wagenschultz said, and stopped.

"Here's the deal, Necho," Friday said. "You cook, that's your business. But what we hear is you also like to make stuff blow up."

"I don't think so," the man said, his eyes darting between Service and Friday.

"You're a tick on a mangy dog's ass," Service said. "We've got two murders, and if we have to fillet your ass in court, that's how she's gonna go down, and I shit you not."

The man's shoulders slouched.

"Where's your lab . . . at your house?"

"Too dangerous."

"Where?"

"Camp off 510."

"You cook white there?"

Wagenschultz nodded.

They put him in the passenger seat and strapped him in. Friday sat behind him.

The hunting camp was fairly remote, just east on Alder Creek Truck Trail, off County Road 510, with Big Pup Creek running alongside the property. The lab was located in a shed in a clearing, separate from the cabin by fifty yards, a wall of cedars between the buildings. *Private, and if it blows, well away.*

The shed door was secured by two padlocks mated with a quarter-inch steel cable. Key-lock, not a combination, more secure. Master brand with thermoplastic covering, designed for use in extreme temperatures, the same kind his own agency used.

"Open it," Friday said.

The man held up his cuffs. "Key's in my pocket."

She slid her hand into his pocket and he grinned and tried to rub against her. She thwacked him on the side of his head with a finger snap and he winced. "Behave, asshole," she said.

Service opened the door and stepped inside. This was not your typical Beavis and Butt-Head operation, which was naturally a disaster. This was organized and clean. A freezer with a lock. "Anhydrous ammonia?" he asked Wagenschultz, who nodded. Service took it all in: metal box for dry ice, packages of lithium batteries, un-iodized salt, mason jars, several expensive coolers, a roll of linen for filtering, triple-neck flasks and other glassware, a stainless-steel container on a counter attached to an electric generator humming just below threshold. *This asshole is big-time.*

"The white?" Service asked.

The man motioned in the direction of the stainless-steel container with his cuffed hands.

Service said incredulously, "In *that,* not underwater?"

"Chill, dude. It's a vacuum, but even the liquid's not so volatile."

"Liquid's no good for explosives."

"I never said I had crystals. What I said was that I made some white, and there it is, man."

Think—remember Anyboner. "Maybe you like to make people *think* you make crystal."

"Could be."

"Women?"

Another nod and a leer. "Just talking about blowing shit up gets them wet, man."

"Then why make it if all you gotta do is talk your way into their pants? What's the point?" Friday asked.

"I think I want a lawyer."

"That's your right."

"There's no meth here," Wagenschultz said.

"Got all the makings in one place; that's against the law and enough for us."

Shaking his head. "Okay, I'm, like, at this Kennecott Eagle Rock dealy, an' like, I stood up and spouted some, man. First amendment shit, right? Afterwards in the parking lot, this chick comes up to me? She says, 'How'd you like to make that mine disappear, *man?*' She tells me if they start to build and dig, they can be stopped. She's heard I'm a chemist, and offers me significant cash for white, but won't pay until I produce, and demonstrate that it works."

The man looked at the far wall of the shed. "Making the conversion was no big deal chemically speaking, but I didn't have the know-how or the equipment to make the crystals. I gotta tell you the truth: The whole thing scared the shit out of me, man."

"You see her again?"

"I got off work one night and she shows up at my truck, wants product. I tell her no deal, she says 'Okay, dude,' and splits—end of story."

"That's not a story—it's a fairy tale," Service said.

"It happened *just* like that."

"No threats, no anger, she just said 'Okay, dude' and walked away?"

"Man, it's the truth."

"What did she look like?"

"Five-ten, big-boned, dark hair and complexion."

Service rolled his eyes. "Lies will fuck you, son. You got a favorite lawyer?"

"No way, man. I can't afford a lawyer."

"With all this? You could hock the damn glassware alone for a small fortune."

"Man, I got no money. I quit the business. I've got to tend bar or I'm fucked."

"This place tells a different story about money, Necho."

"Okay, I did some cooking. I made some money, okay? But *man,* there's, like, cops crawling all over this county. It's not worth it anymore, man. I told myself, get out of this shit."

"A magic reformation."

"Truth."

"Read him his rights," Friday said.

"Wait," Wagenschultz said. "This won't stick."

"You never know," Friday said. "You sure of that description? We're dealing with capital cases, Necho, and if you fuck us around, it just gets worse for you, man."

"Okay, okay—she's five-five, dark hair, wiry."

Service took out a photo of Penny Provo. "Wiry like that?"

Wagenschultz looked at the photo and nodded once. "That's her. Hardcore, calm, soft voice, in charge. Nearly pissed my pants whenever she come around."

"And when you said you couldn't do it, she just walked away?"

"That was the weirdest part, man. She said, 'Lucky for you,' and split."

"Lucky for you?" Friday repeated.

"Three words."

Friday undid the handcuffs and Service said, "Okay, beat it."

The man rubbed his wrists. "Man, it's like fifteen miles."

"Right—git."

"You're not busting me? But *you* brought me here."

"Bring yourself home."

"It's fifteen miles."

"Be glad it's not February."

The man skulked away. Service called Linsenman. "We've got a meth lab off Alder Creek Truck Trail." Service gave him the fire number. "Not Beavis and Butt-Head. This is a significant operation. Call UPSET. We'll need HAZMAT out here. Make sure they know there's liquid white phosphorus in the inventory."

"Holy shit. Prisoners to transport?"

"No, but we know the suspect. UPSET or your people can snatch him later. We'll hang ten until the cavalry shows."

"On it, man."

Service walked Friday out to the Alder Creek Truck Trail to light a cigarette. "What did you hear?" he asked.

She recounted his conversation with the bartender, what she had gleaned from it.

He said, "Kennecott wants to blast a tunnel about a thousand feet into the ground under the river and bring up the ore from there. If someone blows up their shit, they risk causing the exact problem they supposedly want to avoid. What's that all about?"

"What's your point, Grady?"

It was past midnight, now into Wednesday and he was tired. "Not sure yet. *Maybe Provo didn't really want Willie Pete. If not, why was she dealing with Jericho? What the hell is going on? I hate this case.*"

36

Crystal Falls, Iron County

WEDNESDAY, JUNE 7, 2006

It was early Wednesday morning by the time the hazardous materials technicians and county drug people cleared them to go. Service gave the cops Wagenschultz's address in Big Bay and promised to send a written report within forty-eight hours, doubting he'd get to it in that time. Of all his duties, writing reports was the most wearisome for him. Besides, he was pretty sure the man would do a runner, but sooner or later he'd be snagged somewhere by someone for something. The important thing was that the lab was neutralized and they could get on with their own work.

"Food?" he asked Friday as they headed south on CR 510. *She's quiet. Not like her to not tell me she's hungry.* "What?"

"I've got the organizational chart for the Van Dalen Foundation."

News. "I thought your pal Jinger was going west next week."

"Don't be sarcastic. He went early. UPS brought the package yesterday—I mean Saturday. I was up all night with it, which worked out fine because Shigun was up all night."

"Coming down with something?"

"I think he just wanted mommy time. Work and mommyhood don't dovetail so smoothly. Did I mention the chart's not three years old, but current and marked confidential?" She put her head back. "Art Lake's in there. It isn't easy to find, but it's there. Want to see?"

• • •

"Gimme the org chart." While she drank coffee, he leafed through the thirty-page document. "I thought the purpose of an org chart was to quickly show how an outfit fits together."

"Probably why we're not in the business world," she said.

It took a while to plow through everything, but he was able to see that the trust was organized in some general areas, and looked to him like a tree-house built on three support trunks: Education, Health, and Aggregated Properties. Boxes under the latter cited Future Space, Future Time, and Future Earth.

"I don't see anything about Art Lake," he said, grabbing a piece of pizza.

"It's there."

"Are you enjoying this?"

"I might be."

"I give up," he said, dropping the document on the console between the front bucket seats.

She leafed through the pages and gave it back to him. "Top page. See it now?"

"No."

"You like puzzles?"

"Just the ones I can solve."

"You're destined to a life of disappointment," she said. "Aren't you the one always preaching to me about thinking outside the box? Try thinking *inside* the box."

She's a lulu, this one.

"You know what an anagram is?" she asked.

"Jumbled letters?" *Like my brain.*

"Look at the entry, 'Last Carde.' "

"No way that's an anagram for Art Lake."

"*Inside* the box, remember?"

He passed the document back to her and started the engine.

"People tell me Grady Service never quits."

"Shows you how much people know."

"If you don't try, you'll never know the answer," she said.

"I don't need to. We're a team."

"You're trying to guilt me."

"Is it working?" he asked.

"You're a difficult man at times."

"I've heard."

As they got between Channing and Sagola, she said, "Okay."

"Question or answer?"

"Okay is sometimes a word of agreement, sometimes one of submission."

"This time?"

"Do you want the answer or not? The entry, Last Carde, is Art Lake."

"Excuse me, nine letters versus seven. I counted. It doesn't fit."

"In English. If you try *French* it reduces to Lac des Arts, ten letters, which can be scrambled to—"

"Eight letters, which is still too many," he said.

"Not lac *de* Art, but lac d'art,"she said.

How the hell had she figured this out? Was she right? "You deciphered this?"

"It's a gift," she said.

"What is?"

"Puzzles, anagrams, mind-benders. I could do thousand-piece jigsaws alone when I was six."

Between Sagola and Crystal Falls she said, "Your place is closer than mine."

No doubting what she's implying. Am I ready for this? Are we? He looked over at her. "Okay."

"It's Wednesday morning. Is this a workday . . . technically?"

"Are you concerned about that Jell-O mode thing?" he asked her.

"I'm not, but you may be in the morning."

Can't read her, and sometimes I've got no idea what she's talking about, much less what she's thinking. "Maybe we should put this off." *Assuming we both know what "this" is,* he reminded himself.

At the light below the courthouse he needed to turn right to go toward Iron River, or left to go to Simon and Elza's place near Alpha. *Off the dime, he told himself.* He turned left and looked over at her. "This doesn't mean we're joined at the hip."

"No, but you'll be in the ballpark," Friday said with a lecherous grin.

37

Crystal Falls, Iron County

THURSDAY, JUNE 8, 2006

Friday got out of bed and padded into the bathroom. Service looked at the clock twenty minutes later, got up, and knocked on the door. "Is everything all right in there?"

She opened the door with a puzzled look. "*Wha'?*"

"You've been in there a long time."

"I have?"

"Twenty minutes."

"Huh," she said. "Want coffee?"

"It's in the kitchen," he said.

"I *know* that," Friday said, putting on her robe and sweeping past him. She soon returned with a cup.

"Fast enough?" she asked, holding the cup out to him.

He smiled, took a sip, and spat it out. "There's salt in this!"

"Ooh boy," she said, grinning insipidly.

He stalked into the kitchen, got a sponge and a wad of paper towels, went back and sopped up the spill. Friday was back in the bathroom, door open, naked in front of the vanity, tilting her head left and right, "My face is crooked," she announced, and looked out at him. "I'll rustle us up some breakfast," she said.

Salt in the coffee is enough. "No, I'll take care of it."

He fried one egg for each of them, poured small glasses of orange juice, toasted a piece of Swedish limpa rye. She came out to the table and joined him. "My feet hurt."

"Eat, they'll feel better."

She made a sour face. "That's severely illogical, not to mention extremely counterintuitive." She looked at the egg on the small plate. "Where's the French toast?"

"You never said anything about French toast."

"I must have been thinking it," she said, smiled, got up, and limped toward the bedroom.

"Hey."

"What?"

"Your shoes are on the wrong feet."

She looked down. "See, eating *wasn't* the solution."

"You *didn't* eat."

"Sure I did. One egg and toast."

He pointed at the table where her breakfast sat untouched.

She grinned and said, "Well, *duh.* And oops."

He followed her into the bedroom. "This is it, right—that *Jell-O mode* thing?"

"Not pretty, is it?"

"How long does it last?"

"Can't say I have empirical evidence. I'm pretty sure the duration is in direct proportion to the number of my orgasms." She looked up at him. "Which means it's probably going to be a very loooong day."

In the Tahoe she said, "Don't blame me if last night was a work night."

"You'd better stick to simple tasks this morning."

"Like pouring coffee?"

"Point made. Just sit in your chair and look intelligent."

"I can do that . . . but I'd rather look sexy."

"Knock yourself out." *Had to open the door, didn't you? Could've turned right, but you had to go left. . . .* I like her!

Grady Service groped in the center console.

"What're you looking for?"

"Motrin."

"Got a bottle in my purse."

"What else—salt, maybe?"

"Hurts my feelings, but point well taken," she said. "Boy oh boy oh boy oh boy, last night sure was nice."

"Is the next day always like this?"

"Pretty much."

"This is normal?" Service asked.

"For me," she said happily.

A small black bear was sitting splay-legged in the parking lot when he maneuvered the Tahoe into a parking spot. "Is that for real?" Friday asked.

"Sure is."

She said, "That's one big honking dog!"

"Probably because it's a bear," he said.

"Whoops," she said, rolling her eyes.

38

Iron River, Iron County

THURSDAY, JUNE 8, 2006

The Iron County medical examiner called almost as Service sat down. "Vick one, confirm amputation of left arm, below the elbow joint. Scoring on the surviving bone suggests crude surgical technique, hurriedly done. Vick two is estimated at six-eight, but it's a pretty good estimate."

The ME's tone was entirely different now, like he had been reborn. Service shared the ME's information with Friday and Millitor, and leafed through his case notes, looking for loose ends. He found the note he had made to himself: "Pinky Barbeaux to send Art Lake plate nos." He looked at Friday, but spoke to Millitor. "Have we gotten a fax or call from Sheriff Barbeaux of Baraga County?"

"Were we expecting one?" Millitor said.

"I was."

"Don't remember it, eh." Millitor had pretty much assumed responsibility for all the case's paperwork and filing.

Service wrote *License plate numbers?* on a piece of paper and signed his name. He started to hand it to Friday, but Millitor picked it off.

"I'll take care of it."

Friday sighed. "Guess what I'm thinking about."

"French toast."

She grimaced. "Not even warm."

Service grabbed his notebook, went out to the parking lot, and lit a cigarette. The bear had curled up on the grass near a Dumpster, watching US 2 traffic. He walked toward it, trying to get direct eye contact and shaking his hands. "Hey bear, hey bear, hey bear!"

The yearling's ears twitched and it got up, scampered across a side street, up a small hill, and into some oak trees. Service leaned against the building to make sure the young bear didn't come back and dialed the number for Evers Gorsline. The phone rang several times before dumping to voice mail.

Service said, "So much for twenty-four/seven. My name's Service. Words for the day: Last Carde. Call me," and hung up. He found Millitor standing nearby, chewing his cigar.

"You didn't leave no number."

Service said. "Everybody in Chicago's got caller ID, right?"

"You'd think," Millitor said with a grin.

Service called up his own voice mail. Only one message: "This is Gabby, MSP Regional Forensics Laboratory. Got some results for you. Give me a shout." The message was followed by her number. The message was dated two days ago.

He called the number.

"Forensics, Gabby speaking."

"Service, Iron River. Our assay results in?"

"You didn't provide geographic coordinates for the samples," she said.

"Not required. Case security."

"Excuse me, but we're on the same team, Detective."

"The things you learn," he mumbled. "Sorry. What about the results?"

"Six samples. Numbers one through five are vein quartz, but no prezzies and nothing of interest in them. "Where'd you find number six?"

"Case security."

"Yeah, I think you already said that. I'm just wondering, 'cause if it's close to the other sample sites, I'd isolate number six and slap some tight-ass security on that sucker."

What the hell is she going on about? "Why's that?"

"The assay indicates Au 2,300 grams per ton."

He had never been much good with numbers and calculations. "Got a translation?"

"We're talking in the range of five pounds of gold per ton."

"That's good?"

"Rich enough to start wars in some parts of the world."

"But nothing at sites one through five?"

"Nothing significant."

"What about the reference sample?"

"A little better than number six: 2,575 grams per ton. Difference is that the gold in the REFSAMP is visible to the eye. So is number six, but the veins aren't as thick."

"They're from the same source?" he asked.

"No way I can tell that, but I'm guessing they're physically proximate."

"Can you draw *any* conclusions about a relationship between the reference and sample six?"

She was quiet for a few seconds. "Just guessing, but I think a purity test would show they are from the same source, but perhaps not quite in the same location."

"Like they're related underground?"

"Yeah, sure; that's not technical, but that's the general idea, eh."

"Thanks, Gabby."

"Seriously," she said. "If word gets out on what the samples show, you could have a bloody stampede on your hands."

So where did Thigpen's daddy's gold sample come from? Number six had come from an exposed quartz outcrop a mile or so east-northeast of where the remains were discovered, and the remains had been sprinkled with gold dust. Where did the dust come from?

He called the Marquette number again. "Did you get some gold dust with the other samples?" he asked.

"Nope. Were we supposed to?"

"If you had dust, could you do the same assay as for the other samples?"

"Yeah. You sending something up the line?"

"Soon as I can."

"I'll expedite," Gabby said.

He went into the office and grabbed a box with USGS topographical maps. Friday joined him. "Need help? I think I'm back."

"We've got assay results. The reference sample from Thigpen is rich, and my sixth sample is close to it. In the range of five pounds in a ton."

"Is that good?"

He laughed. "We're too much alike. Apparently, it's real good."

He spread a map on his desk and weighted the corners with ashtrays and coffee cups.

"What're you looking for?"

"Not sure."

"You say that a lot."

"Because it's true a lot of the time. The professor said her father wouldn't say where he got Lincoln's gold sample."

"The source of all evil," Friday said, nodding.

"Call her—see if she remembers anything else, something he might have said that would give us a clue."

"Something he said eighty years ago? We're *that* desperate?"

"Think of it as that *clueless,* not desperate."

"That doesn't help," she said, reaching for her phone.

He left Friday and went outside again, this time to call Zhenya Leukonovich, who answered on the second ring. "I met Funke. Did he tell you?"

"The captain has a frenetic schedule."

"He says you're looking at Van Dalen Foundation."

"Captain Funke made this statement?"

"Not in so many words. He's not much for direct answers, but he said you're onto a scent."

"Zhenya thinks the captain somewhat prone to hyperbole and overstatement."

Ducking and weaving—why? "Do you have a copy of the Van Dalen organizational chart?"

"Zhenya chooses not to respond."

"Well, if you happen to come into possession of one, you just might look at page twenty-four, at an entry called Art Lake."

"There is no such entry," she said immediately.

"If you don't have a chart, how do you know?"

"Such data resides in Zhenya's mind, but she assures the detective there is no such entry."

"Bring up the screen in your brain and give it another look. Call me if you figure it out."

"There is no such entry," Leukonovich insisted.

"There is if that chart in your head is dated this year, and you know how to break the code."

"Zhenya thinks it impossible for the detective to possess such a document."

"Improbable, but not impossible. I have it. The entry you're looking for is 'Last Carde.' " He spelled it phonetically for her. "It's an anagram. 'Last Carde' transposes to the French, *Lac d'Art,* which translates to Art Lake."

"Zhenya thinks this is execrable French. You deciphered this yourself?"

"Not me—my partner."

"Remarkable," Leuknovich said.

"Why would Van Dalen be hiding the identity of its organizations?"

"This answer is, of course, obvious."

Not to mè. "When Funke checks in, you might want to share this information with him."

"Zhenya will take the detective's suggestion under advisement."

Service terminated the call and stared at the hill across the road where the bear had disappeared. *Why no sexual tension with Zhenya this time? Always there before . . . not now. I just want to be a game warden,* he thought, the latter the larger insight of the two.

Friday came outside and drew in a deep breath. "I talked to the professor."

"That was quick."

"I need to get into the Tahoe," she said.

He gave her the key and watched as she rooted around in the storage area. When she came back, holding out the key, she had a book tucked under her arm.

"What's that?"

"A hunch. I pressed the professor and she resisted, but she also said something that didn't register until the call was finished."

"Which would be?"

"When I asked where the stone came from, she said she could only imagine."

"Okay." *I don't see the point.*

"You don't hear it?"

Hear what? "Afraid not."

"She didn't say she *couldn't* imagine."

"Tuesday, is this more Jell-O mode?"

"Don't overrate yourself," she said. "And incidentally, I like it when you call me Tuesday." These things said, she left him standing in the parking lot, staring at the door to the Troop post.

He expected a callback from Evers Gorsline, but the day ended without one. *Using Last Carde should have stimulated a response—something. Shit, maybe we aren't so smart. Maybe Last Carde is wrong.*

Millitor left for home and Service drove Friday down the hill to the AmericInn and parked.

"Why are you parking?"

"I thought you'd invite me in."

"It's a weeknight," she said. "We have work to do."

"Want dinner?"

"I'm too busy for food. You're on your own."

Don't think, don't talk, just go. Tomorrow is another day.

Crystal Falls, Iron County

THURSDAY, JUNE 8, 2006

He was vegging on Grinda's deck when his cell phone sounded. The number window said only private.

"Grady Service."

"This is Evers Gorsline. You left a succinct message for me, Detective, tinged with irritation, so let me take care of your question directly. I'm sure you are a fine conversationalist—most detectives are—but as you might imagine, I'm a very busy man. If this Last Carde thing is intended to mean something, I'm afraid it eludes me."

"Last Carde—aka Art Lake."

"You're talking nonsense, Detective."

"You're the attorney for Art Lake."

"I fail to see your point."

"I'm interested in Art Lake."

"You are not alone."

"What exactly is the place?"

"It is a retreat for artists, for exceptionally creative people, a place for them to work without interruptions from the outside world."

"What kind of creative people?"

Pause. "Detective, I have neither the time nor the patience for insipid patter. If you have something to say, please do so now."

"I want to visit the retreat."

"Many share your desire, but residency is by invitation only. People are selected; they do not apply."

"I don't want to be a resident. I just want to see it."

"May I ask why?"

"Police business."

Another pause. "Please don't be offended, Detective, but if you have official police business, and a valid reason, you can obtain a warrant, and we will of course comply."

"I meant this as a friendly call."

"Received as such, Detective, but we each have our own portfolios of responsibility. This conversation is terminated. Please don't call again unless you have a reason."

A polite fuck-you-very-much. The man was smooth, his tone amiable, yet businesslike. *Gorsline had clearly laid out the rules of engagement: Find a legal reason to enter, probable cause to support it, a warrant to flow out of that. What probable cause?*

Art Lake owns the property where the remains were found. A judge will shove this up your ass. The wolf tree is not on Art Lake property. Taide Jarvi, Art Lake—is there a legal business connection?

Elza Grinda came out to the porch and sat beside him, her long curly hair freshly washed. "Am I interrupting?" she asked.

"More like saving me from myself."

"You look troubled."

"Call it stumped."

"You hear about Candi?"

"That she interviewed for stripes in Clinton County?"

"She got the job," Grinda said.

"She'll be a great sarge," he said, his stomach flipping a little.

"Everyone thought—"

"She's my friend and colleague, that's it."

"I didn't mean to pry."

"Of course you did."

"Yeah, I did! Sorry. By the way, Friday's nice. Simon and I both have really good vibes. She good at her job?"

"Seems to be."

"Well, I just wanted to tell you that Simon and I like her."

"I was really concerned about that."

"You can be a real SOB," she said.

"Get anything from your girlfriend on the drug team?"

"No suspects. UPSET thinks it's not an actual drug operation. They're setting up outside too early for a dope crew, and most of the crews up here have gone hydroponic. Hydro THC levels are in the twenty to thirty percent range, and in some places hydro farmers can trade their dope ounce for ounce for coke. Why go outside at all? But some growers up here realize the drug teams have limited manpower, so they're setting up decoys, hoping to draw law enforcement resources to surveillance on dummy operations."

TCH was short for delta-9-tetrahydrocannabinol, the ingredient in marijuana that produced psychotropic effects. "The team's encountered decoys before?"

"Increasingly."

"Some crews set up a decoy and you happened to stumble onto it? And then they beat the shit out of you to add to the authenticity? Bullshit."

"Too many other things to think about to worry about it," she said.

"Have you talked to the partner of the dead guy recently?"

"I told him to stop calling me all the time and to talk to Friday because it's her case."

"He was insistent with you, then nothing? We haven't heard from him."

"Normal mourning progression?" she offered.

"The deceased . . . how much do you know about him?"

"Squat. I interviewed the partner at the bridge and gave the tape to Mike Millitor. Not my case, right?"

"I'll talk to Mike."

"Did I screw up?"

Typical of the most competent officers to continually question their own performance, he thought. "No."

"Cool. How's little Mar?"

"Going through a stage."

"Really."

"She has a vocabulary of two words. It's hard to have a meaningful conversation with your grandpa when your vocabulary amounts to two words."

"Enjoy it," Grinda said. "Soon the words will come in paragraphs—torrents of paragraphs and words. Your life will never be the same again."

"It's good to be the grandpa," Service said.

Grinda went inside.

Service called Friday. "It's Grady. Did you and Mike do a report on the dead man at the bridge?"

"Early on. He and his pal live in Indianapolis. The Marion County, Indiana badges interviewed the widow for us. Her statement is in the files. Ask Mike."

"You were pretty funny this morning," he said.

"Nobody reacts the way I do. I won't blame you if it's too much for you to deal with. The first time it happened to me, I thought I was going crazy. I talked to my doctor and he just laughed, told me I probably release more endorphins than normal."

This was a real thing? "How's the reading going?"

"It's probably a waste of time, but it's good to finish what you start, right?"

"Depends on what it is."

"Is something wrong?"

"The Art Lake lawyer called back. He was polite but made it clear we can't get into Art Lake without a warrant."

"The proverbial probable-cause hurdle."

"There it is," he said. "Are you absolutely certain about Last Carde, Tuesday?"

"Aren't you?"

"I just don't understand how Art Lake fits anything we've got going. I feel it and I sense it, but I can't see it."

"The wolf tree?" she said.

"Not on their property."

"I know," she said. "You want to come over?"

"You've got reading to finish."

"I can read and share space at the same time."

"Thanks anyway."

"Jello-O mode anxiety?"

"Are you kidding?"

"Good night, Detective Service."

"Good night, Detective Friday."

40

Iron River, Iron County

THURSDAY, JUNE 8, 2006

Service sent an e-mail to the Marquette lab, asking that the chain of custody on the gold dust be reviewed. The samples had been sent to Gabby, and pressing by e-mail was all he could do short of driving up there and doing a physical search that would just piss off everyone.

The transcription of Grinda's interview with the dead man's partner, the individual who had discovered the body, was next on his agenda. It made for interesting reading.

> GRINDA: You guys came up here to fish?
> MR. TIMBO MAGEE: [hereafter TM]: Jimbo and I live in Big Nap, and we'd never heard of the Paint until that pamphlet showed up. Usually we fish Tennessee and West Virginia, or even North Arkansas. But the Paint looked interesting, so we decided to drive up and give it a go.
> GRINDA: Big Nap?
> TM: Ya know, Indianapolis? Actually, we live in Speedway, but it's all Big Nap.
> GRINDA: You mentioned a pamphlet?
> TM: It's in my truck; you want to see it?
> GRINDA: Please. I'll make a copy and give yours back to you. Where are you staying?
> TM: Golden Lake Campground.
> GRINDA: Tell me what happened today.
> TM: Jimbo and me parked at the bridge. I went through the woods to get around the holes, and he went upstream.
> GRINDA: Did you hear the shotgun?
> TM: (Shakes his head) There was too much river noise to hear *anything*.
> GRINDA: Speedway?

Service grinned. She was asking questions down one line, then jumping to another line to keep him off balance. *Grinda is good!*

> TM: A little west of downtown—you know, home of the Indy 500?

GRINDA: Indianapolis is a long drive from here.

TM: You got that right. Are you people gonna call Magahy and tell her?

GRINDA: Magahy?

TM: Jimbo's wife.

GRINDA: Notifications will be made.

TM: I could do it. I mean, it feels a little bit my fault, hear what I'm sayin'... that we come up here in the first place.

Service underlined certain passages in the transcript and passed his copy to Friday.

"Claims he never heard of the Paint," she said. "Then he says, 'I went through the woods to get around the holes.' " She looked up at him with questioning eyes.

"If he's never heard of the Paint or been here, how did he know there were holes downstream of the bridge? They aren't visible from the bridge."

"Good question," he said.

She started rereading the transcript.

"Do we have the report from the Marion County people?" he asked Millitor, who dug in a folder and handed it to him.

The report was short and to the point: 1520 EST, 4-30-06, 5700 White Horse Drive, Speedway, Indiana. Senior Detective Woodrow Agnew, Speedway Metropolitan Police Department. "I drove to Mr. Macafee's home on White Horse Drive to inform Mr. Macafee's wife of his death. She met me at the door and informed me that her husband (Jimbo Macafee, 41) had driven to Upper Peninsula, Michigan, three days before (e.g., April 27). Mr. Timbo Magee, Jimbo's partner (age 32), left two days before her husband for unspecified business in the Milwaukee area. They were to meet up in Michigan to fish for trout. Mrs. Macafee (age 29) reacted normally and emotionally when informed of her husband's death. I got water for her and tried to calm her to find out if there was someone who could come stay with her, but she told me she is alone. Her husband and Mr. Magee are owners of Real Stuff Sporting Goods in Speedway. The business was started by Mrs. Macafee's late father, who sold it to she and her husband four years ago. Mr. Magee joined them as a partner last year. Mrs. Macafee was distraught because she said she had to nearly throw her husband out to get him to take some time off to go trout fishing. According to her, Mr. Macafee is a workaholic who does not like to be away. Macafee and Magee work together, and when both are away, she runs the establishment. She says she grew up working the business. Like riding a bicycle."

Service looked at Friday. "The wife said the men departed and drove separately. Take another look at Grinda's transcript."

She read silently. "Magee says 'We decided to drive up.' He doesn't say they drove *together*."

"But it sounds that way in context. *We* didn't know about the river, got the booklet, we decided to try it, *we* drove up. Everything is we."

"It's probably nothing."

"I also wonder about that last statement of Magee's—how he feels like it's a *little* bit his fault."

"Look at the notification report. The wife says *they* had to talk the vick into going."

"I know, but it just seems a little too gratuitous."

"You can't analyze every word someone says."

"Don't want to analyze everything—just the stuff our guts say to question. I'm going to call Detective Agnew and talk to him."

There were office and cell phone numbers at the bottom of the report. The detective answered on the first ring. Service explained who he was. "Got a few minutes to talk about the interview with Mrs. Macafee?"

"It's your dime, and I don't mind thinking some on Magahy Macafee."

Calls her by first name. Why? "Memorable lady?"

"World-class looker, if you like women. Which I do."

"Seems like she had to convince her husband to take the trip."

"Seems like, and I bet I know how," Agnew said. "She called him, and I quote, a 'work-jerk.' "

This was not in the report. *How much else had Agnew excised or ignored.* "Jokingly?"

"There was a smile on her face, but it didn't sound all that playful to me."

"Her husband's partner left two days before him. They drove separately."

"She called Magee *our* partner."

"She seem broken up?"

"You know, the usual burst of tears, red eyes, some snot. I got her a glass of water."

"Is there a reason you noted ages in your report?"

"Mrs. Macafee's the live-wire type. I got the feeling hubby wasn't."

"Did she say why they took on a partner?"

"I quote: 'To infuse cash to enable us to grow.' "

"Happy marriage?"

"Are any?"

"Have you had calls from Mr. Magee?"

"Not really."

"He called here a lot, right after it happened—to Conservation Officer Grinda, our first responder. The case team hasn't heard from him or from the widow since."

"I had one call from Magahy asking when the body can come home. I explained the rules. She didn't seem too happy."

"When was this?"

"Couple of days after the notification."

"You tell her about disposition of the body when you notified her?"

"SOP."

"Have you been to their store?"

"No reason."

Service made a decision. "We might want to drive down there and talk to Mr. Magee and Mrs. Macafee."

"True what I heard, it was a booby trap?"

"Where'd you hear that?"

"From the widow."

How did she know? "When?"

"When she called about the body. She was weighing closed versus open casket, wanted to know how bad off hubby's body would be."

Magee was back home by then. Did Grinda tell him about the booby trap? Had he seen it that day?

"Okay if we drive down? We'll give you a bump if we do."

"Works for me," Detective Agnew said. "That widow's major eye candy."

Service went outside for a cigarette and Friday and Millitor went with him.

"Why don't we just smoke in the office?" Millitor said. "We're all out here all the time."

"Our hosts wouldn't like it," Friday told him, and, "plus, I don't smoke."

Service related his conversation with the Speedway detective. "Something about the widow and the partner is bugging me," he told them. *Could be you're reaching,* he cautioned himself. *But if you don't reach, you can't get the brass ring.*

"You guys ever been to Indianapolis?" Service asked.

"Got a third cousin lives down there," Millitor said.

"I'm thinking there should be a chat with the partner and the widow."

"When do we leave?" Friday asked.

"Not we—you and Mike. This homicide stuff's your ballpark."

"You?"

"Not sure."

"That again," she said with a smile, and went inside, talking animatedly with Millitor. Service went to the radio in the Tahoe and turned his channel to District One's frequency. "Three One Twenty, Twenty Five Fourteen."

"Go," Grinda said.

"Got your cell?"

"Affirmative."

"Give me a bump."

"Three One Twenty."

The cell phone buzzed and Service answered and said, "Did you talk to the vick's partner about the device?"

"Negative, and I told the techs not to say anything to anyone either. Anything else?"

"Thanks," he said, hung up, and went back into the post.

"That trip to Indianapolis . . . I think I'll join you two."

Millitor said, "No need for all of us. I'll stay here in case someone needs to contact the team."

"What about your third cousin?"

"A regular See-You-Next-Tuesday," Millitor said with a grin.

41

Speedway, Indiana

FRIDAY, JUNE 9, 2006

Real Stuff Sporting Goods was in the Turbocharger Strip Mall and marked only by a simple sign, nothing elaborate or expensive: Guns & Ammo, Fishing Supplies, Gunsmithing Services Available. The last part caught Service's attention.

The shop smelled and felt old, not new as the strip-mall location suggested. They walked inside between gun displays, mainly wooden crates with packing straw, marked Shop Special: Surplus Chinese SKS Carbines, Out-the-Door Special: $159.95.

Service knew about ten-round semiautomatic SKS rifles. The Type 56 had a nine-inch folding bayonet. Probably the shipment was genuine surplus from the 1950s or '60s, not ubiquitous recent Chinese knockoffs of their own stuff. How the hell did antique military surplus find its way into the middle of the U.S.? *Might be worth a call to BATF,* he told himself.

They were hardly into the store when a youngish man with gel-spiked hair and an earring approached with an earnest, welcoming smile and a gushing voice that made Service cringe. "Mornin', folks."

His red, white, and blue nametag said Timbo—I Support Our Troops

"Nice shop," Service said, taking out his badge and showing it. "Mr. Magee?"

"I see you that day?" the man asked Friday.

"That was Conservation Officer Grinda. I was elsewhere," she said.

"I swear there were two game wardens there."

"How're you doing?" Friday asked.

"Would do a lot better if you folks were here to tell me you busted somebody."

"Sorry," Friday said.

Service changed the subject. "Sign outside your shop says gunsmithing services are available; what exactly does that mean?"

"I'm the gunsmith, but I don't do any work here; the gunsmithing business is separate from Real Stuff."

"No offense, but you look a bit young to be a gunsmith."

"I grew up with guns. Been in business since I was sixteen, legally since twenty-one."

"Good skill to have," Service said.

"With fewer hunters these days, I sometimes wonder," the man said.

"How's Mrs. Macafee?" Friday asked.

"How do you think she'd be?" he challenged. "She's hurtin', but she'll make it."

"The SKS carbines . . . good price," Service said. "They look like real surplus."

"You know guns?"

"Sort of my job," Service said.

Magee chucked his head. "It's a helluva price."

"Where'd you get them?"

"Gun show deal."

"The ATF been inquiring?"

"Why?" Magee asked, looking surprised. "There's nothing wrong. I got the paperwork, and they ain't automatic."

"No offense. My job to ask," Service said.

The man looked irritated, straining to control it.

"Say," Service asked, "maybe you can answer a couple of questions that have come up about that day."

"I gave the officers my statement."

"Yessir, we appreciate that, but we just need to clarify a couple of points."

Magee shrugged. "Such as?"

"You and Jimbo had never been to the Paint before?"

"That's right."

"Neither of you?"

"I just said that, didn't I?"

"Okay. You left Jimbo at the bridge and went downstream."

"That's what I told the officer."

"How far downstream?"

"Two, three hundred yards, maybe," said Magee.

"While Jimbo went upstream?"

"Guess he didn't get all that far."

"How'd you guys decide who went where?"

"Just decided, I guess. I don't remember how. Does it matter?" asked Magee.

"Not really. You drove up to the U.P. separately, right?"

The man hesitated. "I told the officer that."

"You did, but the way you said it, it sounded like you meant you came up in the same vehicle."

"I never meant to say that."

"Okay. That's why we're here, to clarify," Service said.

"What difference does it make?"

"Probably none, but we've got supervisors who can be pricks about details, and when we get ready to seek the criminal indictment, the prosecutors will double-check everything."

"Does that mean you're getting close to an arrest?" asked Magee.

Service didn't answer, asking instead, "So Jimbo, he went upstream?"

"Like I said."

"Which means you went downstream?"

"Right."

"Through the woods?" Service asked.

"Yes."

"To get around the holes."

"I could've waded the edges, but why waste the energy or get into the water before you have to?"

"I fish for trout, too."

"Dry-fly man?" Magee asked.

"Pretty much whatever works."

Friday said, "You got a booklet."

"I gave it to the officer and she made a copy."

"Thanks, we have it. You got it in the mail, unsolicited?"

"Yes."

"Did it come to you or to Jimbo?" Friday asked.

The man looked confused. "I don't remember. We both get a lot of mail about destination fishing."

"Mrs. Macafee said she nearly had to kick her husband out the door to get him to take time off work," Friday said.

"Jimbo didn't know how to rest and relax. Work, work, work. Yeah, she convinced him, I guess. I guess wives know how to do that," the man added with a wink.

Friday turned to Service. "You want to talk to the Mad Russian?"

"What Mad Russian?" Magee asked.

"The one who sent the brochure. He's got mailing lists. It'll tell us whether you or Mr. Macafee got the brochure."

"What difference does it make?"

Service intervened. "If Macafee got it and he doesn't like to take off work, why'd he even mention it? Seems to me he'd just shit-can it."

Magee nodded. "Maybe it did come to me."

"If we call the Mad Russian, he can confirm it, and then it will make some sense."

"What will make sense?"

"You know . . . what you told Officer Grinda that day?"

The man looked tense. "I just told her what happened."

"You also said something about feeling a little bit guilty."

"That was just talk. He was my partner and friend."

"Of course, which makes it understandable. If you got the brochure and then talked him into it, I can see that. But if the brochure came to him, not you or Mrs Macafee, how could you convince him to go somewhere you didn't know about?"

"Yeah, I'm sure now it must've come to me."

"We'll check."

"Go right ahead. Is this going to take much longer? I've got a heap of work to do."

"Shouldn't be much longer," Friday said, adding, "I'm a plain old cop, not a game warden, and I don't know anything about fishing or any of that outdoor junk."

"Should try it," Magee the salesman said. "Could set you up with our starter kit and our cop discount."

"See," Friday said, "the part I don't understand is if you'd never been to the Paint River, how did you know to go through the woods to go around holes you had no way of knowing were there? Can you help me understand this?"

"There are holes there," he said.

Service said, "There are, but you can't see them from the bridge."

The man rubbed his jaw. "I could see 'em. So could Jimbo."

"He could?"

"Yeah, we talked about them, and he decided he didn't want to mess with downstream so I volunteered to go that way."

"A few minutes ago you said you couldn't remember how you guys made the decision."

"Now I remember."

"In my experience," Friday said, "when an individual loses a friend and partner, and they were the last to be with that person, every detail becomes nearly indelible."

"What's your point?"

"Just sharing my experience with you." She looked over at Service. "Anything else?"

"Not for the moment."

Friday looked at Magee. "I guess that's all for now. We'll be in touch as the evidence suggests."

"What evidence?"

"Sorry—just a generic term."

Service looked at the man. "You a good gunsmith?"

"I like to think so."

"You specialize in routine stuff, or do you do custom jobs?"

"I'm full-service. Depends on what kind of custom job you're talking about."

"I don't know; just a theoretical question, I guess."

"By the way," Friday said, "who told you there was a booby trap involved?"

"Booby trap?"

"Detective Agnew of the Speedway Metropolitan Police told us Mrs. Macafee asked about the booby trap."

Magee's eyes narrowed. "I've got no idea where she got that."

"Not from you?"

"Not from me."

Service nodded for Friday to leave, but he pivoted. "You ever make a booby trap, spring-rig a shotgun?"

"What the fuck is going on here!" the man exploded.

"We'll be in touch," Service said, and the two officers left the shop, stopped outside, and saw Magee hurrying toward the back of the store.

"He seems a bit stressed," Friday said.

"Think the widow might be getting a phone call?"

"Phone records often tell the tale. You need lunch, or shall we see Mrs. Macafee first?"

"I'm good for now," she said.

"You were good in there," he said.

"We make a pretty good team," she said.

"No Jell-O mode," he said.

"Well, we had to work today. Maybe that won't be true tomorrow."

Neither of them laughed.

Weren't you supposed to pick up your vehicle today?"Service asked.

I called them and told them it could be a day or two," Friday said. "Nice thing about being a cop. You don't have to provide a lot of detailed explanations."

42

Rocky Ripple, Indiana

FRIDAY, JUNE 9, 2006

The Macafees lived in a rural village seven or eight miles northwest of the town of Speedway. The modest ranch house sat on the banks of the White River, which had a bit of a muddy look but with a healthy current. In town there had been several vehicles with bumper stickers reading I'M NOT LOST—I LIVE HERE. The two officers looked at each other and shook their heads. Friday mouthed, "Indiana."

Having not called ahead, they pulled into the driveway just as a woman was getting into a white 2005 Lexus. She was wearing Asic trainers, and a turquoise leotard under a loose orange shirt. When they got out of the Tahoe and started toward her, she ignored them, hurriedly scrambled into her vehicle, and started the engine. Grady Service stood directly behind the Lexus and when she started to back up, he smacked the hood with the heel of his hand. She stopped.

Friday knocked on her window and the woman sat staring straight ahead, apparently trying to decide something. Service watched her take a cell phone out of her purse, press a speed-dial number, and start talking. Friday exchanged glances with Service, who said, "Let her finish. She's not going anywhere."

When she was done talking, the woman got out and exhaled. "I called my lawyer. I'm not going though this bullshit alone."

Service showed his badge. "What bullshit would that be?"

"My lawyer will talk for me," she said. "That's what he gets paid for."

Friday took out a small laminated card and began reading the woman her Miranda rights, but the woman said, "Wait! Why are you doing this? Oh my God!" and ran into the house.

"Kinda brittle," Friday said.

"Must be a little birdie gave her a call."

"A birdie with spiky feathers," Friday added, nodding.

Service said, "Let's call Agnew, see if he can break away and join us."

The local detective had begged off the earlier meeting, but now arrived—just ahead of Macafee's lawyer. They had just enough time to talk him through the interview with Magee and Mrs. Macafee's reaction to their arrival.

The lawyer introduced himself as Reuben Hocksinger, the widow's attorney and longtime family friend. "What's going on here?" the lawyer asked.

"We dropped by to talk to Mrs. Macafee about her late husband," Friday said, "and she went ballistic."

"She's been under a great deal of stress. We all have. Jimbo was a fine man."

"We're just doing our jobs," Friday said.

The lawyer said, "For out-of-state events like this, isn't it customary to ask local police to do the grunt work?"

"That's why Detective Agnew is here."

"Woody," the lawyer said.

"Mr. Hocksinger," the detective answered.

"You two know each other?" Friday asked.

Agnew shrugged.

Friday told the lawyer, "We just want to clarify some points with Mrs. Macafee."

"Fine," the lawyer said. "Let me go inside and calm Magahy down. Then we'll make some coffee and you folks can come on in and we'll talk like civilized people."

Service looked at Agnew after the lawyer was inside. "When you notified her of her husband's death, you sniffed something when you talked to her, eh?"

Agnew nodded. "But I couldn't quite get a steady bead on it. I drove over here last night. There was a vehicle here all night. I saw a picture in the house the day I talked to her. I ran the plate to be sure: It was Magee."

"Gives the term partner some deeper meaning," Service said.

"Not like the first time we seen it in our business,"Agnew said.

Ten minutes later the lawyer had them set up to talk at the dining room table, but as soon as coffee was served, Friday suggested they move into the attached garage, and the woman and her lawyer put up some resistance before relenting.

Smart, Service thought. *Great technique for an interview. Move people out of their physical comfort zone.*

In the garage, Friday said to the woman, "You told Detective Agnew that you and Mr. Magee had to convince your husband to take vacation time."

"What are you implying?" the lawyer asked.

"Let your client answer the question," Friday told the lawyer. "We're not in court."

The woman was trembling, rubbing her hands together. "I said that, yes. It was true."

"Okay," Friday said. "Mr. Magee told us about a brochure about the Paint River. That's the pamphlet that got the men interested in driving up there."

"I saw the brochure," the woman admitted.

"Okay. Did that brochure come to you, your husband, or his partner?"

"I don't remember. It was just around, and they got to talking about it. I told them they should just take some time and go and I'd hold down the fort."

"Okay, the brochure was 'just around.' "

"Yes."

"Okay," Friday said. "You told Detective Agnew about a booby trap; do you remember that?"

"I'm not sure."

"You're not sure you told him that?"

"I might have."

"So you knew there was a booby trap."

"I guess I did, and I was worried about how Jimbo would look—ya know, how he'd look for the funeral and all?"

"What kind of booby trap?" Friday asked.

"A gun-thingey, right?"

"A gun-thingey?"

"It was, wasn't it?"

"How did you know what it was?"

Hocksinger intervened. "Where's this going?"

"It's just a background question."

The lawyer looked at his client. "Mags?"

"Jimbo died by a gun, so the booby trap had to be a gun-thingey, right? Timbo told me."

"When did he tell you this?"

"I don't remember. Why is it important?"

"We just would like to understand the time frame."

"I really don't remember. Everything sort of runs together, ya know?"

Friday said, "I do know, and I'm sorry. You're doing fine. Timbo told you your husband was killed by a booby trap?"

"He said something like there mighta been a rigged gun-thingey, a booby trap."

"Might've been a rigged gun? His words?"

"Yes."

"Did he see it?"

"I don't know. You'll have to ask him. Jimbo *was* shot, right?"

"Did Timbo call you before we got here?"

She looked at her lawyer, who nodded, and said, "Yes."

"What did he say?"

"He said you guys were asking a lot of crazy questions, and you don't have a suspect, so you're desperately trying to nail someone so you'll look good."

"He said that?" Friday asked.

"Yes."

Friday said, "Are you sleeping with Mr. Magee, Mrs. Macafee?"

The woman's eyes opened wide. "That's not . . ."

"*Our* business?" Friday said. "Sure it is. If you're sleeping with your husband's partner and you both talk your husband into going fishing to a place he'd never been before, and he ends up dead, that's *exactly* our business."

"It's some sort of nut-group," Mrs. Macafee said.

"What nut-group is that?"

"I don't know—Timbo told me."

"Are you or are you *not* sleeping with him?" Friday repeated.

"No, I'm not."

"His vehicle was here all last night," Detective Agnew said.

"We're finished here," the lawyer said. "Any more questions, you'll have to make it formal. This interview is terminated."

"*His* idea to spend the night?" Friday asked the woman." Or yours because you needed company?

Magahy Macafee looked at her lawyer, who held up his hands and shook his head.

"Okay, we've slept together—what of it?"

"Before your husband died?"

"What difference does that make?"

Friday switched directions abruptly. "So Timbo leaves two days before your husband to do business in Milwaukee."

"What's that got to do with me sleeping with him?"

"Did you sleep with him before he left?"

"Yes!"

"Timbo or Jimbo?"

The woman looked flustered and sighed. "Not at the same time. I'm not one of *those*."

Friday asked, "Do you know what business he had to do in Milwaukee?"

"He didn't say."

"Did he call you while he was gone?"

"I don't remember."

"Meaning you didn't hear from him for what, five, six days?"

"Time's all discombobulated," the woman said. "Ya know?"

"You realize we're going to look at phone records: yours, your husband's, Timbo's."

The lawyer took his client by the arm and pushed her back into the house. "This is over," he said, slamming and latching the door.

Service walked out of the garage and lit a cigarette.

"What're you thinking—the partner's good for this?" Agnew asked.

"Not sure."

"He says that a lot," Friday said. "My gut is telling me they're both involved. We'll need a warrant for phone records. You want to look down here? Could be a prepaid throwaway involved."

Service said, "The call had to come to someone somewhere, if there was a call. Let's do some more spadework before we up the ante on this thing."

"I'll help you with the warrant for the phone records," Agnew said.

"Magistrates down here picky?"

"An experienced cop learns which ones aren't."

Friday said, "Can you talk to Timbo, see if he can show receipts for gas, hotels, a schedule for meetings in Milwaukee, and if he had business, call and confirm times, dates, length, all that?"

Agnew said, "Are you thinking he skipped Milwaukee, headed over your way to set things up?"

"Let's not get ahead of ourselves," Friday said. "He claims he was on business in Milwaukee. Let's give him the chance to prove it. If he can't, we'll move to the next step."

"You two headed all the way back today?" Agnew asked.

"Nope. Morning. Drive's gonna take us about eighteen hours from here."

They had rooms at a Red Roof Inn, Indianapolis Speedway, a mile from the world-renowned track, and they went to the Ginza Japanese Steakhouse, north of the track, for an early dinner. Nondescript place, with inadequate parking, but they were after the lunch and before the dinner crowd. There were no small tables, the place designed more for groups than couples. It was like sitting around a bullring watching the chef do his thing. When no others were seated, the chef came out and began to flip and twirl his knives, and Service said, "I'm sure it's a great show, chef, but save it for the dinner crowd."

The man looked at him. "You sure?"

"Yep." Service looked at the menu and said, "Two spicy tuna sushis, two small salads with sesame dressing."

"Drinks?"

He looked at Friday. "I get to choose? Japanese beer," she said. "It's not very romantic here," she said.

"We're still working."

"You seem troubled."

"My gut's still churning. If Magee and the wife conspired to pop hubby, we'll get them, but what's all the rest of the anti-fishing shit about, and how come Mrs. Macafee and Timbo knew about it?"

"What are you thinking—that Magee is behind the whole deal?"

"You met him. You think he's that smart? I'm wondering when the *FBI Bulletin* warned of the Let Fish Live Free threat?"

"How would he get it?"

"With the Internet you can get all kinds of shit," he said, or maybe it came through Trout Unlimited or the Federation of Fly Fishers, warning their members. I just want to run it down, and once we get that figured out, we'll see where we are."

"Travel day tomorrow, right?"

"Yep," he said.

"I've got a good idea where we'll be tonight," she said. "Let's tell the chef to get the lead out."

43

L'Anse, Baraga County

SATURDAY, JUNE 10, 2006

They drove straight through to Iron Mountain, stopping only for pee breaks, gas, and sandwiches. Friday collected her repaired car a day late and headed for Marquette for the weekend. Service headed north to L'Anse to find Sheriff Pinky Barbeaux to find out why he'd never faxed license numbers from Art Lake. Was he hiding something?

Being a Saturday, Barbeaux was not in his office. The county dispatcher would say only that the sheriff was "Oot, eh."

Barbeaux might very well be out on patrol with his people, but it seemed more likely he was pressing flesh at a local watering hole. It was impossible to know for certain, but eventually he'd have to head for home. *Staking out a colleague sucks, but if the sheriff isn't reachable or going to return my phone calls, what choice do I have?*

The sheriff's house was in the center of Hermansville, an island of high ground surrounded by hardwoods and a cedar swamp that stretched for miles to the south and east. Barbeaux's place was two stories, in good repair, with an eleven-foot-high wire deer fence around his garden, neat piles of firewood somewhat depleted by last winter, a worn Jeep Eagle, handpainted camouflage, tucked along the outside wall of the garage. A high-tech antenna stuck up from the house roof, suggesting a powerful base radio.

The 800 interrupted his thoughts. "Twenty Five Fourteen, Thirty Two Twenty."

Junco Kragie. "Twenty Five Fourteen."

"Just rolling into town from the south. Want coffee?"

"Twenty Five Fourteen, affirmative."

Kragie pulled alongside him, nose to tail, and passed across a dented thermos. "You waiting on Pinky?"

"I need to talk to him."

"Won't be home tonight. His wife left with a guy who owns a trucking company in Kremlin, Nebraska. Pinky's girlfriend is Sulla Kakabeeke. She's a Troop sergeant out of Baraga, lives out on Skanee Road. Pinky's at her place on Saturdays nights if she's not on duty."

"Kakabeeke got an address?"

"Old farmhouse painted lilac." Kragie gave him the address and directions.

"You ever creep the Art Lake perimeter?" Service asked.

"Coupla times."

"Any breaks in the wire?"

"Fixed quick if there are. The folks there seem to take maintenance seriously."

"Do their own work?"

"Don't know."

Service said, "Seems to me somebody around here knows their way around Art Lake. People up here *hate* fences. If they don't cut them, they climb them. Somebody around here knows something, or this is the most secure facility in the entire U.P."

"Nobody comes to mind," Junco Kragie said. "But I'll noodle on it some."

Service found the lilac farmhouse on Skanee Road, as Kragie described it, and the sheriff's SUV parked in the loop driveway.

He was greeted at the door by a short-haired woman in shorts with a square jaw, huge eyes, and the muscled legs of a power jock. "You lookin' for Pinky?" she asked, and pointed at a room. She didn't introduce herself.

Barbeaux was stretched out on a couch and made no effort to sit up. "You're won-drin' 'boot your fax. Figured I'd be seein' youse," the retired DNR lieutenant said.

"I was expecting plate numbers."

"Well, I did some thinkin' on that. That day I was out there, I wrote 'em down with the intent of running them, but it occurred to me I had no reason to do that, eh. If I did, it would be invasion of privacy or me misusing my power as an elected public official. Seems to me abuse of power would apply to you too. Don't blame you for wantin' the numbers, but get me somethin' convincin' on 'em and you'll get the numbers. I intended to call and talk to youse about this. Sorry."

"You want me to get something on people I don't even know?"

"See da problem?"

"Sorry to interrupt," he told Sgt. Kakabeeke as he was leaving. He heard her following close behind him.

"Pinky's a great guy, but he's got this overpowering need to be liked, ya know? And, he wants especially to be liked by a certain individual, maybe?"

Gut-thought: Gorsline had warned him off.

"But me," Kakabeeke said, "I don't know nothing from nobody. Give me some time and I'll get the numbers you're looking for."

"You know what I want?"

"Part of wanting to be liked means the need to talk to someone. Right now, that's me. He told me about the numbers. He tells me everything."

"Thanks," Service said.

"That officer of yours—Denninger? Is she okay?"

"Pins in her ankle, but the docs say she'll recover."

"She gets back, have her look me up. Girl cops up here gotta stick together."

"I'll do that."

Barbeaux had been a great game warden and leader of game wardens. What had changed? Holding elected office? Little government financial support for his operation? Probably a little of everything. People changed, conditions changed—even change changed, the rate, the kind, everything. *You spend your life in green and gray, you stay green and gray. It's like once a marine, always a marine.* He found Barbeaux's behavior both shameful and disconcerting.

Service tried to call his granddaughter, but there was no answer from Karylanne, and as he cruised past the entrance to Art Lake, he turned around and did a second drive-by, looking for something, something not there, something that wasn't, anything, but nothing suggested itself, and his belly continued to insist this place was a key.

There are numerous ways to get inside a facility, some questionable but all technically legal. Heard shots. Saw a moving light inside the fence at night, thought I smelled smoke. First you get inside, then you come up with a rationale. The risk of backlash from such entry was not insignificant, but he'd done it before, stretched the rules plenty of times, and made solid cases because of it. *Not this time. Use your brain, pick everything apart, piece by piece. Go home, get your animals and bearings, regroup. What's the opposite of technically legal?* he wondered on his way to Lehto's clinic to pick up his dog and cat, who hissed and growled at each other all the way to Slippery Creek.

Art Lake takes maintenance seriously, he kept thinking, not sure why.

McCants came by as he sat on the porch with a glass of inexpensive but good Crane Lake merlot.

"Bottle's open on the counter," he said.

She came out with a glass and sat beside him while Newf prodded her with her nose and wouldn't relent until she scratched under the dog's chin.

Service raised his glass. "Sarn't."

McCants touched her glass to his and grinned. "Feels weird."

"Wait until you've got eight officers and all of them whining about their problems."

"I'm actually looking forward to that."

"That's what every new sergeant thinks."

"You pissed or disappointed?"

"About what? You'll do a great job."

"What about the Mosquito?"

"It's bigger than you or me. It'll be fine."

"I'll miss it."

"Once you cross that bridge, forget the U.P. and the past. Keep your mind on there, now, and what's next. We like to make out how special we are up here, but every county in this state has more than enough assholes, and some of them have a lot more assholes per capita than we do."

"Seen the kiddo recently?"

"Last month, but we talk on the phone."

"Those're conversations I'd love to hear," McCants said sarcastically, resting her head against a wall. "Grady, you need to make this place a real home. It's like a damn outpost on Hadrian's Wall."

"Feels like home to me."

"Whatever," she said, not bothering to hide her disapproval.

44

Slippery Creek Camp

SATURDAY, JUNE 10, 2006

Friday called late Saturday afternoon. "You want guests?"

"Plural?"

"Shigun and me. I'm giving my sis the day and night off. I'll drop him off tomorrow night on my way to Iron River."

"There's not much here in the way of creature comforts," he warned her.

"Me, I don't need much, and Shigun's a baby, so what does he know? I finished my reading," she added.

"And?"

"I don't know for sure. We can talk."

His refrigerator was empty and his freezer full of things he had no interest in. He drove down to Rapid River to Viau's Northland, got a bottle of Chianti, makings for a salad, some frozen salmon steaks that cost a small fortune, fresh asparagus to grill, and some of Viau's freshly made horseradish.

He and Newf fished for a couple of hours mid-afternoon, but no bugs were hatching and no fish rising, and he hated dredging bottom with nymphs under a strike indicator. "Skunked," he told the dog, who looked unsympathetic.

Friday arrived with her car packed with baby stuff, and the baby tucked in a car seat like a worm in a cocoon. She wore shorts and a skimpy halter and had her hair pulled back and tied off with a short ponytail. She had two bags with diapers, marked arrivals and departures, and a bag of miscellaneous items about whose function he was largely clueless. There was also a box with cans of Enfamil Lipil baby formula. Another bag contained bath materials, including soft towels and wash rags. Finally, a small bag with Tuesday's clothes.

By the time he got things transferred to the house, Shigun was making a ruckus. "Like his mommy," Friday said with a smile. "When it's time to eat, it's time to eat, no arguments, no compromises, just get me my food, dammit!" She stared at the footlockers with the mattresses on them and raised an eyebrow.

Service held the baby and rocked him while Friday prepared the formula. She did everything with no wasted effort. The baby alternated squawking with staring up at him with wide eyes.

"I'll feed him, get him down for his nap, and then it will be just-us time."

Cat watched the intruding baby from a distance. Newf followed wherever the baby went, sniffing at the infant. In the feline world there were two kinds of creatures: those you could kill and eat, and those who could kill and eat you.

"I was going to breast-feed," Friday said, "but it's just not practical."

"Better for the baby?"

"Some say. Were you a tit baby?"

He shrugged. "No."

When the baby was finally down, she sat on the porch with him and exhaled. "Okay, our turn."

"For what?"

"Whatever you want."

"What about dinner?"

"Shigun will be up in about two hours. I'll give him a snack then. I'll give him his dinner after we eat."

"Before you head back?"

She looked at him and laughed. "Head back *where, ya big dope*? The whole idea is to spend the night *here*—with *you*."

"Did you see a bed?"

"I didn't have to. Elza warned me about your barbaric lifestyle. There's an inflatable mattress in the trunk. I didn't drive all the way out here to the sticks just to turn around, go back, and sleep alone . . . buster."

"Sleep, as in the euphemism?"

"Sleep, as in the all-inclusive word for night activity."

She threw her arms around him and held tight, and they both laughed.

"You said you read Thigpen's book."

"*Books*—three of them. In the first one she talks about a crazy old man from town having a secret place thirty miles north of Crystal Falls and east of Norway Lake. In her story the man has a grove of burl maple trees he carves into beautiful things, from which he makes a lot of money from

Chicago and Minneapolis art dealers. The thing is, he refuses to say where his place is, and nobody in town ever sees one of his carvings, so there's a lot of suspicion and speculation. The little girls spy on him and watch him come and go. He rarely comes back in less than ten days, and always leaves early in the mornings."

"Washington Lincoln as model?"

"Possibly, but that location she's talking about is sort of near Art Lake, right?"

He grabbed a DeLorme and looked. "Yep."

"Could you make it from Elmwood to there on foot?"

"In the old days, that was pretty much the only way people traveled: Foot or canoe, snowshoes in winter, boots in summer. People walked hundreds of miles to do things they needed to do, and twenty- to thirty-mile trips weren't even remarkable enough to mention."

"You get the license plate numbers?" she asked.

"The sheriff's had a sudden onset of legality and morality. Bottom line: no probable cause, no plate numbers." He omitted Kakabeeke's promise.

"Assuming Art Lake's what she's alluding to in her books, we're thinking gold, not burl maple, right?"

"I wish I knew."

"What options do we have?"

"Not many. One thing I'm going to have to do is go back to where I found sample six and take a more thorough look around. You want to go? Might be out there three days, maybe more."

"Excluding the morning fire show, one night wasn't all that bad, and if we're comfortably prepared, why not? We *are* going to be prepared, right?"

"Define comfortable."

"Let's get something straight. Until I met you, my idea of roughing it meant a four-star hotel with Jacuzzi and room service."

"All our stars will be overhead," he said sheepishly.

"Okay, plan B . . . promise me one thing: no porcupine livers, or, failing that, something more to go with them."

"How about fresh brook trout?"

"Never tasted brook trout."

He rolled the asparagus in sea salt and olive oil, grilling it until it had singe marks. He grilled the salmon filets and served them with mustard-horseradish sauce, topped with thin slices of unseeded Thai peppers. They drank the Chianti, which he'd opened an hour before dinner.

The first time she tasted the wine she closed her eyes and said, "Oh my. Definitely not your Chateau Traileur Parc from Wal-Mart."

He laughed out loud.

They put the baby in a porta-crib not far from the inflated mattress and Newf immediately curled up near the crib.

When Friday took off her clothes and slid under the sheets with him, it felt like she was laminating him, and it felt wonderful.

After making love, she whispered, "Sooner or later we have to talk about what all this means."

"All *this*?"

"Right—what it means to us. I don't jump in and out of bed with men."

"Me neither," he said.

She poked him in the ribs. "I'm serious, and I'm nervous."

"Me too." Flippant and dismissive, but he understood what she meant. This felt like something more than he had anticipated, and whatever it was, it felt pretty good—her companionship, the sex, shared work, her smarts, even Jell-O mode, which was unlike anything he'd ever encountered before. As he fell asleep he wondered what condition she'd be in tomorrow. "No pooping," he whispered to the baby.

45

Baragastan

MONDAY, JUNE 12, 2006

Tuesday Friday was at the post with Mike Millitor and Service was headed in their direction when Junco Kragie called on the cell phone. "The name Tahti ring any bells for youse?"

Helveticus "Hell" Tahti had been one of the kings of U.P. violators before Allerdyce and his clan had ascended to the top of the rubbish heap. "Long dead," Service said.

"Got a grandson named Rigel."

"One of your regulars?"

"No. He served in Iraq and was discharged by the marines last fall. Technically he lives on the family homestead on Sidnaw Creek, near the old German POW camp."

German prisoners of war had been lodged at the camp near Sidnaw, and at other former Civilian Conservation Corps camps around the U.P. Some of the German soldiers actually came back to the U.S. and became citizens after repatriation as POWs. "Technically?"

"Yeah—he owns the property, but he may have gone OTG."

OTG—off the grid—meant living in the bush. In the wake of Vietnam there had been several pockets of bush-vets in the U.P., men who couldn't or didn't want to find a way back into society. They were all gone now, dead, assimilated, or moved on. "What about it?"

"I started thinking about Art Lake and remembered I've seen young Tahti out that general way a couple times, and I've heard from others that they've seen him skulking around out there too."

"Out *what* way?"

"I seen him near Bog Lake, south of Forest Highway 2108. That's only a couple of crow-fly miles from the general Art Lake area. Others have seen him out there."

"Where's his homestead property?"

"Caliper Lane, Sidnaw, not sure of the number. It's just west of town. Twenty can probably run an address for you."

"Thanks, Junco. I'll follow up."

"It's a long shot, but the best I can do," Kragie said. "Just not many people out that way."

Service knew that Lansing—Station Twenty—didn't like working from incomplete data, but depending on the dispatcher on duty, he'd probably get some help. Some Lansing dispatchers would do back flips to help officers in the field. Others treated radio calls like impositions and unwanted intrusions into their lives. If he were chief, he would order every dispatcher to spend a week a year in the field with conservation officers to get a feeling for why their jobs existed in Lansing.

"Station Twenty, Twenty Five Fourteen."

"Station Twenty," a female dispatcher responded.

"Run a name for an address and check RSS and CCH."

"Go ahead, Twenty Five Fourteen."

"Name is Rigel Tahti. First name, Robert-Ida-George-Edward-Lincoln, Rigel. Last name, Tahti, Tom-Adam-Henry-Tom-Ida, Rigel Tahti. Twenty Five Fourteen."

"Our computer's a little cranky today," the dispatcher complained mildly.

Service understood. If any other device so critical to human endeavors operated with the reliability of computers, those devices would be recalled by government as shams and scams. Computer companies were allowed a different level of reliability than just about anything else he knew.

Several minutes passed before Lansing radioed back. "Twenty Five Fourteen, Rigel Tahti, eleven-six-eighty, six-five, two-thirty, brown and brown. We have a plate for an '05 Silverado, silver in color, nil, null, and valid."

Nil meant no hits on LEIN, the Law Enforcement Information Network; null meant no outstanding warrants in the system; and valid meant the man's vehicle was properly and legally registered. Everything about the man seemed legal. "Twenty, CCH negative?"

"Affirmative, Twenty Five Fourteen. RSS coming up. Stand by one."

Another few minutes passed before the dispatcher came back on the radio. "RSS shows clear, Twenty Five Fourteen."

Which meant Tahti had no licenses this year for fishing, small game, trapping, deer, nothing, which made it pretty tough to legally live OTG. "Twenty, can you look back?"

"How *far* back, Twenty Five Fourteen?"

"Far as you can go."

"Not quite to Noah and the flood," Lansing said with uncharacteristic humor. Dispatchers and officers were expected to keep radio transactions professional—defined as formal and brief, not chatty and collegial.

Twenty finally came back. "Took him back to '98, Twenty Five Fourteen," the dispatcher said. "Nothing there."

Odd. What the heck was Kragie thinking? "Twenty Five Fourteen clear."

Tahti had not bought DNR licenses in the past eight years—and he would have been eighteen in 1998. Did he go straight into the marines and spend seven years on active duty? The media was reporting that marines, airmen, soldiers, and sailors were being stop-lossed, held involuntarily past their enlistments because of manpower shortages and recruiting shortfalls. How had Tahti gotten out?

Grady Service called Kragie on the cell phone, hoping he'd have a signal, and when the other officer answered, he asked, "Where'd Tahti go to high school?"

"L'Anse. Lived with an aunt named Pechtola. His old man died while he was in grade school, and he moved to his aunt's, his mum's sister. His mum cut out years before with another man."

"You seem to know a lot about him. RSS shows nothing, and he's clean on CCH."

"He was famous around here, a minor celebrity, the all-everything jock. All-state football three years. Tech, Northern, St. Norbert, Lake State, and Grand Valley all wanted him, but he enlisted instead."

"Word is that the military is holding everyone past their enlistment date. How'd he get out?"

"He's a Tahti."

Implying what? Kragie's attitude puzzled him. "You ever bust him?"

"We're paid to be professional not suicidal."

"What's that supposed to mean?"

"The kid was scary."

Scary? "Did he hunt and fish?"

"Word was. Consider his genes."

"But you never had contact with him."

"Happily."

"Theres no RSS record of licenses going back to '98."

"Does that sound like a Tahti or what?" Kragie shot back.

"Did the kid have *any* problems with local law enforcement?"

"Grady, Tahti's the size of a front door and tough as they come. When he played, L'Anse won, a man among boys, a warrior amont pissant wannabes."

Translation: Local deps and Troops had overlooked some of the star athlete's transgressions? High school sports in the U.P. were important—sort of a proxy war between towns for bragging rights. *Probably Pinky Barbeaux or his undersheriff would know more about the young man, but that avenue of inquiry is dry for the moment.*

"You gonna look for Tahti?" Kragie asked.

"Maybe."

"You do, be real careful," his colleague said. "Tahti's Finndian."

Meaning a blend of Finn and Native American. "He favor one side or the other?"

"Double dose of both, I think."

"On tribal rolls?"

"Probably qualifies, but Keweenaw Bay blackballed the hull family back in Hell's time."

No surprise there. Hell Tahti had been a violent man, stabbed to death outside a Covington tavern, the circumstances never fully established, and no arrests ever made. Hell's late son was an unknown, and the grandson seemed to have inherited the family's rep, short on facts, which was not unusual in the U.P. Gossip here sometimes created reputations not supported by facts or reality. *Probably that way everywhere,* Service told himself. "Thanks, Junco."

"I'm serious, Grady. That kid scared hell out of me, and I don't mind saying so. Didn't talk much. Just struck."

Service rubbed his eyes. "Struck who?"

"You understand what I'm saying," Kragie said conspiratorially.

He didn't understand and didn't feel like hearing more. "Later, Junco."

He had several choices. Start at the Tahti property in Sidnaw, or in the area where the former marine had been seen. He delayed a decision and called Iron River to talk to Friday. "I've got a possible lead on someone who might know something about Art Lake. It's a long shot." He gave her the name. "Can you call Baraga County and the L'Anse Troop post and see what their history is with the kid?"

"Is this one of those see-ya-sometime calls?"

"Not exactly. I just don't know how long I'm going to be tied up here."

She laughed. "I talked to the wire company in Milwaukee this morning. They say the wire sample we got off the river matches a stolen lot. I'm not sure where the heck that leaves us, but now we know. Maybe you ought to grab a good night's sleep and start fresh in the morning," she suggested.

"I'm here, I've got everything I need in the Tahoe. Besides, it's a work night."

"Did we ever discuss exceptions to the work-night rule?"

"Not that I recall."

"Okay then. That goes to the top of my to-do list. Who is it you want me to do the background check on?"

"A young man named Rigel Tahti."

"Rigel, like the star?'

There's a star called Rigel? "I guess." He filled her in on the boy and his family and Kragie's peculiar reactions.

"That OTG business doesn't sound like normal behavior," Friday said.

"That's true for most people."

"See you around?"

"Bet on it, and tell Mike where I am, okay?"

"He and I are driving out to Golden Lake campground to see if we can find out if Timbo Magee was there before the killing. The progress in all this is really slow," she added.

"We just have to keep on plugging," he told her. In his experience cases up here were rarely solved easily or quickly.

Grady Service kept two rucks in his Tahoe—a small one for his regular police work, and a much larger version for longtime pursuits and survival in the woods. It had been a while since he'd been in a sustained stalk, and he went through the pack to make sure he had everything he needed. What the pack kit didn't include was luck, and he knew he'd need this more than anything else. If he couldn't find Tahti, or if he did and the man knew nothing, he'd have to hope that a Troop sergeant named Kakabeeke would come through for him.

CHAPER 46

West Iron County

WEDNESDAY, JUNE 14, 2006

None of the cases were coming together, but Grady Service could feel in his gut that they were winnowing possibilities, and often this was all the progress you could hope for until a new piece of evidence or new meaning for something old suddenly lit the day and pointed you to an inescapable conclusion.

The Rigel Tahti lead was one he wanted to follow up. Before doing so, his gut nagged him to get back to the woods to the area where they had encountered the Willie Pete. He thought about going alone, but he had already asked Friday.

"You sure about this?" he said to her.

"Hell no, but you promised no porcupine entrails."

"Did you talk to Baraga County about Rigel Tahti?"

"Had problems with his grandfather, not young Tahti. I talked to the Troops and tribal cops—all the same story."

Why's Junco Kragie so negative about the Tahti boy?

"Are we headed for the same place?" Friday asked.

"Plan to start where we stopped. This time we'll drop your vehicle ahead of us and hike to it."

"Properly outfitted, right?"

"Define properly," Service said.

"I'm not joking."

"Me either."

She rolled her eyes and snorted.

Service left his truck in the same place as last time, but took a new and more direct route to where the "firestorm" had taken place. The fire had been relatively small, but its footprint was obvious. He still wondered if the fire had been intended to block their way or to attack them. He had no feeling one way or another.

Friday looked though the woods over ferns nearly as tall as her. "I doubt I'd ever get used to working out here," she said.

"It's an acquired taste," he said.

"I bet."

He aimed them in a general direction that continued the route of march from the previous rocky abutment on the crazy woman's property, which meant a long uphill slog. It was hot, and mosquitoes swarmed in the shade of the overhead canopy. Friday slapped at the insects but never complained, and she kept pace easily.

Moving along a gentle slope, Service slowed down and tried to work along the southern edge.

"Looking for rocks?" Friday asked.

"Yeah."

"Pet rocks?"

"With quartz veins. They should be visible."

"White?"

"Could be pinkish too."

"Game wardens are trained in geology?"

"Not one lick."

"What are you trained in?"

"Optimism," he said. "And determination."

"That's a curriculum?"

"Shut up and look for rocks, Tuesday."

• • •

They walked up to Friday's vehicle after 10:30 p.m. Service had found two more rocky protuberances. Both showed veins that seemed to have been removed, and in both locations he broke off samples from the small rock channels, put them in evidence bags, marked them, and stuffed them in his pack. The gap at the second site was sixteen inches wide in places, and he found some shards of white quartz, which he bagged.

"We're not going to spend the night in the woods?" Friday said. "No brook trout dinner?"

"Another time," he said.

"You spending the night with me?"

"No time. I'm going to drive over to Marquette, leave the evidence for assays. I want to be there when they open in the morning."

"Your sleep habits need serious attention," Friday said, taking off her pack.

"I've heard that."

"You'll be hearing it again," she said.

• • •

Personnel began to trickle into the state police lab at 0700. Service went with them and found most with eyes that were still slits.

A woman said, "You'd be?"

"Grady Service."

"And you've got more samples for assay, and you need the results ASAP, right?"

"You're psychic?"

"No, I'm Roxy, and I'm experienced in working with cops. A rush job on this will be a week to ten days. We have to farm out this sort of thing."

"Perfect," he said.

"Yeah," she said with a groan. "Peachy, too."

The woman seemed tired and, he guessed, overworked. Everyone who worked for the state carried a bigger workload nowadays, and he wondered if this had a negative effect on his own cases. State budgets had been cut to the bone. When you went past bone, you killed the patient. He wondered how close the state was to such an outcome and shuddered to guess.

47

Baragastan

THURSDAY, JUNE 15, 2006

Grady Service got the names of others who had seen Rigel Tahti and drove to the Bog Lake area to talk to two individuals.

According to Kragie, Asdis Henriksdottir worked at the casino in Baraga. She was forty-something, and Service immediately recognized the name as Icelandic. The short-haired woman was dressed in shorts and Birkenstock sandals, her toenails painted bright blue; she wore a halter top that didn't hide much, and lived in a year-round house on a forty-acre parcel off Norway Lake Road, where it intersected Forest Highway 2460.

"Officer Kragie told me you've seen Rigel Tahti out this way."

"I din't tell 'im dat so he'd go blabbin' it around, eh," she answered. "Youse know what people say about dem Tahtis: Get on dere wrong side and youse got youse a problem, hey."

"Ms. Henriksdotter."

"I ain't no *Mizz*. Youse can call me Asdis. The name means goddess in the old Norse language, or so my folks told me. I'm a Miss. I was married onct, but the hubby was a lazy bugger, so I sent 'im packin'."

"Rigel Tahti?" Service said, trying to get her back on track.

"Yeah, I seen him, okay? Fact is, I seen 'im coupla times a week, always in same place, 'boot quarter-mile below where da Norway Lake Road joins da Forest Highway. Dere's big bunch a hemlocks on west side of road. Seen him right dere. You want a drink, some coffee, somepin'?"

"No thanks."

"I work up casino. Youse gamble?"

"No."

She grinned. "No problem. You come see me sometime, won't be no gamble, eh?" She winked at him and he hurried to get away from her.

The second witness was also a woman, this one elderly, slow-moving and cautious.

"Mabel Tiles? I'm Detective Grady Service of the DNR. Officer Kragie told me you've seen Rigel Tahti around here."

The Tiles's place was south of where Henriksdottir had seen the man. It was small and didn't look like it was insulated for year-round occupancy. The woman had her hair bunched under a white kerchief, and wore a red plaid jacket and hiking boots that looked well used.

"Yes, I've seen him just north of here, by the hemlocks," she said. "He's stopped in here a couple of times, and made wood for me. Nice, polite young man."

"You're not afraid of the Tahtis?"

"You listen to gossip up here, you'd never meet anyone."

"When was the last time you saw him?"

"Yesterday he stopped by. Walks all the way from his place in Sidnaw."

"Does he say where he's going?"

"Nossir, he's not real talkative. I get the feeling he's a troubled young man."

"He was here. Did you see which way he walked when he left?"

"I walked out to the road with him."

Service asked him to show her, and she did. The condition of the tracks told him that her story of timing was accurate. Rather than start at the hemlock grove, he decided to start here and asked permission to leave his truck, and the woman had agreed.

The going was slow at first, and it took him four hours to cut fresh tracks, which moved steadily southeast from Bog Lake across low rises and ridges and kept a more or less steady course, veering only to avoid escarpments and the hazards of endless muskeg bogs. Mostly the trail stayed with contours, sometimes crossing open, rocky areas. But Grady Service was always able to locate traces again on softer ground or in weeds and grasses, and as he hiked he felt certain that the person ahead of him was neither trying to obscure his track, nor throw off followers. The boot print was the same here as at Tiles's place. *Has to be him.*

He wouldn't call it an easy trail to follow, but neither was it difficult. Overall it showed the tracks of someone who seemed to know where they wanted to go and was not paranoid about being followed, all of which didn't add up to OTG behavior.

Six hours after leaving his Tahoe, Grady Service saw a man sitting on a boulder, rendered orange and pale green by lichen patches. The man was staring out at an expanse of muskeg, black spruce, and wild cranberries. Using his binoculars Service saw that the man was clean-shaven, with long legs, a thick neck, and big black boots.

The man walked another two hours, the route finally ending at a cabin cut into the side of a hill and overlooking a beaver pond with black water. The cabin was made of blackened logs, its yellow chinking showing a dire need of serious attention. The metal roof was rusted orange-brown, but there was a shiny new metal chimney poking up.

Service estimated the cabin at twelve by eighteen feet. The man went inside, came back out, lit a cigarette, swatted at insects, and went back inside. Smoke soon began to snake from the metal chimney.

He had left the Tiles's place at 0900, and it was now going on 6 p.m. If Tahti had been at the Tiles's place yesterday, what had taken him so long to get here—if this was his intended destination, and not an intermediate stop? *No way to know until you talk to the man.* He found himself thinking about Tuesday and told himself to stop. It had been a long time since a woman had actually intruded into his thoughts, and he wasn't sure how he felt about this development.

Grady Service found a place above the cabin in some ground-hugging junipers and slept against a cedar snag until first light, ignoring the insects trying to devour him. With light hinting in the east he eased down to the cabin and found a place to the left of the door, which finally eased open a few seconds after 5 a.m. The man stepped outside in his underwear, stretching and yawning.

Service said, "DNR. Good morning." He held his badge out so the man could see. You Rigel Tahti?"

The man had short hair, military style, just starting to grow out and looking raggedy. "Morning," the man said with a smile and nod. "Yah, I'm Rigel. You lost?"

Unstartled, no apparent nervousness—a simple question and greeting.

"Philosophically or geographically?"

The young man grinned. "Let me take a leak and then we can talk."

Business complete, Tahti said, "You're a long way from somewhere."

"How far is Art Lake?" Service asked.

The man cocked an eyebrow, his first sign of concern. "They sic you on me?"

"They?" Service asked. "I've got some tea bags in my ruck if you can supply the water."

"Water, fire, evaporated milk, even some sugar. Come on in, but watch your head. This place wasn't built for people our size."

Tahti was not at all what he had been led to expect.

Water boiled and tea bags steeping, Service said, "You have some sort of problem with Art Lake?"

"Was my *ukki* had issues with them."

"*Ukki?*"

"My grandpa Tahti. *Ukki*'s a Finnish word."

"That would be Helveticus Tahti."

"Hell himself. You knew him?"

"My old man did, long time back."

"He was a mean sonuvabitch, but he was always good to me after my old man died."

"You say he had problems with Art Lake?"

"They stole property from him."

"He call the police, get a lawyer?"

"That wasn't Hell's way, and what would have been the point? The Art Lake people had all the skids greased around here in those days."

"What sort of property?"

"Personal hunting and trapping territory—deer, bear, rats, beavers, otter, his sugarbush, berries, south of the lake."

Sugarbush was a Native American term for maple trees, their traditional source of sugar. "He owned the land?"

"Not exactly, but everyone in these parts knew it was his winter territory."

"Ownership by use."

Rigel Tahti smiled and nodded. "That describes it. It wasn't the sort of land he thought anyone would actually ever spend money for—especially city whites."

"I got a sense that maybe you've had your own trouble with the Art Lake people."

"Figured that's why you humped all the way out here."

"Nope, I was just passing by."

Tahti laughed out loud. "Sounds like a line of bull to me. I wouldn't call what happened real trouble."

"What *would* you call it?" The kid seemed intelligent, well-spoken, friendly, and not in the least bit hinky.

"A by-product of urban sprawl. I bought some land out here while I was in the service. It touches Art Lake property. They don't like having anyone so close. I bought the land from a friend of my aunt's, and later she heard that Art Lake wanted it and their lawyers confronted my aunt's friend, but I'd already bought it legally, and done's done."

"They could've made you an offer."

"Nope, but they did fire a couple of warning shots in my direction."

"*At* you, or in the general direction?"

"I heard the rounds nip the tree branches. Two shots, one to my right and one to my left, bracketing me. I took them as a message for me not to come any further north, even on my own land."

"You should have called the cops."

"Like I said, Art Lake has influence, and I'm a Tahti. Who would be believed? Why waste everyone's time? No harm, no foul. I got their message."

"But you thought they called me."

"It's how they do things, I hear."

"You just let them shoot at you and slough it off?"

"I was in Fallujah," the young man said matter-of-factly. "The hajis were always sniping at us. Over there we considered it a form of intercultural communication," he explained with a wry grin.

"This place is a long way from nowhere," Service said.

"How'd you find me? This shack isn't easy to locate."

"Luck," Grady Service said. "How much land do you have here?"

"I inherited four hundred acres from my dad and bought another hundred and twenty while I was overseas."

"The cabin looks like it's been here a while."

"It was one of Hell's trapline shacks. He had a dozen of them all over the U.P. After Art Lake took his hunting land, he moved here, just a little bit south of them, and kept at it. He was pretty stubborn. I used to snowshoe out here with him in wintertime when I was just a wee guy. I loved being in the woods with him."

"You've got a house in Sidnaw."

Tahti narrowed his eyes and his young face hardened. "You seem to know a lot about me."

"How'd you get out of your enlistment? We keep hearing bout stop-loss."

Tahti took on a vacant stare. "My discharge was honorable, but let's just say that we had some brass who didn't appreciate some questions I asked, which they construed as criticism. I thought I was raising legitimate issues on behalf of my guys. They didn't. All of my buddies were held over, but they cut me loose. Who are you, and what exactly do you want?"

"I've got some questions," Service said.

"What kind of questions?"

Service considered pressing the man, but decided not to. "I was hoping you'd been inside the Art Lake property, but that doesn't matter anymore. You've given me a way in."

"I don't understand."

"Shots fired, reckless discharge of firearms."

"But I haven't filed a complaint."

"It's not necessary when public safety is at issue. You told me about it, now I'll have to look into it."

"I don't want trouble. I just want to be left alone."

"To live off the grid?"

"Why the heck would I do *that*?"

"You know how word goes around up here. You've been spotted out this way several times."

Tahti shrugged. "The gossip up here is pure bullshit. I'm engaged, and my fiancée would like to have a camp out here, so I've been coming out to look for a good cabin site and figure how to cut a road into it. She's a grad student at Northern, and I'm enrolling in the fall on the GI Bill—if it comes through. I've been waiting a long time already. I could afford it on my own, but it seems to me it's a matter of principle. I did my duty, now Uncle Sam needs to step up and do his. I filed before I was discharged, and they've made me re-file twice more since I got out. I figure they're just yanking my chain because they can."

The GI Bill had been similarly plagued in the wake of Vietnam. This kid did not seem at all like an OTG type. "I didn't think you had the look of a buckskinner," Service said, "and you're not the first vet to be screwed after the dirty work's done."

"I've had enough of living rough. You a vet?"

"The Suck, same as you," Service said. "You ever buy a hunting license?"

"I always hunted and fished with Hell when I was a little guy, and he didn't buy licenses. Said his birth certificate was all he needed. After he got killed I got into team sports and had no time for the woods, but I'm going to start again. My fiancée hunts and fishes," he added proudly.

"Have you ever actually talked to the Art Lake people?"

"Only seen them at long range."

"And you've never been on their property?"

Rigel Tahti stared at his boots. "What's the statute of limitations on trespass? Hell took me in there more than once. Like I said, he couldn't tolerate fences, and felt the territory was his to use."

"Do you remember what you saw inside?"

"It was a long time ago and I was scared, sneaking in with him."

"Still."

"Big log building on a rocky hill, a pond created by the dam on the feeder creek, which is where we went in. There was a long skinny pond with little log cabins built along the banks, almost at the water's edge. Big brook trout in their pond."

"Ergo, your grandfather's interest?"

"We took a lot of them out of there, that's for sure. He poached inside their fences all the time—his idea of payback, I guess. Hell was big on revenge when he felt he'd been wronged."

"Did Hell ever tell you anything about the Art Lake people?"

"Called them Commies," Rigel Tahti said. "Anybody who didn't think his way was a Red in his mind."

A common attitude in Helveticus Tahti's heyday. "They ever come on to your property?"

"Not that I know of, but I haven't been out here that much."

"You ever walk their perimeter?"

"Not with guards hanging around."

"You've actually seen guards there?"

"I've heard their voices from time to time, but you can't see through their fence."

"Where were you when they shot at you?"

"Northeast corner of my property."

"You saw muzzle flashes?"

"No, but like I said, I heard both shots, and having been in Fallujah, you get a good feel for what's coming from where, or your ass ends up dead."

"Did Art Lake have guards in your grandfather's day?"

"Yes, and word was they were always recruited from outside, never locals."

"The guards live on the grounds?"

"Can't really say for sure."

"How'd you and your grandfather get through their fence?"

"We paddled a canoe up from the Perch River, stashed it in the tags and cattails, and waded up to their outlet dam. The bottom was firm, the water shallow. Ukki said the amount of water coming over the dam was decreasing over the years. He wasn't sure why, but it really pissed him off to think they might dry up that pond and kill all those fish inside the fence. The dam was an easy way in, and I don't think the Art Lake people ever realized it was a weakness. Ukki specialized in exploiting the weaknesses of others."

"I'm going to talk to the folks at Art Lake about the shots fired. You want to make out a formal complaint?"

"Why would I do that?"

"Why'd you join the marines?"

"It seemed like the right thing to do. My dad served in Korea, my ukki in World War Two. *Ukki* was captured in the Battle of the Bulge and was a POW in Germany until 1945. He was a lawless SOB, but he was also a patriot. I think they both expected me to serve."

"Write down what happened and I'll take it from there. Having your statement will help me to get a warrant if it comes to that." *Which I hope it does.*

"I hope you know what you're doing," Rigel Tahti said.

"Want to show me where you were when the shots happened?"

Having seen the site, Grady Service concluded the Art Lake people had fired blindly, or, as Tahti thought, the shots were meant to warn. Either way, it had been reckless behavior, and Service knew he had grounds at least for a visit to Art Lake. Added to this, the old poacher's shack was inside the 450-foot no-hunting-or-shooting buffer law, which meant no shooting within that distance from occupied buildings without the occupant's permission. Of course, it could be argued that Tahti's shack wasn't fully occupied, but it was a wedge he could use, and he intended to do just that.

L'Anse, Baraga County

FRIDAY, JUNE 16, 2006

Pinky Barbeaux was jawing with a couple of his deputies when Service walked in. The deputies departed without being dismissed and Barbeaux offered him a seat and a cup of coffee, both of which he refused.

"The people at Art Lake took a couple of pot shots in the direction of Rigel Tahti," said Service.

The sheriff showed no reaction.

"Someone needs to talk to the Art Lake people," Service concluded. "It's more your bailiwick than mine."

Barbeaux didn't move. "I think I prefer to leave the matter in your capable hands," the sheriff said.

"You'll have an easier time getting inside than I will."

"I won't argue that, but don't assume my getting in would be a gimme."

"You won't be talking to Gorsline, letting him know I'm coming?"

"Whose team do you think I'm playing for?"

Service left the question unanswered.

Barbeaux added, "Gorsline sort of expects a heads-up on such things—a matter of courtesy."

"And the price of new patrol vehicles?"

"That's not fair, Grady."

"Fair or not, it's a fact. I understand your position, Sheriff, but you can always blame me after the fact for not being a team player."

Barbeaux chewed on his bottom lip. "I won't call Gorsline, but have you got any notion of what can of worms you could be opening?"

Odd question. "Is there something you need to tell me, Pinky?"

"Just that we've got a nice balance in this county. Sometimes the status quo ain't all you'd want, but it's the best you can get."

"I doubt my visit to Art Lake will create anything like a tipping point."

The sheriff's face suggested deep skepticism.

49

Art Lake, Baraga County

FRIDAY, JUNE 16, 2006

Service considered several scenarios and decided to keep it low-key, a simple follow-up on a citizen complaint. As a precaution, he asked Kragie and del Olmo to hover in the area while he went inside.

Like the fence around the compound, the front gate was threaded with some kind of ballistic green fabric, which made it impossible to see inside. Service wondered who had the fence concession as he picked up a telephone from a box on a stripped cedar post and pressed a button.

"Who are you?" a female voice asked.

"Michigan Department of Resources, Detective Service."

"Do you have an appointment?"

"No, but someone in there does—with me."

"And who might that individual be?" the voice inquired without emotion.

Service growled. "It's not gonna go this way. I have a complaint of someone shooting firearms recklessly from inside this compound. If I have to get a warrant, I can play it that way, but if it goes that way, I won't be coming in alone. Right now I just want some questions answered, but I gotta tell you, your attitude is beginning to rub me the wrong way."

"Please stand by," the voice instructed. Service lit a cigarette and stared up at a surveillance camera staring down at him from a post above the gate. He wondered what sort of discussion was under way inside.

Friday called him on his cell while he waited. "Golden Lake doesn't open until a month after the trout-opener, late May through October first. There's a resident campground host couple all summer, but they don't start until just before Memorial Day. Mike and I talked to the host. He's retired and lives in Corpus Christi in the wintertime and comes up here summers with the wife. He said before and after official campground openings campers are still required to register and pay on the honor system. He says Ottawa

National Forest personnel pick up the registrations and money. The host said not everybody follows the rules."

"Anyone get paper on our boys?" Service asked. Campers in various Michigan campgrounds had to fill out camp registration forms and openly display them near their campsites. Passing national forest personnel, COs, deputies, or other officials tore off the bottoms of the forms and held onto them in case emergency notifications were needed. Over the years Grady Service had delivered bad news to too many camps to count.

Friday said, "Mike and I can call around and see if anybody might've."

"That would be good." Do the work, he reminded himself. *Do every little scut task, no matter how inconsequential it seems.*

"Where are you?" she asked.

"Waiting at the Art Lake gate."

"You think they're going to let you in?"

"I think that question is under active discussion."

"Have you got backup?"

"Kragie and del Olmo are in the area."

Service heard a hum in the electric gate motor, said, "Later," and closed his cell phone. A young woman with thick yellow hair squeezed through the gate opening and the gate immediately closed behind her. She wore frayed cutoffs and a white T-shirt emblazoned with the word OEDIPUSSY.

"Detective, I'm Alyssa Mears, retreat coordinator. What can I do for you?"

Early thirties, small-boned, muscled, obviously fit; her dark blue eyes beamed directly at him, with no apparent anxiety over his presence. The closed gate suggested that her appearance was perfunctory, and that he was not going to be admitted. "We have a report of firearms being discharged from your property."

"There are no firearms on this property, Detective, and even if there were, it is not illegal, I believe, to discharge weapons on private property."

"It's not legal if the discharges endanger neighbors, or if the discharge is within the 450-foot buffer protecting other private property."

"There are no neighbors near here," the woman said.

"You're wrong. You have a security detail here."

"Is that a statement or a question?"

"Don't play games with me."

"We have security *technology* on the premises."

"And if a breach is detected?"

"We would call 911 and notify the authorities."

Petite, polite, polished, resolute. "The state requires that for a complaint such as this, I come onto the premises and investigate. I've already looked at events from the other party's perspective," he said.

"I'm sorry, Detective, but you can't come inside. It's just not allowed."

"Maybe so, but I have state laws to follow." Her attitude pissed him off. "Call Gorsline and tell him what's going on. Tell him if I don't hear something PDQ, I'm going to call for a warrant, and we *will* be entering, with or without your consent."

"A warrant based on a single individual's allegation?"

"That's the way the system works. We don't look lightly on the reckless use of firearms."

"I must repeat, Detective: There are no firearms on the premises."

"What we have here is something between intentionally aiming a firearm without malice and discharging a firearm without malice. Now if somebody intentionally fired a shot at an individual, the implications are different, and the charges would be far more serious."

"I'm telling you, there are no firearms here. This is a wild goose chase—or is it something else? A fishing expedition?" she asked, staring hard at him.

"You also just told me that I'm here because of an allegation by a single individual," Service said. "I never said how many people complained, or how often, which makes me think you know exactly what I'm talking about. And is there something inside I'd be interested in fishing *for*?"

"You said you had a report, singular. If there had been more than one, I assumed you would have chosen the plural. But you didn't. I'm a very good listener, Detective."

"I guess this is going down the hard way," he said, adding a theatrical sigh to suggest he didn't want to take the formal path.

"Do what you must, Detective."

"How many people are on the premises at the moment?" he asked.

"That's privileged information," Mears said.

"Well, tell them if anyone tries to leave, they will be detained and questioned. I want everyone who is here now to remain here until my business is concluded."

The woman cocked her head, picked up the telephone, and commanded the gate to open, sliding through it as soon as it was wide enough to admit her slender frame. Service tried to peer past her, but she was too fast, and moved like a cat.

He called Kragie and told him what had happened. "I hate to tie up you guys, but I need you and Simon to sit on the front gate until I get the warrant."

"Uncooperative, are they?" Kragie asked.

"But polite."

"Lousy combo, polite and uncooperative. You want us just on the gate?"

"For now. I don't think they'll do anything until they talk to their lawyer."

"Did you find Rigel Tahti?"

"I did. He's not like his *ukki*."

"What the hell is that?" Kragie asked.

50

L'Anse, Baraga County

FRIDAY, JUNE 16, 2006

County magistrate Huw Nugle met Service at the courthouse annex on North Third Street. About sixty, with long white hair and scarred knuckles, the man made it clear he didn't like being held over past normal hours on a Friday.

"Art Lake, eh?" Nugle said, reading Service's affadavit and request for a search warrant. "I ain't so sure about this deal, Detective. Reckless discharge? Cripes' sake, stand around here any weekend night and you can hear guns a poppin' all over da bloody county, eh? You considered the source of the complaint?"

"Rigel Tahti served in Iraq and has an honorable discharge. Does the county have a beef with the man?'

"Just his low-life pedigree," the magistrate said. "Only reason he ain't got a sheet is mebbe 'cause he ain't never been pinched by youse guys."

"Never caught or never charged?"

"Pretty tough catchin' them Tahtis, them being a buncha slimy snakes. Whoever pigstuck old Hell did everyone a favor."

"The grandson is not the grandfather. Last time I looked, there's no guilt by accident of birth," Service said forcefully. He didn't like Nugle's attitude. "Which part don't you like about the family—the red part or the Finnish part?" he lashed out.

The magistrate looked perplexed. "Art Lake does a lot of good in the community."

"Doing some good makes them immune to the law?"

"You've got no cause talking like that," Nugle said. "I'm stayin' past my quittin' time for a bunch of trumped-up shit." Nugle tapped his chin with a ballpoint pen. "Judge Kallioninen will have to be the one to sign this, and he ain't available until Monday morning, which means you're out of luck, bucko."

Service knew Kragie and del Olmo were patiently waiting at Art Lake.

"Where is he?" Service asked.

"Her, not him," Nugle said. "Her Honor spends weekends at her camp up on the Abbaye."

The magistrate's tone left little doubt that he was passing the buck in the hope Service would just go away and come back Monday so the judge could deliver some major kick-ass. Nugle seemed to be making his view on female judges quite clear: He didn't care for the concept.

"Okay, where *exactly* on the Abbaye is *Her Honor*?" asked Service.

The Abbaye Peninsula stuck into Lake Superior to the northeast of town, splitting Keweenaw and Huron bays. Service had visited the peninsula many times over the years, but could never get a meaningful translation of the French word. Technically it was said to pertain to an area controlled by an abbot, and this usually implied isolation and celibacy, which made the naming at least half accurate, because it was very sparsely populated.

"She's a smidge south of Finlander Bay," Nugle said with a sneer, handing him an address and camp number on McBeth Road. "Wun't call ahead, I was you. Save gettin' your keester kicked twice that way."

51

Abbaye Peninsula, Baraga County

FRIDAY, JUNE 16, 2006

The judge's camp was a fairly new and substantial cabin, situated in old-growth cedars and tamaracks above an expanse of naturally terraced sandstone that stretched gradually down to a rocky beach, and the dark blue waters of Huron Bay.

He parked next to a small Toyota SUV on the grassy lane that led up to the house, and got out.

A barefoot woman came out wearing a red apron, her hands covered with flour. "If you're lost, I'm not one of those gadget geeks with a neutered voice to tell you how to find the public outhouse. If you've got business with me, identify youself, and state your purpose. I've got baking to do, and I take it seriously."

She was about his age, tall, with short black hair in a pageboy, and long arms. "DNR, Detective Grady Service, Your Honor." He held out the draft warrant.

"You shaking that paper at me like I'm an ill-tempered dog?"

He laughed.

"I'm glad to be the source of your amusement, Detective, but that's not an answer."

"I need a warrant signed, Your Honor."

"You see the magistrate?"

"Huw Nugle said you'd have to sign it."

"Mr. Passive Aggressive," she said. "He tell you I don't appreciate being interrupted at home and that I'd chew off your head?"

"Something along those lines."

She sighed. "I wear a dress and high heels under my robe just to remind the likes of Huw Nugle that women do the same jobs as men in these times, and he can't turn the damn clock back. I'd rather wear slacks and tennis shoes, but a woman's got to make her points when she can. You agree?"

"I'd agree to just about anything to get this warrant signed, Your Honor."

She pursed her lips and looked him over. "I like candid, Detective." She wiped her hands on her apron and reached out for the paperwork. "Let me have a look."

The judge immediately looked up at him. "Art Lake?"

"Yes, Your Honor."

"Pinky know about this?"

"I told the sheriff I was going out there to investigate the complaint and asked him if he wanted to take it. He turned it down and I asked him not to call ahead."

"I bet that twisted his BVDs," she said. He agreed.

"How much do you know about Art Lake?" she asked.

"Not much. Artist retreat, whatever that is, apparently very exclusive, owned and operated by a foundation out of Chicago."

"That's pretty much the extent of what we know," the judge said, "but Art Lake spreads their money and largesse around the area strategically, which they believe entitles them to some privacy."

Service expected her to refuse to sign the warrant, but she took another angle.

"Did your complainant actually witness the alleged shooter or shooters?"

"No, ma'am. You can't see through the Art Lake fence."

"Then said complainant can't prove the shots came from the Art Lake property."

"He served in Fallujah in Iraq, and said he got real familiar with fixing the origin of sniper shots. I served in Vietnam and had a similar experience. Over time, you get so you know where shots intended to kill you—or those meant to get your attention—come from."

"Granted, but you have no probable cause to enter buildings," the judge said. "You will restrict your search to the grounds, and if that yields something, we'll look at another affadavit with a warrant with greater reach. That float your boat?"

"Yes, ma'am, Your Honor." It would get him inside the compound, and right now, that's all that mattered.

"Hand me a pen and give me your back," the judge ordered. Service did as he was instructed and felt her scratching the pen against his back.

"Call me Taava. I happen to know who you are, Detective. That's the thing about reputations up here: They can open doors or close them. You've been around a long time, and you're one of the game wardens judges up here love to gab about. Twinkie Man, right?"

"Yes, ma'am," he said, accepting the pen and the warrant. He once arrested a man for poaching who claimed that excess sugar had made him break the law. After that, a lot of cops and judges around the U.P. began referring to him as Twinkie Man.

"All of us in the law enforcement community were very sorry to hear about your lady and your son," she said.

"Thank you."

"I deleted dwellings from the writ. Grounds only, Detective, but if you get something, come back to me and I'll open that place like a ripe fish. You wonder why I'm so agreeable?"

He nodded.

"Have you met Gorsline, Art Lake's too-smooth-by-a-mile mouthpiece?"

"I talked to him on the phone."

"Make you want to take a shower afterwards?"

"Pretty much."

"There's more to this than what you're telling me, right?"

"Yes, ma'am," he said, and took her through all that had happened from the second day of trout season until now. By the time he finished he was helping her pull a cookie sheet out of the oven and finishing a cup of raspberry-flavored coffee and she was staring vacantly at Lake Superior and shaking her head.

"The people up here are good folks, and the U.P. is absolutely one of God's most beautiful natural creations anywhere. That aside, I swear we're a mega-magnet for assholes and troublemakers. Let Fish Live Free? What the hell is wrong with people? We've got starving kids, economic problems big enough to choke the world, and the zanies are worried about *fish* feeling pain?" She paused and took a breath. "Out of judicial propriety, I think I'll say no more. You've got your warrant, Detective Service. Do your duty."

It was just before 10 p.m.

He drove away from Judge Taava Kallioninen's place thinking she was a helluva person and probably one very hard-ass adjudicator. All in all, the U.P. had some peculiar personalities on the bench, but most of them were pretty solid, and more were supportive of the DNR than weren't.

He called Kragie on his way south. "Any activity down there?"

"Not that we've seen. You get the warrant?"

"Sitting on the seat next to me, and I'm on my way now."

"This ought to be interesting," Kragie said. "You want us to hang around?"

"Absolutely. Should be there in forty minutes at the outside."

52

Art Lake, Baraga County

SATURDAY, JUNE 17, 2006

The three officers pulled their vehicles up to the compound's gate. Service got out, used the outdoor phone, and held the warrant up to the lens of the surveillance camera.

Alyssa Mears eventually slid out through the gate. *Looks like a teenager,* he told himself. He handed the paper to her. "Open the gate," he said.

She took a pair of reading glasses out of her shirt pocket and put them on. "First I read, then we'll see," she said with complete external emotional control.

"Everything seems to be in order," she said after she finished reading the warrant. She looked up at the camera, nodded, and the gate slid open.

Service got into his Tahoe and drove in with Mears walking beside his front left fender. A dirt-and-grass two-track led about two hundred yards back to a three-story wooden building that looked like a grand sportsman's lodge from a different era, something built and maintained by someone with beaucoup resources and not interested in scrimping. The house was built on bedrock and below, as Rigel Tahti had reported, there was a long, narrow pond with small cabins strung along the shore, including one directly below the main lodge. There were no outbuildings or sheds in sight, and no vehicles in evidence.

"I'll accompany you," Mears announced as he got out of the truck.

"I don't think so," Service said. He checked to make sure they all had digital cameras and good batteries in their 800s, and sent Simon south along the west perimeter, and Kragie south along the eastern fence. At the south end the two men would turn toward the middle and the three of them would meet in the center of the south boundary. "Bump me if you need anything," he told them. "When we're done I want to be able to piece together a fairly accurate map of the grounds. Use GPS, look for footprints, vehicle prints, loose brass, anything man-made where it shouldn't be."

Mears had left them and was standing next to the porch of the main building. Again Service looked for vehicles and saw none. "Who else is here?" he asked her.

"Ginny and me."

"Is Ginny a guest?"

"She works for me."

"Just the two of you?"

"Disappointed?"

"Introduce us," Service said.

"Is that necessary?"

"It is. Did you talk to Gorsline?"

"That's not your concern, Detective."

Translation: She has. "Guns inside?"

"There are no firearms on these premises," the woman said.

"Then you won't mind if I look around inside."

She grinned. "Nice try. We've got nothing to hide, but your warrant says 'Grounds only.' Please adhere to the specifications of your warrant."

No rancor, but his ploy had not worked. Usually it got him permission to get into vehicles and dwellings. Either she had a legal background, or she had been well prepped. It had taken the better part of six hours to deal with the magistrate and get the warrant from the judge, and now it was evening and the mosquitoes were swarming in the humid air. "I'd like to meet Ginny," he said.

Ginny was small and wiry and squinted like the prescription for her contacts was no longer right. Unlike Mears, she avoided eye contact. "Identification?" Service asked.

Ginny looked at Mears, who nodded.

Service read the driver's license: Virginia Czuk of Palinko, Illinois. Current, and the description and photo matched her. "You live here, Virginia?"

"It's Ginny," the woman said. "Yes."

"What's your job?"

"Assistant coordinator."

"Like Alyssa?"

"My assistant," Mears said, interrupting.

"Hierarchical organization," Service said. "I thought nonprofits operated differently than General Motors."

"Artistic chaos, or a commune populated by eccentrics—is that what you mean?"

"Those aren't my words," Service said. "I'm just trying to clarify. Just the two of you, or are you between guests? Or are guests just not in the compound at the moment?"

"Just us," Mears said.

"You're not making this easy," Service said.

"Easy isn't in the warrant," she said. "It's nothing personal, Detective. We each have a job to do."

Mears was clearly in charge and uncowed. "Penny Provo around?"

Mears blinked and tried to hide it. Czuk visibly flushed.

"She here?" he repeated.

"There's just Ginny and me," Mears said.

Clearly, Provo's name had registered reactions. *Press now, or search first?* He opted for searching, leaving them to stew on Provo's name.

• • •

It was after midnight when the three officers convened on the southern fence.

"Big-ass chunk of land," Simon said. "Varied terrain, lots of gullies, swales, ravines, and some major nasty underbrush. They keep the foliage thick along the fences, have paths paralleling them, about three yards in, with trails to the fence itself here and there, but no peepholes or signs of duck-throughs. Maybe they use periscopes?"

"Prints?"

Simon del Olmo shook his head. "Would take a lot longer and a lot more of us to do this carefully," he said.

Kragie added. "Nothing along the east fence."

"You look at the dam?" Service asked.

"Quick look but didn't linger. Got a spillway, and another concrete block with a culvert splitting the outfall, steel grate over the culvert."

"Diameter?"

"Four foot, give or take."

Odd setup; worth a closer look? he asked himself.

Service led his colleagues to the area close to where Rigel Tahti thought the shots had originated. It was dark and hot, and although they looked hard for signs, there was nothing obvious.

"Maybe they were in front of the fence," del Olmo suggested.

Service mopped the sweat from his eyes. He hadn't considered this angle. "You guys want to swing around the outside when we get out of here, look around?"

Kragie said, "I think we're wasting time. These people seem almost anal about procedures and upkeep."

"Humor me," Service said. "If you wanted to use a rifle to scare off someone, how would you do it?"

"Offset the aim a few feet to hit branches and make some noise, close enough to frighten, but by a wide-enough margin to make sure a piece of bark didn't kangaroo and hit the target. I'd shoot off a stand to make sure I hit what I intended," Simon del Olmo said.

"Branch?"

"Something less flexible. The fence might work, especially against a post."

The fence again. Who had installed it, and when?

"Swap sides on the way back, Simon north along the east, Junco north along the west. Look for a manufacturer's name, a brand, lot number, anything."

"What about you?" del Olmo asked.

"I'm heading for the dam."

It was just after 2 a.m. when he released his partners to head back to the north. They were all tired and frustrated, but he welcomed some time alone to think without distraction. When they got back to the main building they would go outside and circle the fence to look at the area where the shooting allegedly had taken place.

The warrant was a one-time shot. Probably he could stretch it for another day, but Mears and Art Lake were strict constructionists, and it would be a battle to extend it.

He zigzagged his way north up the middle of the property, shading east a bit with the intention of intercepting the outlet creek where the dam was. *How the hell had the Tahtis gotten inside? Is the setup different now than it was back then? Had the Art Lake people plugged a security hole?*

He became aware of his shadow about fifteen minutes after separating from del Olmo and Kragie. The shadow had exquisite sound-suppression skills, but his night vision gave him an edge, letting him pick up motion where most people couldn't. *Paralleling me? Mears? The other one? Choice to make: Confront or be aware, and watch the watcher? No. Stupid to conduct solo recon and try to guard your six. Safer to deal with it head-on.* Course of action decided, he began angling toward the shadow, trying to calculate a place where he could pinch off the route along the fence, and pounce.

Workable plan, he told himself, just as something caught him hard and low behind his head and dumped him straight down into pine duff and dirt, mashing his nose and causing his eyes to flood involuntarily with tears.

A female voice, right at his ear, whispered, "What the fuck is your *problem, man?*"

Not the shadow. He was still seeing the shadow when this happened. Someone else, someone he'd not seen. Two people out there. He tried to will the cobwebs out of his brain, touched his upper lip, felt blood, tasted salt, spit quietly. "If you wanted to talk, you just had to say so," he whispered. "Penny Provo, right?"

"I was warned you're stubborn."

Warned! "You are Provo," he repeated. "Warned by *whom*?"

She popped his head again. "Man, names mean shit."

"You're undercover," he said softly.

"Keep your fucking voice down," she whispered back.

"Things have been bugging me since the beginning. As good as the army says you are, you've left more tracks than a moose at a muddy waterhole in a drought. I asked myself, why is she so sloppy? Hike Funke showed up in Kenton, which is right next to Left Testicle, Mars. We have good photos of you, know about your interactions with the meth chef in Big Bay, have a perfect description from your Guard mates. There had to be a reason beyond gross incompetency. The army says most walkaways are caught fast. You've been away for almost a record length of time. Finally it dawns on me: You're laying tracks for a case. The question is why, and what case?"

"Stubborn and imaginative," she said. "You're sabotaging the gig."

"I haven't done anything."

"Being here, inside, that's everything. All the silent alarms are going wacka-wacka dingdong. Lots of questions will be asked. I'd gotten past all that shit; now it will start up again."

"I could help," Service offered, and thought he heard her chuckle.

"There was all sorts of optimism and confidence at the Little Big Horn and the Alamo, and it didn't mean shit for either," she said. "You have no idea what is going down."

"Enlighten me."

"You want to help, get out and stay the fuck away from here."

"What's in it for me? I've got cases to deal with. A man was killed on the river, shots were fired from this compound, and another man was murdered."

"Shot at and shot are not synonymous," the woman said. "All locals need to stay the hell away from here."

"Who did the shooting?"

"Who do you think? *I did,* and I always hit what I shoot at."

"Even with spring guns?"

"Jesus, that shit down on the river? Those guns had nothing to do with this, *nothing.*"

"There was more on the river than spring guns."

She said, "You need to back off. The spring guns were set by someone else, not us."

"You used the word *this.*"

No response this time. "What about the wolf tree?"

"The *what*?"

He described the cause of Dani Denninger's injuries.

"No clue, man. There'd be no point."

"Deterrent?"

"If so, didn't work for shit, did it? It's got you and your people crawling all over the place."

"Mears runs the show here?"

"Hardly."

"Let Fish Live Free."

"They're real," she said. "And totally irrelevant."

"What *is* relevant?"

"Man, this is not a bonding moment. You need to get the fuck off the property and stay away before you destroy everything we've done."

"I'm not good at walking away."

"No shit, Sherlock."

"Why approach me at all?" he asked.

"Professional courtesy—I don't know. If you leave now, this may settle down for me."

"This—you keep saying this. What about Rankin Box?"

"What about him?"

She doesn't know. "Dead, and not of natural causes."

He heard her breath catch. "Not in the media," she managed.

"You know the drill on murders."

"I saw Box. Nice old man. He was fine the last time I saw him."

"Why did you see him?"

She sighed with frustration. "Spring guns."

"You said—"

"Original plan called for spring guns with blanks, but we dumped that notion. The plan changed direction. Then some asshole set up spring guns with live ammo. Bad serendipity, man. Karma of the sucky sort. Without those guns, I doubt you'd ever have shown up here."

He couldn't argue. "Allerdyce?"

"The old pervert?"

"Says he sold you some traps."

"Bullshit. I wanted information and he wanted to get it on, and I told him to get lost."

"You met with him?"

"No, it was all done by phone."

So Limpy had lied. Somehow he found this comforting, a natural law being obeyed. This he'd have to follow up on. "Hike Funke showed up in Kenton, no explanation, but there had to be a reason. The only thing I can think of was you, or someone like you."

"Control freaks," she said with disgust. "This thing is close to finished. You need to move out and stay away."

If this was all legit, he could understand her concern. "You're not inside alone," he added.

"This is not a group exercise," she countered.

"Fooled me. I saw your shadow, but missed you."

"My *shadow* . . . ?"

Palpable fear in her voice, borderline high alert, not fear. "To my right," he said. "Our right. I was angling for an intercept when you jumped me."

Moments later, silence only. Mosquitoes buzzing languidly. *She's gone, just like that; here, not here. The shadow shadowing a shadow, or something like that. Which one am I?*

He got up, brushed himself off, blotted the bleeding lip, which had begun to swell, and resumed trying to intercept the dam. Just five more minutes and he might have had more information from Penny Provo. Had he blown her cover? No way to judge.

He had just reached the dam when a voice ahead of him declared, "That's it. You're done here, Detective."

It was Ginny. "You're into the next day, and you're finished. You want back, get another warrant."

"*After* I look at your dam," he said.

"That is *not* going to happen."

"I say it is."

"Sorry, Grady," a voice said, and Service turned to see Pinky Barbeaux. "Warrant says for yesterday. It's tomorrow by that standard. People have their rights. It's time for you to go."

Service looked at the sheriff. "Just on my way out."

Ginny Czuk said, "You're a twisted piece of work."

"You admire that," Service told her. Funny shift in attitude. Mears made Czuk out to be her hireling, but she wasn't acting the role right now, was nowhere in sight, and the sheriff was clearly taking his lead from Czuk. The stuff you learn, he noted in his mind.

"Get out," she said. "Now."

"I'll be back," Grady Service said.

"I don't think so," the sheriff said.

"You talk to the judge?" Service asked.

Barbeaux shook his head.

"I *will* be back," Service said icily to Czuk.

North Bear Town Road, Baraga County

SATURDAY, JUNE 17, 2006

As Grady Service drove away from Art Lake just after 5 a.m., a man stepped calmly onto the road and held up his hands. He was small and compact, with long gray hair, wearing blue jeans, work boots, a camo boonie hat, and a badge hanging from his left shirt pocket.

Service stopped the truck in the middle of the road and got out. "Joe Kokko," he said, greeting the man.

"Bojo, Twinkie Man. What're a couple of old warhorses like us still doing stumbling around the woods?" Joe Kokko was a full-blooded Ojibwa from Isabella County in the lower peninsula, a longtime federal law enforcement man for the Ottawa National Forest, a former helicopter pilot in Vietnam, with two tours and a chest-full of medals for heroism, and a one-time state trooper who had graduated in the same Academy class with Service and Treebone. They had known each other for a very long time and had rarely worked together. Service couldn't remember the last time he'd seen the man.

"You lost, Joe?"

"Nah. I was working my way down an old two-track, stopped to take a piss, and heard your tires. Glad it's you. Been looking to run into you for coupla weeks."

"I have telephones."

"Yeah, well, maybe I had some thinking to do before I got in touch. Pinky told me you might be down this way."

"So, here I am. What's up?"

"*Maingan mitig,*" Kokko said.

"Wolf something? My Ojibwa vocab ain't what it once was."

"That wolf tree bit one of your officers?"

Kokko was known as a plodding but thorough officer.

"You got something for me on that, Joe?"

"Young fella, Keweenaw Bay lad."

"He got a name?"

"Not ready to say it just yet."

"Because you're missing some facts?"

"Because he's fourteen—just a kid."

"He'll be treated as a juvenile, I'd think."

"White juvie ain't the same as tribal juvie."

"I don't think the law makes such distinctions, Joe."

"The courts do," Kokko said.

Service couldn't argue. An Indian kid in a white court would fare about as well as a black kid. "What do you want?" Service asked.

"Cops write the charges."

"You want a deal? Is that what we're talking about?"

"Let the tribal courts handle it. Probation, released to the care of his grandmother, and to me as his P.O."

Service took a guess. "His grandmother special to you, Joe?"

"My old lady without the paper."

"One of our officers was seriously hurt, Joe."

"I know."

"I can't promise anything till I talk to the boy." He felt Kokko studying him.

"Both the boy's parents," Kokko said, putting a thumb in his mouth and tilting his fist upward to mimick a bottle. "Bad lushes, hopeless. Kid's a good boy, and smart. Get him away from his parents to his grandma and me, he'll do fine."

"We're not social workers, Joe."

"Way I see our job with kids is, if we can keep one going in the right direction, we need to do whatever we can to make that happen."

"Do I get to talk to the boy, decide for myself?"

"Go easy on him. He's scared to death of you, heard you're the windigo warden, out for revenge."

The Ojibwa believed that windigos stalked the land in winter and were cannibals. "Wonder where he got that notion?" Service said.

Kokko smiled. "Let me go get my truck out of the woods and you can follow me. We'll cut west through Baraga, then north all the way to the north end of Bear Town Road. Betty's got a small place on Kelsey Creek."

"Betty?"

"Betty Lachoix."

• • •

Thirty minutes later they were standing in front of a small house that sat on a low rise over a sparkling creek. A boy with blond hair was standing on the porch with an older woman.

Kokko said, "Officer Service—Betty Lachoix and William Satago."

The woman said, "I'm *okomissan,* his grandmother." She touched the boy's shoulder. "You look the man in the eye and tell him what it was you done."

The boy looked up from the floor. Service could see him trembling. "I set them traps that hurt the lady."

"What traps?" Service countered harshly.

"For the wolves," the boy said.

"Wolves are sacred to your people."

"Din't do it for my people," the boy said. "Did it for the lady with the money."

"The lady with the money?"

"She give me the traps, said she'd give me five hundred dollars for a dead wolf."

"Any dead wolf?"

"Any wolf come into the area where I set my traps."

"She say why?"

The boy shook his head and looked at the ground again.

"He figured if he got enough money, he could give it to his mom and dad and they'd let him move in with me," Lachoix said. "He wanted to buy his freedom."

"They wouldn't wonder where the money came from?"

"*Gawashkwebidi,*" the boy mumbled.

"Alcoholics," the woman translated. "Drunkards. They're never gonna get loose."

Service rubbed his eyes and tried to think. A wolf tree set by a fourteen-year-old-boy who was being paid by an unknown woman who wanted wolves dead? Pretty damned outlandish, but this was the U.P., and outlandish sometimes seemed perfectly feasible. "You get any wolves?"

The boy shook his head. "Your lady got hurt and you took my traps."

"How long had it been there?"

"Just that day."

This jibed with the estimated time of death for the deer the boy had used as bait. "You kill the deer?"

The boy nodded.

"The traps belong to your father?"

"The woman give them to me."

"This woman have a name?"

"She didn't say one."

"What did she look like?"

"Short, dark hair, old."

"How'd you meet her?"

"Fishin' the Slate River with my friends. She give us beer."

"You drank beer?" Betty Lachoix asked, alarm in her voice.

"My friends, not me," the boy said quickly. "She told me just before she left the river she wanted to see me later, not my friends, because any under-age kid that would drink beer from a stranger couldn't be trusted."

"Did you meet her again?"

"Just outside the state park."

Just north of the town of Baraga. "She make the wolf tree offer then?"

"No, first time we just talked. We met again about a week later, and I said yes, and she give me the traps and a hundred dollars. She drove me to where she wanted the trap set and told me to put a red mark on a tree outside the state park if I got a wolf, and she'd get in touch with me."

"How?"

"She never said, and I never got no wolf."

Service looked at Joe Kokko, who raised an eyebrow.

Service said, "The wolf tree was set all the way down by Art Lake. How'd you get down there?"

"My old man's four-wheeler. He's always too drunk to use it."

"Did the woman give you any idea why she wanted this exact location?"

"Nope."

"And you didn't ask," Kokko added.

"What's going to happen to me?" the boy asked.

"A woman was seriously injured," Service said. "A conservation officer. She almost lost her leg."

Tears began to dribble from the boy's brown eyes.

"She'll keep the leg, but it's serious, and I'm not going to kid you, William."

"I didn't mean for nobody to get hurt," the boy said. "I just needed that money."

Kokko said to Service, "The boy ain't learned the difference between want and need. We might want two assholes, but we only *need* one."

Service shot a look at Kokko. "Did you tell your grandmother about this beforehand?"

"No, she would've got real mad at me."

"Where'd you get the deer?"

"Down in that area."

"I'll talk to the prosecutor," Service said, looking at the boy's grandmother. "He's going to move in with you?"

"Yessir, if you turn this over to the tribal court, I think they'll take care of it."

Service loathed turning matters over to tribal courts. Some of them were good at upholding the laws, but magistrates in other tribal jurisdictions ignored all charges transferred or lodged by white law enforcement. He looked at the boy. "You ever see this woman, besides in your meetings?"

"Just them times."

"Anything special about her?"

"Just dark hair and old, and she wasn't so big, eh."

"Not so big. Like skinny?"

"Not skinny."

Service dug out a photo of Penny Provo. "This her?"

The boy held the photo in both hands and stared hard. "Nossir."

Service took back the photo. "Where are you staying now, William?"

"Here," Betty Lachoix said. "He's not going back to that house again. His folks want to see him, they can come here sober."

Service tried to evaluate what he'd heard. "How'd you know how to set up a wolf tree, William?"

"The woman give me a pitcher."

"Like a schematic?"

"I don't know that word," the boy admitted sheepishly.

"Like a drawing," Service amended his statement.

"Yeah, really fancy."

"Fancy?"

"Done by somebody really knows how to draw," the boy said.

Service and Kokko talked by their trucks. "How'd you get on to this?" Service asked.

"Heard about the wolf tree, started nosing around. Wolves are sacred in these parts, so I figured no tribal adult would be doin' this. I heard some kids alluding to this and that, and some kid who'd done something, and I just kept track of who was doing the talking, and who they hang out with, and when I found five or six of them hanging with the one who was always silent, I guessed it was William. I confronted him, and he confessed. I think guilt was getting to him."

"What's so special about the area west of Art Lake?" Service asked.

"Not a thing I could point to," Joe Kokko said. "Doesn't make a lot of sense, does it?"

"Not yet," Service said.

Kokko smiled. "Ever seeking justice, Twinkie Man."

"You're not?"

"End of this year I'm filing my papers. Tribe here talked to me about head game warden for them, but I told them I just want to settle down with Betty and raise William and hunt and fish to make up for all the time I lost over all these years. Tribal CEO told me if I run across you, to let you know they'd be interested in talking to you about the job."

"Me, a tribal game warden? I *have* a job, Joe."

"Just passing along what I got told. Working with the tribe's a dang good job," Kokko added. "The state's in rough shape."

Jesus, is he recruiting me? "Thanks for the pass-along."

"You going to turn the boy over to the tribal court?"

"Probably. Thanks for coming forward with this."

"You want to go down and walk that wolf-tree country, I'll go with you." Kokko handed him a business card. "Just call. Ain't a lot of routine in our line of work."

54

Abbaye Peninsula, Baraga County

SUNDAY, JUNE 18, 2006

It was mid-morning, and Grady Service found Judge Taava Kallioninen sitting on her front deck with her feet up and a book open in her lap. She was asleep, mouth open, drool pooled in her left dimple.

"Judge?"

The woman inhaled and snorted loudly, looked up at him, and wiped drool off her lips. "This must be a pretty picture, eh? How'd the search go?"

"It got cut short. Pinky showed up to tell me I'd been in there long enough."

"You had a day. That usually means a full twenty-four hours."

"It wasn't specified," he said.

The judge rolled her eyes. "Hardball chickenshit time, eh? You get anything?"

He told her about the shadow episode and being jumped and talking with the woman he was pretty sure was Penny Provo, including his theory that she was a government plant.

"Sounds like she wanted you out of there pretty bad."

"She was pretty blunt."

"Why not do what she asks?"

"I don't know that she is who she says she is, or even who *I think* she is. She assaulted me. That's grounds for a new warrant," he said.

The judge looked up at his face. "Nice lip," she said. "Detective, I'd like to help you, but if there's a buncha federal stuff going on, I'd hate for us to blunder in and kick over the apple cart. Let me make some calls and get back to you, okay?"

"Is this a kiss-off?"

"Nope. This is what I call a matter of jurisdictional prudence. Are you and your people done looking around the perimeter?"

"No, Your Honor."

"Okay, then. You're good to go on that, and I'll work on clearing a path to get you back inside; agreed?"

No choice. "Yes, Your Honor."

55

Allerdyce Compound, Southwest Marquette County

SUNDAY, JUNE 18, 2006

Limpy looked shocked to see him. "Youse shoulda calt ahead," the old poacher said. "Woulda strapped on da feedbag."

Service reached out, grabbed the old man's collar, and pulled him onto the porch. "You *lied* to me. That made me really, really happy. I was almost buying the reformed man routine, but you lied."

"I din't lie about nuttin' to youse," the old man complained, trying to twist away.

"Penny Provo."

"What about her?'"

"You never sold her any traps."

"Like hell. Met her in Gwinn, did the in-out, sold her traps."

"I talked to her. She called you 'an old pervert.' Said she talked to you on the phone was all."

"Ain't no way," the old man said. "I sent dat girlie away wid big smile onner kisser."

Service stared at the old man, felt sick to his stomach. *Jesus. Why is my gut telling me to believe Limpy Allerdyce? God!*

He took out the army photo of Provo and held it out to Limpy, who looked at it.

"My s'pose to know dis girly?"

"That's Penny Provo."

Allerdyce cackled. "Not da one I plugged."

"You talked to her on the phone and then you met her?"

"Never talked on phone. She sent message."

"How?"

"Envelope left on tree out by park-spot."

"You still have it?"

"Nah, burned it."

"Shit," Service said, the word slipping out before he could contain it, and he felt Limpy's hand patting his back.

"S'okay, sonny. Ain't none of us perfect, even on our best day."

The Provo in the photo was not the Provo Allerdyce had met, and not the woman who'd given traps to William. So who was she?

He thought back to his strange meeting with Penny Provo and how she had rabbited when he told her about the shadow, and the bottom of his stomach began to fall away and his thoughts began to turn dark.

"You doing anything today?" he asked the old poacher.

"Why?"

"Want to take a ride?"

"Where to?"

"Could use another set of eyes in the woods."

"Let me get my pack," the old man said. He did not gloat, did not make an issue out of being invited, and Service wondered what this behavior portended.

"Back tonight?" Allerdyce asked.

"Not sure," Service said. "Why?"

Allerdyce came out of his cabin with a pack on this back and a bedroll curled over the top and lashed into place.

"No firearms," Service said.

"Felon," Limpy Allerdyce said. "Can't have 'em."

I must be insane. Desperation as the mother of insanity. Have to bounce this off Tuesday, see what she thinks.

56

Perch River, Baraga County

SUNDAY, JUNE 18, 2006

Late in the morning, Service stashed his truck a mile from the river, on the edge of a swamp not that far from Frodo the Finn's place, and he and Allerdyce made their way through the dense cedar swamp to the river.

The wind was out of the southwest when they got to the Perch River. "There's a feeder stream that runs out of Art Lake over a dam. I want to wade up the stream, look around," Service explained to the old man. *I can't believe I asked Limpy to come with me!*

Allerdyce said nothing and followed along. As they reached the opening to the feeder just to the south of where they had intersected the river, the old man whispered, "We got a stinker somewhere close."

"Stinker?"

"Somebody done crossed over the Sticks, like in them Geek mitts. Underground now, but it ain't planted too deep."

Service shook his head, trying to clear his mind. There was no way to predict anything Allerdyce might say, or to clearly translate it. "You mean a dead body?"

"Jes said dat, din't I, sonny."

"You can smell it?"

"You *can't*? Your old man woulda."

Great—now I get comparisons to my old man.

"Let's find the dam."

"You go ahead," Limpy said.

An hour later Grady Service reached up to grasp the grate across the culvert in the Art Lake Dam and found that it was hinged, but with encouragement could be swung up. It was rusted pretty badly, but the hinges were there, with no sign of recent use. Something old. He was just about to take some rope and try to dislodge it when Allerdyce appeared out of the shadows. "Better come see, sonny."

The body was in a black plastic bag, buried two feet down and covered with loose dirt and rotted logs. "Pewtered," Allerdyce said. "Early on, not advanced. Dis jes been planted, I'm tinkin."

Service dug cautiously, got to the plastic, used his knife to split it, spilling out even more noxious fumes, which caused him to gag, but he kept looking, worked his way up to the head, uncovered the face: Penny Provo! There were sparkling specks on her face, and he used forceps from his pack to lift specimens of the material, which he put in a plastic evidence bag in his pack. The smell was beyond description, and he would have loaded his nose with Vicks if Allerdyce hadn't been with him.

• • •

The remainder of the night was a classic goat rodeo. Service called the L'Anse state police post for their local foreniscs technician, but Pinky Barbeaux intervened and insisted that the Baraga County medical examiner officiate on the scene. Then the U.P.'s senior Troop commander out of Negaunee called Barbeaux and they got into a shouting match, and all the while Limpy Allerdyce and Service babysat the rotting body, awaiting backup and technical support.

Service asked Barbeaux to ask Art Lake if the ME and EMS could come in through Art Lake property to make the body recovery easier, but Art Lake refused permission.

It was not until just before official sunrise that others arrived at the body site and immediately began to track over the place like a herd of clowns in a third-rate circus. Service finally lost his cool and ordered them all to "sit on their fucking asses and not move unless and until the ME told them to."

"You'd think somebody'd at least have brung us coffee," Allerdyce complained.

"You'd think," Service said, agreeing with his companion.

"You know the stiff?"

"Penny Provo," Service said.

"Ah," Allerdyce said. "Yer pitcher don't do her no justice."

"Death does?"

Allerdyce chuckled, breaking loose mucous and causing himself to cough violently until he hocked and launched a major loogie onto a beaver stump.

Within an hour of sunrise the humidity was rocketing upward.

"Gone cook us out here today," Limpy said.

Service still couldn't understand how the old man had smelled the body from the river, but Allerdyce was a phenomenon in many ways, and not easy to explain in any context.

"Who you think pop her?" Allerdyce asked.

"No idea. Let's wait for forensics."

"You smell the ice cream?"

Ice cream? Now what was he talking about? Service opened his hands, inviting the old man to finish his thought. "You smelled ice cream? Was this before you found the body or afterwards?"

"When you dug 'er loose."

The Baraga County ME was an elderly man who moved slowly and looked exhausted in the humid morning air. He begged a cigarette and Service gave him one. "Female, twenty-five to thirty-five, GSW to the back of the head, one round, small caliber; thirty-two maybe, but could be as small as a twenty-two caliber. Time of death looks like maybe twenty-four to thirty hours ago. Got to get her back to the lab to nail that down."

"Signs of a struggle?" Service asked.

"Nope, back of the head. Doubt she knew it was coming."

"Foo-foo juice?" Limpy Allerdyce interjected.

Service poked at the old man to make him shut up.

The doctor nodded and smiled. "Yah, faint traces of something sweet and familiar, not sure what. The old sniffer ain't what she used to be. We'll look at everything during the autopsy. Anything else interest you fellas?"

"She killed here, or elsewhere?" Service asked.

"Let the techs finish their work to be sure, but I'm thinking elsewhere, and buried here."

Pinky Barbeaux approached Service almost timidly. "Sorry about the other morning."

"Fuck off, Pinky."

"Hey, no need to cop an attitude."

"Had my way, I'd kick your ass right here."

"I'm not talking to you until you cool down."

"Don't bother talking to me at all, asshole."

"You taking this *personally*?"

"I take *everything* about *my* job personally, Sheriff."

"You maybe should give Judge Kallioninen a call this morning."

Service turned away from the sheriff.

"Dat da one usta be one of youse guys in green, eh?" Allerdyce said.

"Don't remind me."

"Dis what you brung me along for?"

He wasn't sure why he'd brought Allerdyce. Fate was as good an answer as he could come up with. "Get your stuff," he told the old man. "We're gonna take another hike."

Limpy grinned. "I like walking."

They were almost to the southern limit of the Art Lake fence when the voice of Alyssa Mears broke their silence. "Stay clear of the fence, Detective. And keep away from our creek outflow."

Allerdyce craned to see the woman, but the fence hid her. "You know dat one?"

"Yeah," Service said.

"You got pitcher?"

"Of her? No. Why?"

"Voice sounds real f'miliar."

No time to sort out the old poacher's fantasies and musings. "C'mon, we've still got a way to go," Service said.

●●●

They found Rigel Tahti's body on the dirt floor of his grandfather's cabin, which was filled with flies.

Service peeked in, saw the body, went inside to be sure Tahti was dead, and that determination made, withdrew outside, where he gagged for air and used his 800 to report the death and ask for yet more assistance.

"You think they took a long time this morning," Service told his companion, "watch how long this will take. We're about as far from anywhere as we can get."

"Me," Allerdyce said, "I'd just shoot up da old Deer Clip Trail. Cuts Forest Service road just below Baraga County line, in Iron County."

"A mapped road?"

"No, jes old two-track now, but good hard ground, easy to get across if you got good spares. It don't get much traffic anymore. Called Deer Clip Trail in da ole days. Loggers usta use 'er."

"Except for you."

"Guess I been down 'er some. I like ole roads."

Service called Barbeaux and gave him instructions, and Barbeaux's undersheriff, a man called Boveneck, called back moments later to confirm the directions, saying he was a lifelong resident of the area and he had "never heard of any goddamn Deer Clip Trail," and when Service said it had been Limpy Allerdyce who'd provided the instructions, the undersheriff had said, "Oh," and hung up.

Allerdyce was off in the bush and came back with a handful of roots and put them in water and made a fire and boiled the roots. "Sassafras," the old man said when the tea was done. "Cleans your blood and makes your man-part stand at attention—not dat Limpy needs dat kinda help, eh."

Service couldn't help laughing. He was too tired for anything else, and when Tuesday Friday called, he was still laughing.

"We're hearing about all kinds of bodies up where you are. One of them isn't yours, is it?" she asked.

"Limpy Allerdyce just gave me sassafras tea," he said.

"Are you okay?"

He started laughing uncontrollably again.

Limpy took the cell phone away from him and said, "Da dickteckera-tive's kinda bushed. He'll call youse back," and closed the phone.

Service looked at the old man. "She isn't going to like that."

Allerdyce shrugged and poured more tea for himself.

57

Harvey, Marquette County

MONDAY, JUNE 19, 2006

Service called the captain and outlined the most recent developments, including the discovery of the two bodies and the whole line of experiences he had had regarding gold ore veins. The captain listened attentively and said, "See Jen Jeske, at the ore sample repository, over by the maintenance garage in Harvey."

At the repair shop he found a female fire officer reading the latest edition of *The North Woods Call.* She had blonde hair and wore a yellow Nomex shirt.

"Jen Jeske?"

"Second tin building east of here," the woman in yellow said. "I think I saw her going into the office earlier."

"Second tin building to the east and straight on till morning," he said, joking.

The woman in Nomex looked up at him."Yeah, *that's* a real hoot."

A weathered brown-and-white wooden sign on the tin building said MICHIGAN GEOLOGICAL SURVEY—CORE SAMPLE REPOSITORY. A smaller sign, handwritten, said, HOOT'S HOUSE.

When he stepped inside he found himself among twenty-five-foot-high stacks of musty wooden boxes painted blue and orange and white, and on the floors, more wooden boxes filled with ore samples that looked like colorless stone candles. The place felt like something out of an *Indiana Jones* movie.

A diminutive woman was in an office at one end of the tin building, seated at a desk, staring at a computer.

"Hoot's House?" he greeted her.

"Yeah, I'm Jeske."

"Service, DNR Law Enforcement."

"The butt-kicking detective in the flesh, eh. Lots of stories goin' 'round about youse."

Butt-kicking detective. He cringed. "I've got some weird questions."

The woman smiled encouragement. "My specialty. Let 'em rip."

He unfolded the 1:24000 quadrangle map he had taped together and explained the overall situation, including specific assay results.

"Where's the last outcrop you talked about?" Jeske asked.

He pointed to it. "I don't know if there was gold there at one time, but someone definitely excavated what looks to me like a vein."

"Get a sample of the surrounding rock. If there're traces, the tests will show it," Jeske said.

"Tests are already in the hopper," he said.

Jeske picked up a pencil and a set of dividers and a plastic navigation plotter and began to draw lines between Service's sites.

"What's with this place?" Service said. "I've never heard of it before."

"By law, if you drill in Michigan, you need to provide coordinates and send drill core samples to the state."

"Even if you drill on private property?"

"Environmental liability the way it is nowadays, you'd be dumb or myopic not to alert the state, but it's not legally required, especially if you're not activating a mine."

"Meaning?"

"Volume, depending on the ore. Over volume X, you're mining. Under X, you're not."

'Loophole?" he said.

"Depends on your viewpoint."

Lines complete, she stepped back to get a wider view of the charts.

"You have records of everything in the state here?" he asked.

"Mining records back to the last quarter of the nineteenth century, core samples from the early twentieth onward—if the mine owners complied with state law, which not all of them did."

"You have records on gold mining?"

"Not exactly. The required state records are by mine, not by ore body, and I'd have to go to every entry to find what's in each mine. But I've also got some folders by ore. They're just not complete."

He wasn't sure if this stop was worth his time.

"Sonuvagun," Jeske said in a hissy voice.

"What?"

"Had an old-timer swear to me once that Peter Paul's mine in Iron County was a red herring—that the real strike was north of there, which lines up with your finds. Peter Paul's claim is south of your travel line."

"That's significant?"

"Not sure, but it intrigues the hell out of me. Back in the 1920s an old army vet who had served in France claimed he'd struck a rich vein of bedrock ore in the western Huron Mountains. The thing is, he was shell-shocked and in and out of reality, ya know? The man spent an entire winter in the mountains and stumbled into L'Anse one spring. Lost all his toes on his left foot and all the fingers on his right hand to frostbite. Damn lucky he didn't die. He came out with a half-pound of nuggets, nearly pure, the richest assay seen in state gold history."

"In the western Hurons?" he asked.

"Ironically, he couldn't remember precise or general locations, and he died that summer from complications following surgery. Somehow those nuggets ended up here. Want to see?"

"Sure."

He held some of the nuggets, noticed they were pink in hue. "So his mine is lost?"

"More or less, but you know how things work up here. Locals know a helluva lot more than they let on, except to each other. Word in L'Anse was that the strike was beween the Arvon slate quarry and Henry Ford's logging operations in Alberta. The mineralogy isn't right for gold in that area, but veins can run underground for miles and miles and pop to the surface in some strange places."

Service studied the map and mentally extended Jeske's pencil line. The extension seemed to pass through Art Lake property. "Any possibility the gold wasn't ever in the Hurons?"

"Sure, but exactly where is another issue."

He made a circle with his finger, southwest of L'Anse. "Any mines in this general area?"

"Fifty to sixty of them, mainly exploratory holes, but there are also eight or nine mine shafts."

"Gold?"

"All ores. Years back a Michigan Tech team surveyed everything—hundreds of mines and tunnels. It's all in the computer now as an interactive map. You want to look at the area, I can put you into the database and you can have at it while I try to get some work done."

It took him three hours, looking mine by mine, but in the end he built a mind picture. One of the mines he looked at, called Leftover, was just west of Art Lake.

Jeske looked at his printout and went to her folder. "They were looking for gold, but it was a dry claim."

"That's in your folder?"

"No, in the codes. Leftover was opened in 1930, shut down in 1932."

"A mine opened during the Great Depression?"

"People do dumb things in good times *and* bad," she said.

"Did the mine owners own the land, or was it state property?"

"State-owned, mineral rights leased by Taide Jarvi Explorations out of Chicago, a subsidiary of Last Carde Enterprises."

"Huh," Service said out loud, his heart racing as he repaired to the computer. "Will this thing give me GPS coordinates?"

"No, just geographical coordinates. You'll have to convert. You know how?"

He shook his head.

"There's a pull-down menu in the program. Select GPS and Map."

He did as instructed and wrote down the coordinates. "I've taken up enough of your time," he said.

"I don't mind. I'm glad to help."

"One last thing," he said. "Hoot?"

She blushed. "I was in a basic Geology 100 class at Northern, and I bet my friends I could get the whole class hooting in one minute."

"Hooting?"

She made a godawful sound, pumping her arm like a piston. "Hooting," she said. "I won fifty bucks. The day I graduated I walked onto the stage at the Yooper Dome to get my diploma, and the whole student body hooted me. I just about died!"

Service liked Jen Jeske. "Thanks."

When he looked at his AVL in the Tahoe he saw that the wolf tree and dry mine were almost identical coordinates, and he smiled and called the Baraga County registrar of deeds, identified himself, and got immediately to the point. "Van Dalen Foundation owns Art Lake, correct?"

"Yessir."

"When did they purchase the property?"

The man left the phone and came back minutes later. "There's not one answer for that. They bought parcels over time, a little now, a little later, and so forth."

"Where was the first purchase, the second, et cetera?"

"I'll have to go back to my files. You want section, township, range, or GPS?"

"Everything."

An hour later he had it all written down, and the man was sending a package of hard copies to his office in Iron River.

Sitting in his Tahoe he dropped electronic markers on everything into his AVL. The initial Art Lake property was that with the pond and the dam.

He called the registrar back. "Art Lake. There's a pond on the property. Has it always been there?"

The man grunted. "Have to ask the owners about that. Our data doesn't show that kind of thing."

What the hell are you looking for? he asked himself as he headed the Tahoe toward the state police lab.

58

Marquette, Marquette County

MONDAY, JUNE 19, 2006

Gabby was in her lab, a tray of slides in front of her. "You," she said when she saw him.

"In the flesh."

"Bad choice of images in this joint," she said.

"You said assay results in seven to ten days."

She reached for her desk diary. "You delivered the slides on the fifteenth. They teaching you game wardens new math or something?"

"It's pretty important."

"Everything here's important. How about I call the lab and check?"

"That would be great."

"Yeah," she said, "but will you still love me in the morning?"

After the phone call she turned and faced him. "June twenty-second, guaranteed."

He made a mental calculation. "Seven days."

"Truth in advertising," she said. "You want the results by phone, e-mail, or snail mail?"

"Can you call me and put the paper in the mail?"

She scribbled a note in her planner. "You've got it. Will you have phone coverage out in the woods?"

"Hard to predict."

"I'll leave a message on your voice mail and double with your e-mail."

59

Baragastan

TUESDAY, JUNE 20, 2006

Word came from Indianapolis that the two sporting-goods lovebirds had confessed to conspiracy in the death of Jimbo Macafee, but Friday didn't seem the slightest bit elated at the case break.

Last night he'd told her, "You should be happy."

"The Box case is still out there," she countered.

"Enjoy your successes."

"Like you?"

He rarely basked in success, but he'd not known her long enough for her to know this about him, and her knowing bothered him. Was she asking people about him, or was she prescient?

This morning he again called Zhenya Leukonovich and was surprised when she picked up on the first ring. "You still on Van Dalen's ass?" he asked.

"Zhenya neither confirms nor denies."

"Are you aware that Penny Provo has been found dead?"

He heard the air go out of the IRS special agent. "What are you telling me?"

"We found Provo in a shallow grave just off Art Lake property. An autopsy is under way."

"Foul play?"

"One small-caliber bullet in the head—about as foul as it gets. I met her, you know."

Another sudden exhalation. "Explain."

"I had a search warrant for Art Lake's grounds. She intercepted me at night and we talked."

Silence on the other end.

"She didn't deny being a plant," he said.

More silence.

"She yours, or Hike Funke's?"

"Zhenya will arrive in Michigan tomorrow. Where will you be, Detective?"

"Where they pay me to be—out in the woods."

She hung up without further comment.

He considered asking other COs for help, but decided to perform the next task alone. He called Junco Kragie. "Did you ever go back and check the wolf tree site?"

"Once."

"Anything?"

"Not that I seen. Why?"

"Just jumping through hoops," Service said. "Dotting my i's, crossing my t's . . . shit like that."

"Roger that," Kragie responded.

Something said by the boy William Satago had stuck with him, and he telephoned Betty Lachoix. "Grady Service. Is William around?"

"He just finished cutting the lawn and is sitting down for iced tea."

The boy came on the line. "What?"

"You told me about a drawing. Did the woman give it to you, or just show it to you?"

"Just showed it."

"She say why?"

"No."

"Could you re-create it?"

"Already done that."

"You did?"

"Figgered a wolf might could mess up the sets, so I come right home and drew up what she showed me."

"You still have the drawing?"

"In my bedroom."

"Give it to Betty, William. I'll be by to pick it up."

"Is that all?" the boy asked.

"Thanks, William."

•••

Service parked a long mile from his intended destination and came at the site from the boggy swamps to the south rather than from the roads to the north. Ground always looked different in daylight than at night, and it took him a while to work out the exact location where they'd found Dani Denninger, but eventually he found the tree where the deer had been cabled, and he saw the damage to the bark from where the cable had been looped.

Kragie had sent the cable and traps to the Marquette lab. No fingerprints, no nothing. The boy, William, had been meticulous in avoiding signs or incriminating evidence, and the DNR lacked the resources of some of its sister law enforcement agencies—the sort of sophisticated state-of-the-art high-tech resources necessary to crush a crime scene with technology, all in support of the investigators. In the DNR they had their brains, and not a lot else.

Someone who knows about wolf trees. The kid knew, didn't he? Need to ask. Woman who paid the kid was not Penny Provo, and it wasn't Penny Provo who approached Allerdyce. Close to something, his gut said. *But what?*

"Holy cow," a voice said.

Junco Kragie was in full camo, not ten feet away.

"I liked ta shit when I seen your silhouette," Kragie said shakily.

Overreaction? "What're you doing out here?"

"Same as you," Kragie said, sitting down. "That Denninger kid's a little fleshy-flashy for my taste, but she's one of us, eh. I keep thinking there's got to be a reason for a bloody wolf tree, so here I am on my pass days. Had it in mind to take this place apart, inch by inch. You?"

"Great minds," Service said, causing Kragie to look puzzled.

"Same idea occurred to me," Service clarified.

"How long you been here?"

"Not long. Been sitting, noodling the case, trying to find angles and options."

"Do any good?"

"Not yet."

"If somebody asked you to set up a wolf tree, could you do it?"

"Now . . . maybe," Kragie said.

"Now?"

"Yeah, since we found Denninger and we seen the real thing."

"You'd never seen one before?"

"Just the drawing Station Twenty put out to the field."

"Lansing sent a drawing?"

"Last year after deer season."

Shit. He hated computers and e-mail, and did a less-than-satisfactory job of staying abreast of electronic traffic. "You still got a copy?"

"On my computer, back in my truck. We going to look around here now?"

"Changed my mind. How about we go look at that drawing?"

Kragie shrugged. "Sure."

Back at the officer's truck Service looked at the drawing on the screen and asked Kragie to e-mail a copy to him.

"You want to go search now?" Kragie asked after sending the document.

"No, I've got some other things to look into first."

"Mind if I do some looking around on my own?"

"Just be careful."

60

North Bear Town Road, Baraga County

TUESDAY, JUNE 20, 2006

Betty Lachoix invited Service in for iced tea and gave him the boy's draw-ing, which he took out to his truck. He called up Kragie's e-mail and com-pared the two renderings. *Damn near identical. What're the odds?* he asked himself.

He sat in the truck and thought hard. *What're the chances someone out-side the department has the DNR drawing? And if so, how'd they get it?*

He called Sheena Grinda on her cell phone. "You remember the wolf tree sketch Station Twenty sent out?"

"Came to us after last deer season," she said. "What about it?"

"Public document?"

"Not hardly. Would serve as a blueprint for every wolf-hater in the state."

He scratched his jaw and lit a cigarette. *Someone involved in this from the inside?* The thought made his stomach flip. A year ago he had broken a case featuring some unethical internal behavior, and it had been the most unpleasant task of his career, from start to finish. He didn't care to repeat the experience, but neither could he write off theoretical possibilities just because they might be unpleasant.

"Man," he said out loud, and telephoned Friday.

"You headed south?" she asked immediately.

"Not yet."

"Call when you start," she said.

"You bet."

The boy had seen a photo of Penny Provo and rejected it. There remained other possibilities. An inner voice told him there was an answer close at hand, but he couldn't pull it up.

He drove to Art Lake, pulled up to the gate, and announced to the video and intercom that he was there to serve a search warrant. When the gate slid open and Alyssa Mears came out, he snapped a digital photograph of her.

"Asshole!" she snapped. "Where's your warrant?"

Her grace and poise were gone. "Must be some mistake about that," he said, heading back to his truck.

He called Lachoix on Bear Town Road and arranged to meet her and William again.

William Satago looked at the digital photo and shook his head.

"You're sure?"

"That's not the woman."

Service grunted. Theoretically that left only Virginia "Ginny" Czuk, who worked for Alyssa Mears. He was standing with the boy when Kragie called.

"I got something down here you'll want to see," the other officer said.

"At the wolf tree?"

"Hundred and fifty yards south of where you and I were earlier today."

"What is it?"

"Better you come and look," Kragie said. "Look for my sticks." Sticks were natural markers officers used to subtly point trails for others.

"Rolling," Service said, holstering his 800-megahertz radio and heading for his truck. The juxtaposition of the ultramodern talk-just-about-anywhere commo system and the ground sticks once used by Native Americans made him shake his head. Other police agencies might be in the twenty-first century, but a game warden, to be effective, needed to step in and out of a lot of centuries and use whatever he could find and jury-rig.

He called Friday en route. "Kragie's got something near the wolf tree."

"Grady, the drug team called. They found plat books in a safe in Box's house marking dope plots in four counties."

"He was killed over drugs?"

"Maybe. The stuff on the plat books has been plotted on different scale maps. There are a few marks that don't align with the drug fields."

"What are they?"

"I'm not much on map interpretation, but they look to me like your outcrops."

Jesus. "Do you have copies of that new stuff?"

"They left us a set."

"Hang on to them."

61

Baragastan

Mid-morning, and hot. It took an hour of slow walking and sign checking to find Kragie, who was sitting on a cedar blowdown that looked relatively recent.

"What've you got?" Service asked.

Kragie took him to where the uprooted tree's root-ball had torn loose, allowing him to crawl down into the hole the uprooting had created. "Careful, this ain't stable. I was down here earlier, poking a stick in the dirt, half-assed, and it gave way." Kragie pointed at a black hole opening into the earth.

"You look inside?"

"Yeah, and you should too."

Service got down on his hands and knees and took his SureFire light off his utility belt, and shone the beam into the hole. "Rock," he said over his shoulder to Kragie.

"Look *straight* down."

Service looked. "Timber."

"Hewn timber, flat sides," Kragie said. "Looks like an old mine."

"How old?"

Kragie shrugged. "Can't tell. Need someone out here who knows about such things."

"You ever hear of mines in this area?"

"Rumors about way back. You?"

"Maybe."

"We ought to call in backup and technical support," Kragie said.

"No time for 'by the book,' Junco. We need to go in there," Service said. "You got rope in your ruck?"

"Some, and in back of my truck."

"Let's start with what we have. You can play anchor."

With a makeshift harness, Service opened the hole a bit wider and Kragie lowered him into it. Only eight or nine feet of vertical descent before his boots hit solid ground.

"I'm down," he called up, looking around. He was in a squarish tunnel, all rock, with a few rotten timbers. The tunnel looked blocked to the east, but open to the west.

"I'm undoing the rope," he called up to Kragie.

"I wouldn't."

"It'll be okay." He unknotted the rope and walked three, then four steps west, using his SureFire. Immediately to his left as he faced west he saw an area exactly like those he'd found in some of the quartz outcrops in Iron County. The image in his mind was that of a carefully excavated tooth awaiting a filling. He moved his face close and shone the light in the dust and saw sparkles. He scooped some of the dust from the area into a plastic bag and saw a green mineral with wispy white stripes piled up on the tunnel floor. He bagged a sample of the mineral too. It weighed next to nothing, and was stringy, like a woven basket coming apart.

The blockage to the east didn't look solid, and neither did it look old. He wasn't sure why, but his heart was really racing now.

Back in the light Kragie said, "Anything I should know?"

"Definitely an old mine."

"What else?"

"I wish I knew."

He needed to get the new samples to Gabby in Marquette, and somehow she needed to dump the "seven- to ten-day service" mantra and get this assay done most ricky-tick. Tonight he wouldn't be able to get back to Iron River, and Friday probably was not going to be happy about it.

"You hear about the feast at Pinky's?" Kragie asked, breaking his train of thought.

"Feast?"

"All county law enforcement's invited. Word's going 'round that Pinky's going to retire and he's throwing a party on Sunday."

"Kinda sudden," Service remarked.

"Yeah, lots of people are thinking that," Kragie said. "I had calls from our guys downstate. They're invited too."

"Our guys, as in downstate COs?"

"Yeah."

"How'd the word get to them?"

"He's got a list. Most retirees do, so they can stay connected. Guys send stuff to retirees all the time. You get an invite? It was by e-mail."

"Haven't noticed one."

"Should be a good time. Peel the politician's hat off Pinky and he's a good guy."

"I bet," Service said, wondering what had led the sheriff to the seemingly sudden retirement decision. "Don't say anything about today," Service told his colleague.

"No problem. We done here?"

"I don't want to leave the site unattended."

"We don't have the bodies to sit on it."

"Can you cap it with plywood or something?"

"Explain."

Service did. He wanted the hole covered so nobody would slip into it – or find it.

"I'll get Simon to help me," Kragie said.

"What are you going to do?"

"Heading to Marquette."

"Man, you cover *beaucoup* ground."

Yeah, Service thought. *All velocity and no direction until now. Was a break in the making? It sure felt like it.*

He called Friday again. "I'm going to Marquette, then to you in Iron River."

"Shall I have breakfast waiting?"

"You're in a motel room."

"Mickey D's is in walking distance."

"That's not a breakfast place. Can you get on your computer?"

"For what?"

"Get everything you can find on Virginia "Ginny" Czuk of Illinois. If she's got a sheet, let's see it all."

"I knew I wouldn't get any sleep tonight, but didn't think it would be because of a computer."

"I'll make it up to you."

"You've got that right, brother."

62

Allerdyce Compound, Southwest Marquette County

WEDNESDAY, JUNE 21, 2006

Service called Gabby on his way to Marquette and met her at the lab.

"I'm going to try to accelerate your results," she said, accepting the latest assay requests.

"Is it possible?"

"I hope so—you're exhausting me," she said, adding, "What is it this time?"

"More rock with something taken from an empty vein. Also some dust from the same source, and some green rock from the floor of an old mine."

She looked at the green substance. "The green is serpentine; the white stuff is asbestos. This combination is commonly associated with gold-bearing ore."

His heart skipped. "Can dust be carbon-dated?"

"Not with the specificity to tell you how old your mine find is, if that's what you're thinking."

"Don't waste time on the floor dust."

"I can't promise this will actually go faster."

"Do the best you can," he said.

• • •

Limpy Allerdyce answered his cell phone. "Grady Service. I'm on my way to your place, and I don't feel like hiking all the way back to the compound. Meet me in the parking area."

"Why?"

"Just meet me."

"Might as well," the old man cackled. "Youse wokened me up."

Service got there before Allerdyce, who came through the darkness without a light. Even with his superior night vision Service told himself he'd have a hard time in a cedar swamp at night. Despite his age, Allerdyce moved fluidly, a true creature of the darkness. And he was carrying a thermos.

"Youse want coffee?"

"Thanks. That sounds good."

"Night fuel for wardens and violators," Allerdyce said.

Service couldn't help smiling. He took out his digital camera and thumbed his way through the photographs. Once again he showed Penny Provo to Allerdyce, who said, "Girl from da grave, not da girl met me."

When the photo of Alyssa Mears came up, Allerdyce chuckled lasciviously. "White and tight, eh."

"You know her?"

"She's da one met me in Gwinn."

"You sold her traps."

"Wun't nothin' illegal in dat."

"Not saying there was."

"Den we done each other," the old poacher said. "Long time boom-boom. Youse were in Vietnam, 'member boom-boom?"

He rarely thought about Vietnam. "You seen her since Gwinn?"

"Nope, but she's da voice we heard da night we found da stiffs."

"You're certain?"

"She's one a dem likes ta sit on top, bark orders, eh. Like a jockey strap."

"She never gave you a name."

"Nope. Figured it was like dat New York writer talked, you know, da zipperless fuck."

Service stared through the darkness at the old violator. "Erica Jong?"

"I ain't much for names. Dere anyting else, sonny?"

"Nope."

They finished the coffee and Allerdyce took his thermos and faded into the night.

Allerdyce had been with Mears; he could testify to that. The boy William Satago had dealt with Ginny Czuk. Why the division of labor? Not important now. Evidence of conspiracy. What the hell was Penny Provo doing in there, and who sent her?

He punched in Friday's phone number. "I'm forty-five minutes out, wildlife permitting."

Tuesday Friday laughed and said, "Step on it!"

63

Iron River, Iron County

THURSDAY, JUNE 22, 2006

Grady Service had never been easily startled, but when Zhenya Leukonovich opened Tuesday Friday's door at 7 a.m. in the AmericInn, the detective
found himself speechless. He looked past Zhenya to Friday, who held out
her hands in a gesture of helplessness.

"Zhenya said she would be here, and here she is. She arrived late last
night," the IRS agent announced.

"Where did you call from the other day, *Sagola*?" he shot at her. Sagola
was only thirty miles east of Iron River.

"This is an irrelevant topic," Leukonovich said. "Tell Zhenya about
Provo."

"She was yours?"

"First you talk, then we shall see."

"The fact that you seemed totally surprised by her death suggests Zhenya
is not as well wired as she assumes. If there's to be talk here this morning, it
will be two-way, not one," said Service.

Leukonovich nodded her head once and Service took her through the
saga of the late Penny Provo. "She was too obvious in leaving a trail," he said.
"It took a while, but it finally dawned on me that there might be more to her
than the obvious."

"Your talents are wasted in your backwater career," Leukonovich said.

"Was Provo yours?"

"Zhenya resides in a world where resources travel like tides, rising
and falling, ebbing and flowing. Who owns the tide? It is a world one must
quickly accept or be lost."

"Yes or no?" he asked with a growl.

"Technically no, and operationally, partially. She was army CID on loan
to a joint FBI-EPA task force. The effort had gotten nowhere until we introduced principles of forensic accounting."

"Meaning you?"

"Yes."

"FBI *and* EPA?" he asked.

"An unholy and tenuous alliance."

"Domestic terrorism?"

"A plague of cases mostly old, with a recurring cast, a repertoire company, if you will. It finally dawned on someone to ask where the finances came from to enable such sustained operations."

"Chicago," Friday said.

"Surmised, but not yet confirmed," the IRS agent said.

Service said, "Provo's mission."

"Now failed."

"Van Dalen Foundation sponsors domestic terrorism?"

"Zhenya harbors doubts."

"But you sent Provo in."

"Neither my choice, nor my order. Isaac Funke sent her."

"A decision above your pay grade," Service said. Parroting something Leukonovich liked to trot out when no detailed or reasonable explanations seemed feasible. "Gorsline runs the Van Dalen Foundation. He's dirty?"

"Not by customary definition," Leukonovich said.

"Zhenya, I'm in no mood for guessing games."

"Gorsline has nothing to do with extremist eco-terrorist agendas or operations."

"Don't make me pull teeth."

"Elements under Gorsline within the trust organization are involved. Not him."

"Art Lake."

Leukonovich nodded. "Evidence suggests that for a long time, funding for extremists came solely and physically from Art Lake."

"High-grade gold," Grady Service said.

"*Extremely* high-grade. Unprecedented in state mining history—this ore merits up to five nines on the purity scale."

"You have assays?"

"Isaac Funke met Provo, who provided the samples."

"Alyssa Mears and Ginny Czuk," he ventured.

"Two of numerous pseudonyms, adherents of enforcing their vision and views at any costs, believers in hard-green direct action."

"I've done a background check on Czuk," Friday said.

"Save your energy," Leukonovich said. "You will find nothing. Under these current names, the women are as clean as octogenarian nuns."

"What was Provo's exact mission?"

"To locate the ore, and she failed."

"She provided samples."

"Without seeing the actual vein or learning where it is. They run very efficient security, with state-of-the-art procedures."

"Their security's not that state-of-the-art. Provo got inside."

"Only to die."

"Is there evidence to warrant going in? Provo provided the samples for assays."

"We do not know the provenance of the samples," Leukonovich said with a hint of emotion Service read as anger and anguish. "Even the most political of federal judges would be hard-pressed to interpret the evidence as probable cause," she said with an almost audible sigh.

"In forensic accounting your investigations sometimes look for back doors, right?"

"Zhenya would undoubtedly employ a more precise and technical term."

"I know where Art Lake's back door is," Service said, "no technical term needed."

"Such a thing is impossible. Zhenya has analyzed exhaustively."

"From your office."

She raised an eyebrow in protest.

"Boots in the dirt," Grady Service said. "In my world, that's what counts most."

When Leukonovich finally left them alone, Service got into the shower and Friday went down to the lobby and fetched coffee.

"I've never seen such a strange woman. She didn't even look at me." Friday said when he came out of the shower. "Her eyes say she'll devour you. Is there like…history between you two?"

"Business and professional history only," he said. *Did one describe prior sexual tension and sparks as history?* "She is, I'm told, the top agent in the IRS. She helped me break a big case last year."

"Have you really found a back door, whatever that is?"

"Could be," he said, sitting on the edge of the bed, "but I need the lab to finish some things for us before we take the next step." Declaration complete, he lay back, folded his arms across his chest, and was asleep.

64

Iron River, Iron County

THURSDAY, JUNE 22, 2006

When Grady Service awoke alone, it was nearly noon. He went into the bathroom to take a leak and saw writing on the mirror, in lipstick: office, babe!

Babe. It sounded right, but he had no idea what it meant, or implied.

He called Karylanne and she picked up immediately. "It's Grady," he said.

"It's your Bampy," Karylanne said, obviously to Maridly. He was too groggy to protest.

"We had you MIA," the mother of his grandchild said.

"Just out and about. What day is this?"

"Things are *that* bad? It's Thursday."

"I'm in a fairly complex case. Couple of weeks should sort it out. You want to bring Mar to Slippery Creek, or me to come up there?"

"No classes right now," Karylanne said. "We'll drive down to your place."

"I'll call as soon as I can nail down some pass days. Put the kid on."

He heard cooing and slobbery sounds on the phone receiver. "You know who this is, Maridly?"

"My Bampy!" the little girl shrieked into the phone.

Her Bampy? "Yeah, close enough," he said, a lump in his throat. "I'll drive up to you guys after this breaks," he told Karylanne.

• • •

Friday and Mike Millitor were in the office at the post.

"She tell you what's going on?" Service asked the Iron County homicide detective.

"Something about back doors. She wasn't so precise, eh."

Service changed directions, looking at Friday. "Where are the maps from the drug team?"

She bent down to open a box, took them out, and began unfolding them.

Service walked over, leaned over, and began looking. After a while, he smiled at her.

"Your outcrops?" Friday asked.

"Sure looks like. Who had the maps?"

"Gogebic County found them at Box's place. They also found a name on a slip of paper."

"Name?"

"Tikka Noli."

"Mr. Willie Pete himself."

"Turns out Noli allied himself with green groups to hide his dope operations. There were substantial plant colonies near where the burning deer appeared."

"Who marked the outcrops on these maps, and why?"

"We don't know," Friday said.

"Where's Noli?"

"Still lodged at the county jail," Millitor said.

"He lawyer up with Sandy Tavolacci?"

"No, his lawyer is out of Oak Park, Illinois."

"That's Chicago, right?"

Friday nodded. "Western suburb."

Not Sandy? Huh. "Name?"

"Rosemary Slick."

"Solo wolf or pack lawyer?"

"Not sure."

"Find out, okay?"

"I'm all over it," she said, turning to her phone.

The maps, gold dust and ore, Provo, Box, Mears, Czuk, Art Lake, Gorsline, Van Dalen—his gut told him that all the pieces fit, but he couldn't see how yet. The only real outliers were the two old bodies unearthed by Newf at Elmwood.

"Beloit, Singe, and Merriman," Friday said, closing her phone. "Guess who one of their clients is."

Service grinned. "Van Dalen Foundation."

"We're on a roll," she said.

"Does the Slick woman handle Van Dalen?"

"Not that I can discern," Friday said. "But you can ask her yourself. She's in Crystal Falls."

"I could kiss her," Service told Millitor.

"I ain't stopping youse," the detective said.

"I'd have to cut off your lips," an unsmiling Friday said. "By the way, Noli's four-wheeler?"

"What about it?"

"One of the tires has a missing chunk, and the print matches casts taken from where you heard it that morning."

"Does Noli know this yet?"

"I don't think so."

"Cut off my lips," he said. "What would you do if I had no lips?"

"Make do," she said.

65

Crystal Falls, Iron County

THURSDAY, JUNE 22, 2006

The lantern-jawed Rosemary Slick carried herself like someone who trolled courtrooms looking for fights with any and all takers.

"Who're you?" she asked Service, ignoring all social conventions and pleasantries.

"Detective Grady Service, Wildlife Resource Protection Unit, Michigan Department of Natural Resources."

"I hope like hell they pay you by the number of letters in your bona fides," she quipped. "What the hell is a game warden doing in my client's business?"

No verbal sparring here, Service told himself. *She wants to punch it out, go toe to toe right from the bell, see if she can get an edge on me.*

"To begin with, your client tried to kill me."

"You have an expansive imagination. Perhaps you've spent too many hours alone in the forest. My client was protecting his crop."

"You mean his *dope.*"

"I mean potatoes and rutabagas. My client is not in the dope business."

"Won't argue that," Service said.

"Discretion and so forth?" Slick countered.

"Not at all. I'm not a lawyer. I collect evidence and refer cases to prosecutors."

"It's the same system everywhere," she said.

"What I know is that the day my colleague and I were assaulted, there was a four-wheeler nearby. Casts from the tire prints are identical to the tread on the tires of your client's all-terrain vehicle."

Unintimidated, the woman leaned forward. "And you can testify that you saw my client riding said phantom machine? He reported it stolen a month before."

"The day I asked him about it, he told me the machine was at his house in Gaastra." Service laughed. "Welcome to the Upper Peninsula. It's standard practice up here. You think you're in trouble, you stash your toy assets—four-wheelers, snowmobiles, motorcycles—report them stolen, and collect the insurance money. Your client screwed up his timing on this one."

"You have no proof of that."

"We will."

"Is there a reason you are taking up my time?" Slick asked, shifting tones.

He told her about the plat books and maps, and she denied her client had any knowledge of such things or any involvement in the drug business.

Stonewalling all the way. "You represent Van Dalen Foundation?"

"My firm does, not me. I've never had that honor."

"And you probably won't," Service said. "Van Dalen's about to go down in public flames. The IRS is all over them."

Slick blinked but remained silent.

"Call the home office. I'm sure they'll confirm."

"My client has no connection to Van Dalen," she said, after a long pause to collect her thoughts.

"Really? Ask him about the X's marked at certain points on the maps and plat-book pages. When Van Dalen goes down, it will be like the *Titanic,* sucking down everything close to it, vendors included."

"Are you an attorney?" she asked.

"Nope."

"I didn't think so."

"Phone home," Service said, "for your own good." He dropped a business card on the table and left.

66

Iron River, Iron County

THURSDAY, JUNE 22, 2006

When Grady Service walked into the post ten minutes after Friday, she handed him a slip of paper, which said, "Gabby at Forensics."

He punched in her number. "Service here."

"Got it."

"First batch?"

"*Everything*. I know a prof at Northern with a lab. He did the assays on the last batch, and I'll send the evidence out to our regular vendor too, but we can trust this quickie alternative."

"And?"

"Gold traces in all the samples you provided. But the last one is purest of all. You want the reports by e-mail or snail?"

"Both. Can someone drop hard copies at the DNR Regional Office?"

"Thy will be done," Gabby said. "Anything else you need yesterday?"

"Won't know till tomorrow," he countered.

"Tomorrow's yesterday is today," she said.

"Thanks a lot, Gabby. Peace be upon you,' she said, hanging up.

Service looked at Friday. "Someone mined those various outcrops for veins of almost pure gold."

"Damn," she said. "Noli?"

"Not sure." He took a pad of paper and began sketching a wolf tree.

"What's the weekend look like?" Friday asked.

Thought I'd crash a party. Interested?"

"Seriously?"

67

Skanee Road, Baraga County

SUNDAY, JUNE 25, 2006

They met in the parking lot outside the L'Anse post. Sergeant Sulla Kakabeeke in civvies, her shift over, was standing beside her personal Ford 150 truck.

"Pretty sudden, his retirement decision," Service said to her.

"I guess," Kakabeeke said.

"License plate numbers?" he said.

She sighed. "I can smell where this is going, Detective. Pinky's one of us, and more to the point, one of *you*. He just wants to retire quietly."

"With a big party, while bodies are still on autopsy tables?"

Kakabeeke looked sad. "You know he couldn't have had anything to do with any of that Art Lake mess."

"Define *mess*," Service said. "Personally, I'm having a helluva time with all this."

"You know what I mean. It's not in him to do anything illegal. For crying out loud, he didn't *create* the Art Lake deal; he inherited it from his predecessors."

"Admirably defended," Service said. "But Pinky still needs to answer some questions."

"He'll get a lawyer to protect his retirement."

"I don't care if he calls in the pope."

"This is really hard for me," the Troop sergeant said. "I care about Pinky."

"You think it's equally reciprocated?"

She looked off in the distance and chewed her lip. Her right hand was lightly tapping her hip.

"The IRS is about to be all over this thing," Service told her. "Their ability to dig surpasses all of us put together. Money leaves a trail. Why the retirement party at your place and not his?"

"He prefers to keep his Hermansville place private."

"And you've never found that odd?"

She nodded.

"He give a reason?"

"Yeah—he's got things people don't need to see."

"Such as?"

"He inherited a lot of money," she said, a catch in her voice, and the hint of a deep frown etching her face.

"The IRS will sort that out pretty fast. You don't believe the inheritance story?"

She shook her head solemnly. "Vegas a couple of times a year, Jamaica every winter; we've lived a pretty good life together since we met."

"On his inheritance?"

Kakabeeke opened her hands, begging understanding. "You can't live in cop mode every second of your life."

"He sent out invites for the party."

"Did it all himself."

"To whom?"

"All county law enforcement and some downstate cops."

"I never got one."

Kakabeeke stared at him. "Seriously?"

"See you out there," he said, and went to his truck, leaving her to her own thoughts.

Friday looked at him. "What was that all about?"

"Tell you later."

• • •

Pinky Barbeaux looked at Grady Service and shook his head. "Didn't expect to see youse today," the retiring sheriff said.

"You want to take a walk, and talk to me?"

"Think I'd rather get swarmed by pine beetles."

"This has to be done," Service said.

They walked through a grove of second-growth Norway pines behind Kakabeeke's house. "You want me to read the Miranda card?" Service asked.

"That won't be necessary," Barbeaux said.

Grady Service took the laminated card out of his shirt pocket. "I'm becoming a strict constructionist on legal procedures," Service said. Then he read the retired DNR lieutenant his rights.

Barbeaux said, "Let me say this about those bodies and all that—I don't know nothing about any of it. And I want my lawyer."

"Alyssa Mears," Service said.

"I know her, of course."

"Biblically?"

"You've got a filthy mind."

"You trade a lot of e-mails with former department pals?"

"We're a family and a community. You know that."

"Sometimes it's eyes-only internal stuff."

"No comment."

"Like the wolf tree drawing."

Barbeaux looked away.

"Computer geeks," Service said. "They can find stuff in hard drives, who sent what, who got what, like that. No idea how, but they can do it with all sorts of tricks."

"I got nothing to hide," Barbeaux said.

"That's good. You think Ginny Czuk can say the same?"

Intuition had fueled his math. It had been Czuk with the sheriff when Pinky told him his warrant had run his course. Why her and not Mears, if Czuk was just an assistant? No, Czuk was something more, and she was pulling Pinky's strings. Czuk had to be the one who gave the wolf tree instructions to William Satago, the drawing, which originated with Pinky Barbeaux. There had to be more to this for Pinky than new patrol vehicles and departmental equipment. *Did Kakabeeke know, or just suspect he was on the take?*

Barbeaux's paste-on gregarious facade had begun to crack.

"Czuk hired a Keweenaw Bay kid to set up the wolf tree. You gave her the drawing."

"Why do you assume it was me?"

"Plain as a moose in a fridge. You didn't deny the allegation. You tried to find out what I based it on. Shame on you, Pinky. This is basic Interviewing Suspects 101 stuff. We've got two bodies, one of them a federal agent. All federal hell is about to be visited on Baragastan. The IRS is going to peel you and Van Dalen like cheap onions."

"Okay, maybe I give da girl da wolf tree thing."

"Why?"

"Was interested."

"You banging her?"

"I want my lawyer."

"Kakabeeke seems nice, but I don't think she'll ignore this, and when she hears you were banging that young woman, she'll suddenly recover some of her lost memories and suspicions," said Service. "Talk to me, Pinky. At this point there may be room for some dealing. Once the feds swoop in, forget it."

Barbeaux sighed. "I give her the sketch. But I swear it was just because she's interested. She hikes a lot and didn't want to stumble into a trap."

How'd she even know about such a thing? The Ontonagon event had never been made public. "Before that memo came out, Station Twenty circulated some photos of a wolf trap found in Ontonagon County."

"Yeah, I give her those too."

"How much is Gorsline paying you?"

"Gorsline?" Barbeaux said, and Service suddenly felt light-headed. *Gorsline is the center of gravity for this, right? Has to be.*

Kakabeeke joined them and Service said, "Sergeant, let him enjoy his party. Then haul him to the county and book him on three open murder charges. I'll be in later to talk to the prosecutor and supply details. Between now and then, he gets no phone calls until you book him."

"And you?" Kakabeeke asked.

"Digging," he said. *Literally.*

68

Baragastan

It was not yet 5 a.m. on Monday morning.

"Hoot," Service greeted Jen Jeske as she crawled out of an unmarked black DNR truck driven by Marquette County CO Alvin "Leadfoot" Leader.

Jeske looked at Service and held up one of her hands, which was shaking. "I thought the speed of light was a buncha Hollywood Star Trek crap," she said. "Never been so scared in my life."

Service said, "Everybody feels that way after they ride with Alvin."

"Why the heck am I here?" the woman asked. "Your officer showed up at my house, said you needed me urgently, and here I am."

"Thanks. It is urgent."

"It better be. We've got eight people coming to dinner tonight. Am I gonna make it back to cook, or should I call my old man and tell him to go to plan B?"

"Better make the call," Service said. "*Is* there a plan B?"

"Plan B means he's on his own to figure it out."

He had no way to estimate how long, but he was sensing a very long day and probably a night ahead of them. Friday and Millitor were with him, along with conservation officers Simon del Olmo, Elza Grinda, Junco Kragie, and Sergeant Willie Celt.

Another vehicle pulled up, and Judge Taava Kallioninen got out with a coffee mug in hand.

"Your Honor," Service said.

"I was a Troop before law school," Kallioninen said. "Sulla Kakabeeke and I are longtime friends. She told me what went down at the sheriff's get-together when I showed up to make my official, pro forma appearance. I figure you're on the cusp of something big, and given Van Dalen's past record with lawyers, I figured it wouldn't hurt to have me on the scene and at your side. Objections?"

"None, Your Honor."

Service introduced the judge to everyone and explained what he hoped to accomplish. Turning to Jeske, he asked, "You bring the information?"

"Yeah, we're definitely on state land here, and there're no mineral leases—not now and not in the past—at least, none I can determine."

"You inspect mines for the state, right?" he asked.

"New operations, for the Department of Environmental Quality, but not for engineering or employee safety."

"But you've been down in hardrock mines."

"More times than I care to remember," Jen Jeske said. "I'm sensing here you want me to go underground and evaluate your blockage, to see if it's possible to get past it."

"You're psychic."

"That's one way to look at it," she said. "How deep am I going?"

"Ten feet max."

Kragie nodded agreement.

"That's good," Jeske said, "because the really deep stuff seriously creeps me out, especially if there's been a collapse."

Jeske went to the Marquette officer's unmarked truck, fetched her equipment bag, put on a helmet with a light mounted to it, grabbed a loop of line, a small pack, and a long-handled hammer with a pick on one end.

"You come prepared," Service said.

"My gear goes everywhere I go—just in case. Where's the opening?"

Kragie and del Olmo had hidden the entrance with plywood, covering it with dirt and debris, but the board was off now, the hole revealed.

"You already been down there?" Jeske asked Service as she looped line through her harness belt and worked her way down to the opening.

Service nodded.

She straddled the hole and shone her flashlight into it, then knelt and pulled a respirator out of her pack. "How long were you below?" she asked Service.

"Not long," he said.

"There's another respirator in my big equipment bag. Help yourself. Are the walls reinforced?"

"Yes, but it's mostly solid rock."

"Correction: solid except for the collapse."

He shrugged.

She handed one end of her line to Kragie, gave a thumbs-up, and disappeared into darkness.

Below they could hear her hammer tapping rock.

When Kragie helped her back up, her face was covered with sweat and dust. She accepted a bottle of cold water from Friday. "Good news, bad news," she said after a long pull on the liquid. "It's definitely open past the slide, but I can't tell how far. There could be another blockage to the east."

"Good or bad?" Service asked.

"Depends on who goes with me. It's a tight squeeze down there."

"I'm going," Service said.

"You'll never fit."

"That's what they always told Harry Houdini."

"This isn't a stage trick."

"You've got that big hammer."

"Plastic explosives maybe would help, but I couldn't even handle a cap gun as a kid. Jen Jeske don't do bang-bang."

The judge stepped forward. "Please explain to a layperson what's going on."

"Public land," Service said. "There are no leased mineral rights here, which means this is an illegal operation, and I'm going to bet that it leads east under Art Lake property, and that in fact they have been mining this for a long time. I'm also betting I don't have enough probable cause for search warrants, so if we go in underground and it pops out at Art Lake, we will have entered legally and legitimately."

The judge smiled. "You might have a future in the law," she said.

"I'm already in the only part of the law that interests me," he said.

Friday nudged him. "I'm a lot smaller than you. Let me go."

"No argument on size or pluck," he said, "but at this time, this tunnel is a DNR-DEQ issue, not one for the state police."

Service guessed that any of the COs would volunteer to go in his place, but he was determined to see this through. His case, his job. "If I can't get through, one of you will have to try. Draw straws or something," he said, putting on the respirator and the night goggles head harness he'd dug out of the Tahoe.

"We don't have a helmet big enough to fit over that rig," Jeske said.

"I need eyes, not a brain bucket." Even superior vision would be worthless in total darkness underground.

Service looked at Jeske and she looked back and said, "Do everything really slow, okay?"

There were no good-byes or good lucks.

He nodded as Jeske lowered herself back into the opening, and when she was gone, he gave a thumbs-down to lower him to Kragie and del Olmo, who anchored his rope as he dropped into the old mine.

Crammed against each other at the bottom, Jeske said, "I've got a low-lumen red penlight. Will it screw up your night-vision gear?"

"Just try not to point it right at me."

"It's really, really tight from here," she said. "I shit you not."

He looked at the blocked area. "Tight for you?"

"Not bad, but for you . . ." She didn't finish her sentence.

"I'll hold my breath," he said.

"Spoken like your average half-witted caver."

"Humor can be a good thing," he told her.

"Hold that thought—see if it helps."

"You go through and I'll watch. When you get to the other side, talk me through."

"I repeat, take it *really* slow."

After a while he saw a glint of light. "How far?" he asked.

"Eight feet," she said. "There's a forty-degree angled shelf on your left, and maybe a foot from the lip of that to the right rock wall. Fourteen inches, max. That enough?"

"Before we find out, how about moving down the tunnel where you are and see how far it's clear?"

When she returned fifteen minutes later, she said, "I walked seven minutes. No problem. There's some debris on the floor, but nothing insurmountable. The footing sucks, is all."

Service took off his shirt and pants and gunbelt and put everything in a pile, pushing it ahead of him with his boot.

"Can I do this standing up?" he asked.

"I can't imagine how."

"I can't crawl on my side."

"Then try it standing up," she said.

Though it was cool underground, sweat poured off him. *No way to crawl. Too big, too inflexible, not limber enough. Too damn old.* He eased into the opening. The ledge tilted upward from the top of his thighs. "Okay," he said, trying not to grunt.

"Okay what?" Jeske shot back.

Too tight to talk. Tilt upper body to parallel the sloping shelf. First take off your Night Vision Device. Loop the NVD over your right arm. Make a fist, put it in the middle of your forehead to serve as a bumper. Move one inch at a time. Hit my elbow. "Fuck." *Shut up. Discipline. Can feel blood on elbow. Shit.*

"You doing okay?" Jeske called softly to him.

"Peachy."

Ten minutes later he finally cleared the last inch of blockage and immediately squatted, Jeske's red light illuminating him as he put the NVD back in place.

"Nice 'wears," Jeske said, shining her light on his underpants.

"This tunnel better take us out," he said. "I'll never get back through that."

"The way ahead is clear as far as I followed it. But the footing's tough, very uneven and slippery."

Service put on his pants, shirt, and utility belt. "Let me lead," he said.

"I'm used to moving underground."

"Are you used to ducking bullets?"

"You win," she said, patting his arm. "Unassailable logic."

Service wished they had radio contact with the surface, but on Jeske's advice, he'd left the 800 with Friday.

Clothes on, equipment in place, Service said, "Your GPS work down here?"

"Nope."

"Paces then. I figure if we go more than two hundred meters, we'll be past the Art Lake perimeter fence."

"I'll do the counting," Jeske said.

"It doesn't have to be exact," he said.

"It won't be."

Later he heard her voice close behind him. "Three fifty, and we've been descending since about pace one hundred," she said, veering northeast, "best as I can tell."

"You can sense that?" He had no sense of direction underground and was in no moody to experiment. Or if he did, he didn't trust it.

"No, I always carry a button compass. It's not worth beans if there's any iron, but it always spins like a Sufi master when that happens, and so far, no spinning, so I think we can trust it."

What the hell was a Sufi master? "Okay, keep moving."

Along the way they passed a number of tunnels branching left and right. Mostly Service paid no attention, but at one of them he ducked right and moved until he hit a dead end. Jeske stayed right behind him. *Damn NVD. No depth perception.* He turned off the device and said, "Use your light."

"On what?'

"The rock face."

She shone her light past him and said, "Holy cow!"

"More specificity, please," he said.

"Look at the groove in the wall. Four inches wide, two feet deep. That's amazing. Never seen anything quite like that. Rare as hell," she continued, "but not unheard of. Could very well have been almost pure ore. You know about Silver Islet, off Thunder Cape in Lake Superior?"

"No."

"Copper discoveries made on the mainland. Prospectors went a mile or so into the big lake to put down observation markers, and one of them noticed galena. A few whacks with the pick and there's pure silver. The vein was twenty feet wide, and the men stripped it with crowbars. But the vein dropped straight down the middle of the island into the lake, and engineers found a way to tunnel down to recover the ore. In ten years they took out a million and a half ounces. There's still silver down there, but nobody wants the risk or expense of getting it out. This vein is like that one. Beyond belief."

"But people know about that island."

"Yes, but there are other deposits here and there that nobody ever hears of. They're maintained as private resource banks."

"If gold was sold, someone would know," Service said.

"Presumably, but a lot of precious gems and metals get moved off the official tax books."

Damn. No wonder Leukonovich and the IRS are on this thing.

Two and a half hours after bypassing the blockage, the tunnel began to angle upward until it suddenly ended. Service looked up, saw metal-bar ladder rungs built into the rock.

"I'll go up," Jeske said, and moved past him.

"There's a platform here, and six more feet of tunnel, ending at a big iron door."

"I'm coming up," he said.

It was cramped above, so he took off his NVD and used his SureFire to examine the door.

"Old hinges," he said, running his hand over the nearest one. "Old, but solid as all get-out."

"Do we just knock on the door?" Jeske said.

"No. You go back to the others. Explain to the judge what we found and how far we've come. Tell her it would be sweet if our colleagues came through the Art Lake gate and found their way to the other side of this door so I can get the hell out of here."

"That might take a while."

"I've got plenty of time."

"I could stay," she said. "I'm used to being down here."

"If someone opens the door, they are not going to be happy campers to find one of us. Go talk to the judge, Hoot. Tell her what we found and what we need, and don't let her say no."

"What if she won't listen to me?"

"Tell Friday, and tell the judge she'll have to personally dig my ass out of here. And leave your fancy hammer if you can get by without it."

She handed it to him. "Why?"

"Maybe I'll dig for gold," he said.

69

Baragastan

MONDAY, JUNE 26, 2006

The SureFire had new batteries, and he had a backup supply of four more in his pack. He got up close to the bottom hinge on the door and used his knife to test it. There was a small gap, mostly rusted in. The hinge seemed to be riveted or welded. Weird. The four hinges had six-inch-long pins. Jeske's hammer might work, but the handle wasn't long enough to get good leverage, which left force as the only alternative.

He descended the ladder to search for a rock with some heft, and when he found one, he climbed back up. He had just positioned the pick end on one of the hinges when there was a metallic thump on the other side of the door and it began to screech open. Acting on instinct, he dropped down the ladder into the tunnel below, moved to the first side tunnel, and stepped into it, his heart pounding. *Too damn soon for the cavalry.*

He heard whispers but couldn't make out voices or words. Tone, however, was clear: *Somebody was spooked. Then he heard muffled thumps. Footsteps? Somebody coming down the ladder, dropping the last few feet? Why come down here? Someone small enough to get out past the blockage, the way Jeske had gone? Or someone who didn't know there was a blockage? Jesus.*

He eased out of his hiding place and advanced back to the ladder. There were two lumps at the base of the ladder. *Bodies!* He moved closer and looked. *Mears and Czuk, with no obvious wounds or marks. And no pulses— bodies not warm. Dead a while. Geez.*

He knew he should wait for Jeske and help, but maybe he had an opportunity here. He unholstered his SIG Sauer and climbed the ladder. When he got to the door, it was open. *What the . . . ?* The chances that the two women had died instantaneously and simultaneously of natural causes were nil. There was only one assumption: Someone had killed them and dumped the bodies.

Why leave the door open? In a hurry, not expecting visitors. Or not caring one way or the other—that's possible too. Keep your ass moving. Now he *really* wished he had his radio.

The door opened into a storeroom, the walls solid rock with worn stone steps leading up. At the top, another door, this one closed, but not locked. *Somebody left in a big-ass hurry.*

Had Jeske gotten to the judge yet, and, more important, convinced her to send in the cavalry? *No probable cause issues now.* The bodies he'd found changed all calculations and procedural go-slows. He was in the heart of Art Lake. The mine was illegal and connected to them, bodies dumped in the mine as he stood there. *Slam-dunk.*

Slow down, he reminded himself. He tried the door. From one knee he unlatched it and pushed lightly. *Nothing.* Then he shoved it open violently and went through with his weapon up and ready, his heart pounding. *Still nothing.* He exhaled slowly and looked around. Metal boxes and tools, boxes empty. More stairs to his right, this time made of wood—cedar, aged silver.

And another damn door. It's like a human rabbit warren down here.

Beyond the next door, a sort of living room with bookcases and more rock walls, only these had some wall paneling in places. Old stuff, needing replacement. *Weird.* How many levels had he climbed up, and how many more to go? Jeske's story of Silver Islet flooded his mind: how engineers had taken a ninety-by-ninety-foot slate island and dug straight down hundreds, maybe even thousands of feet. Every time they'd stopped on the way in, she'd talked more about Silver Islet, and he understood. She was afraid, trying to think about something else. He didn't blame her. He was plenty scared too. *You're still underground: Keep moving up.*

There were windows on the next level, looking down on the pond with the cabins around it. *A storybook scene . . . except for all the dead bodies. Why does someone kill, then dump bodies close to the open bottom door? Closed, it might take forever to find them. Door open, it would take only one person with a flashlight looking down the old ladder. Left open intentionally? He* pondered this as he moved. *Somebody wants the bodies found and attention diverted, so they can boogie?* In a flash he had a pretty good idea where it would happen.

He pushed through doors and rooms, looking frantically for a door to the outside, and popped onto a stone porch. He was in the main building.

He leapt to the grass and side-hopped downhill, trying not to fall on his ass. When he hit flatter ground, he ran hard for the pond's spillway on the east perimeter, and when he got there, he bent over to catch his breath, listening for sounds that would say help was on the way. *Nothing. Still alone.*

He looked around on the ground for signs, tracks, anything, but the ground was pancake-dry and hard. He clambered across the spillway and looked down into the stream. No signs in the bottom gravel or mud. Was he ahead of the game suddenly? *Or had he misread the whole damn thing? Shit. Is there another way out of the compound, one I don't know about? Shit, shit, shit. The property is immense, doofus. Someone can go over or under the fence virtually anywhere.*

Heart still racing, he tried deep, slow breathing to get it under control, and a new thought froze him. Mears had told him their security was high-tech. *Monitors, sensors, and alarms in the mine? If so, they know the place has been breached.*

A swish of grass interrupted his thoughts. Not a breeze, the weight of a body moving. To his left.

When Pinky Barbeaux suddenly appeared by the spillway, Service was afraid he'd been busted, but the sheriff looked back over his shoulder in the direction he'd come, with panic in his eyes.

"Stay where you are, Pinky." *How the hell had he gotten away from Kakabeeke?*

"Ya bloody fool," Barbeaux said, snapped erect, shuddered with a shocked look on his face, and fell forward into the creek between the dam proper and the spillway, his blood immediately turning the water red. Pink. *Holy shit—Pinky's blood is pink. What the hell? Stay focused, you jerk. Why did you have to open your mouth. You had time. Whoever got to Pinky knows you're here now. Shit.*

He slid down off the dam structure and eased into the cattails, only to bang his shin on something metal. He glanced down. *Canoe painted with cattails.*

One minute later he heard the surge of creek water and readied himself as Sven Lidstrom, Frodo the Finn himself, lunged through the cattails for the canoe. When the man got both hands on the vessel, Grady Service struck him on the head, sending him to his knees in the water.

Lidstrom was a small man, but resilient, and he tried to retaliate almost immediately. But Service got the man's arm, twisted it behind him, and dumped him unceremoniously facedown in the swamp, holding him underwater while the man flailed wildly. After a decent interval, he jerked the man out of the water, cuffed him, and threw him in the canoe.

The eco-terrorist turned sweetgrass entrepreneur somehow got to his knees, put his hands above his head, and dove forward. *Should have searched the fucking dam and everything around it,* Service yelled silently as he heard a thump in the distance and felt the canoe sway wildly and the earth under the swamp surge. Seconds later it began to rain debris, and a cloud of red-black dust began to spiral into the sky. Service understood. The mine was gone, and most of the main building with it.

Lidstrom stared up at Grady Service. "No bodies, no evidence."

"We'll figure something out, asshole."

"I've got nothing to say until my lawyer gets here."

"Is your lawyer Gorsline, or Taide Jarvi?"

"Fuck you, pig."

"Eloquence at its zenith, Frodo."

When the dust settled from this mess, he was going to call Summer Rose Genova and let her know that her instincts about people needed some serious work. He knew Lidstrom would go mute, had been in the system before, understood the rules of the game.

There was no way to get Lidstrom back over the dam onto Art Lake property alone, and Friday had his radio. He pointed his SIG Sauer at Lidstrom's head, and the man's eyes widened, but he was suddenly grinning. "Do it, dude. It ain't that hard."

"I know," Grady Service said. In a career of violent confrontations with violators and criminals, he had never discharged his weapon at one of them. He lifted the barrel past Lidstrom's head and fired two shots into the water. "Frodo, dude, we're gonna have beaucoup company most ricky-tick."

70

Crystal Falls, Iron County

THURSDAY, JULY 6, 2006

Gorsline had not yet been charged with anything, and remained in custody in Crystal Falls. He had been almost immediately fired by the Van Dalen Foundation for allowing illegal activities to happen on his watch. The foundation wanted to limit damage to its reputation.

Gorsline insisted he did not know Lidstrom, and so far, Lidstrom had not admitted knowing Gorsline.

Zhenya Leukonovich assured Service that a warrant with multiple counts was coming from DOJ, not just to the foundation, but also to Gorsline and other lesser officials. She had already located a fund with nearly $100 million in it, and evidence suggesting the gold ore from Art Lake and the area had been sold to some sort of mob-related fencing operation in New York. Gorsline would do heavy time.

Pinky Barbeaux had been buried quietly. No official DNR or state police honor guard gave him an assist down what the local Ojibwa called the road of souls.

Baraga County's undersheriff was appointed to serve out Barbeaux's term.

Sergeant Sulla Kakabeeke had suffered a bad concussion from Barbeaux's escape. She announced she was retiring, and made a full statement to the prosecutor about everything she knew and had suspected about the late sheriff.

Magahy Macafee and Timbo Magee, the Indiana lovebirds copped to murder two and were given life sentences in Hoosierland.

Lidstrom, aka Frodo the Finn, was awaiting trial on one count of homicide for killing Pinky Barbeaux, and a lot more. His New York trial attorney had made his bones defending Weathermen back in the sixties and seventies.

It was impossible to determine who had killed Penny Provo, Rigel Tahti, Alyssa Mears, Ginny Czuk, or old man Box. The five homicides would be left open and eventually fade to cold cases.

Lidstrom was wrong about evidence. The forensics people found traces of Mears and Czuk, and quickly identified them through DNA. Identities confirmed, there was an outside chance the killings of Czuk and Mears could be pinned on Lidstrom, but this was a long shot at best.

On Monday, Grady Service and Tuesday Friday had driven to Crystal Falls to meet with Gorsline before the feds moved him somewhere for further interrogation.

The Chicago man looked unconcerned. "You know, of course, that Lidstrom put it all on you," Service said. "The gold was sold to raise cash for the movement, but he says you were the organizer, money manager, sympathizer, and the brains."

"The man's ego would never allow him to say that."

"You don't know him, but you know his ego well enough to say that? He's already said it. Somebody will have to pay, counselor. If it were me, I'd plea-bargain here where there's no capital punishment. Once the feds pick up the ball, you'll get the out-of-here needle for sure. The feds loathe losing agents to scumbags."

Outside the jail Friday said, "You don't know what the heck the feds are planning."

"Neither does he, and in any event, it doesn't matter. This way we give Gorsline something to think about. We'll do the same with Lidstrom in Marquette." Lidstrom had been moved a week ago.

"You play dirty," she said.

"Only on the job," he replied.

"The two bodies your dog found," Friday said.

"I'm guessing Washington Lincoln found the gold, and Van Dalen somehow caught wind of it and came north. Van Dalen probably killed Washington Lincoln and Roland Denu, and he may very well have killed Sheriff Petersson, too. But we'll never know for sure. I'm guessing Van Dalen used the gold to launch his empire."

"So long ago," Friday said.

"History has a way of popping into the present in strange and unexpected ways," he said. This would turn out to be a prescient statement.

"Why're we driving north and west when we live north and east?" she asked.

"To see my granddaughter."

Friday stared at him. "Does this signify something about us?"

"You're the ace detective. Detect." He shook his head and began to laugh out loud. "Jell-O mode?"

"Let me remind you it's a work day, Detective Service."

He looked at his watch and smiled. "Won't be in half an hour."

About the Author

Joseph Heywood is the author of *The Snowfly* (Lyons), *The Berkut, Taxi Dancer, The Domino Conspiracy*—and the seven novels comprising the Woods Cop Mystery Series. Featuring Grady Service, a detective in the Upper Peninsula for Michigan's Department of Natural Resources, this series has earned its author cult status among lovers of the outdoors, law enforcement officials, and mystery devotees. Heywood lives in Portage, Michigan.

For more on Joseph Heywood and the Woods Cop Mysteries, visit the author's web site at www.josephheywood.com.